The Wrong Kind of Blood

DECLAN HUGHES

The Wrong Kind of Blood

JOHN MURRAY

© Declan Hughes 2006

First published in Great Britain in 2006 by John Murray (Publishers)
A division of Hodder Headline

The right of Declan Hughes to be identified as the Author of the Work has been asserted
by him in accordance with the Copyright, Designs and Patents Act 1988

I

Grateful acknowledgement is made for permission to reprint the following material:
Excerpt from 'Adam Raised A Cain' by Bruce Springsteen.
Copyright © 1978 Bruce Springsteen (ASCAP). Reprinted by permission.
International copyright secured. All rights reserved.
Excerpt from *The Zebra-Striped Hearse* by Ross Macdonald.
Vintage Books, Random House Inc. Copyright © 1962 Ross Macdonald.

A CIP catalogue record for this title is available from the British Library

Hardback ISBN 0 7195 6745 9
Trade paperback ISBN 0 7195 6840 4

Typeset in Plantin Light by Servis Filmsetting Ltd, Manchester

Printed and bound by Clays Ltd, St Ives plc

Hodder Headline policy is to use papers that are natural, renewable and recyclable
products and made from wood grown in sustainable forests. The logging and
manufacturing processes are expected to conform to the environmental regulations of the
country of origin.

John Murray (Publishers)
338 Euston Road
London NW1 3BH

To Kathy Strachan

Blood.

The last time, they'd pressed the sharpened points of their sheath-knives into the flesh of their thumbs, and let their blood mingle, and smeared it on each other's foreheads till it looked like burning embers. They were brothers for sure then, bound fast as any natural-born siblings. But embers turn to ashes, and blood doesn't always take.

And look at them now. One is still alive, but barely; the other wishes he had never been born. And look at all that blood. Planning a murder in advance doesn't guarantee that you cut down on blood, although it can help. But when it just happens, in the heat of rage and with the available means to hand – a wrench that can smash a mouthful of teeth, open up an eye socket, splinter a cheekbone; a screwdriver that will gouge through gristle and nerve, puncture liver and spleen, sluice blood from a torn throat – when murder just happens, you wouldn't believe how much blood there can be.

Forensic scientists classify bloodstains under six separate headings: drops, splashes, spurts, trails, smears and pools. And they're all here: drops on the stone floor, splashes on the walls, spurts on the striplight and across the ceiling, trails as the dying man tries to evade his killer, smears on the car bonnet and the garage door, and at the end of it all, the wine dark pool of blood seeping out beneath the dead man.

The murderer cries, weeps at what he has done: involuntary tears, a spasm, not of remorse, but of shock, of relief, of exhilaration at the brave new world he has wrought, a world with one man fewer living in it. He wipes the tears with the backs of his hands, the sweat from his brow, the snot from his streaming nose. His breath still comes in sharp, shuddering gusts, like sobs. He sinks to his knees, leans his head back, shuts his eyes.

Look at him now. Look at his face: blood matted around his hairline, in his eyebrows, in his moustache; blood collecting in the folds of his neck and in his ears; blood anointing him the chosen one, the first murderer, his brother's killer. Look at the happy savage, who's discovered the fatal flaw in God's creation: if Cain could rise up against Abel and slay him, what's to stop the rest of us?

I

What hast thou done? the voice of thy brother's blood crieth unto me from the ground.

Genesis 4:10

I

The night of my mother's funeral, Linda Dawson cried on my shoulder, put her tongue in my mouth and asked me to find her husband. Now she was lying dead on her living-room floor, and the howl of a police siren echoed through the surrounding hills. Linda had been strangled: a froth of blood brimmed from her mouth, and her bloodshot eyes bulged. The marks around her neck were barely perceptible, suggesting the murder weapon had been a scarf or a silk tie. Cyanosis had given her already livid skin a bluish tone, deepest at the lips and ears, and on the fingernails of her hands, which were clenched into small fists. They lay stiff in her lap, and her eyes gaped unseeingly through the glass wall towards the sky; her corpse looked like some grotesque parody of the undertaker's art.

The siren's howl reached a deafening crescendo and then stopped. As the car doors slammed, as the Guards stomped up the drive and began to pound on the front door, my eyes looked out past Linda's, out at the grey morning sky, then down along the cliffside, down between the stands of spruce and pine, down among the great Georgian houses, the Victorian castles and modern villas of Castlehill, down to where this all began, barely a week ago.

~

We were standing on the terrace of the Bayview Hotel, watching a bloated old moon hoist itself slowly above the sea. Out in Dublin bay, the city lights flickered in the haze. Across the road, framed by gorse thatched cliffs and a scrubby pebble beach, the railway station stood deserted, the signal stuck on red. Everyone else who had been at the funeral had gone home, and I was waiting for Linda to finish her drink so I could drive her home. But Linda didn't want to go home. She untied her hair and shook it down, then back from her face. She narrowed her dark eyes, forced her brow into a frown and set her red lips in a small pout, as if, all things considered, she definitely agreed with what she was about to say.

'I can't take it,' she said. 'I can't take another night on my own in that house.'

Something in my eyes must have warned her that now was not necessarily the best time to be making her problems my problems.

'Oh Ed, I'm sorry,' she said. 'Tonight of all nights, this is the last thing you need.' She began to cry suddenly, deflatedly, like a lost child too sad to panic. I took her in my arms and lent her my shoulder. The sea was silver grey beneath the moon, and it glistened like wet granite. The railway signal changed from red to amber. A mild breeze blew the clean balm of eucalyptus up from the hotel garden below. I could feel Linda's cold cheek brush my neck, and then her warm lips were on mine, and she was kissing me. I kissed her back, and then moved her cheek alongside mine and held her. Her body went rigid for a moment, then she tapped me twice on the back, like a wrestler ready to submit. We separated, and she finished her drink, dabbed her eyes and lit a cigarette.

'I'm sorry.'

'No need to apologize.'

'It's just . . . I'm really worried about Peter.'

Peter Dawson was Linda's husband. I'd been at school with Linda; her husband had been a child of three when I left

6

Ireland. I hadn't seen either of them for over twenty years. Kissing another man was an unorthodox way of expressing concern for your husband, but then Linda had always been known for doing exactly as she pleased, and nothing I could see in her face or figure suggested much had changed, in that regard at least.

'You said he was away on business.'

'I don't know where he is. He's been gone four days now. He hasn't called me, they haven't heard from him at work.'

'Have you told the police?'

'No, we . . . I didn't want to.'

'Why not?'

'I suppose . . . I suppose I thought the police would make the whole thing more real, somehow. And I've been half expecting Peter to just walk back in the house as if nothing had happened.'

A fresh drink suddenly materialized in Linda's hand; she must have snagged a waitress by means I didn't notice – or understand. I gave in, ordered a large Jameson from the girl and lit one of Linda's cigarettes.

'You say that as if it's happened before. Has Peter disappeared like this in the past?'

'Not for four days. But occasionally . . . well, we do have the odd row. And Peter's favourite response has always been to storm out. You know how marriage is. Or do you? It's been so long, I don't know if you . . . I don't really know very much about your life, Edward Loy.'

'I was married, yes.'

'And?'

'It didn't take.'

'Were there children?'

'A little girl.'

'I suppose she's with her mother? You must miss her. But of course you do, what a stupid thing to say.'

An express train crashed out of the cliffside tunnel and blazed through the station. The carriages were brightly lit, and crammed with passengers. I wished I was one of them, and that I was on that train now, hurtling into the night.

My whiskey arrived. I splashed some water into it and knocked half of it back.

Linda was still talking.

'Tommy Owens was saying he visited you out there.'

'I wouldn't have thought you kept up with Tommy Owens.'

'I saw him in Hennessy's the other night. And no, I don't go there much either, just when I'm feeling . . . even more trapped than usual.'

'Hennessy's. Is it still the same dump?'

'Whatever you want, you can get it in Hennessy's. God knows how they never closed the place.'

'We used to think Hennessy had a friend high up in the cops.'

'If he has a friend. Anyway, Tommy said you found people who were missing. You helped a family find their daughter.'

'I did some work for a guy who traced missing persons.'

'Well, I just thought . . . and I know you must be in bits with your Mum and everything, but if you could even have a think about it, Ed, I'd really, really appreciate it.'

In case I didn't understand just how she might show her appreciation, Linda moistened her lips with her tongue, wrinkled her button nose a little, and threaded an arm around my waist. Her breath smelt yeasty and sweet, and her scent was all grapefruit and smoke and summer sweat. I wanted to kiss her again, and was just about to, when her drink slipped from her hand and smashed. It left a jagged, gleaming scrawl on the terrace flagstones. With the charmed timing of the accomplished drinker, Linda turned, caught the waitress's eye and, flashing a wry smile of expiation, summoned a replacement. I quickly waved some semaphore of my own, and began to persuade Linda that it was about time to bring the day to a close. She was still very thirsty, and took some persuading, so I had to remind her that it had been my mother we had buried that morning, and she began to cry again, and apologize, but finally I got her down the front steps of the hotel. We crunched along the gravel drive, past rows of palm and yucca. Eucalyptus loomed at either side, and fat sumacs squatted on the lawn. There wasn't a native tree in sight. Linda sat into the passenger seat of my hire car, and we drove in silence along the coast road past Bayview village. The coconut musk of gorse was thick in the warm night air. It smelt like incense, and I had a flash of the church that morning, of the seething thurible glinting in the light, of the coffin and the cross and the faces in the pews, faces I half remembered but knew I must know.

> *Change and decay in all around I see;*
> *O Thou who changest not, abide with me.*

I turned inland by the Martello tower, cut through the old pine forest and began the climb up Castlehill Road. Near the top, Linda juddered into sudden life.

'Next left here, Ed.'

Just before we reached Castlehill village, I swung the car down a granite-walled slip road and halted in front of a set of black security gates. Linda ran her window down and pressed some digits on a credit card-sized keypad she took from her purse. The gates swung open and she pointed to the furthest of the five new detached white houses in the development. I parked in front of the deco-styled property, which had curved exterior walls, a carport, a large back garden and a view reaching from the mountains to the bay. The barred gates swung slowly shut behind us.

'Nice,' I said.

'Peter's father built them.'

'Must feel safe up here.'

'Sometimes I wonder whether the gates are to keep intruders out, or to keep us in.'

'It's hard being rich.'

Linda smiled. 'I wasn't complaining. But the last thing you feel is safe.'

Her smile, which hadn't reached her eyes, vanished. She looked frightened, and the moonlight flooding through the windscreen showed the lines in her tired face.

'About Peter . . . and I know this is not the right time, Ed –'

'Tell me what makes you so worried about him. What do you think has happened?'

'I don't know. I . . . come in for a drink, will you? Or a coffee.'

'No thanks. Tell me about your husband.'

A silver Persian cat had emerged from the dark, and was padding from house to house, setting a searchlight off on each front lawn as he went. He looked like he was doing it on purpose, out of badness.

'Peter's been in trouble for a while now. I think he's being blackmailed.'

'Over what?'

'I don't know. There've been phone calls. People hanging up when I answer.'

'An affair?'

Linda shook her head.

'I'm pretty sure it's a money thing. A business thing.'

'How is the business?'

'Are you kidding? Have you not heard about our great property boom?'

'Just a little. Prices have shot up, right?'

'They're still shooting. These houses here have doubled in value in the five years since they were built. It's wild.'

I had barely been forty-eight hours in Dublin, and quite a few of those hours had been spent either in the funeral home or in the church, but Linda must have been the fifteenth person to reassure me about the vibrancy of the local property market. It was like being trapped at an estate agent's convention. Everyone took care not to appear too triumphalist; the boom was spoken of as an unbidden but welcome blessing, like the recent stretch of unexpectedly good weather. But boasting was boasting, however you tried to dress it up. At least Linda had the excuse that her father-in-law, John Dawson, was one of the city's biggest builders. Cranes bearing the Dawson name seemed to be trampling at will all over Bayview and Seafield; I could see three from where we sat. My first view coming in on the plane wasn't of the coast or the green fields of North Dublin; it was of four great Dawson cranes suspended above a vast oval construction site. It looked like they had just dug up the Parthenon, and were laying the foundations for another shopping mall.

'Peter's the company accountant?'

'Financial controller, they call it. Same difference.'

'So if business is booming, what's his problem? Gambling? Drugs?'

'Gambling, I doubt. Drugs, occasionally. But for fun. No more than anyone else we know. He's not an addict. He probably drinks too much. But I'm no-one to talk.'

'So what did he need money for?'

'He said something about having to be "ready for opportunities as they arose". I don't know what he meant.'

'Has he any other business interests?'

'A few apartments dotted around the city. Tax-incentive investments. They're let through a property agency. And a bunch of stocks and shares, a whatdoyoucallit, portfolio. Although maybe he's cashed them in. He was in a panic, like a controlled panic, the last few times I saw him.'

'A controlled panic?'

'I know, aren't we all? I know it sounds a bit vague, but . . .'

She shrugged, and let her words trail away.

'When was he last seen?'

'He went on-site at the Seafield County Hall renovation on Friday last. He had to go through the budget with the project manager, then he was due to meet me for a drink in the High Tide. I was about twenty minutes late, by which time Peter had gone. I haven't seen him since.'

'Does he have a cell phone?'

'A mobile? It just rings off.'

A swollen, dark-tanned blond man in a white towelling robe appeared in his doorway and waved his fat hands at the silver cat, who ignored him. The man padded to the edge of his driveway, folded his pudgy arms across his belly and frowned across at my car. I returned his frown until he broke eye contact. When he saw Linda, he turned and retreated into his house, red-faced and breathing deeply from his night's work.

'Fucking busybody,' Linda said. 'It was his idea to have the gates built, but since they went up, the fall of a leaf has him rustling his curtains or lumbering down his drive. Try and give a party, he's reporting every strange car to the police.'

'How are things between Peter and his father, Linda? Do they get along?'

'They don't see a great deal of each other. John Dawson doesn't concern himself with the day to day much any more. Only time he ventures out in public is to race meetings.

Otherwise, he's like a recluse, himself and Barbara, rattling around that huge house at the top of Castlehill.'

'So no great father and son rivalry?'

'Not really. Not that Barbara hasn't tried to drum some up. She's always said Peter should have made his own way, that his father had come from nothing and made it to the top, that Peter had it easy all his life. At least his father didn't have to put up with you as a mother, I always want to reply.'

'I saw Barbara at the removal. She looks well for her age.'

'She's discovered the secret of eternal youth. Goes to a clinic in the States every summer, comes back looking five years younger.'

'Did Peter take what his mother said to heart?'

'I think so. I know it hurt him. And maybe . . . I mean, buying the apartments and things, that's only recent . . . maybe that's an attempt to strike out on his own. His "opportunities". But for God's sake, he's only twenty-five years old, I mean, give him a chance, you know?'

'Anything else you can think of?'

'Well. That Friday. Peter and I were actually meeting to . . . Talk About Things, you know?'

'What, a divorce?'

'God, no. Maybe a . . . a trial separation, isn't that what we used to call it? Back in the days when we were young, and it didn't really matter. But Peter still *is* so young. Which is great in some ways,' said Linda, baring her teeth in a hungry grin which left me in no doubt which ways she meant.

'But outside the bedroom?' I said.

'Outside the bedroom, we had nothing left to say to each other.'

The silver cat settled in Linda's porch and began to howl. Linda turned to me and took my arm.

'Can you find Peter?'

'I don't know. To start with, I'd need his bank and phone records and a bunch of other stuff. But the truth is, most likely, he doesn't want to be found.'

'You don't know that.'

'No, I don't. But adults who go missing, it's usually because they want to. And if they don't want to be found, well, it can be very difficult. But I'll think about it. OK?'

Linda leant across and kissed my cheek, and crinkled her face into a smile, as if to reassure me she was being brave. Then, having agreed that we'd talk again in the morning, she got out of the car and walked up her drive. The cat leapt to his feet and rubbed himself against her slender, black-stockinged calf. She pointed at the security gates to open, and I turned the car and headed back up the slip road. In the rearview mirror, I could see Linda in her doorway, smoking a cigarette. When I made the turn onto Castlehill Road, she was still standing there, moonlight pale on her face, her bright hair wreathed in smoke. Her sweet smell clung to my skin, and her salt taste to my lips, and I realized how much I'd wanted her all evening, how much I still wanted her now. I gripped the wheel and hit the gas and drove away without looking back.

2

My mother lived in a red-brick semi-detached house at the foot of Quarry Fields, a leafy road halfway between Bayview and Seafield. Quarry Fields wasn't much of a neighbourhood when I was growing up. The Somerton flats were around the corner, and Fagan's Villas, where my mother and father had been brought up, or dragged up as they put it, was just across the main road. Now Somerton was long gone, Fagan's Villas had a four-wheel drive on every inch of kerb, and a house in Quarry Fields was worth more than I'd believe, or so assorted mourners had been keen to assure me.

Yet for all that had changed, the streets felt familiar, as if I had never left. Familiar but strange: I was driving back to my mother's house, but she didn't live there any more; she was spending her first night alone in a freshly dug grave, in sight of the stony beach at Bayview she used to take me to as a child. When they lowered her coffin down, I looked out to sea and remembered the first time she visited me in Los Angeles: how I took her to Zuma Beach, out past Malibu, how she smiled when she smelt the ocean, and clutched my hand in excitement, how we swam together the way we always had, and never would again.

I parked the hire car outside the house and opened the rusting black gate. An unruly hedge of holly, yew and cypress shielded the overgrown front garden from the road, while untended rose bushes sprawled across the drive.

Crumbling brick work and rotting window frames and missing roof tiles told the same story: the place had become too much for my mother long before the end. Not for the first time that day, I thought I should have come back sooner; not for the first time, the mocking futility of the thought made me flush.

As I tried the keys in the storm porch door, I heard a shuffling on the gravel behind me. In the glass of the door, I saw a shadow move. Over my left shoulder, something glinted in the moonlight. Threading the keys through the fingers of my left hand, I drove my right elbow as hard as I could into the centre of the shadow. At the same time, I slashed out with the keys in the direction of where I figured the shadow's arm was.

A thick grunt, a scream of pain and a crash of metal on concrete later, and I turned to see Tommy Owens on his knees, vomiting into a rosebush. His left hand was soaked in blood, and a semi-automatic pistol lay in a bed of night-scented stock by the boundary wall.

~

Tommy Owens, having damned me for a fascist and a psychopath, having cleaned and bandaged his wounds and rinsed his mouth out with Listerine, and having refused to concede there was anything remotely reckless in his brandishing a gun in my ear, was sitting in the living room making light work of my duty-free Laphroaig.

The squat hunk of black gun metal that sat on the coffee table beside the whisky was a Glock 17. Next to the Glock sat a magazine chambered for 10 rounds of 9mm ammunition. Unlike the whisky bottle, the magazine was full.

'Where did you get the gun, Tommy?' I said, not for the first time.

'It's nothing. Fuck sake man, state of this gaff. Hasn't changed since I was working for your oul' fella, what, twenty years ago? More.'

'It's not nothing, Tommy. It's a gun.'

'I mean, your old lady had some money, didn't she? Arnotts couldn't've paid that badly. She'd've got a staff discount anyway. Carpets, curtains, it's like the B&B from hell. And these radiators, I mean, no disrespect, but I bet they sound like a fucking whirlpool when you turn them on.'

Tommy finished his scotch and reached for the bottle. I got there first. I'd babysat enough drunks for one day.

'Hey, come on man, I'm in shock here, and it's your fault.' The 'man' unstressed, in the Dublin way; ages since I'd heard it.

'Tommy, tell me what you're doing with the gun. Or I'll call Dave Donnelly and ask have you a permit for it.'

Tommy's face contorted into a sneer of scorn that, combined with his narrow eyes and wispy goatee beard, made him look even more like a weasel than usual.

'I saw the pair of you in the churchyard today, very cosy with the cops all of a sudden. Detective Sergeant Donnelly.'

'He was paying his respects, Tommy. More than you bothered to do.'

'I can't do the church, man, can't hack the whole church thing. But I was around, you know, watching you all after. Visited the grave this afternoon too.'

'Did you? Why didn't you come down the Bayview?'

'Hotels? I don't do hotels, man. Churches, hotels, no way.'

Tommy had always been like this. Anything mainstream, anything aimed at people Tommy probably still referred to as 'straights', any venue that seemed, however implicitly, to endorse the way the world worked, and Tommy would have none of it. This ruled out not only hotels and churches, but supermarkets, night clubs, restaurants, pubs (with the sole exception of Hennessy's), and cafés. When he came to stay with me in LA, after his marriage had fallen apart, he refused to go anywhere except an illegal late-night shebeen in Culver City that was noteworthy (a) because we were the only white faces there, and (b) because there had been five murders connected with it in the nine weeks of its existence. That I knew of.

'Very sorry though, Ed. Your old dear. A real lady, she was.'

'The gun, Tommy.'

'Yeah. I was gonna tell you anyway man. Because I was hoping you could, like, mind it for me.'

'I could what? Are you out of your fucking mind?'

'All I want you to do is hide it somewhere, for a few weeks, till all the malarky dies down.'

'What malarky? Tommy. Where. Did. You. Get. The. Gun?'

'It's just a . . . I've been doing a bit of work . . . for the Halligans. I know, I know, but it's nothing, just a bit of . . . delivery work, you could call it, collecting a package in Birmingham and bringing it home type of thing.'

There was a phrase I remembered from my childhood. In fact, I probably heard it first, like so much else, from Tommy Owens. It went, 'I may be thick, but I'm not fucking stupid.' I sat there and stared at Tommy grabbing the bottle and pouring more whisky, and as he gulped it down, I wondered just how fucking stupid he could be to get involved with the Halligans.

'They're not that bad these days, you know man? Well, Leo is, Leo's still the same animal he ever was, but Leo's in jail and everyone hopes he rots there, even his brothers. And Podge is Podge, fair enough. But George is sound, know what I mean?'

'George Halligan sound? The same George Halligan that broke your ankle by stomping on it?'

'Ah, that was ages ago. We were only kids. I stole his bike, for fuck's sake. Anyway, drugs, it's all just a business thing. I mean, if people wanna take coke or E or whatever, they do, middle-class people – (the venom Tommy reserved for the words middle class was impressive to behold) – whoever, it's supply and demand, it's no different from working in the, in the drinks industry.'

'Except people working in the drinks industry don't get maimed and murdered as a matter of course.'

Tommy drained his glass, grimaced and said, 'I know, that's the fuckin' problem, that's why I need you to hold the gun.'

I took charge of the whisky bottle again, and told Tommy that the bar was closed and wouldn't reopen until he told me the whole story. After a great deal more railing and vituperating, Tommy finally explained that his invalidity benefit wasn't enough any more, that his ex-wife was screaming for higher maintenance and if he didn't up the payments she was going to stop him seeing his daughter no matter what any court said. He'd tried to go back to work but had only lasted a day and a half, it wasn't that he couldn't work on cars any more, he was a mechanic to his fingertips, he had just gotten too slow for any garage owner to employ. Then he'd been in Hennessy's one teatime trying to cash a benefit cheque but the right barman wasn't on, and when his ex came in for the cash and he didn't have it, she started screaming at him in front of everyone, calling him a loser and a malingerer and all this, in front of his daughter, I mean, fuck sake, and George Halligan walked up to him, 'The shekels I owe you, Tommy,' like old buddies, and through to the bar with him. Five hundred notes. That shut his ex up. So Tommy asked Podge Halligan how he can repay the debt, and the trips to Birmingham began, very straightforward, different location each time, collect a package, fly home from another airport, Manchester,

Liverpool, wherever. Hand the goods over, get paid, everyone's happy.

'And the gun, Tommy?'

'I'm getting to it, right? Anyway, I'm back from Birmingham last night, and Podge calls me, says, come up to the house. One of those new jobs the other side of Castlehill.'

'The golf club side?'

'Near the old golf club, yeah. Big red-brick things with swimming pools and hot tubs and all this. Some boyband cunt owns one of them, George and Podge Halligan are next-door neighbours there. A million plus, they went for. Anyway, never been asked before, so up I go, and this big bolts-in-the-neck lad in a tracksuit shows me into the lounge, tells me they're all in George's having a party. He goes next door to get Podge, and I'm starting to get nervous, something's up, something doesn't feel right.'

'Were you raking off the top?'

'Not so's you'd notice, Ed, I always replaced it with talc or whatever. Just enough for a few deals in Hennessy's.'

'In Hennessy's? And you thought the Halligans wouldn't find out? Even when they lived in the Somerton flats, the Halligans used Hennessy's as a second home.'

'I don't know what I thought. But I'm telling you, I was thinkin' now. Straight into the kitchen, out the back door, over the wall and leg it through the golf club back to Castlehill Road. Only I didn't, I waited, and in comes Podge, all smiles, a bit pissed, howya Tommy, welcome home, good man, all this. He gives me the shekels, then he opens a drawer and takes out one of those olive-green canvas army bags, says I'm doing very well, and it's about time I moved up the ranks. Bit pissed as I say, actin' like The Boss, you know? I said nothing, he winks and taps his finger to his nose, says "Be in touch, Tommo," and off he goes.'

'And the gun was in the bag?'

'The gun and the spare clip.'

'The spare clip?'

I picked up the Glock and weighed it in my hand. It was loaded. I snapped the magazine out. Two rounds were missing.

'Have you any idea what it was used for?'

'No-one's been hit. At least, no-one that I know of. But we may just be about to find out. Or it could've been used shootin' rabbits.'

'But it could be you being set up.'

'Well, that's the point. That's why I'm here, case a corpse turns up and the cops get a tip-off.'

'But that doesn't make sense. I mean, the cops get hold of you, you can take Podge Halligan down, what you know about him.'

'Unless the corpse is a civilian. In which case, the cops have me, they've a gun that matches, forget about the Halligans.'

'Or unless he meant what he said, that you're rising up the ranks, and in a couple of days, you'll get the nod to hit someone.'

Tommy shook his head, a forced smile on his face. He looked frightened.

'I don't know which is worse, Ed, being set up for murder or being asked to commit one. I mean, I'm not a . . . I could-n't fire a gun. Fuck sake.'

'So in case it's a set-up, you want me to hold it?' I said.

'Sure, 'cause it's all very well, oh you can tell the cops all about Podge Halligan, but what about my old dear? My sister? My kid? If they can't get at me in jail, they'll get my family. And then they'll get me eventually, Ed. No, the cops'll hear nothin' from me. But if you have the gun, all they have is a tip-off, nothin' to back it up, and we're grand.'

'Except you've got Podge Halligan on your trail. Maybe he knows you've been stealing from him, he's out to close you down.'

Tommy leapt to his feet, too excited to stay in one place for long.

'Why hasn't he just hit me? He could, any day, nothin' I could do. So fuck that, I'm not gonna, what, bail out, go to England or whatever, never see my daughter, just on the off-chance that . . . I mean, if he wants to, he will. Maybe he doesn't know anything. Maybe he doesn't have a plan. He's just a drug dealer and a knacker, not . . . not fuckin' Napoleon, you know?'

I looked at Tommy clumping around the room, a marked limp still from where his ankle had been smashed. Twenty-five years later, and the Halligans still hadn't done with him.

'Will you hold on to it, Ed? And we'll see what happens.'

'And if he wants you to hit someone?'

'Maybe we can warn the target, get him out of the way. Then I'll say I can't find him.'

Running the length of one wall in the living room there was a sideboard, with ornamental plates and bowls, jugs, candle-sticks and lamps piled on top. Below there were two cup-boards flanking a chest of drawers. I opened one of the cupboard doors, took a pile of plates out and pushed the gun and the two magazines in to the back, then replaced the plates and shut the door.

'What happened to the bag, Tommy?'

'What bag?'

'The olive-green canvas bag the gun was in.'

'Oh yeah. I got rid of it. Too conspicuous, swingin' a bag around the street.'

'As opposed to swinging a gun around my head.'

'Ah, that was just a bit of crack, man.'

Tommy's face creased into a smile.

22

'Listen, thanks for this, specially the day that's in it and so on.'

'The day that was in it was yesterday. It's three in the morning tomorrow now.'

Tommy looked hungrily at the whisky bottle, then shook his head, as if thinking better of it.

'Are you sticking around, Ed?'

'I've to sort out the house. What to do about it.'

'But are you going back to the States?'

'Pretty much, yeah. Haven't had time to think, Tommy. I've had the funeral all day, Linda Dawson all evening and now you.'

'Linda Dawson? What did she want?'

'I can't tell you.'

'Don't get hooked in there. Steer clear man. Big trouble. Poor little rich girl, black widow spider.'

'I can look after myself.'

'All right. Friendly advice spurned, don't blame me. One more thing. Let me see your garage, man.'

At this stage, it seemed easier to do what Tommy wanted than to ask him why he wanted it. I led him out through the kitchen, unlocked the back door, turned down the passage and slid the bolt on the rear garage door.

Inside there was a car covered in dust-darkened tarpaulins. Tommy began to haul on the heavy old cloths, and together we got them off.

Beneath was an old saloon car, racing green with curved lines, tail fins and a tan leather interior.

'I knew she'd be here,' he said, a note of triumph in his voice. 'Everything else is as it was, why shouldn't this?'

'What is it?' I said.

'She's an Amazon 122S. A Volvo, from the days when they weren't built for mummies to fill full of kids and dogs and shopping and all. 1965, I think. I worked on her with your old man.'

'It's a beautiful car.'

'Your oul' fella was no angel, but he had a lovely way with a motor.'

When Tommy Owens failed his Inter Cert., my father took him on as an apprentice in his garage. So while the rest of us were still slaving away in school, Tommy was earning money and buying a leather jacket and a motorbike and getting the girls. But then my father ran into some money problems and his garage shut down. Not long after that, he walked out of the house one evening and was never heard of again. And not long after that, I found out that my mother was seeing another man, and that's when I walked out. I took a flight to London, and then another to Los Angeles, where I stayed. Eventually, I paid for my mother to visit, and she told me that it was just one of those things, and I told her that it was none of my business, and she said that, given the way my father had abandoned her, she was entitled to whatever comfort she could find, and it was all over and done with now, and I agreed and apologized and that was the end of that. But I never went home. Every year, I'd arrange for her to come over. She was there when I got married, and she was there for the christening of my daughter Lily, and she was there for the funeral. Lily, who had fair, tangled curls and the wrong kind of blood, died two weeks short of her second birthday. After that my marriage fell apart, and so did I, and the next time I saw my mother it was the day before yesterday, and she was lying in a coffin in the funeral home. I slipped her wedding ring from her cold hand and looked inside the rim. My father's name, Eamonn, was engraved there. I pushed the ring back on her finger. When I kissed her forehead, it was like kissing a stone.

I suddenly felt very tired. Tommy was underneath the bonnet, muttering to himself. I said, 'Tommy, I need to get some sleep.'

Tommy said, 'This is in amazing nick considering. Do you want me to bash her into shape for you?'

'Sure. If it means I can ditch the hire car, go ahead.'

I closed up the garage and saw Tommy out. He promised to return first thing in the morning to get going on the Volvo, so I gave him a key. I doubted whether Tommy's first thing actually took place in the morning, but if it did, I didn't want to be around for it. I locked doors and switched off lights and was climbing the stairs when the doorbell rang.

Fuck it. Whatever Tommy had forgotten, he could live without it for the time being. I continued upstairs, went into the bathroom and brushed my teeth. But the ringing wouldn't stop, and soon it was joined by a pounding on the door. I went downstairs, put on the hall light and opened the door, ready to reef Tommy out of it. But it wasn't Tommy, it was Linda Dawson. Her hair shone bright in the moonlight, and her brown eyes glowed.

'I'm sorry, Ed,' she said, her voice hoarse and cracking, 'but I told you, I just couldn't take another night alone.'

It turned out, neither could I. I took her hand and pulled her into the house. I pushed the door behind her, and shut out the light.

$\sim$

We clung to each other in the dark. At one point, thinking of all that had happened in the past few days, my eyes filled with hot tears. Linda held me until they passed, and then until I slept.

$\sim$

I woke just before dawn. She was sitting in a chair in the corner of the room, naked, smoking a cigarette and staring at the moon. She turned to me and smiled, and said, 'Go back to sleep.' So I did.

3

When I awoke the next morning, Linda had gone. I washed and shaved, dressed in the black suit I had been wearing for the past three days, and the last clean white shirt I owned. Then I called the airline to find out what had happened to my luggage. Between putting me on hold several times, and passing me to three different people, I was told variously that it had been found and would be couriered to me that day, that it had been mistakenly re-routed back to LA, and that the person who deals with all this type of thing wouldn't be in until later, and I should ring back then. Ireland hadn't changed that much after all. I made some tea and toast and had it sitting outside beneath the pair of male and female apple trees in the back garden. They stretched out their branches towards each other, but never touched. They had been there as long as I could remember.

I went indoors and looked around the house. Nothing had changed from my childhood, and now everything was torn and frayed, chipped and stained and damp, and all over a smell of must and mould, a spoor of neglect, of decay. Tommy had been right: state of the place. I sat on the stairs and looked at the telephone. It was an old black bakelite telephone with a brown cord that looked like a coarsely woven shoelace. Beside it on the cheap pine table, there was a bowl of pinks and an address book. The pinks had a sweet, spicy smell that reminded me of summers long ago, and of my mother. The address book was open to my name. The woman who lives next door, a Mrs Fallon, had found my mother collapsed in the porch and called an ambulance. Then she looked up 'Loy' in the address book and called me in Los Angeles. By the time I got the message and rang St Vincent's Hospital, my mother was dead. On the evidence of these rooms, it felt like she had been waiting for that death for a long, long time.

The phone rang.

'I tried you earlier but it was engaged. I didn't want you to think I'd just ducked out on you,' Linda said. Her voice was husky, her tone a little too bright.

'It's still too early to think anything much,' I said.

'I know what you mean. I have those papers you asked for. You know, Peter's phone records and so on. Do you want to come over and get them?'

I told her I'd see her later and hung up. But I didn't want to see her later. I wasn't sorry we'd slept together, far from it, but I knew if I set out to find the husband of a woman who had just shared my bed, we would both be sorry soon enough. Besides, I had a train to catch.

~

The DART – Dublin Area Rapid Transit, as nobody calls it – shares thirty miles of the railway track that runs up the east coast of the country, from Rosslare in the south to Belfast in the north. I took a train to Pearse Station. I crossed Westland Row and followed the horde of office workers filing in the back gate of Trinity College. The campus doesn't exactly provide a shortcut to the city centre, but I guess a walk through an Elizabethan university first thing in the morning might not be the most stressful way to start your day. As I strolled through College Park, past the Old Library and across the cobbles towards Front Gate, I thought about what my life would be like if I had studied medicine here like I was supposed to, all those years ago. The road not taken.

On College Green, I turned south past the Provost of Trinity's House (dream address: Number 1, Grafton Street) and walked through Dublin's upmarket shopping quarter. It had a sleek sheen to it now, a brash, unapologetic confidence about itself that had been thin on the ground in Ireland twenty years before. It also had a derelict in every doorway: most stores hadn't opened yet, but security personnel were beginning their patrols, so the homeless were gathering up their cardboard boxes and bedding, ready for another day of whatever you did when you had nowhere to go and nothing to do once you got there.

At the corner of South King Street and Stephen's Green, I was expecting to see Sinnott's, where Tommy Owens and I once drank, and which I had dreamt of over the years, but it had been replaced by a towering white shopping mall with fussy decorative work around the windows and roof that made it look like a giant wedding cake. Sinnott's had migrated down the street, transforming itself during the journey from an atmospheric old Victorian pub with a long dark bar counter into a generic American-style sports lounge.

I passed a sleek brushed-chrome and glass tram standing on the corner of the Green, cut across onto Leeson Street, checked the address on the card I had been given at the funeral and climbed the steps of a Georgian terraced house. There was only one bell, for Doyle & McCarthy, Solicitors, and I pressed it.

After a short wait at reception, I took a lift to the second floor and was greeted by the slim, rangy, navy-suited figure of David McCarthy.

'Edward Loy, good morning, sir,' he said, his tone crisp and breezy. I followed him into a large conference room and we sat across from each other at a long, polished table. Light streamed in through the high sash windows and reflected off the diplomas and degrees that hung behind glass from the picture rail on the opposite wall.

'Nice to see you this fine morning,' David drawled, taking a black Mont Blanc fountain pen from his breast pocket and laying it on a pad of lined A4. 'Do I take it this means you want me to sort out the old house for you?'

David McCarthy's older brother Niall had been in my year at secondary school, and they had both showed up at the funeral. Niall was an accountant, David a solicitor in his father's practice. Both possessed to the full the exemplary traits of the South County Dublin professional: an obsession with rugby and golf, an all-year tan, a complete lack of imagination and a tendency to precede every other noun with the qualifier 'old'.

'You do indeed, David,' I said. 'I want to sell up and move back to the States as soon as I can.'

'Right. Well, we'll try and make that as soon as possible for you. First off, even though both parents died intestate, it's a straightforward old chain: your mother inherited the house from your father, and you inherit it from her; indeed, you've had a right to one third of it since your father died.'

'That's just it though. My father isn't dead. Or at any rate, he may not be.'

'Lob that past me again?'

'He went missing. They never found him, or a body.'

'But that was a long time ago?'

'Over twenty years.'

'Right. Well, seven years is all you need. And obviously you're going to need the old death certificate. So the first step is to have your father declared dead.'

For a moment, I couldn't speak. I got up, walked to a window and looked down into the street.

'Ed? Are you OK?'

'David, I . . . I'm not sure I'm ready to do this yet.'

'I understand perfectly. Day after the old funeral, many emotions, not the cleverest to rush into big decisions.'

'Maybe if I got back to you in a few days.'

'Absolutely. Take your time. And if there's anything I can do in the meantime . . .'

David was rising, as if the meeting was over. I went back and sat down again, and after a moment, so did he.

'Well yes, there is, that's partly why I . . . I'm not exactly burdened with cash right now, so I was hoping to get some sort of document from you that I could take to the bank, let me borrow against the value of the house. Strictly short-term, of course.'

David cleared his throat and looked down at his Mont Blanc. He tapped it gently on the pad of lined paper.

'Right. Well, I can state to the bank my opinion of your intention to initiate probate. But only in an individual capacity. In terms of a document on behalf of this practice, I'd need you to have commenced the process, and only then would Doyle & McCarthy be positioned to give them a sensible estimate of how long it would take before you'd have your hands on the deeds.'

'And that's the kind of letter the bank would need?'

'I can't speak for every bank manager. But in my experience, that's the only type of assessment upon which they'd be prepared to make, ahm, a cash advance.'

His voice had taken on a more distant, strained tone, as if the phenomenon of someone needing money was one he had heard of but regretted having to encounter directly. He unscrewed the cap of his fountain pen and then screwed it back on again. I stood up, smiling, as if to reassure him that being broke was really no big deal.

'Not to worry. Well listen, thanks anyway, David, and I'll probably be back in to you soon enough.'

David walked me to the lift.

'Thanks indeed, sir,' said David. 'See you round the old campus.'

We shook hands before the doors closed. I took the lift down and walked back the way I'd come, head down, angry and embarrassed with myself. It had never occurred to me that I would need a death certificate for my father. In LA, I had simply put him from my mind, dead or alive. That's what LA is for, to forget your past. But as soon as I got back to Dublin, I thought I'd see him on every street corner. I expected him to be at the funeral. I wasn't ready to declare him dead, not yet. Not before I had some inkling of what had happened to him. It looked like I'd have to stick around after all. And since I'd had to borrow the airfare to get here, the first thing I was going to need was a job.

I walked down Westmoreland Street, crossed onto O'Connell Bridge and stared down into the green water of the Liffey. It didn't smell any more – in my childhood, the only respite from its seemingly perpetual stink was when the aroma of burnt hops from the Guinness Brewery up on James's Street enveloped the city in a warm narcotic cloud. The North Quays too had changed: there used to be so many abandoned and demolished buildings that Bachelor's Walk and Ormond Quay looked like a mouth full of ruined teeth; now a row of smart new restaurants and enhanced shopfronts seemed to testify that cosmetic dentistry had finally arrived in Dublin, as no doubt it had. There was money on these streets, after all, and the people who had it were wearing it on their backs, and around their wrists and necks: why not in their mouths too? What was the point of having money if no-one knew you had it? For too long, the Irish knew the shame of not having an arse to their trousers; no-one could ever be allowed to think that again, and if that meant a carnival of ostentatious vulgarity and greed, well, didn't we wait long enough for it? Wasn't it no more than we deserved? Didn't it prove we were as good as anyone else? And anyone who said different was only a begrudger.

I followed the river down Burgh Quay to Butt Bridge and looked past the grey limestone dome of the Custom House to the new cathedral of economic prosperity in Dublin: the International Financial Services Centre, a gleaming complex of blue-tinted plate glass and grey steel. It was a powerhouse for banks and brokers and all manner of money makers, and it made Dublin look like any other city. I guess that was the point: at one stage in our history, we tried to assert a unique Irish identity by isolating ourselves from the outside world. All that did was cause half the population to emigrate. Now we preferred to avoid distinctive national characteristics of any kind. Having once been anxious to prove that Ireland was not a colonial province called West Britain, we were now sanguine about our re-colonisation, resigned to our fate as the fifty-first State of the USA.

There was a noise behind me and I turned. Three grey-faced, snuffle-nosed wraiths in grimy navy and white sports-wear had encircled me. Maybe if I hadn't heard them above the traffic's roar, they would have made a move, but head on, their eyes fell away. They were carrying fast-food restaurant cups full of bright yellow liquid you were supposed to think was lemonade, but which everyone knew was methadone. The woman was nudging the taller of the two men, but he was staring fixedly at the ground. The smaller man was nodding and grinning vacantly at me. He had scabs on his eyebrows and beneath his lower lip where his piercings had become infected.

I took a pack of cigarettes from my pocket and said, 'All right for smokes, are you?' They each took a couple, and I nodded at them and walked off towards Tara Street station.

'Big fucking deal. Think you're it now, do ya? State of ya,' the woman shouted at my back.

'Thinks he's fuckin' it now, so he does,' one of the men agreed.

Dublin, where no kindness goes unpunished.

I got the DART back and walked down to my mother's house. I didn't feel comfortable about keeping a gun belonging to Podge Halligan there, whether what Tommy Owens had told me about it was true or not. I took the Glock 17 and the ammunition from the sideboard, wrapped them in an old towel and put them in the scuffed leather bag I'd managed to keep from the airline's clutches. Coming out of the house, I could hear Tommy at work in the garage. I locked the gun in the boot of the hire car and headed for Castlehill.

~

Pale hardwood floors and bare white walls made the open-plan ground floor of Linda Dawson's house look even larger and emptier than it already was, like an art gallery waiting for an exhibition. A floor to ceiling plate-glass window ran the length of the curved back wall. Through it you could see half the county, from the mountains to the sea, all over Bayview as far as Seafield Harbour, and beyond it to Dublin Bay itself.

Linda's hair was wet, and her face glowed; she wore a short black silk robe and her feet were bare. She stood at a granite counter beside a stainless steel double-doored fridge. A crystal jug of mint leaves and a bottle of Stolichnaya rested by her elbow; a bunch of keys hung on a hook above the counter, with a small sign that read 'Car keys, you idiot'. Linda threw ice cubes and mint leaves and grapefruit juice into a tall glass.

34

'I'm having a drink. Grapefruit screwdriver. Are you interested? Or is it too early for you?'

'I'm interested. But it's half eleven in the morning. The only people it isn't too early for are sitting in doorways with cuts on their heads.'

'Is that a yes or a no? There's a pot of coffee freshly brewed.'

'I'll have the coffee, please. Milk, no sugar.'

Linda poured a large slug of vodka into her glass and brought me a mug of coffee. She sat on a cream-coloured sofa that ran along the back glass wall, tucked her bare legs beneath her and gave me a smile. Her eyes looked out of focus somehow, as if this was not the first drink she'd had, or she'd scarfed some tranquillisers, or both. Her black robe probably had a lot of uses, but keeping her soft brown body covered was not one of them.

'So tell me, Ed – what do you want from me?'

'No, tell me what you want from me. Are you sure you want me to find your husband?' I said, trying to keep my eyes fixed on hers and failing.

'I told you last night. Of course that's what I want.' She smiled again, aware of the effect she was having. 'It's not all I want though.'

'It's not all I want either. But as I'm going to be working for you, I'm afraid it'll have to do. Because if I'm sleeping with a man's wife, I tend to lose interest in her husband. So maybe you could put some clothes on. Then we can talk about Peter.'

Linda's smile vanished in an instant. She flushed, and seemed to flinch, as if she'd been slapped. She stood up and left the room without a word. I wished for a moment that I'd had that drink.

Out in the bay, the first few sails dotted the sea. They gleamed pearl white in the powder-blue haze. Seagulls swooped down the cliffsides and skimmed across the rippling tides. It was turning into another improbably glorious day.

Linda returned wearing a black trouser suit. She sat down on the sofa again and said, 'I hope this is sober enough for you. All my dun-coloured sacks are at the cleaners.'

She took a long hit of her drink. She looked frightened again, but there was defiance in the set of her red mouth, and a flash of anger in her eyes. Before I had a chance to, she brought up the subject of money.

'Since you are going to be working for me, I suppose we better sort the practical side out first. What is it they used to say in the movies, twenty-five dollars a day plus expenses?'

'That must be the silent movies you're thinking of. Last job I worked, I got a thousand dollars a day.'

'A thousand dollars? I thought you said you were the monkey. You helped the organ grinder out.'

'That's how it started.'

'And then what happened?'

'The organ grinder died, and the monkey took his place.'

Linda's hand went to her throat, and her eyes widened.

'You didn't tell me that. How did your boss die?'

'He was murdered.'

'Did you get the guy who killed him?'

'His wife killed him.'

'His wife?'

'It's nearly always the wife. And yes, I got her.'

Linda finished her drink and lit a cigarette. Her hands were shaking. She made them stop.

'Weren't we talking about money?' I said.

'How does seven fifty a day sound?'

'It sounds fine. All right then. Did you get those records?'

'They're all gone,' Linda said. 'I checked his home office this morning. Bills, correspondence, personal photographs, they've all been taken.'

'I thought you said they were here.'

36

'I thought they were.' She gestured towards a pile of box files on the kitchen table. 'Everything is on file with Peter, right back to his birth cert. But these boxes have been cleaned out.'

I looked at the four box files. Each one was clearly labelled: Bank – Statements/Cheque Books; Eircom/Vodafone; Property; Shares. And each one was empty.

'There's no sign of a break in, so . . .'

She waved a hand in the air and shrugged, as if to suggest that it was a mystery, or that Peter must have taken them himself, or that she was already so out of it that she didn't care what had happened to them. Then she nodded her head violently, as if ordering herself to get a grip, and sat forward, staring at the floor, her hands clenched in small fists between her knees. It was exhausting watching her change personality and mood every thirty seconds, and impossible to know if it was guilt, or fear, or just the blithe shapeshifting of a drunk.

'Can I see his office?'

'It's upstairs, last door along.'

The white hall curved in a spiral up the stairs. I walked to the end of the landing and opened the door to Peter Dawson's office. The wooden blinds were closed, so I flicked the lights on. An entire wall's worth of shelving was crammed with box files encompassing every aspect of Peter's life. There were files dealing with school, university and work; files labelled 'Swimming', 'Tennis' and 'Sailing'; there were even files devoted to stamp collecting, football cards and the boy scouts, and two files stamped 'Scrapbooks – Pop' and 'Scrapbooks – Sport'. Linda was right: Peter had his entire life filed away up here. I worked my way through each box, checking the contents off against the labels. The only other files that were empty, apart from a couple of unmarked boxes, were two labelled 'Family 1' and 'Family 2', and another marked 'Golf Club'.

The desk was a pale oak table with no drawers; an Apple Mac G4 Computer sat on it, its semi-spherical white base and floating monitor looking stridently last-word-in-design. While it was booting up, I looked around the rest of the office. Two year planners hung on one of the side walls, marked with things like 'Argus Vale – 64 Apts, Town H'ses – Sept 2006' and 'Glencourt Comm'ty C'tre – 18 months'. The shelf full of books housed mostly sports and business biographies and a few sailing manuals.

There was a photograph on Peter's desk, of two men and a racehorse. One of the men was plump and tanned and looked pleased with himself; he wore a waxed jacket and a tweed cap. I couldn't remember his name, but he hit it big in property in the sixties; the papers used to call him 'Ireland's First Millionaire'. The other man was thinner than when I saw him last, and his small, cold eyes peered suspiciously from beneath the brim of a black fedora: John Dawson, Peter's father.

I sat at the desk and gave the Mac a quick once-over, but the files seemed almost entirely work-related: spreadsheets and profit and loss accounts and so on. If the secret to Peter's disappearance lay buried in any of that, I'd have to hire a specialist to wade through it all. I opened Word and worked through the Recent Documents option. Most of them – saved under titles like hhhh, or lllll – had evidently been trashed, leaving only the dialogue box: 'The alias "hhhh" could not be opened, because the original item could not be found.' The most recent document had been saved as 'twimc', but it opened to a blank page. I wondered whether Peter had saved the title without getting any further, or if its contents had been deleted by another hand. I located it within the documents folder and checked: Date created: Fri, Jul 16th, 1.27 p.m.; Date Modified Tue, Jul 20th, 12.05 p.m. Just after midday yesterday, someone had wiped whatever had been written there, but hadn't put the document in the computer's virtual wastebasket.

I got down on the floor to see if there was any interesting litter, but the whole place was spick and span, as if it had been cleaned and dusted that day, and the stainless steel wastebasket was empty, but for the fossil-stain of an apple core on its base.

I had a quick look in the other upstairs rooms: a large, white-tiled bathroom, two bedrooms furnished in a spare, impersonal style that suggested they were for guests, a third bedroom full of art books, a silver Apple laptop, oil paints, sketch pads, and canvases stretched on wooden frames, and the master bedroom, which had the same stunning view as the living room, with the addition of a massive abstract canvas on the opposite wall. The painting, two great glowing swabs of red and orange, had a dark, passionate intensity that was violent and melancholy in almost equal measure, and if I hadn't known that Linda had probably painted it in an afternoon, I'd have thought it was a genuine Rothko. When she was still at school Linda used to make a tidy sum knocking off copies of the old masters and selling them to the kind of people who felt a Renoir or a Monet suspended above the mantelpiece would set their suburban lounge off a treat.

Downstairs, Linda was eating a banana and drinking a cup of coffee – time out from her drinking. She looked at me, her gaze a little clearer now.

'Did you find anything? Was there a break in?'

'I don't know. There are three more empty files here.'

I put them on the table. 'The two marked family . . .'

'Peter kept all his photographs in those. His mum and dad's wedding, his childhood snaps . . . are they gone too?'

'What about "Golf Club"?'

39

'Don't know what that's about. Peter wasn't in any golf club. He didn't play golf.'

'Sure he hadn't taken it up?'

'Certain. We still . . . we hadn't become complete strangers. Not yet, anyhow.'

Without knowing I was going to ask it, I said, 'Did you and Peter make a decision not to have children?'

Linda flushed and stared into her coffee for a moment. Then she shook her head and, in a strained, brittle voice, said, 'No, they just didn't come. My fault. Left it too late, maybe. And now I'm . . . sterile? No, barren. A Barren Woman. And . . . I guess the air seemed to go out of the marriage after we found that out. I offered Peter a divorce, but he said no. He probably should have said yes, 'cause we've been . . . winding down ever since.'

'And you were meeting on the Friday to talk about a separation. Did Peter know that was on the agenda?'

'I'm sure he did. He must have. Why is this relevant?'

'Because it gives Peter a reason to take off. Avoid the conversation, and by the time he gets back -'

'She'll have worked it all out by herself. That what you'd do?'

'That's what most men do. Lie low until the storm passes.'

'And are you most men?'

'I tend to lead with my chin. But this isn't about me.'

'Four days. No. He'd have called. Left some message. He wouldn't leave me to worry like this. He's a very considerate man. That awful mother of his had it bullied it into him.'

'What about Peter's parents? Have you spoken to them?'

'They think I'm overreacting. Barbara said maybe he just needed a break from me. "You know the way men can be." Then she said if I was really worried, she'd get John to ring the Garda Commissioner. Whatever good that would do.'

'Does Dawson have that kind of pull?'

'That's the whole point, he used to. Story goes, that's how he did his first big land deal, the houses up on Rathdown Road, back in '77. Friends in high places, the right palms greased. Those days are gone. Barbara thinks they still have the clout, but I doubt it. Better if they know as little as possible.'

'They'll get to know soon enough if I go round asking a lot of questions.'

'Maybe. You'd be surprised just how isolated they've become.'

'Do you ever use Peter's computer?'

'I have a laptop of my own.'

'Because someone was on it yesterday, at midday. A document titled t-w-i-m-c was adjusted – wiped clean, if there was anything in it to wipe.'

'Midday. I was at your mum's funeral.'

As if I was accusing her. Maybe I was.

'Anyone else have a key?'

'Agnes. The cleaner. But she came today.'

'Where would she have put the trash?'

Linda smiled. '"The trash." You mightn't've lost your accent, but there are still a few giveaways. Out here.'

She led me out the front door and around the side of the house. A small wooden shed stood behind a young beech tree. Inside the shed, Linda pointed to a grey wheelie bin.

'What are you looking for?'

'Anything that might have been in Peter's office. The waste-paper basket, on the floor.'

A bunch of newspapers lay at the top of the wheelie bin. I took out an *Irish Times*, spread it on the floor of the shed and tipped the first bag of garbage on top.

'I'll leave you to it,' Linda said, wrinkling her nose, and went back in the house.

I worked my way through two small bags full of crushed orange juice and milk cartons, plastic tonic-water bottles, apple cores and lemon peel. And an awful lot of cigarette butts, ash and vacuum-cleaner dust.

The third bag contained a Jo Malone grapefruit cologne atomizer, a Dr Hauschka Quince moisturizer bottle and an old toothbrush – so at least we'd made it upstairs. I sorted through used cotton buds and peppermint teabags and eventually salvaged three receipts and two crushed index cards. I had a quick look in the car port, where a red and black Audi Convertible sat in factory fresh splendour, entertained a few rancorous thoughts about people with too much money and knocked on the front door.

After washing my hands and face, I showed Linda my haul. Two of the receipts she identified as hers; they were for buying art materials from a shop on Harcourt Street.

'It's good you're still painting, anyway,' I said.

'I'm a Sunday painter, Ed. I teach Art at the Sacred Heart in Castlehill now.'

'Really? That's –'

'Yes, isn't it? Disappointed alcoholic lady teacher. A suburban cliché, is what it is. This is from Ebrill's, that's a stationery shop in Seafield. It's itemized too: envelopes, two reams of white A4, address labels. Thrilling stuff.'

Linda went to the fridge, collected the grapefruit juice and the vodka and brought them back to the table. She mixed herself a very strong second drink and downed half of it.

'*Slainte*,' she said, and grinned with bad girl bravado.

I laid the index cards out on the table and flattened them. They were both lists. One had four items:

Dagg

T

L

JW

The other had fourteeen names.

'You recognize any of these?' I asked Linda.

'There's a Rory Dagg who's a project manager with Dawson Construction. No-one else rings a bell.'

'You said Peter was at the Seafield Town Hall renovation last Friday. Was Rory Dagg on-site?'

'Could have been.'

'Because then, this L could be you. This could be a list of people Peter was to meet that afternoon.'

I looked at the other list: Brian Joyce, Leo McSweeney, James Kearney, Angela Mackey, Mary Rafferty, Seosamh MacLiam, Conor Gogan, Noel Lavelle, Eamonn Macdonald, Christine Kelly, Brendan Harvey, Tom Farrelly, Eithne Wall, John O'Driscoll.

The T could be Tom Farrelly. The L might be Leo McSweeney. But who were they? Had they anything to do with a golf club to which Peter Dawson didn't belong?

Linda shook her head. Her eyes were gone again, lost in a mist of booze. I was tempted to join her. It looked safe in there; miserable, but safe.

'Anything else? His car?'

'It's in the garage. There's his boat.'

'He sails? With a club?'

'The Royal Seafield.'

'Did you check it?'

'He doesn't go out much any more. He used to crew for other people. I think the fact that his father bought him the boat put him off using it. But it's moored in front of the club-house all summer. The Dawsons still count at the Yacht Club.'

'I'd better have a look at it. What's she called?'

Linda pretended she hadn't heard me. 'What?' she said.

'What's the boat called?' I said.

She shook her head, and smiled down at her drink.

'It's really stupid. He named it after this awful Beach Boys song that I . . . that we both used to like. The *Lady Linda.*'

She looked up at me with a start, as if she had just woken up in the middle of herself, and was dismayed by what she had found. Her smile dissolved, and her face reddened, and she turned away and began to cry, great wrenching sobs this time. I didn't know whether she remembered how much she had loved him, and missed the feeling, or whether she was ashamed that she didn't feel more, and I didn't know how much the booze had ramped up all those feelings, but it was a long time since I had seen anyone look so frightened, and lonely, and lost.

4

The Royal Seafield Yacht Club is one storey above a basement. Since the basement is right on the water, and the club is situated hard at the base of Seafield Harbour, and it was built in the high style of the 1840s so that the fashionable rich might have a fitting location to amuse themselves, it's as impressive a one-storey exterior as you might see.

It's impressive inside too, with high ceilings and fancy coving and ceiling roses and chandeliers and classical columns and what have you.

The staff are not unaware of this, which is presumably why I had been waiting in the foyer for twenty-five minutes, studying a brochure extolling the club's virtues and watching a procession of men in navy blazers with gold buttons and women in navy sweaters with gold stitching pad about in deck shoes from, as far as I could surmise, the Dining Room to the Formal Bar to the Club Room to the Informal Bar to the Commodore's Room to the Billiard Room to the Forecourt. The club secretary, whose name, the brochure told me, was Cyril Lampkin, had been considering my request to see Peter Dawson's boat for all this time. Linda had phoned ahead to arrange things, and I had Peter's club identity card and the spare keys to the storage booths on the boat, but it seemed Cyril Lampkin was still weighing the evidence.

Cyril Lampkin was a strange looking fellow. About thirty-five, he was wearing a burgundy velvet dinner jacket with a matching burgundy and turquoise paisley bow-tie. He had a lightly freckled pink pate, across which an inverted question mark of carrot-coloured hair had been plastered. He had soft pink skin which dimpled at his cheeks and in clefts behind his double chin, and a pale gold moustache shaved equidistant from nose and upper lip. He was filling in at the desk, he told me, because the girl who should have been there had gone into hospital to have a baby, his tone making it clear that he did not think much of babies or the people who had them. He greeted every personal inquiry and phonecall, many evidently from club members, with a symphony of eye rolling, sighing and tongue clicking. If it wasn't for the fact that he was getting in my way, I would've enjoyed watching Cyril in action, if only to try and figure out just what it was he thought he was doing.

'Of course, it would be so much simpler if you were a club member, Mr Loy,' he said, a smile of pity on his shining face.

As he had just informed two club members who had tried to book dinner for that evening that bookings could only be taken over the phone from five fifteen precisely in the Dining Room, no he could not pass on booking requests, that was all there was to it good afternoon, I doubted that my being a member would have helped all that much.

'Well, seeing as I'm waiting, perhaps I could get a sandwich and a cup of coffee at the, um, the Informal Bar,' I said, trying to pitch it as humble as possible.

'I'm afraid not, Mr Loy. For one, you are not a club member. And for two, you are not wearing a tie.'

'There are plenty of people inside not wearing ties,' I said.

'Club members, Mr Loy. If you were familiar with the regulations, you'd know that dress code on Wednesdays until four thirty is: informal for club members, semi-formal for club members' guests –'

46

'And strictly formal for Cyril Lampkin,' I said, gesturing at his burgundy evening clothes.

'I am hosting an antiques event at two forty-five in the Commodore's Room,' said Cyril haughtily. 'As to the question of Mr Dawson's boat, I'm afraid it's a very busy day today, and I wouldn't dare take one of our boatmen away from his duties. Perhaps later in the season, and if you were accompanied by Mr Dawson himself. And if there's nothing else, Mr Loy, I have work to do.'

Cyril had been treading a fine line between amusing irritant and pain in the neck. He had just crossed it. I slapped my hands down on the reception desk, leant into his face and hit the volume control.

'No, Cyril, what you have to do is listen to me. Peter Dawson's wife, Linda, is concerned about her husband's whereabouts. She has authorized me to act on her behalf by searching his boat. Both she and I wish to conduct this business without worrying her father-in-law, who is as you know a loyal and generous friend to the Royal Seafield. But if you continue to obstruct me, I'll call John Dawson and let him know all about it. I'm sure the Commodore will be interested to hear from Mr Dawson on the subject. Now are you going to get a boatman to take me out to Peter's boat, Cyril, or do I have to strip down and swim out there myself?'

It's fair to say that by the end of this little speech, I was shouting. Looking around, I was glad to see that we had attracted something of a crowd. On top of the navy blazers and sweaters, there was a younger contingent, the men in rugby shirts, the women in navy and white striped tops. Maybe there was a club uniform, graded by age. I wasn't thinking about them, however, or about Cyril Lampkin, who was staring goggle-eyed at me, his jowls working like a bull-frog's, or even about the tall, wiry, dark-haired guy in shorts and a life jacket who had materialized at my side, and who looked like he could make things difficult for me if he felt like it.

What I was thinking was, 'This is what I do, and I haven't done it for far too long.' It had been eighteen months since I had worked a case, eighteen months during which I had lost my daughter, my wife, my apartment and my job. I ended up tending bar in a dive in Venice Beach, sleeping on a friend's floor, drinking every cent I made, thinking little and feeling less, trying to make connections between events that don't connect and probably never would. I never would make sense of why my daughter had to die. I probably never would discover what happened to my father. But I did have a fair chance of finding Peter Dawson, and if I did, it would close one broken circuit, remake one connection that had been broken. And even if I didn't, it was good to feel the stir of blood in my veins again.

Cyril Lampkin said, 'You leave me no option, Mr Loy; I'm going to telephone the Commodore.'

I thought of school, and being threatened with the head-master, and I began to laugh. A hand nudged my arm.

'It's all right, Cyril, I'll look after this. Come on, Mr Loy, I'll take you out to the Dawson boat.'

It was the tall dark fellow with the life jacket.

Cyril Lampkin said, 'Colm, ah, indeed, well, Colm, I didn't want to distract you from your duties, but if you think it fit for a non-member, ah, to be summarily authorized . . .'

But Cyril's voice had already begun to fade. Colm led me through the Club Room, down two sets of stairs and out on to a dock. We sat into a small wine-coloured launch, he started the motor and we set off across the harbour. We crossed a number of swinging moorings at the front of the clubhouse until we came to a medium-sized cruiser. At the fore of the boat, the L had dropped off, leaving it named the *ady Linda*.

'Here we are,' said Colm, grinning at me. 'You were having fun, weren't you?'

'I hope I didn't get you into trouble with your boss,' I said.

Colm laughed scornfully. 'Lampky? Lampky's no-one's boss. Lampky's just the club wanker. His mummy's left the club some huge sum of money in her will, but in return they have to employ Lampky, and he just blunders around, getting in everyone's way. Normally it's not a problem, he doesn't interfere with the sailing, and as for all those blazers in the clubhouse, well, they're just wankers too, they deserve someone like Lampky telling them when to wear a tie and what hand to wipe their arses with.'

'I'd've thought the club would be keen to keep John Dawson onside.'

'Dead right they are. But Lampky doesn't like the idea that anyone might gain influence through money. But it's all right when he does it, because Lampkins back to Queen Victoria's time have been members of the Royal Seafield.'

Colm laughed again, and shook his head.

'Ah, the wankers like all that though, portraits on the wall, the glorious tradition, all that codology. Still, they pay their fees, and half of them never sail at all, they just sit around eating and drinking, so the more the merrier to be honest. If I want a drink I'll go up the town a stretch; the pint is shocking in the club bars. Not to mention all those double-arsed old dears and wankers in rugby shirts braying in your ear.'

I laughed. 'Is that how the club divides up: sailors and wankers?'

'That's how the world divides up, far as I'm concerned. Speaking of which, are you going to take a look around the boat or what? 'Cause Lampky was right about one thing: it is a busy day.'

I slipped Colm a twenty and said I'd be five minutes. He

looked at the money for a few seconds, and I wondered whether he was going to hand it back. Then he nodded at me, and said, 'It's a Hunter 23. Twenty-three feet, four berths, and it sits here all summer, waiting to be used. I'm not religious, but it's a sin to own a craft like this and not sail her.'

'Is Peter much of a sailor?'

'He knows his way around a boat. Quiet chap, you wouldn't talk much with him. But he can handle himself well, always places in competitions. Or used to, he hasn't been out in a while.'

'Has anyone been out in the boat recently?'

'Anyone else? Not that I know of. I could ask the other lads, if you like.'

I told him I'd like, climbed on board the cruiser and went below. There were sofa berths at the fore of the boat, behind the anchor-well. These berths had a saloon table between them, and their brown cushion seats lifted off to give stowage space beneath. Fore of the engine-well on the port side, there were lockers, a small toilet and four pine shelves running the length of the boat. There was a cooker halfway back on the starboard side, and aft of this, a double berth cabin. And there wasn't a single other thing on board: no cutlery or crockery, no waterproofs or sweaters, no blankets or bedding, no books or maps, no compasses or navigational instruments, no clock, no radio. There wasn't even any dust. I ran a finger over the table. It smelt of ammonia and pine. Someone had cleared the place out, and recently, and cleaned up afterwards. They'd made a thorough job of it too, like they were scared of what they might leave behind. But you can never cover your tracks, not entirely. There's always a human trace remaining. The job is, to find it.

I felt about in the engine- and anchor-wells, and checked to see if there were any flaps or pockets in the storage pods beneath the sofa berths. I looked beneath the mattress in the aft cabin, and knocked to see if either of the bedroom lockers had false backs. I checked the hanging wall lockers on the port side, and the floor to ceiling locker aft of it – and finally spotted something. In the tight space between the locker and the wall, a few tiny fragments of blue plastic were caught on the corner of the locker, at about chest height. A few more scraps lay on the floor. It looked like a plastic bag had been wedged behind the locker, and then ripped out. I could see more scraps a bit further in. I tried to reach my hand into the space, but it wouldn't fit.

I went up and asked Colm if he had any tools, but those he had – screwdrivers, spanners, wrenches and so on – were too bulky to be of any use. I borrowed a torch though, went back down below and shone it behind the locker. In addition to the blue plastic scraps, I could see something else, what looked like a scrap of glossy paper.

My belt was new, and the leather in it was still quite stiff. I took it off, doubled it and, holding it like a rod, dragged it behind the locker a few times. It brought out more blue plastic, and some dust, and finally the scrap of paper.

It was a fragment of an old photograph. On the back, written in red felt-tip pen, was:

ma Courtney

3459.

The photo was of a mixed group, all dressed up and very young, two men and four women. It looked like one of those shots they take after the wedding photographer is done, when everyone crams into the picture around the bride and groom. I didn't know whose wedding it was, and I didn't know any of the women, but I recognized the two men. Someone had drawn a circle around their heads, again with a red felt-tip pen. One man looked like John Dawson. The other was Eamonn Loy, my father.

5

Seafield Town Hall stands at the top of the main street. You can see it from the harbour, and walking right up the town towards it gives you a sense of how the town used to fit together. It's a substantial late-nineteenth-century granite clad building with a clock tower, council chambers and public reception rooms. At least, it once was all those things. Now, it's a McDonald's. I stood outside it feeling utterly bewildered, like George Bailey in Pottersville. My heart had been pounding since I had found the photograph of my father and John Dawson; now sweat sparked on my face and down my back, and my throat was dry as cardboard.

An old man in a black beret and a tightly belted navy raincoat divined, in part, the source of my confusion, commiserated with me, and directed me to the 'new' town hall, which he assured me was, in fact, over twenty years old. I thanked him and followed his directions as far as the nearest pub. Hidden down a side street, The Anchor wasn't the kind of place that did food, not even sandwiches; the barman didn't catch your eye; the exhausted-looking men huddled in silence over their pints looked at you once and turned away. I ordered a double Jameson, topped it up with water and drank it off in three or four swallows. I could hear the rustle of newspapers, and the ticking of an old clock. When I walked back on to the street, my hands had stopped shaking.

I had arranged to meet Rory Dagg, the project manager of

Dawson Construction's town hall refurbishment, but I still had some time. I stopped off and bought a pre-paid mobile phone in a main street shop and had it loaded with call credit. I called Linda and Colm the boatman and Tommy Owens and left my number with them. Then I walked back down to the Seafront Plaza and bought a roast-beef and horseradish bagel from one of the cafés ranged along the walkway. I sat at an aluminium table with two Chinese girls and washed down the food with a bottle of the Dublin Brewing Company's Revolution Red Ale. The sun was out, and the plaza was thronged with people: office workers grabbing lunch, young mums with buggies passing the time over lattès and iced teas, tourists poring over maps or writing postcards. I felt strangely at home there. And then I realized why: because this scene reminded me more of Santa Monica, of West LA, of California, than of the Ireland I had left. The only thing that felt truly Irish was the shambling couple with the baby in the buggy and the toddler walking alongside. They were both in their early twenties: the guy had heroin cheekbones and grey skin, and he used his full arm to smoke, as if his cigarette was a barbell; the girl's hair was dyed copper and her eyes were pinched against the smoke from the cigarette she held in her mouth. The baby cried and the toddler whined, and as the guy shouted variations on 'He wasn't fucking there' into his mobile phone, the girl kept her head down and tried to placate the now-howling toddler at her side, and as they weaved through the prosperous, cosmopolitan crowd, jostling other buggies and lurching against tables, spitting and swearing, I thought how this did not remind me at all of California. In California, they would have employed security to ensure that people who have money to spend never have to look at people who don't. I couldn't remember whether it was better never to see people like that at all, or to see them and pretend they aren't there.

I sat and looked at the two photographs I had collected. Linda had given me a shot of Peter Dawson, his face engorged and glistening. His deep blue eyes were shot with blood, his cheeks flecked crimson, his damp lips swollen into an anxious pout. For all the ravages of alcohol though, he looked like nothing so much as a startled boy, as if he had lost control of his life, and had no idea how to get it back.

The fragment I had found on Peter's boat had presumably come from one of his empty 'Family' box files. My father and John Dawson looked young and slim and careless in it, their pints of stout held aloft, their eyes shining, their mouths open in song or celebration. I stared at the photograph and cast down the years, trying to recall a time when I'd seen my father's eyes shine like that. I came up empty.

I finished my beer and walked down to the car park near the yacht club. I found my hire car and fed the meter and took a flyer exhorting me to Save Our Swimming Pool from beneath the windscreen wiper and put it in my pocket, then I went back up the hill and turned down a slip lane into the County Hall and Civic Offices, a set of three seven-storey concrete and glass bunkers ranked parallel to, but out of sight of, Seafield Main Street. Two cranes flanked the central bunker, and a builder's sign informed me that Dawson Construction were undertaking this refurbishment with the help of the European Union Structural Fund and the National Development Plan, that Rory Dagg was project manager and, in a spray paint addendum, that Anto sucks big dicks.

And that looked like it was going to be as far as I would get. White and blue police tape ran from both legs of the builder's sign to surround the town-hall bunker, assorted police vehicles were parked in the forecourt and a Guard in uniform stood by the sign.

'What's going on?' I said.

54

'Police business,' said the Guard, his thin lips sucked in over his teeth.

'I have an appointment with Rory Dagg, the Project Manager,' I said.

'Police business,' said the Guard again, his lips disappearing into his small mouth. He looked like he was afraid someone was going to steal his teeth. 'No entry to the public.'

'I've an appointment with Rory Dagg,' I repeated. The Guard didn't bother to reply to that. I didn't blame him. We stood there in silence for a while, and then the town-hall door opened and two men came out. Both wore hard hats. One wore a fluorescent yellow site jacket over a tan corduroy coat, green and navy plaid shirt, fawn chinos and pale tan Timberland boots. The other was Detective Sergeant Dave Donnelly. Dave saw me and came over at once.

'Ed Loy, the very man. I believe you're here to meet Rory Dagg. Something do to with an investigation you're running?'

Dave looked quizzically at me, the expression on his broad, open face poised somewhere between amusement and professional suspicion.

'That's right, Detective,' I said.

Dave gestured for me to come under the police tape. He led me over towards what I assumed was his car, an unmarked blue saloon that may as well have had 'Cop' sprayed all over it in gold paint. He leant on the roof, lit a cigarette and grinned at me.

'What the fuck are you up to, Ed?' he said, his tone friendly but direct. 'What's all this private cop shenanigans?'

I shrugged. 'That's what I did, in LA. Missing persons, paper trails, divorce, a little bodyguarding. Bit of everything, really. I started out working for someone, then set up for myself.'

'And now you're doing it here? Dagg there says you told him Peter Dawson is missing. Why didn't Linda Dawson come to us with it?'

'That's what I told her to do. But you know yourself, Dave, grown man disappears for what, five days now, it's not exactly priority police business, is it?'

'And how did you get involved in this anyway?'

'After the funeral, up at the Bayview. Everyone else went home. Linda stayed and got drunk. She needed someone to look after her. She begged me to look for Peter. She was very upset. Eventually, I said OK.'

'You could've done without all that yesterday.'

'You're telling me.'

There was a silence. We both looked down the hill to the sea. The high-speed ferry was powering briskly out of the harbour, sending great waves of surf billowing across towards Seafield Promenade.

'You don't have a licence to operate as a private detective here, Ed.'

'I didn't know I needed one. Look, if you want me to tell Linda you've warned me off, fine. I could do without all this today as well,' I said.

Dave looked at me again. He ran a hand along the bristles of his close-cropped, salt-and-pepper hair. 'It'd be something to do, though. Take your mind off the funeral and everything.'

'There's that.'

'Were you any good at it? You know, out in LA?'

'I made a living.'

'And you'd turn anything you found out over to me?'

'Can't arrest anyone myself.'

'If you step on any other copper's toes, I don't know you.'

'And I don't know you, Dave.'

I had known Dave Donnelly all my life. We were in primary

school together, and if the whole class had been asked back then how we'd all end up, the one person we'd have got right was Dave. He wasn't the cleverest, or the funniest, or the best at football, he just had a quiet authority, that Captain of the School quality that made you anxious for him to approve of you.

Dave laughed, took a last drag on his smoke and tossed it away.

'Come in and have a look at this, Ed. This is a good one.' He headed towards the town-hall door, and I followed, signalling towards Rory Dagg that I'd catch up with him in a minute. Busy on his mobile phone, Dagg waved me on.

Nodding to the uniform on duty in the foyer, Dave gave me a hard hat and we took the lift down. The doors opened and Dave stepped out onto a scaffolding gantry, part of an interlocking grid of walkways that crisscrossed the entire basement. All the walls and partitions had been knocked down, leaving one vast room. The floor above was being supported by great steel girders. 'They're excavating. Lowering the foundations,' Dave said. 'Ceilings too low down here, or structural damage or something. But they've been ripping up the concrete, and look what they've found.'

In the centre of the room, about eight feet below us, a police medical team were gathered around a steel gurney, gingerly rubbing clumps of concrete from a partially clothed corpse. A police photographer took snaps, and fingerprint and forensic teams dusted and swabbed, but their presence seemed incongruous. It looked less like a crime scene than an archaeological dig.

'It's male,' said Dave. 'Buried in the foundations, so it goes back to what, '81, '82. Earlier, maybe. Came out of a huge slab of concrete intact, like a fossil. And his clothes have been preserved. That's as much as we know . . .'

57

'Dental records?'

'Or false teeth. And we find who was on the missing persons list at the time. Million to one we identify him at all. Mind you, the pressure'll be on. This is the kind of shit the press love.'

I looked down at the corpse again, a tattered scarecrow caked in grey dust and gravel. Another of the missing. Maybe it was my father. The dates would fit. Maybe if I stared at him hard enough, he might give up his secrets. And maybe it was just another bundle of dry old bones.

'I wonder if Dawson carried out the original construction,' I said.

'They didn't. I'm not sure who did, but your man Dagg out there has been tut-tutting over the state of the original job. Said it was real cowboy stuff.'

'Shit, Rory Dagg. I'd better go and talk to him. Thanks for letting me see this, Dave.'

'All right, Ed. Take it handy now.'

I left Dave climbing down a ladder to join the team gathered around the body. Descending to the dead to shorten the odds from a million to one.

Rory Dagg was outside sending a text to someone on his mobile phone. When he saw me, he picked up his silver laptop and a transparent plastic tubular case containing what looked like architect's plans and began to move towards the main gates.

'I'm sorry to have kept you, Mr Dagg,' I said.

'Walk with me, will you?' he said, his voice a quiet drawl, his manner easy and efficient. 'I've another site to check in on, and all this has made me late. Donnelly didn't give you any idea when they'd finish up, did he?'

'He didn't. But I can't see it taking too long. Twenty years in a concrete block probably doesn't leave too much work for forensics,' I said, affecting an insouciance towards the freshly exhumed corpse I certainly didn't feel.

We headed up the main street towards the old town hall, that is to say, McDonald's. Dagg's phone beeped, and he read an incoming text as he walked. He was in his mid-forties, had the wiry build of a swimmer and the high colour of a drinker; he wore his greying curly hair short. He looked like a civil engineer, or a university lecturer; in fact, as he told me, he had been both, but had set up in project management when the building boom started, because there was money to be made, 'and I knew the job. My father was a foreman for Dawson's years ago.'

'Is he retired now?' I said.

'He's dead these ten years. Are you working with the police, Mr Loy?'

'In a manner of speaking. I'm investigating the disappearance of Peter Dawson, on behalf of his wife, Linda.'

Dagg looked up from a text he was composing.

'I didn't know he'd disappeared. I saw him only the other day.'

'Peter was supposed to meet his wife in the High Tide, just after he'd finished with you. You're one of the last people we know to have seen him. What business did he have with you?'

Dagg sent his text, put his mobile in his jacket pocket and shrugged.

'The usual, I suppose. He came on-site and asked his questions about budget overruns and unforeseen expenses. Each of the site supervisors said his piece. Then he rolled off a bunch of bills to pay for nixers. Last week it was a sparks and a couple of chippies we had to call out when some genius kango-hammered through a fuse board. The odd unofficial bonus, site security, because tools kept walking. That was it, I think.'

'Was that the usual? I mean, it sounds a bit hands-on for a financial controller.'

'Yeah. Well, truth be told, Peter Dawson isn't really the financial controller. The real work is done by Hanly Boyle, they've been Dawson's accountants since the beginning. Peter's title is what you might call an honorific – you know, because he's the boss's son.'

'That must be humiliating for him.'

'I don't think it was initially. Easy money, free house, his boat, a beautiful wife: we should all be so humiliated. But in the last few months, he's seemed less and less satisfied.'

'Was there anything out of the ordinary about him that day?'

Dagg thrust his chin forward and grimaced in thought.

'He was actually quite – not distracted, preoccupied. Energized. As if he was excited about something. And once we were done, he was off, you know, all business.'

'How was he dressed?'

'Cream chinos, white shirt, navy sports jacket. It's his uniform.'

Dagg's phone rang. He found it and checked the number that flashed up. 'Sorry, I have to take this,' he said, and then barked into the phone, 'I said sit outside his office, not ring his office . . . that's 'cause they're liars, they say the permits are in the post, but they never are . . . all right, once more with feeling: GO TO COUNTY HALL, SIT OUTSIDE JIM KEARNEY'S OFFICE, DO NOT COME BACK UNTIL YOU HAVE THE PERMITS.'

Dagg looked at me, still glaring, then raised his eyebrows, rolled his eyes and grinned. We had reached his car, a black '94 Volvo estate, parked down a laneway leading to an old terrace of small redbrick cottages.

'I know,' he said, 'I should have a brand-new four-wheel drive with bull bars and all the rest. But they're hell to park. And they make you look like a gobshite.'

He loaded his stuff onto the back seat, then looked over the roof of the car at me. 'I don't like spoilt rich kids, Mr Loy. And maybe it's not his fault, but that's what Peter is. He doesn't understand work, or money, or responsibility. He plays at his life. How he holds on to that wife of his, I'll never understand.'

'Sounds like you'd like to hold on to Linda Dawson yourself,' I said, my tone light.

'I'm married with three kids,' Dagg said, without indicating whether that was a reason for or against an interest in Linda. He didn't sound like the most content of family men.

Dagg looked at his watch.

'I've really got to go,' he said.

'One last thing. The refurbishment at the town hall. Do you know who did the original work?'

'Whoever they were, they deserve to be in jail. That's partly why we're here, there are structural fissures that . . . the whole place could have caved in by now.'

'Can you remember the name of the builder?'

'Not offhand. But I have the plans back in the office, I can find out for you.'

We exchanged mobile numbers and I walked back down the hill. As I reached the slip lane for the town hall, I was nearly run over by Dave Donnelly's unmarked blue car. He had slapped a flashing red light on top, and the car screeched past me into traffic and swerved around the corner towards Bayview.

6

The barman in the High Tide said he wasn't working last Friday, but one of the girls who had been was due on in twenty minutes. I ordered a bottle of beer and drank it at the bar. The High Tide was two storeys above the Seafront Plaza, and had been decorated in a bland modern style, with large abstract daubs on the eggshell walls and coffee and cream tones in the soft leather furniture and polished granite fittings. At four o'clock on a Wednesday afternoon, there were three jowly, balding suits drinking brandy and smoking cigars, two over-dressed women in their forties with a bottle of white wine and a bunch of fancy carrier bags, and a party of women in their twenties clutching pints of lager and bottles of alcopops and making a lot of noise. After they had sung 'Happy Birthday' for the ninth time, replete with obscene variations, the barman had a word with them, and after they had sung it a further five times, they tottered out in a cloud of hilarity, heels clicking and phones beeping, their shouting voices echoing back up the metal stairs as they crashed out onto the street.

A church bell began to toll, and I walked over to the side windows and looked up towards St Anthony's. A hearse was pulling into the churchyard, and a crowd of people parted to let it pass. I wondered whether the concrete corpse in the town hall would ever be taken to a church, ever be given a name and blessed before it was returned to the earth.

I was about to ask for a Jameson when a short, plumpish girl with blonde highlights and too much orange make-up on her pretty face told me her name was Jenny, and that the barman said I wanted to talk to her. I showed her the photograph of Peter Dawson and asked if she remembered seeing him.

'Not really,' Jenny said. 'Friday at six? I mean, the place is black at that hour.'

She looked again at the photograph, and shook her head. I ordered the Jameson, a double with water. When she brought it, she said, 'He wasn't with your man with the limp, was he?'

'Maybe. What did your man with the limp look like?' I said.

'Bit of a mess, to be honest with you. He had a combat jacket on, real scruffy like, not a designer one or anything. Long hair, a little goatee beard. Bit of a shambles, bit of a dopehead.'

'And the limp?'

'Ah it was desperate, poor fella. One of those, you'd think at first he was puttin' it on, know what I mean?'

Tommy Owens. The T on the list. I drank half the whiskey neat. It seared the back of my throat and filled my nose with its sweet smoke.

'And he was with the man in the picture?' I said.

'I wouldn't swear to it. But he was a smart looking, business kind of guy. Big head of curly hair, yeah. I remember thinkin', they're an odd couple. Are they cousins, or gay or somethin'?'

'Well, they're not cousins anyway. What happened then?'

'I don't know, it was black in here like I said, I was runnin' around like a blue-arsed fly. Next time I noticed, the guy in the photo had gone, and Scruffy was there with this woman, well out of his league I'd've thought.'

'What did the woman look like?'

'Honey blonde, hair piled high, expensive lookin' black clothes. I mean, she was old, must've been at least forty, but she looked well on it. Discreet. Tasteful. Most people in here with money, they wear it on their backs, know what I mean like?'

Linda.

'And were they here long?'

'I didn't see them again. I had a smoke break at seven, when I came back on they were gone. Or she was gone anyway. I was lookin' out for her. I was gonna ask her where she got her hair done.'

I paid for the Jameson with a ten, drank the rest mixed with water and left the change as a tip. Coming out onto the Seafront Plaza, I looked across the sea towards Bayview Point. There was some kind of commotion down on the promenade, with a crowd gathered, and what looked like flashing lights. I headed that way, and pushed across the grass through the summer throng of joggers, dog walkers and ice-cream eaters. A horde of rubberneckers had gathered behind the bandstand around the second set of white and blue police tape I'd seen that day. There to secure the scene were two uniformed Guards. One looked like he was taking witness statements from about half a dozen people. The other was my blabbermouth friend from the town hall, the Guard with no lips. I marched straight towards him, tapping my mobile phone.

'Detective Sergeant Donnelly,' I said, nodding meaningfully.

He threw a glance to his rear, looked at me uneasily, then nodded and lifted the tape to let me through. The tape sealed off the centre point of the promenade, where a set of stone steps leads down to the sea. Beneath the promenade, there's a lower walk which gets drenched by the waves at high tide. The tide was turning now, and it was on this lower walk that the burly, squat figure of Dave Donnelly stood, inspecting the body of a man sodden and distended by the sea. I was halfway down the steps when a woman in a charcoal-grey suit appeared from the other side of the walk and blocked my passage.

'Sir, this is a crime scene, you've no business here, please leave the area,' she said.

She was about five-five, with short red hair and piercing green eyes; her body was slender but powerful-looking, like a tennis player's. Dave Donnelly turned around.

'Move back up the steps, sir, now. Now!'

I did as I was told. Dave joined us on the upper promenade, an expression of incredulity on his open face.

'Loy? What do you think you're doing here?' said Dave.

The only thing I could think of was the truth.

'The Guard on duty let me through, so I thought I'd come down and have a look. Body just wash up?'

The redhead had been staring at me; now she turned to Dave with a grin of derision.

'You know this clown, Detective?'

'I used to,' Dave said.

The redhead was Detective Inspector Fiona Reed. Dave explained briefly who I was. Fiona Reed didn't look impressed.

'You realize you risked contaminating a crime scene? If you have the experience DS Donnelly says you have, you should know better,' she said.

'That body looked like it went in the sea a few days ago,' I said. 'Thousands of folk would have walked back and forth along upper and lower promenades since, the weather we've had. No forensics to speak of, I'd say, except on the body itself.'

Behind DI Reed's back, Dave Donnelly was rolling his eyes.

Reed put her hand on my forearm and squeezed. She had quite a grip.

'Don't be a smart alec, Loy. Especially when you know fine well you've just behaved like a prick. And don't think because

65

you used to be friends with Dave, you can tag along after him.'

She tightened her grip on my arm, then released it. Dave was trying to suppress a grin. He wasn't trying very hard.

'Now get out of here, and let the real detectives do their work.'

I did my best to look abashed. It wasn't difficult. My arm felt like someone had closed a door on it.

'I'll see him to the tape, DI Reed,' Dave said.

She looked at him, then back at me, shook her head once and walked away. Dave set off towards the lipless guard. I followed.

'You're some fuckin' eejit, Ed,' Dave said. 'You don't want to make an enemy of Fiona Reed.'

'I know I don't,' I said.

'You just have,' Dave said.

'Have you an ID on the body, Dave?' I said.

'It's not Peter Dawson anyway.'

'Does that mean you know who it is?'

We reached the tape. The lipless guard didn't like me any more than DI Reed did, but at least he kept his hands to himself. The police photographer had arrived, along with the forensic team I had seen earlier at the town hall. Behind them a tall, raven-haired woman in a long black dress was being led along by a female Guard. The woman wore dark glasses, and as she approached the promenade, she stumbled, and laid her hand on the Guard's shoulder for support.

'That's Mrs Williamson. I better get back,' said Dave, turning to go.

'Dave? Would it help if I said please?'

He turned back and said, 'You're supposed to be a detective. Work it out for yourself. And don't pull a stunt like this again, Ed.'

Then he was on his way across to join Mrs Williamson.

When I got back to the car, I checked the index cards I had found in the Dawsons' bin. No Williamson there.

The other list read:

Dagg

T

L

JW

The T was Tommy Owens. The L was Linda. But before Linda arrived, Peter took off – to meet JW? Perhaps – except, who was JW? Could the W stand for Williamson?

I took the photographs from my pocket. The flyer I had found on my windscreen came with them. It highlighted the failure of Seafield County Council to ensure the survival of the community swimming pool, and warned of the danger of this public amenity being sold to private developers. It proposed a public meeting at the bandstand on Seafield Promenade, and a march from there to the pool. The flyer closed: 'Issued on behalf of the "Save Our Swimming Pool" campaign by Noel Lavelle and Brendan Harvey, Labour Party Councillors, Seafield County Council.' The names seemed familiar.

I looked through the list of fourteen names again: Brian Joyce, Leo McSweeney, James Kearney, Angela Mackey, Mary Rafferty, Seosamh MacLiam, Conor Gogan, Noel Lavelle, Eamonn Macdonald, Christine Kelly, Brendan Harvey, Tom Farrelly, Eithne Wall, John O'Driscoll. There were the Labour pair. What about the rest? Were they all local councillors? Another name on the list rang a bell: James Kearney. I got Rory Dagg on his mobile and asked about the Kearney whose office you had to sit outside to get building permits.

'That's Jim Kearney, yeah, what about him?' Dagg said. I could hear the chattering of small children in the background.

'Is he a local councillor?'

'No. But he works for the Council. He's the planning officer.'

'Could you . . . if I read a list of names to you, could you say whether they have any connection with Seafield County Council?'

'Depends how long the list. I'm solo here with three kids under five.'

I ran through the list, excluding Harvey and Lavelle.

'Yeah, most of them are either councillors or council officers.'

'What's Seosamh MacLiam?'

'An epic pain in the hole, that's what he is. Anti-developer, anti-builder, anti-fucking anything that wasn't built two hundred years ago. We'd all be living on the side of the road if it was left to the same Mr Williamson. Only he wouldn't want any roads either.'

A crash sounded down the phone, then a piercing scream and child's wailing.

'Gotta go,' grunted Dagg, and broke the connection.

Mr Williamson? Seosamh MacLiam. Of course: MacLiam – Son of Liam – is the Irish for Williamson. And Seosamh is the Irish for Joseph. I'd been away so long I'd forgotten Ireland has a language of its own – even if most of the Irish prefer not to speak it. And Mrs Williamson was his wife, now his widow, come to identify the body.

Joseph Williamson.

JW.

Peter Dawson's disappearance and the Councillor's death looked like they could be connected. It was time to talk to Tommy Owens.

～

When I drove along Seafield Promenade, MacLiam/ Williamson's body had been strapped to a gurney and was being loaded into the back of a Garda medical vehicle. An RTE TV crew were filming, and as I passed, I saw DI Fiona Reed flipping a reporter's microphone out of her face. I turned off the coast onto Eden Avenue – twenties and thirties villas hidden from the road by great sycamore, ash and horse-chestnut trees, their branches aching with green in the evening sun. In Quarry Fields, kids played on skateboards, and in the drive to what I hadn't yet gotten used to calling my house, wearing a pair of battered old combat trousers and a 'Give 'Em Enough Rope'-era Clash T-shirt, Tommy Owens was wax polishing the 1965 Volvo.

When he saw me, he came close and spoke in a low, urgent voice.

'Ed, the gun is gone. I checked the sideboard –'

'It's OK, Tommy, I've got it.'

'You've got it with you? Or –'

'I'm looking after it. Don't worry.'

Tommy looked up at me from beneath furrowed brows. I winked at him and turned back to the car.

'Jesus, Tommy, are you done already?' I said. 'Good work.'

'Most of the work was done twenty years ago,' he said, a slow smile of pride spreading across his face. He made a long speech about pistons, rods and rings, camshafts and carburettors, bearings and bushings, transmission gaskets and seals. I nodded like I had a clue what he was talking about, and he said, 'You haven't a clue what I'm talking about, have you?'

'No,' I said. 'But if you give me the keys, I'll be happy to drive the thing.'

'It's gonna need maintenance, Ed, and if it's obvious you haven't a notion, you'll be ripped off, any garage'll think, here comes some rich cunt with his weekend hobby, let's make him pay.'

'I'll worry about that later, Tommy.'

'Just be sure that you do. Anyway, there she is.'

'Thanks.'

I went into the house, picked up the Laphroaig, glasses and a jug of iced water and brought them outside. Tommy was sitting in the porch, rolling up a three-skinner, heating a small block of dope with a cigarette lighter and crumbling the edges into the tobacco. I sat beside him and poured a couple of drinks. A woman in her thirties came out of the house opposite with her two young children. At her gate, she looked across the road at us. I offered a smile and a wave, but she whipped her head away and hurried her kids out of our sight. I guess two middle-aged men drinking whisky and rolling joints on a porch wasn't her idea of adding value to the neighbourhood.

Tommy smoked the joint about halfway down, until his eyes were red and watering and a smile had ploughed its way into his face. He offered it to me, but I waved it back at him, and he finished it off. He nodded and laughed a little, and took a hit of his drink.

'So Ed, what did you get up to today man? Have a swim, get any sun?'

'I spent my day asking people questions, Tommy. See, I'm looking for Peter Dawson.'

'Peter Dawson? Why, what's happened to him?'

'According to his wife, he's gone missing.'

'His wife? And what, has she hired you to find him? I warned you about Linda Dawson, Ed –'

'But you didn't tell me you were with her in the High Tide last Friday.'

Tommy's grin had become a mask. 'Was I? I can't remember.'

'And minutes earlier, you were drinking with Peter Dawson. Making you the last person to see him before he disappeared.'

'If you say so man. I bump into a lot of people. Maybe I should keep a diary, log what everyone says, case they go missing and I'm the only one who knows what their last words were. Only thing, I'd better warn them not to talk shite to me all the time.'

'Tommy, what were you doing with Peter Dawson?'

'Just . . . bumped into him in the street, you know? Thought we'd have a quick jar.'

'In the High Tide? Don't bullshit me Tommy, there'd have to be a very good reason for you to go into a pub like that.'

Tommy tipped his head back and grimaced. 'I know, Jaysus, the state of the place, like drinking in a fucking hairdresser's.'

'So? What was that very good reason?'

Tommy drank some whisky, took a gulp of air into his lungs and exhaled slowly.

'Peter owed me money. I was meeting him so he could pay it back.'

I burst out laughing.

'Sorry, millionaire's son owes you money? What did he borrow, twenty quid?'

Tommy frowned, as if he were about to get on his dignity, then laughed it off.

'All right man: truth? Weekend deal for Mr D: fifty-bag of dope, fifty-deal of coke.'

'Yeah? This you scamming the Halligans, creaming off the top of their stash? Or is that what you do now, Tommy? Are you one of Podge's dealers?'

'What if I am?'

'A drug dealer. For a gangster. That it?'

'It's not as if . . . I mean, it's just dope, coke, E: consenting adults all the way. Not as if I'm hanging round the playground pushing smack to schoolkids.'

'What did you talk about?'

'Nothing much. I just wanted to get out of there.'

'But you didn't, did you? You stayed.'

Tommy looked quickly at me, as if wondering which lie to tell, then stared at the ground.

'Peter was . . . agitated. Excited, you know. Like something big was about to happen.'

'What? He wasn't branching into the drugs trade himself, was he?'

'I don't know. Not drugs. Anyway, he got a call on his mobile. Whoever it was wanted to see him earlier than they'd arranged. He asked me to stay and tell Linda he'd call her later.'

'So you met Linda that night? She never mentioned it.'

'Nah, she wouldn't,' Tommy said, with sour emphasis.

'And how did you find her?' I said.

'The usual. "Lady Linda talks to the little people." This expression on her face, like someone might spot her talking to me.'

'Was she drunk?'

'I've never seen Linda Dawson drunk.'

'Really?'

'I don't mean she doesn't drink all the time. But she can hold it. She'd drink you and me under the table. It's a useful part of her act, though.'

'What act?'

'Her whole "I'm a sensitive soul on the edge" bit. Sobbing and then being brave about it, she's so lonely, she can't take much more. She does it in Hennessy's about once a month. Then she goes home with some dupe who's given her a shoulder to cry on. It's pathetic.'

'Sounds like it's personal, Tommy,' I said.

Tommy flashed me a look of cold rage, then drained his glass and sat with his head down, breathing heavily through his nose.

'Tell me this: what's the deal with that marriage? How did the most beautiful girl in Bayview end up with a bloated rich kid like Peter Dawson?'

Tommy held his left hand up and rubbed thumb against index and middle fingers.

'Makes the world go round,' he said. 'Linda did the whole arty thing in her twenties. Tried to make a go of it as a painter, went out with mad beardy blokes, lived in dives, suffered for her art. She didn't make it. After ten years, she thought, time to trade that dream in. And she was determined it was going to be a cash deal. So she went after Peter Dawson.'

'Surely she had a wider choice. Rich men form a queue for a woman like that.'

'Ah yeah, but she wanted to be sure, you know?'

'Sure of what?'

'Sure she wouldn't fall in love with the guy. And with Peter, that was guaranteed, at least as far as she was concerned.'

'What kind of woman would want to guarantee herself a loveless marriage?'

'The kind of woman who doesn't have an ounce of love in her,' Tommy said bitterly. 'The kind of woman you should have nothing to do with, Ed. Steer clear, man, steer clear.'

The dope and the whisky had proved no match for Tommy's nerves: he was tapping his feet and nodding his head, as if the arrhythmic vibrations of his past were working their way through his bones. He was bound up with Linda and Peter in ways I didn't know about yet, but there was no point in asking him straight out: Tommy would always tell a lie in preference to the truth, as much out of habit as strategy. Better to drop a hard fact and see if it caused a ripple.

'Tommy, do you know a local councillor name of Seosamh MacLiam?' I said.

Tommy gave me his thinking face, meaning either he was checking his dope-addled memory or he was stalling.

'Because they fished him out of the sea today.'

That did it. Tommy looked like someone had walked across his grave.

'Joey Williamson is dead?'

'I think that's who Peter Dawson was due to meet the day he disappeared. Probably it was Williamson who called his mobile when he was with you in the High Tide.'

'Jesus. I don't believe it.'

'Did you know him, Tommy?'

'Everyone knew him, he was . . . well, he was a councillor, but he was really sound, you know? Against the developers, the builders, he led the protests when they were going to build on that old Viking site in Castlehill. He was in favour of legalizing weed too.'

'What was Peter Dawson's connection with him? I understand he wasn't exactly Mr Popular with the building trade.'

'I don't know.'

'You weren't really in the High Tide to sell Peter Dawson drugs, were you? What were you meeting him about, Tommy?'

He stood up and dragged his ruined leg halfway across the garden. The sky had clouded over now. It was clammy, and the midges were beginning to bite. Sweat glistened like sequins on Tommy Owens's darkening face.

'What is this, Mr Private Fucking Dick? Do you think I know where Peter is? What the fuck are all these questions for?'

The swear-words rang out like chimes of menace in the hot suburban night.

'Keep your voice down. All I'm trying to do is get to the facts.'

'Well you don't have to give me the third degree while you're doing it,' Tommy said sulkily. 'Fucking Gestapo tactics.' He was pouting like a thwarted boy, and I smiled in spite of myself.

'I haven't pulled your fingernails off yet, have I?'

'Only a matter of time,' said Tommy, but he smiled too, and tossed his head like a dog, as if he was trying to shake his mood away.

His mobile rang – the ringtone was the eleven-note riff to Thin Lizzy's 'Whiskey in the Jar', a record we played to death as schoolboys, proud they were the first Irish band to make it onto *Top of the Pops* – and he hobbled as far as the gate to answer it. When he came back, he wasn't smiling any more.

'That was Podge Halligan,' he said. 'He wants to meet me tonight, in Hennessy's. Bring the gun and everything.'

'Did he say why?'

'"And we'll take it from there." That's all he said.'

'What do you think he meant? Is it a loyalty test, or does he want you to use the gun?'

'Maybe both,' Tommy said. Fear showed in his tiny eyes. 'I can't do it, Ed, I can't . . . what am I gonna do?'

He sounded like he was going to burst into tears. I felt a surge of anger flood my brain: at Tommy Owens's weakness, his inability or refusal to do anything to help himself, his complacent assumption that whatever lie he told or drug he sold, whatever act of small-time criminality he committed, everything would be fine – despite all the mounting evidence to the contrary.

The dark-green Volvo gleamed in the sun. I walked around it, running my hand along the bodywork, tapping on the windows and opening and closing the bonnet, as if I were a prospective buyer, inspecting the car for flaws. Even if there had been any, short of a flat tyre I wouldn't have been able to spot them. The car had belonged to my father, had evidently been a source of pride to him, and maybe on some level I was trying to feel that pride too, feel some vibration, some distant echo of the man he was. But it was useless. I didn't know enough about my father, and I didn't know anything about cars, and all I ended up feeling was foolish on top of angry, like someone trying to look as if he knows what he's doing and failing. Sweat pinpricked my brow and the roots of my hair.

'I've got to go,' I said. 'Have you got the keys?'

'Do you want to drive it now?' Tommy said.

'No, I want to put it in a museum and charge admission. Have you got the keys?'

'They're in the ignition.'

Of course they were. Being angry makes you behave like a fool, but realizing it doesn't make you stop. I got in the Volvo and started the engine. Tommy came around to the driver's window, eyebrows aloft in his anxious face.

'I'll meet Podge Halligan for you, if you like,' I said.

'Oh God, man, would you?'

Tears actually did appear in his eyes, and he reached into the car and clutched my arm.

'Provided you tell me the truth: why did you meet Peter Dawson on Friday?'

Tommy exhaled slowly.

'To give him money.'

'Tommy, for fuck's sake —'

'Not my money.'

'Who did it come from then?'

Tommy looked around him, then leant in the window and spoke softly in my ear.

'George Halligan,' he said.

7

The clutch on the Volvo was a bit stiff, and the engine roared, and it rattled as I picked up speed, but it was a smooth ride, and I hit sixty for a short stretch coming along the coast road past Bayview. The sun had dropped behind the hill, and a fresh salt breeze gusted in off the paling sea. I passed the train station and pointed the car up the drive of the Bayview Hotel. A smart wedding was in full swing, and refugees from the dance floor, the men in disintegrating morning suits, the women in pristine charcoal and aubergine two-pieces, spilled out onto the terrace and sat smoking in the grounds. I parked the car and went to reception, where a TV was announcing the death of Seosamh MacLiam.

Before I left, Tommy Owens told me he assumed the money – a 'bag of cash', he called it – was some kind of sweetener from the Halligans to Peter Dawson – for what, he didn't know, but the Halligans ran legitimate site security for builders all over the southside, so it could have been a tender for future work in that line, or a bribe to help them keep the contract. He denied being a bagman for George Halligan, and said that was the only time he had made such a payoff. We agreed it made sense for him to lie low in Quarry Fields tonight.

I got a telephone directory, sat in the shade of an old eucalyptus to the rear of the hotel, ordered a pint of Guinness from a passing waitress and began to work my way through the list of councillors and council employees. It took a while, as there were several entries for most of the names. Three weren't listed at all – Leo McSweeney, Angela Mackey and the planning officer, James Kearney. Brian Joyce and Mary Rafferty weren't at home, but I got office numbers to ring in the morning.

Excluding MacLiam/Williamson, that left eight calls. Local politicians the world over resent the fact that the national media doesn't report their many opinions and activities in the detail they believe they deserve, or at all, so I identified myself as Sean O'Brien of the *Irish Times*, ringing to get their reactions to the death of their Seosamh MacLiam. The reactions in the first six cases were similar: shock, dismay, a brief tribute, its generosity proportional to the political persuasion of the speaker. In each case, I asked whether they felt MacLiam's close relationship with Peter Dawson of Dawson Construction was unusual for an anti-development candidate; Noel Lavelle, Conor Gogan, Christine Kelly, Tom Farrelly, Eamonn Macdonald and Brendan Harvey all denied any knowledge of the relationship, with Lavelle and Harvey going on to say they'd be amazed if any such relationship existed: they had worked closely with MacLiam on many planning and rezoning appeals, and on the recent campaign to save the swimming pool; indeed, Lavelle said MacLiam was anti-builder 'to a fault', echoing Rory Dagg's verdict.

The next call I made was to Eithne Wall, but someone had got to her first. She had rung the *Irish Times* and been told they had no reporter by the name of Sean O'Brien working for them. She said she had caller ID on her telephone, and she was going to report my mobile number to the guards. I had blocked my number from showing on a caller ID display, but I hung up anyway. At least one of the first six councillors I had spoken to had something to lose. I needed to get to my last man before he was got at.

John O'Driscoll had a wavery, slightly camp Dublin accent, and a precise, formal manner, as if he were dictating to a secretary. He sounded nervous, so I decided to see if I could work out why.

'Sean O'Brien of the *Irish Times* here, Councillor O'Driscoll. We're just wondering in the wake of Councillor MacLiam's murder why your name keeps coming up, linked with Peter Dawson of Dawson Construction?'

There was a long pause.

'Councillor O'Driscoll?'

'I have always been happy to listen to the public when it comes to any planning and development decisions, and to act in the interests of the common good, and that remains the case in relation to Seafield Swimming Pool, Castlehill Golf Club, or indeed any other proposed development.'

I had found an empty file in Peter Dawson's office marked 'Golf Club'. I asked O'Driscoll why he had mentioned Castlehill Golf Club, but he was in mid-flow.

'I have no special connection with Peter Dawson. Nor had I any with Councillor MacLiam, whose tragic death is a blow to us all. My thoughts are with his wife and children at this sad time.'

I tried again.

'Councillor, could you expand on your remarks about Castlehill Golf Club?'

But O' Driscoll had hung up.

~

Carmel Donnelly (O'Rourke as was) gave me a hug, looked me up and down, grinned and said, 'Jesus, Ed Loy, you look like shit.' She was a big-boned woman with wide, knowing eyes and full lips. Her face had a few lines now, her chestnut hair was threaded with grey, and her clothes were flecked with milk and children's food, but she had a crooked, crinkle-eyed smile and a way of looking at you that made you feel like you'd missed your chance with her, but only just. Carmel and Dave had been together since they were sixteen; like Dave becoming a cop, it was one of those things you knew was meant to be.

'I'm sorry about your ma, Ed. Mine died last April. No-one tells you how awful it's going to be, doesn't matter what age you are. For a year, I'd wake in the middle of the night and cry my way towards dawn. Dave had to sleep downstairs, he couldn't handle it.'

Her eyes filled with tears. She raised her palms in the air, shook her head and smiled. There were kids' paintings on the walls, holiday snaps in frames, the remnants of a meal on the table. In the divorce cases I'd worked, they always talked about 'the family home' and they were almost always lying; the parents hadn't had enough love, or luck, or guts, or whatever it is you need to create one. Dave and Carmel had managed it though. I looked at photographs of the children: three boys of about four, six and eight, and a little girl with a shock of fair curls.

'What age is the girl?'

'Sadie's just two. You've not been tempted?'

I shrugged, and gave what I hoped looked like a wistful smile.

'Never too late, for men anyway,' Carmel said. 'Although it gets much harder on the knees.'

There was a loud crash upstairs, followed by shouts of glee and howls of pain.

'I wouldn't always recommend it but. Dave's out back. I hope you have some good news for him; he told me you were behaving like a prick.'

Carmel swept upstairs to calm the mayhem that had erupted. I went out to the back garden, where Dave was having an argument with an eight-foot rose bush. As I approached, Dave freed the last root, picked the bush up and heaved it in my path. I went down fast and, after pricking my hands on the rosebush's thorns, lay there beneath it.

'That's for making a clown of me today, you bollocks you.'

'Are you happy now?' I shouted.

'No,' Dave said. 'But at least I don't look as fucking stupid as you do.'

He picked the massive rose bush off me and offered me his hand. I got up without his help and brushed petals and leaves from my clothes. Blood oozed from my torn hands. Dave was far from being a stupid man, but he had an amazingly stupid grin on his big open face.

'Fiona Reed take a dim view then, did she?' I said.

Dave was on me in a flash. He grabbed my lapels in his huge fists and pulled my face up to his. I held his wrists hard.

'Don't fuck with me, Ed. I've been on the Force since I left school. I've been Detective Sergeant for five years, looking at Inspector pretty soon. And I've got where I've got through results, through police work, not politics. Being known as a good cop, not an office jockey – that's what matters to me. So when you compromise me in front of a senior officer, when you risk contaminating a crime scene as if you've got my say-so, it's bad. You can fuck off back to the States and do what-ever it is you do there, but this is my life here, so don't make a mock of it. Understand?'

'I understand. Now get your fucking hands off me.'

Dave let go of me, and I shoved him away and turned back towards the house. Carmel was watching through the kitchen window. I flung her a big false smile, and turned to see Dave doing the same. Caught rapid. For the second time that day, a woman rolled her eyes, shook her head and left us to it. Dave's face subsided into a bulldog scowl.

'What do you want, Ed?'

'Was Seosamh MacLiam murdered? When was he reported missing?'

'That's police business.'

'So is this. I think the last person Peter Dawson met before he disappeared was Councillor MacLiam. I know Dawson was carrying a lot of money at the time, money that came directly from George Halligan. I think that at least one, probably more, of Seafield County Council were involved with Peter Dawson. And I think it might have something to do with Castlehill Golf Club.'

'That it?' Dave said, breathing heavily.

'So far.'

'That's a lot of thought and fuck all else.'

Dave turned his back on me and went towards the house. But Carmel hadn't left us to it after all; she came out with two bottles of beer and put them on the patio table. She said something to Dave and went back in the house. Dave sat down at the table and grabbed a bottle. I joined him and tipped the other bottle to my lips.

'Carmel says I should be patient with you, seeing as how you've just lost your mother,' Dave muttered.

'I'm not asking for any favours,' I said.

'You are, though.'

Dave tipped the bottle back and took a mighty swallow. It was Czech beer, Staropramen, cold and very strong. He wiped the foam off his mouth with the back of his broad hand.

'Also, Carmel thinks I don't have any friends.'

'Why does she think that?'

'Because I don't.'

He didn't have to explain. Cops seldom had friends. They had the tribe of other cops, who understood, and they had marriages, and that should be enough, although it rarely was. We drank in silence for a while.

'Give me a fact, Ed,' Dave said, his tone the opposite of expectant.

'I know for a fact Halligan gave the money to Dawson.'

'The Halligans have run Dawsons's site security for years. All above board.'

'What, are the Halligans legitimate now?'

'Not exactly. But they've businesses that are. Every cent of drug money they bring in gets laundered so quickly – rental apartments, taxis, a hairdresser's, a pub – even the Criminal Assets Bureau weren't able to touch George Halligan.'

'They're still drug dealers, aren't they?'

'You should know. Isn't your old mate Tommy Owens a mule for them?'

'And you just let them operate?'

'That's what the National Drug Unit said a few years ago. My Superintendent, Casey, was happy to keep the relative peace, but the NDU barge in, "zero tolerance, let's get the drugs off the streets", you know, to fill this month's political quota. So a couple of dealers do two or three years, they get Podge sent down for five on possession of firearms, and what happens? Headbangers from all over the city see a gap in the market, come out here sniffing round the Halligans's patch. Blanchardstown, Blackcross, Clondalkin, Charnwood, they're all trying to take over. Result? Total mayhem. Fifteen killings in two years. 'Course, the NDU have fucked off to do good elsewhere, you know, some big splashy half-a-million-worth-of-cocaine-seized news item, oh well, that'll be the drug problem solved for ever then, thanks lads. Meanwhile, we have to wait for Podge to get out. When he does, he sorts the whole thing. Don't get me wrong, Podge Halligan is a scum-sucking piece of rubbish and I can't wait to see him mouldering in his grave, but until we get the resources – and the laws – to sort the drug problem, we just have to handle it. Which means turning a lot of blind eyes. Which is by and large what the public wants – I mean, who buys all the coke and E? Middle-class people. If we cut the supply there'd be an outcry.'

'What about heroin?'

'The Halligans don't sell heroin. Different story if they did.'

'You sound as cynical as Tommy Owens.'

'Dozy gobshite. He's not sharp enough for this carry-on, he wants to get shot of it. Tell him I said that.'

'What's the story with Castlehill Golf Club?'

Dave shrugged.

'It was sold to an outfit called Courtney Estates, along with the surrounding land. About forty acres, all told. They've applied for it to be rezoned high-density development.'

'What is it at the moment?'

'Agricultural. If it goes through, Courtney Estates will make a profit of about one hundred and eighty million.'

'Nice. And who are these lucky Courtneys?'

'No shortage of lucky Irish property developers these days.'

'Is there much opposition to their imminent good fortune?'

'Sure. The Greens, Labour, all the usual suspects. And MacLiam most of all. That's why, if you're saying Peter Dawson was paying him off, forget about it. MacLiam's whole deal was No Development: he was the comfortable-classes' darling. Woolly jumpers, traditional music, the bit of Gaeilge. And his legalize cannabis thing fitted with their ex-hippie image. No way would he want to risk blowing that.'

'Maybe he needed the money.'

'His wife is a trust fund girl. Remember Jack Parland? "Ireland's First Millionaire"?'

The beaming man in the waxed jacket and tweed cap.

'There's a photograph of him and John Dawson on Peter's desk,' I said.

'Sure he was Dawson and all's hero. Anyone who wanted to make a few bob out of property and didn't mind the corners they cut looked up to Parland. He's into all sorts now, banks, airlines, newspapers, everything. Anyway, Aileen is Parland's youngest daughter. MacLiam didn't need money.'

'Was MacLiam dead before he went into the sea?'

'They haven't done the autopsy yet. He was bruised and battered, but that could have been the rocks. They don't have a time of death either. Now, what else have you got?'

I told him about the stolen files in Peter Dawson's office, including the empty file marked 'Golf Club', and about John O'Driscoll's automatic linking of Seosamh MacLiam and Dawson to the proposed development at Castlehill Golf Club. It sounded a little flimsy in the retelling, and Dave was openly sceptical.

'An empty box file?'

'All of his financial and phone records were cleaned out. And Linda said Peter doesn't play golf.'

'I've seen him in Bayview Golf Club many's the time,' Dave said. 'And I'm not saying local councillors aren't bent, but there's been so much scandal recently about money changing hands in return for votes and tribunals investigating planning corruption that councillors all over Dublin are running for cover. I'd be surprised if they were taking major backhanders in Seafield.' Dave shrugged. 'Doesn't sound like much yet, Ed.'

'What time was Seosamh MacLiam reported missing?'

'He wasn't. But he didn't come home on Friday night. His wife never heard from him again.'

Same night as Peter Dawson. It had to be more than coincidence. Not that I believed in coincidence.

On my way out, Carmel said I must come round soon for a spot of dinner. Dave grunted some unenthusiastic agreement. Then there was a loud crash from upstairs, followed by high pitched cheers and squeals.

'If those shaggers wake little Sadie . . .' said Dave, and he bounded into the house.

'"Little Sadie,"' smiled Carmel. 'She has him wrapped around her finger. That girl'll break his heart.'

I muttered something about women wearing the trousers, and gave what I intended as a knowing grin, but something in my eyes must have betrayed me.

'Ed? Are you all right?'

'Ah, you know,' I said. 'The funeral and everything.'

I turned away and waved and made it to my car before Carmel could ask me any more. Because it wasn't my mother's funeral, but the funeral eighteen months before of my two-year-old, Lily: the tiny white coffin, the stricken face of my wife, the ashes vanishing onto the ocean, and nothing to make it right, nothing.

That girl'll break his heart.

~

Night was falling as I drove down to Bayview. I took a left off Strand Street opposite the Catholic Church, parked in Hennessy's car park, walked in the back door of the pub and ordered a double Jameson with water on the side from a barman in a black Nirvana T-shirt with a shaved head and metal studs in his nose, cheek, eyebrow and tongue. The last time I had been in Hennessy's I was still at school, I was going to university to become a doctor, I was learning about women, and how to drink, and talk, how to live, I had two parents and, even if I didn't get along with one of them, it was nothing that couldn't be solved or survived. I was looking forward to my life. Everything had changed in the years since. Hennessy's seemed pretty much the same though: the exhausted, threadbare carpets, the brown leatherette seats split and slashed and oozing foam, the jukebox playing, still, unbelievably, 'Hotel California'. A haze of patchouli oil, cheap perfume and sweat hung in the air. Despite a ban on all smoking in pubs, the smell of tobacco and dope still clung to the walls. Dazed looking people in plaid shirts and bikers' leathers sat drinking abstractedly, as if they were waiting for something to happen. Two women with tattooed arms and unfocused eyes drank pints of cider and spoke to each other in intense whispers while three grimy infants swarmed on the disintegrating rug beneath their feet. A party of teenage Goths in green-hued white face, all spiked hair and black velvet and lace and crows' feathers, were nursing identical sticky dark burgundy drinks – rum and blackcurrant, I guessed – and stroking pale blue packages of French cigarettes. None of them spoke, or even looked at each other.

The barman brought me my whiskey. I sploshed water in, drank half of it and asked him for a pint of Guinness. By the time my pint was ready, I had finished the Jameson, so I ordered another.

'Another double?' the barman said, looking me in the eye.

'Yes please,' I said.

'Drinking to forget?' he asked.

'I can't remember,' I said.

I chased the second whiskey with the stout and had to stop myself from nodding my head and clapping my hands. The booze was doing its work, throbbing its adrenalin back beat at the base of my chest, shooting its crystalline connections around my brain. For a brief moment, I was exactly where I wanted to be: sitting on a bar stool in the narcotic blear of Hennessy's lounge, in plain sight and completely invisible.

Hennessy's had always been Bayview's little secret. Never mind the drugs, and the underage drinking, Hennessy's was simply where you came if you didn't fit in. Daddy's little princess never came here, but her sister did, and she came with something to prove. It was the one place guaranteed to be free of rugby, golf, of competitive sport of any kind, and of the people who played it. Hennessy's clientele was pretty ambivalent about basic functioning, let alone competition. Now, when Bayview was being transformed into a theme village of estate agents and over-priced restaurants, of art galleries and bijou shops selling designer chocolates, New-World wine, French furniture and Italian shoes, Hennessy's was more than ever an antidote to the piss-elegant gentility of it all.

From where I stood I could see across the gantry to the Public Bar, as it would have been called years ago. Little more than a broad corridor, the bar in Hennessy's made the Lounge look like a Holiday Inn. It was in part a class thing. When my old man moved out of the council house in Fagan's Villas and bought his own home he vowed that he would never be seen in Hennessy's Bar again. He was leaving all that behind. But it was also a no-class thing. The bar had always had a bad reputation. We grew up hearing of it as a place full of people who would stab you for looking at them. I remembered it lined with sullen, beaten, vicious men, their faces purple and grimacing from alcohol and cigarettes and hopelessness. It didn't seem much different now. Gusts of joyless laughter drifted across the gantry. The man I was looking for stood with his back to me, at the centre of a ring of snickering sycophants. He was broad shouldered and thick necked, and the muscles in his over-developed back and massive arms rippled beneath his tight white T-shirt. He wore a white baseball cap, and every inch of visible flesh was sunburnt and tattooed in those Celtic designs that look like a lattice of black metal tridents.

I must have been staring, because one of his cohorts nudged him, and he turned around and looked at me. I hadn't seen his face for a long time: the pig eyes, the snub nose, the oversized mouth, the features all compressed together in a permanent jeer in the centre of his large round face. He pointed a stubby finger at me, mouthed my name, took off his hat, swept it down and across his chest and bowed his head. Then he turned away and muttered something, and his lackeys yelled with ugly laughter.

Change and decay in all around I see . . .

But Podge Halligan would always be a prick. He was bigger than us, but it was all fat; he used to be the one Halligan everyone could beat up. Half the time his brothers wouldn't even come after you in revenge. They beat him up all the time as well, figured that was what he deserved. So Podge hung around with kids three and four years younger than him, and beat them up. Soon he had his own little gang. They preyed on the very young and the very old. When Podge was fifteen, he and two twelve-year-old mates mugged a seventy-six-year-old man for his pension. Only the man was a World War II veteran, the twelve-year-olds ran away, and the old soldier broke Podge's right arm and three of his ribs. After Leo broke his left arm for making a show of them, the other Halligans decided it was time to take Podge under their wing. He might be more hindrance than help, but at least they could control the embarrassment factor if they were keeping an eye on him.

I got another double Jameson, from a tiny girl in crimson plaits this time, and drank it staring at Podge Halligan's back. I went around the lounge and in through the side door that connected with the bar. My shoes clicked on the old tile floor. I walked up to Podge Halligan, chest out, fast enough for him to come off his stool and through his ring of thugs to greet me.

'Ed Loy, lookin' good man,' he said, his reedy voice too high-pitched for his bulk.

'Well Podge. Looking good yourself. Working out and so on. You're not a fat cunt any more. Where does that leave you, just a cunt now, are you?'

Podge was so taken aback he began to laugh.

'Fuck's sake, Ed. Nice to see you an' all.'

Podge stepped back, and his boys began to move between us. I held them off.

'I'm here for Tommy,' I said.

'Who?'

'Tommy Owens. You asked him to meet you here. I've come in his place.'

Podge flexed his shoulders and rolled his massive neck.

'You got here early, Ed. Suppose that's on account of you not being a crippledy prick like Tommy. What does that make you, just a prick, are you?'

Podge's boys yelled with sycophantic laughter. Podge's face glowed burgundy with stupid glee. I could feel the whiskey heat in my chest. My eyes were boiling. I stepped up to Podge again.

'This is a warning, Podge. Don't fuck with Tommy Owens. Got me? If you're trying to set him up for something, it's not gonna work, all right?'

Podge was still beaming.

'Set him up? For what? I know lads, to knock him down, like a skittle, wha'?'

I grabbed Podge by the T-shirt, and heard the material rip.

'Tommy doesn't have the gun any more. So forget about it, OK?'

Podge stopped laughing. He turned around and said, 'Noel' to the barman, a burly fifty-year-old in a tight grey jumper. Noel vanished into the lounge and slid the gantry doors shut.

The first punch came from a blue baseball cap on my right, but I had to take it, as it was the tall guy on my left with the nose ring I needed to stop first. I jabbed Nose Ring twice in the Adam's apple with my elbow, and having let my jaw ride with two punches from Blue Cap, I stepped inside the third and smashed him in the face with my forehead. I grabbed him by the ears and headbutted him again. I heard a crack, and could feel the squish of cartilage and the hot spray of blood against my forehead and in my hair. I pushed him down and stepped away. Nose Ring was holding his throat, still gasping for air. There were three others, but Podge moved in front of them. He hit me once full in the stomach and I doubled up and dropped to my knees, winded, desperate for breath. I felt the whiskey rising, and before Podge could kick me in the face it was slopping out of my mouth onto the cold tiled floor. Beer followed it, and a bunch of other stuff followed that, until at last I was hacking up yellow green bile.

'Ah Jaysus. Mind me fucking Nikes, you messy cunt ya,' said Podge.

'Get him into the car park, we'll do him there,' said Blue Cap.

'Leave him alone now, and stop behavin' like a bunch of fuckin' knackers,' said a crisp voice. I looked up at a wiry, dark-haired man with a small moustache in a black chalk-stripe suit, a blue shirt with a white collar and a red tie with a jewelled tie pin.

'Edward Loy, you're an awful man. Don't tell me, it was a bad bag of nuts. I've warned Noel about keeping them past their sell-by date,' said George Halligan.

Noel appeared behind the bar as soon as George used his name. Podge Halligan leant into George and whispered something in his ear. George shrugged, raised a hand in front of his brother's chest, whispered some instructions to Podge, then waved his hand in the direction of the lads. George took a card from his pocket and wrote something on the back of it. I was on my feet now, tasting bile. Podge came up to me.

'We'll see ya, Ed, righ'?' he said, sliding his tongue over his thick lower lip, his expression caught between a glare and a leer. Podge took the card from George and padded out towards the car park, his boys following.

'You should never write anything down in my line of work,' said George, replacing his pen in his breast pocket, 'but the problem with Podge is, he lives in the permanent present tense, know what I mean? He forgets what you tell him as soon as he's out the door. They should never have taught Podge to read, then he'd have to fucking remember. But everyone is promoted one level above his ideal competence, isn't that right Ed? Noel, Remy with ice, bring this man a pint, he needs to settle himself. And shift some little lounge-person out to mop up that scutter.'

George Halligan ran his hand up and down the lapel of my jacket, then looked at the label.

'Nice piece of cloth. What is it? Boss? Ah yes, very reliable, the Germans, not unlike their cars; if you can't afford a tailor, Boss is perfectly adequate. Could do with a tie though, Ed. I don't like this open-necked shirt shenanigans, it's just a fad. And now ties are a reasonable width again, there's simply no excuse.'

George Halligan led me to a small table inside the door. I sat down and leant back against the wall, then quickly sat up straight again. My head was reeling.

'Afraid you'll spill?' said George. 'It's the worst, isn't it? Ah, you'll be grand. Now, first off, very sorry about your ma. And maybe it's a bit early for you to be out on the razz, mind plays tricks on you when your old lady dies. That said, no need to go making a cunt of yourself in here, bar in Hennessy's not your style Ed, leave it to Podge and his little pals, lucky I came along at all, otherwise they would've fuckin' *had* you.'

Noel brought me a pint of Guinness and George Halligan an ice-filled balloon glass of brandy. The brandy fumes made me queasy. Sweat stung my eyes. I tipped the cold pint to my lips and let a third of it slide down my throat.

'Kill or cure, Ed, kill or cure is the only fuckin' way. Good man. Now, Podge tells me you've come all over protective of Tommy Owens. I understand, I've tried to help the same Tommy out myself. But you know as well as I do that the only time Tommy Owens is definitely not lying is when he's asleep, and that the major difficulty in catching Tommy Owens in a lie is that he's never even sure himself when he's telling the truth.'

'He's not lying about the gun. A Glock 17, I saw it myself.'

'But how do you know where he got it from? Podge says he knows nothing about it.'

'Podge always tells the truth, does he?' I said. 'I can imagine that all right.'

George Halligan winced in mock pain.

'You might have a point there. Sadly, I am not my brother's keeper. But he tends not to lie to me. At least, not intention-ally. Anyway, in the event Podge was to be carrying out hits, which is certainly not a class of behaviour I could condone, the last person in the world he'd think of using would be Tommy Owens.'

'That's why we figured he was setting him up. A body would be found, the cops would get the tip off, and lo and behold, the gun that did the deed would be found on Tommy.'

I swallowed some more of my pint. George leant in close and dropped his voice.

'Sounds a bit elaborate for Podge. And don't forget, I brought Tommy in. Felt sorry for the fucker, what with his daughter and all. Despite his invalidity benefit being cut off because he's not an invalid any more, he's just another lazy bollocks who doesn't want to work for a living. Tommy's under my protection, you could say.'

'Do you still feel guilty about crippling him then?'

George exhaled very suddenly. The playful light had suddenly drained out of his eyes, and he looked tired and irritated.

'Listen,' he said, pointing his finger at my chest, 'if I hadn't done him, he'd be brown bread now.'

'How's that? For stealing your bike? That a capital crime back then?'

'He didn't steal my bike, he stole Leo's bike. Leo was a cunt for knives at the time, sure he stabbed the Doran young one a few weeks later, remember? He was looking for Tommy and he'd've cut his heart out if he'd found him. So I got to him first. And it had to be brutal, otherwise Leo would've steamed in regardless. How was I to know the bones wouldn't knit back together properly?'

George Halligan looked as ruffled as I imagine he ever got.

'So you do feel guilty,' I said.

'I always liked Tommy,' George said. 'And he never really held it against me, the ankle thing. Which I appreciated. So I've tried to look out for him, when I could, you know?'

George Halligan drained his brandy, raised his eyebrows in what he probably intended as a humble smile and ran index finger and thumb along his moustache. Compared to his brothers, George gave the closest impersonation of a human being, but it was an impersonation, nothing more. I looked at his shirt: pale blue with white collar and French cuffs. Only two kinds of men wore that shirt: CEOs and gangsters. I still had enough in common with Tommy Owens not to be sure which kind I disliked more.

'How's Peter Dawson?' I said.

George's eyes narrowed. He waited a beat too long, then said, 'Who?'

'Peter Dawson,' I said. 'You know, Dawson Construction?'

George nodded.

'Of course. But I don't really deal . . .'

'You run site security for Dawson's, don't you?'

'A company in which I have an interest, Immunicate. But as I say, I don't really deal with the day to day.'

Maybe not. But affecting not to know Peter Dawson's name was pushing it.

George set his head in a listening position, leant forward and put his elbows on the table and his hands together, as if expecting more.

'Doesn't matter,' I said. 'I'll see you around.'

'I look forward to it,' George said, rising to his feet. 'Buy you lunch next time. Do a little business, you and me. Eye on the future. I mean it, Ed.'

I turned my back on him and walked towards the door, and for the first time noticed that there were other people in the room: a couple of old boys in caps seated at the bar, and a bunch of people sitting in a snug to the left of the exit. I held my hand up and grimaced, acknowledging the contribution I had made to their evening's entertainment. A couple of young lads in sportswear made a whooping sound, somewhere between a jeer and a cheer. No-one else even smiled. Several of their faces seemed familiar, but that had become such a feature of the past few days that I had almost stopped noticing it. As I left, George Halligan crossed to acknowledge them, and was greeted with low murmurs of fealty, like a feudal lord.

8

I parked about a hundred yards back from the turn off for Linda's house, in the speckled shade of a great sycamore. The sun was setting behind the hills to the west, washing the sky a grapefruit pink. I waited for half an hour or so, and then a black Mercedes convertible turned down the slip road. I counted to ten, started the engine and followed it, rolling in through the gates in its wake. I didn't want Linda to know I was coming. I was tired of hearing her tell me lies. This time, I wanted to catch her off guard, so that at least she didn't have time to make up a second set of lies to explain the first.

When I got out of the car, the driver of the Mercedes – a trim, sporty blonde who looked thirty-five, but was probably fifty – stood on the road, watching me. I pointed towards Linda's door, and she immediately turned and went inside her house. I looked around. No sign of life in the pudgy neighbour's house, and no car in his drive. And Linda wouldn't recognize the Volvo. I went quickly around the side of the house. Security lights came on, but I was betting the Persian cat set them off so frequently Linda had stopped paying them much attention. I made it to the shed behind the beech tree and looked up at the side windows. What lights I could discern were low, and seemed to be coming from the rear. I worked my way round to where the house had been cantilevered above a long sloping garden to give an unhindered view of the bay, and ducked down behind an unwieldy clump of St John's

Wort. Linda was standing by the white sofa in her living room, smoking a cigarette and staring out to sea. She was wearing a short black cardigan over a low-cut purple silk top, a tight black skirt that fell just above the knee, black stockings and black high heels. Her golden hair was piled high on her head, and her lips were the same blood-red shade as her fingernails. She looked like a quiet night in was the last thing on her mind.

Tommy Owens had said Linda Dawson could drink us under the table, that it was a useful part of her act. I tried to square that, and the sight of her tonight, dressed for the fray, with the Linda I had seen thus far: drunk and tearful, a lost and lonely soul at the end of her tether. Then when she stood up and walked across the room to answer the telephone, the sway of her hips drained my mind of thought, and I had to look away to catch my breath. It was a stiflingly humid night. Across the bay, the city lay dark and mysterious beneath its shimmering lights, like a great cathedral lit only by candles.

I went round to the front of the house and knocked on the door. Heels clacked on the hardwood floor, and Linda's voice said, 'Just a minute.'

When she unlocked the door, her face betrayed no surprise at seeing me; if anything, she looked relieved.

'Hey Ed, look at you. How'd you get through the gates?'

'I played follow-your-neighbour. She didn't seem bothered about a strange man showing up uninvited on your doorstep.'

'What do you mean by that?'

'What do you think I mean? You're not exactly dressed for church there.'

'What, that I'm some kind of Anytime Annie, strange men always welcome at my door?'

'Are you?'

'I don't know what business it would be of yours if I were. I hired you to find my husband, not investigate my morals.'

'A jealous lover might have an interest in seeing your husband disappear – permanently.'

A flicker of what looked like fear crossed Linda's face.

'I don't have any . . . there's no-one who fits that description.'

'Are you sure?'

'Certain.' Linda wet her red lips with her tongue and smiled. 'On the other hand, I seem to remember you mounting a fairly intensive investigation of my morals last night. How did that work out for you, Ed Loy? Did you get what you wanted?'

The smile stayed on her lips, but there was a challenge in her eyes. I suddenly felt less like a detective than a jealous lover myself, in thrall to the pulse of my own stupid blood.

'Yes, thank you,' I said. 'Did you?'

'I always get what I want,' said Linda, baring her teeth. 'Then I always discover it wasn't what I wanted at all. That what I really wanted all along . . . was a drink.'

She was standing inches from me. I could smell, I could almost taste, the make-up on her face, her grapefruit scent, the smoke on her breath.

'What happened to your lip?' she said.

'I bit it,' I said.

She touched my cheek with her cold hand, then turned back into the house.

I found her in the kitchen, where she was filling a jug with lime juice and rum, and dropping sprigs of mint into a bowl.

'Mojitos,' said Linda. 'Want one?'

'Sure,' I said. 'And while you're mixing it, you can fill in some of the gaps in the story you told me.'

'What gaps would those be?' Linda said.

'How you met Tommy Owens in the High Tide just after Peter left. How he must have told you he gave Peter a bag of cash from George Halligan. How you know much more than you're telling me about that, and about everything else. How if you really give a damn about finding your husband, you'll tell me all you do know.'

Linda was pounding the mint leaves together with sugar and water. She stopped, her head bowed, and appeared to be sobbing.

'And you can cut out the tears, Linda. I'm not sure I believe them any more.'

She looked up and glared at me, her dry eyes flashing.

'Why didn't you tell me you had met Tommy that night?'

Linda looked away and shook her head.

'Why did George Halligan give Peter money?'

'I don't know.'

'Was Peter trying to develop land around here? Castlehill Golf Club, for example?'

'He might have been. If he was, he didn't tell me about it.'

'How well do you know George Halligan?'

'I don't know him at all. I know who he is, obviously; everyone does.'

'But you can't think of any reason he'd give Peter all that money?'

'Are you sure he did? If all you've got to go on is Tommy Owens's word, I wouldn't count on it.'

Linda piled the mint and sugar syrup into the jug, added sparkling water and ice and stirred the mixture with a long spoon.

'What did you and Tommy Owens talk about? Why does he hate you so much?'

'Because long ago, before my marriage but during his, we slept together – once, after a drunken party, or maybe during the party, I don't remember. It was one of those mistakes you make, at least for me it was, but Tommy thought it was the real

99

thing, so he went home and told his wife, and their baby was a year old at this stage, and the wife threw Tommy out, and he hounded me and stalked me until I had to be very cruel indeed to get rid of him, and his wife never took him back, and that's why he hates me.'

Linda poured two Mojitos, topped them off with sprigs of mint and gave me one.

'I'm surprised he didn't tell you all about it. Or do men not talk about stuff like that?'

'Not men like Tommy and me, anyway,' I said.

'Up,' she said, lifting her glass. We both drank. The Mojito was cooling, and it kicked like a Spanish mule. She took the jug and sat in the living room. I followed her through. Her scent was so intense, I felt I was tracking her.

'Who are you all dressed up for, Linda?'

'You, Ed. And luckily, you came.'

She topped up my drink and patted me on the shoulder. But her eyes darted anxiously towards the front door, and I wondered what the deal was: if someone was due here, or if she was expected somewhere else.

'What else do you want me to tell you?' she said.

'Tell me about Seosamh MacLiam.'

'That's the council guy who drowned, right? God, that was awful. Three sons.'

'Were Peter and he close?'

'Not that I know.'

'Was the money from George Halligan a bribe for MacLiam?'

'As I say, I wouldn't know.'

'You never seem to know much about Peter, do you? It's as if you were leading separate lives.'

'That's pretty much the truth. And we had finally worked up the courage to acknowledge that fact.'

'Tommy says you never loved Peter to begin with. All you wanted was the money.'

'Tommy thought I couldn't love anyone else because, deep down, I loved him. So deep down, he was the only one who knew about it.'

'That isn't exactly a denial.'

'What am I, on trial here?'

'So you didn't know Seosamh MacLiam either.'

'Again, I knew of him.'

'Peter planned to meet someone with the initials JW after you that evening. JW – Joseph Williamson – it's the English version of Seosamh MacLiam. Did you know anything about that meeting?'

'No. Wait. He said he might have to duck out for five minutes, to sort out some site problem. But that's all it would be, five minutes. And he didn't tell me who it was.'

Five minutes. Time enough to give a bag of money to an incorruptible councillor to persuade him to alter his vote on a zoning decision for Castlehill Golf Club – a decision that would destroy MacLiam's reputation and his political support, made by a man married to a very rich woman. Then he took a phone call and vanished into thin air. None of it made any sense.

I stood up and walked to the window. The moon looked swollen, fit to burst. My stomach ached from where Podge Halligan had hit me, and my head throbbed from where I had nutted Blue Cap. I finished my drink. Linda stood behind me and put her hands on my shoulders.

'I can't get anywhere if you don't want to help me. You have to tell me what you know,' I said.

'I can't tell you everything, Ed. I'm not sure I know myself. What I think might have happened . . . what I'm afraid happened . . . you'll have to find it out. I *want* you to find it out.'

I turned around and searched her eyes. I don't know what I was looking for there: trust, honesty, some sign that she was on the level. All I saw was the cold glow of fear.

I headed for the front door. Linda followed, stopping to rummage through the drawer of a cupboard in the hall until she found a key pad for the security gates.

'You know you shouldn't be driving,' she said.

'Drunk driving was the national sport when I left,' I said. 'What happened? Has there been a sudden outbreak of civilization?'

'Not exactly. Maybe just the appearance of it.'

But when I hit the air, my legs nearly went from beneath me. Still. Drive with the windows open and no harm done. Linda walked down the drive with me, hissing out for her cat. When she saw the Volvo, she came over to admire it.

'It was my father's,' I said. 'You know he used to run a garage with John Dawson. They grew up together.'

A light came into Linda's eyes.

'There's something Peter started to say: "It all goes back to Fagan's Villas." Do you know what that means?'

I shook my head.

'I don't know that he did either,' she said.

Linda opened the gates for me. I pointed the Volvo out through them and headed up the slip road. I pulled beneath my sycamore on Castlehill Road and lit a cigarette.

'It all goes back to Fagan's Villas.' That's where my mother and father grew up, and John and Barbara Dawson too. They were kids together, fifty odd years ago. It all goes back to there. But what? What all goes back? The body found buried in concrete in the foundations of Seafield Town Hall? A photograph of my father and John Dawson? The fact that two box files marked 'Family' in Peter Dawson's office had been emptied of any other photographs that might show the two men together? I sat and smoked and waited.

After half an hour, a charcoal grey Lexus with tinted windows swept down from Castlehill and swung in towards Linda's house. After another fifteen minutes, I left the car and walked down the slip road to the security gates. The Lexus was parked outside Linda's darkened house. I took a note of the licence plate. The other thing I took note of was the security firm responsible for monitoring this little gated community. The name emblazoned on the gates was 'Immunicate'.

~

I was pulled over at the bottom of Castlehill Road. Two uniformed Guards approached me. They looked at the car for a while, then one of them came to my window and tapped on it. I rolled down the window.

'Nice car, sir.' He had pale blue eyes and thin lips set in a supercilious smirk it would have felt good to slap off his face.

'Thank you,' I said.

'Do you know you've no tax or insurance?'

'Yes. The car was fixed up today, and I couldn't wait to take it out.'

'I suppose you've no driving licence either.'

'Of course I have a licence,' I said. 'Just not on me. My name is Edward Loy. I came home from America for a funeral. So everything's been a bit . . . you know . . .'

'Yes. Have you had a drink tonight, sir?'

'I have, oh yes, a drink or two,' I said. 'Or three. Even.'

'Step out of the car, please sir.'

I thought about this, and decided that stepping out of the car was not what I wanted to do. What I apparently did want to do, in the few seconds available to me while the smirking Guard stepped back to allow me out of the car, was turn the key, put the car in gear and swerve left and out of the way of the other Guard, who was running for their car and slapping the light up and the siren on as I tore down past Bayview and along the main Seafield Road by Fagan's Villas and cut into Quarry Fields.

I parked in front of the house, to make it easy for them, and ran inside, where several things struck me, more or less simultaneously:

1. Someone had ransacked the place from top to bottom. Every cupboard had been emptied, every couch and armchair rent asunder, every table and chair smashed in pieces. The floors were ankle deep in broken crockery, torn books and ripped upholstery.

2. I had parked in the space the hire car had been in, which meant that the hire car was gone. The hire car with the Glock and the ammunition I was holding for Tommy Owens in the boot.

3. There was no sign of Tommy Owens.

4. The siren was getting closer. Once it stopped, the police would arrest me and then I would spend the night behind bars in Seafield Police Station.

I went out and sat on the porch. Tommy Owens had left a couple of fingers of Laphroaig in the bottle. I drank the whisky in the moonlight while I waited for the police to arrive.

9

A cab collected me at the airport and brought me to the house. The garden was well tended, with red and yellow roses, and the hedge was neatly clipped. I walked up to the front door and rang the bell. The man who answered was my father as he had been in his twenties, when he had just married. He looked at me politely, but without recognition. My mother joined him at the door. She was in her twenties also, and pregnant. They stood there together for a while, as if they were posing for a photograph. My mother smiled at first, but the smile soon faded, and the longer I stood there, the more frightened she began to look. Then she looked older, her hair white, her skin like crêpe. Then my father stood in front of her, and indicated that I should go. Then he was shouting at me, and pushing me down the drive. Then he was older too, and in his anger, the bones in his face pressed against his shining skin. Then his eyes turned black, and sank into their sockets. Then he vanished, and my mother slammed the door on me, and I stood in Quarry Fields, not knowing who I was, or where to go, or what to do.

~

In the morning, I was given a cup of tea and sent to wait in an interview room with walls the colour and texture of old porridge and dark grey carpet tiles and community centre chairs and table. At half nine, Detective Sergeant Dave Donnelly came in, leaving the door open.

'How's the head this morning, Ed?' he said, his broad face expressionless, his voice hoarse. He wore fawn flat-fronted Farah slacks, a white short-sleeved shirt open at the neck, the buttons straining against his barrel chest, and a loosely knotted grey suede tie with fresh egg yolk on it. He hung his grey jacket on the back of the chair, sat across from me and rested his elbows on the table, his massive forearms forming a triangle with his clasped fists.

'Not so bad, Dave,' I said. 'But that's 'cause I'm probably still drunk.'

Dave smiled tightly but said nothing. We sat in silence for a while. Then Detective Inspector Fiona Reed appeared and shut the door behind her. Dave fished a cassette tape from his jacket pocket and put it in a big double tape deck mounted on the wall above the table.

'Let's just leave the tape for a moment,' Reed said.

Reed was looking at me. I looked at my hands. For some reason, each of my fingers was stained black. Then she turned to Dave, who immediately lit in to me.

'You had quite a time yesterday, Ed. Trespassing on a crime scene, drinking with known drug dealer Tommy Owens, brawling in Hennessy's with local hoodlum Podge Halligan and his gang, a cosy little chat with George Halligan – that's Seafield's criminal contingent pretty much used up, I think. Then round it off with driving five times above the alcohol limit, without tax, insurance or a licence, resisting arrest and assaulting a police officer – tell me, was it your birthday, by any chance?'

'I had a lot on my mind, Detective. I don't remember assaulting –'

'You pushed Garda Nolan into a rose bush. His face looks like a cat scratched him. A cat that escaped from a zoo.'

'Garda Nolan. Is he the smirker?'

'Not this morning. What the fuck did you think you were up to? I mean, I know you just buried your mother, but . . . fuck's sake, man, you can't be runnin' round actin' the bollocks like that. Apart from anything else, driving pissed out of your mind.'

I was about to make an excuse, something about how, instead of having the space to grieve after the funeral, I had spent the day trying to solve other people's problems, but I didn't. I remembered tracking down a hit-and-run once who'd killed a mother and her three-year-old boy. He said he'd been drinking because it was the anniversary of his wife's death, drinking at her grave. He ran over his victims on his way home from the cemetery. When I rang for the police, he began to cry, not for the mother, or the little boy, or even for his dead wife, but for himself, for the sadness of his own drunken, self-pitying life. That's what I had done after my daughter died. First I got drunk to numb the pain, and then I got drunk to preserve the pain, and after a while I was using the pain as an excuse to get drunk, so I wouldn't feel pain or anything else.

'You're right,' I said. 'It was inexcusable. I assume I'll be going before a judge this morning?'

Fiona Reed was staring at me like I was something the sea had washed up. Dave moved to the wall by the tape machine and leant against it, rubbing his palm against the nap of his tightly cut salt-and-pepper hair. The blood had drained from his face, and his eyes were red. He looked like I felt.

Reed turned to him and said, 'All right.'

Dave switched the tape player to 'record.'

'Interview Room 2, Seafield Garda Station, July 22nd; Detective Inspector Reed, Detective Sergeant Donnelly present; interview with Edward Loy commenced 09.45 a.m.,' Dave said.

'I didn't knock someone down, did I?' I said, fairly certain I hadn't, but needing to wrest some control of the situation back my way.

Dave sat down and rested his elbows on the table again. He pushed his mouth into his fists, then rested his chin on top of them. He started to speak, then stopped and looked at DS Reed, who nodded.

'DS Donnelly interviewing Mr Loy. Can you account for your movements after you left Hennessy's Pub last night?'

'I went to Linda Dawson's house in Castlehill. I was there about half an hour, maybe longer.'

'What is the nature of your relationship with Mrs Dawson?'

Mrs Dawson.

'She hired me to find her husband.'

'Hired you in what capacity?'

'As a private detective.'

'Are you licensed to work as a private detective in this jurisdiction?'

'No.'

'But you represented yourself to Mrs Dawson in that capacity.'

'She was already aware that I had worked as a private detective in the United States.'

'So you would characterize your relationship with Mrs Dawson as strictly professional.'

'What's all this about? Is Linda all right?'

'Just answer the question please.'

'I suppose so.'

'Meaning you're not sure?'

'Meaning I saw her for the first time in twenty years two days ago at my mother's funeral. It's a bit early to be talking about "relationships". Is Linda all right? Because if –'

'And after you left Mrs Dawson's house?'

'I drove back down the hill and into the Garda checkpoint.'

Fiona Reed's lips were pursed; her green eyes were blood-shot and red-rimmed; her flame-coloured hair stood on end. She lifted her finger and pointed it at me.

'Peter Dawson's body was discovered last night, on his boat. He was shot at least twice. A Glock 17 was found at the scene,' Reed said.

With a missing person, you always know whether there's any hope or not, but you always suppress that knowledge in case it interferes with your investigation. I think I had known Peter Dawson was dead from the moment Linda asked me to find him.

'Mr Loy makes no verbal response,' Dave said for the benefit of the tape.

'Your prints were found all over the boat. And on the gun,' Reed said.

My prints? So that's what the stains on my fingers were. The last Laphroaig must have switched my lights out com-pletely.

'I searched the boat from top to bottom yesterday,' I said. 'Like I told you, I was looking for Peter Dawson.'

'Your prints are on the murder weapon.'

'You assume it's the murder weapon. You couldn't have done ballistics yet.'

'We spoke to the boatman.'

'Colm? Well, there you are.'

'He said you came up from below looking for tools. He said you went back down, that you were there long enough . . .'

'Long enough to what? Shoot Peter Dawson twice with a witness fifteen feet away?'

'You could have used a silencer.'

'And what? I left the gun behind to incriminate myself, but took the silencer with me, because it had sentimental value?'

I had a sudden flash. One of the faces in Hennessy's Bar, among the crowd who rose to greet George Halligan, was Colm the boatman, Colm who went up the town a stretch if he wanted a pint.

'How did your prints come to be on the gun?'

Reed, the finger in my face again.

'Was there any blood?' I said.

Dave looked at the floor.

'Answer the question, Mr Loy –'

'Were there any shell casings?'

Dave looked away. Reed pursed her lips.

'I'm betting no. That means he wasn't murdered on the boat. What about time of death? But you probably haven't had the post-mortem results yet.'

Reed's green eyes never left me; her gaze was unsettling, but I wasn't going to let her know that.

'So what is all this?' I said. 'Do you really think I killed Peter Dawson?'

Dave stood up and knocked his chair to the ground, rolling his huge shoulders as he moved.

'Your prints are all over the Glock, you were placed at the crime scene before the discovery of the body, what are we going to do? Tell Superintendent Casey not to worry, we were at school together? How did your prints come to be on the gun?'

'I really couldn't say.'

Dave crashed his huge fists down on the table and began to shout into my face. 'Don't give me any rigmarole here, Ed, just answer the questions I ask like a good man. Or we're gonna have some trouble, you and me.'

Dave sat down and flashed me a quick grin. Some of that had been for Reed's benefit, but by no means all. I tried to figure out just how much I could tell them without landing

Tommy Owens in it. I didn't think Tommy was capable of murder, but I wouldn't have thought he was drug dealer material either. I realized I didn't really know anything for sure about Tommy any more, but that didn't mean I was going to offer him up to the cops on a plate.

'I think the gun came from Podge Halligan,' I began.

There was a knock on the interview room door. Reed raised the finger she was fond of pointing and flicked it towards Dave. 'Don't go away now,' Dave said, and went out.

'Interview suspended while DS Donnelly leaves the room, 10.07 a.m.,' Reed said, hitting the pause button on the tape player.

It was stuffy and warm in the airless room, and I could smell my own scent rising, a toxic cloud of booze and sweat and smoke. My skin was crawling, and I wanted to scrub it with a can of bleach and a wire brush. I tried to focus on the danger I was in, but all I could do was wonder whether Linda would be upset or relieved to hear of her husband's death. And whether it would come as a surprise to her. And whether all that would mean I wouldn't get to sleep with her again. Fiona Reed was gazing at me like I was something that had crawled up out of a drain. I was wondering how I had managed to excite quite so much of her hostility on such a short acquaintance when Dave came back in to the room with two sheets of paper, one of which he passed to his boss.

'DS Donnelly returns to the room, distributes copies of preliminary post-mortem report, interview resumes, 10.11 a.m.,' said Reed, after releasing the pause button.

'Peter Dawson's body had already passed through rigor and begun to decompose. Which sets the estimated time of death at least five days ago, if not more,' said Dave.

'He was last seen on Friday at about six in the evening,' I said.

'And this is Thursday morning,' said Reed. 'What time did you get in from LA?'

'Sunday afternoon, about five thirty. So not only did I not do it, it looks like I couldn't have done it.'

'Just about,' snapped DI Reed.

A silence followed this outburst. I smiled. Reed nodded at Donnelly.

'All right. The two bullets retrieved from his body are 9mm Parabellum. The Glock 17 is chambered for the Parabellum 9mm round. It has a 10 round magazine with two bullets missing. We don't have ballistics confirmation yet, but I think it's safe to assume the bullets came from this gun. So – Mr Loy – once again – how did your prints get to be on the murder weapon?'

DI Reed came crashing in.

'Because it's not just the finger on the trigger, Mr Loy, as I'm sure you know. You think the gun came from Podge Halligan. What's that you're telling us, in the time you could take from your mother's funeral you were handling weapons for the Halligan gang?'

'All right. Who else's prints are on the gun?' I said.

'Who else's prints? You tell us,' Reed said.

'Because this is what I'm trying to say, it's a set-up by the Halligans, they're trying to frame this guy, just like they've tried to frame me.'

'What guy, Ed? We need you to say the name,' Dave said.

They were pissed off with me, and I didn't blame them, but Dave was as straight as they came or no-one was. Tommy would get a fair shake from Dave – and if he had killed Peter Dawson, there was nothing I could do to protect him, and nothing I wanted to do either. I wasn't as optimistic about Reed, but Dave was going to be compromised through his relationship with me if I didn't give them something. So I told them about Tommy's unexpected arrival at the house on Tuesday night, about how he claimed to have come by the Glock and all the rest, leading up to the gun being stolen with the hire car last night, when I was on alcoholic manoeuvres.

'So let's get this straight: Podge Halligan or one of his boys shot Peter Dawson, then gave the murder weapon to Tommy Owens and he brought it to you? Why?' said Reed.

'Why bring it to me? He was scared he was being set-up for a murder. And now it looks like he was.'

'Alternatively, Tommy killed Dawson himself, then brought you the gun –'

'Why would he do that? Why didn't he just dump the weapon, if it had his prints on it? Or wipe it clean before he gave it to me?'

'Maybe the gun itself is significant – whoever owned it –' Dave began.

'I doubt very much this gun is legally registered to anyone,' said Reed. 'It's probably a reconditioned piece.'

'The third possibility is that Tommy took the gun without Podge Halligan knowing about it,' I said. 'I went in and pretty much told Podge I was holding it for Tommy. They have Peter Dawson's body since Friday, trying to work out when and where to dump it. While I'm in Hennessy's with George, they go to Quarry Fields, trash the place, find the Glock in the boot of the hire car.'

'And then Podge took it and placed it with Dawson's body in the boat? How would they get access to the Royal Seafield? I don't think they're members, Ed,' said Dave.

I shrugged. I wanted to take a crack at Colm the boatman myself.

'All I know is, there was no gun and no dead body when I looked the boat over at lunchtime. It had been scrubbed clean.'

'Did you find anything?'

Just a photograph of my father and John Dawson.

'Nothing,' I said.

'Any idea where your pal Tommy Owens might be now?' asked Reed.

'You've tried his mother?'

'He didn't come home last night.'

'He's not a killer, Inspector Reed.'

'We've evidence that says he did it, and nothing to link the Halligans to it.'

'That's how a good frame works.'

'Why should we suspect a frame?'

'I'll find him. And I'll prove he didn't do it,' I said.

Reed exhaled quickly, a silent, mirthless laugh. She waved that finger at Dave again.

'Interview ends, ten thirty-five,' said Dave. He leant across and switched the tape off.

'Don't forget, we have you here on a number of charges, Mr Loy. You may not be in a position to be finding anybody,' said DI Reed.

'Shouldn't I be appearing before a judge this morning, to answer for my sins?'

'You certainly should.'

Reed stared at me for a moment, then pursed her lips and headed for the door.

'Unfortunately, the charges won't stand,' Dave said, shaking his head sadly.

'What?'

'Procedure wasn't followed correctly.'

'How do you mean?'

'Garda Nolan put the wrong date on the arrest form,' Dave said. 'A caution and you're free to go.'

'What about Garda Nolan?'

'Garda Nolan will have to learn how to do his job properly. Just get the car taxed and insured, Ed. And don't be drinking like a girl, and if you do, don't be driving like a cunt.'

'Is that my official caution?'

Reed turned back to me.

'No, this is,' she said. 'Peter Dawson is now a Garda inquiry. We'll look after all aspects of it, and that includes tracking Tommy Owens down. You keep out of it, Mr Loy. No ifs or buts, no outside assistance invited or appreciated: just stay away. Do you understand?'

I looked from her to Dave. No ifs or buts, no nods or winks there; they were warning me off for real.

'I understand,' I said.

I had always been a convincing liar.

10

I got a take-out cup of coffee and sat on a bench on Seafield Pier, watching seagulls swoop and shriek, and boats fill their sails and gust in and out of the harbour. The mackerel were running, and two men in a small green fishing boat out in the bay looked like they were pulling them out of the sea with their hands. The Garda Crime Scene teams had left the Promenade, but the Royal Seafield Yacht Club was still swarming with police.

I called Linda, but she wasn't answering; I left messages of sympathy on her home and mobile phones, and asked her to call me when she felt up to it. I tried to make my voice sound crisp and businesslike, but it didn't fool me; I hoped it would-n't fool her either.

I called Tommy Owens's mother, who said she hadn't seen Tommy for two days, and didn't sound particularly bothered about it. Then I called his ex-wife, Paula, who said she hadn't seen Tommy for two weeks, that he owed her money and that he was a malingerer and a useless waste of space. The only other place I could imagine Tommy being was Hennessy's; when I called there however, the barman told me Tommy had been barred. I said I found that astonishing, and asked had anyone ever been barred before. He said he didn't think so, he had worked there twelve years and he didn't know what you had to do to get barred, but whatever it was, Tommy must have done it: the word had come down from Noel Senior, and

Noel Senior hadn't kept Hennessy's open for fifty years by telling anyone his reasons.

I walked around Seafield until I found a menswear shop. I bought another black suit, five more white shirts and a supply of socks and underwear. In the supermarket I got new potatoes, peas in the pod, lemons, oatmeal, flat-leaf parsley and a roll of black refuse sacks. I went down the Pier and bought two mackerel at a stall that guaranteed all the fish it sold had been caught fresh that morning. I bought half a dozen newspapers in a newsagent's. Then I walked back to Quarry Fields.

In the house, I began to fill the refuse sacks with the debris from the break in. As I filled each bag, I took it out and threw it in the garage. The furniture downstairs hadn't been in great shape to begin with; now it was well beyond repair. I tossed broken chair frames and table legs in on top of the refuse sacks. I would have to hire a skip to get rid of it all, but I didn't feel up to it today. The writing desk in the back room had been smashed to pieces too, and it was only after I had cleared it away that I remembered it was where the family photographs were kept. All the snaps it had contained were gone. The fragment I had found on Peter Dawson's boat was now the only photo I had of my father. Someone was trying to remove all trace of my past, just as they had removed all trace of his.

∼

I sat on the living-room floor and looked through the newspapers. They were having a field day, and who could blame them? DEADLY TRIANGLE blared the *Daily Star*, with reports on 'much loved councillor' Seosamh MacLiam, Dawson and the 'Concrete Corpse' found in the town hall. I'd almost forgotten about him, and I suspected he would drop right down the priority list now. If he'd been dead (and buried) that long, he could wait a little longer for justice. TROUBLE IN PARADISE announced the *Irish Independent*, with many sidebar features on the upscale Bayview–Castlehill 'Top People's Seaside Suburb', where the luxury homes of top Irish rock stars, film directors, barristers and CEOs formed the exclusive enclave the reporter claimed was nicknamed 'Bel Eire'. The *Irish Sun* took up this theme: BLACK DAY IN BEL EIRE, it screamed, claiming 'sources close to the Garda investigation' said that Seosamh MacLiam had been dead before he went in the water, and detailing the rise and rise of John Dawson's construction business. The *Irish Times*, the national 'newspaper of record', confined itself to a brief report on page four which was so circumspectly written, presumably to spare the feelings of the families, or possibly the paper's readers, and so apparently anxious not to prejudice any criminal prosecution that might ensue, that it was hard, having read it, to be sure if anyone had been killed, or had died, or indeed, if anything had happened at all. The *Times* did however mention that John Dawson had been one of a group of businessmen who in the seventies and eighties had clustered around the figure of Jack Parland, Seosamh MacLiam's father-in-law.

Most of the papers speculated that the simultaneous murder inquiries would prove too much for Seafield Garda, and that while the investigation would remain based at Seafield Station, the National Bureau of Criminal Investigation would almost certainly be drafted in to assist. I wondered if Dave would appreciate the help. I wouldn't in his shoes; I'd see it as them muscling in and stealing my case. But it was his case now, nothing to do with me any more.

It was uncomfortable sitting on the floor, so I thought I'd see if lying on it was any better. That's where I awoke, to the sound of the doorbell. One side of my body was numb, and when I finally managed to haul myself to my feet, the blood rushed from my head and set me reeling. The sun had set, but it wasn't dark yet; the dusty house was thick with blurred shadows. The doorbell rang again, continuously this time. I ran a hand through my hair, rubbed my eyes in an attempt to persuade them to stay open and opened the front door to Peter Dawson's mother, Barbara.

Someone had once told Barbara Dawson she looked like Elizabeth Taylor, and she had taken it to heart. Her hair was golden brown now, and cascaded in lush folds over the top of a loosely tied aubergine scarf. Her eyes were large and brown, her aubergine lips wide and full; her skin was pale bronze and firm around eyes and chin, and it shone with a pearly glow. She wore a black linen trouser suit over a black top that revealed a hint of black lace cleavage, stood about five-six in heels and exuded a sexuality that would have been potent in a woman thirty years her junior. Barbara Dawson, with a matching aubergine scarf around her neck, was sixty-four, a year older than my mother had been; there were tears in her eyes as she embraced me.

'I'm so sorry about Peter, Barbara,' I said, aware that I still stank of booze and smoke and sweat.

'It's a terrible tragedy,' she said, dabbing at her eyes with a small silk handkerchief that matched her scarf. 'My family thanks you for all you did, Edward.'

'I'm afraid I didn't do very much,' I said.

'You did what you could, child. I believe we all did. I'm afraid there was a limit to what could be done.'

She smiled brightly, pressing her lips together with her teeth and nodding, as if to say how brave we must all be. I nodded my head, but I didn't understand. Barbara spoke as if Peter had finally succumbed to a slow-working disease, as if his death had been expected for months.

She held the handkerchief to her nose and looked around

her, batting her heavily mascaraed eyelids. I was about to apologize for the state of the place when Barbara, in a terribly grawnd Dublin-on-its-best-behaviour accent, said, 'Daphne certainly kept the house looking lovely and tidy.' I looked at her to see if she was mixing it deliberately, but we were still standing in the hall and her gaze was fixed on the chipped wooden banisters, so I decided she was trying to be polite without having much practice at it.

'Actually, we've just had a break in, Barbara,' I said, walking her into the kitchen. She stood in silence just inside the door. I asked if she wanted some tea, or a drink, but she shook her head. I wasn't sure what to do next, so I took the mackerel out of the fridge, unwrapped them and laid them on the draining board.

'They destroyed all the furniture, so I can't offer you a chair,' I said, trying to fill the silence. 'But the only thing they took was the family photograph albums. Every single photograph of my mother and father. Right the way back to their wedding and before. Don't you think that's weird, Barbara?'

Barbara Dawson was clutching a small black leather purse in her immaculately manicured, aubergine-nailed hands. One hand shot to her mouth in an expression of distress, then clutched at her tiny chin.

'It's barbaric, Edward,' she said. 'That you don't have so much as a memento of your mother. Barbaric, that's what it is.'

Her eyes kept flickering uneasily towards the mackerel, as if they were still alive, and could at any moment make a jump for her.

'Fresh today,' I said. 'Leaping into the boats, they were.'

Barbara Dawson shuddered. 'Your mother, God rest her, her father and mine were both fishermen. I grew up with the house stinking of fried fish: herrings, mackerel, ray, God help us, the reek'd be in your hair and beneath your nails, and never enough hot water to scrub it away. I swore when I had a house of me own, I'd never fry another fish, nor ea' anny neither. Eat any either,' she quickly corrected herself. Her accent had slipped back briefly to Fagan's Villas, where she and my mother had been next-door neighbours. She shuddered again, a more elaborate, full-body spasm this time, with one hand on her breastbone and one to her nose to fan away the imaginary odour of fish straight from the sea. I remembered my mother saying of her, tartly, 'She should've gone on the stage, that one. Only in a big theatre, mind, and you'd have to sit at the back.'

'All I have is this,' I said, showing her the torn photograph I had found on Peter's boat. 'Look, my father, Eamonn Loy, and John Dawson.'

The blood seemed literally to drain from Barbara's face. She looked as if she had seen a ghost.

'Are you all right?' I said. 'I didn't mean to give you a fright.'

'It's all right, child,' she said, her voice suddenly very low and deliberate. 'It's just such a land, seeing your poor father like that, after all these years.'

'I guess it must be thirty-five, forty years ago,' I said. 'Somebody's wedding, maybe?'

But Barbara had looked away, and was staring out the window. The male and female apple trees stood in the centre of the unkempt back garden, their hard green fruit showing no sign of ripeness.

'There's something written on the back,' I said, turning the photo over and showing her. 'See:

'"*ma Courtney*

'*3459.*"

You don't know who that might have been, Barbara, do you? Someone called Courtney? From the old days?'

Barbara shook her head, her lips set.

'I flung that past as far from me as I could, Edward,' she said. 'Haven't kept so much as a photograph. Don't like to see anything that reminds me. I date my life from the year John built the bungalows over on Rathdown Road, and we moved up to Bayview Heights.'

My mother had always tracked my father's decline from the moment the Dawsons moved to Bayview Heights: suddenly, John Dawson had outpaced him. Bayview Heights was considered very much more the thing than Quarry Fields, and with each passing year, the Dawson construction business grew and grew until finally, to crown their triumphal ascent, John and Barbara bought a Victorian mansion in extensive grounds at the top of Castlehill. When John Dawson put up the money for my father to open a garage, it was viewed by everyone as an act of loyalty, a tribute to where they had come from. My father had been drinking heavily for years, and working fitfully, and had it not been for my mother's job behind the perfume counter in Arnotts, the family would have gone under. The garage represented one last chance for my father, but as so often with people who need one last chance, he probably didn't deserve it, certainly hadn't prepared for it, and blew it comprehensively and, it seemed, wilfully. I put the photograph back in my pocket.

Barbara was fumbling with her purse. She took a brown envelope from it and thrust it at me.

'My family thanks you,' she said, her eyes full of tears, 'and I thank you.'

I took the envelope. Inside, there was a wedge of hundred euro notes.

'What's this for? I can't take this,' I said.

'For all you did, Edward,' Barbara said. 'You've been a great help to Linda.'

'I didn't do anything. I didn't find Peter. I don't know who murdered him.'

'If it was murder.'

'If it was murder? He was shot twice, Barbara. What are you saying?'

'The police said it could be suicide.'

'The police what? Detective Donnelly said a suicide can shoot himself twice?' I said.

'Superintendent Casey said it was perfectly possible. The trigger finger can go into spasm. They're waiting for the pathologist to complete the post-mortem.'

'And how did his body get on to the boat? It wasn't there yesterday, I searched it myself. Someone must have moved it there after he was dead.'

Barbara shook her head, then raised her eyes to heaven, as if that was one of those mysteries only God Himself could solve.

'Why would Peter commit suicide?'

'Living in the shadow of a great man like his father,' Barbara said, her voice tremulous, her tone solemn and elegiac. 'Every passing day, the boy would feel increasingly diminished by comparison. And then of course poor Linda couldn't have children. So all in all . . .'

All in all, what? It's what he would have wanted? It's better this way? Barbara sounded as if she was talking about another mother's son entirely, like a churchyard ghoul tying a neighbourhood tragedy up in cod-psychological ribbons and bows. Maybe it was shock, or grief shackled by the steeliest of self-control, or that she did consider her son an inferior manifestation of his father, who was better off dead by his own hand. Whatever it was, it was scaring the hell out of me.

'I don't know what the details of the post-mortem were, Barbara,' I said. 'But when I spoke to DS Donnelly and DI Reed, they were treating it very much as a murder inquiry.'

Barbara smiled tolerantly.

'Yes, well, Superintendent Casey . . .' she purred, as if seniority of rank were the only deciding factor. 'Of course, we may never know exactly what the circumstances were. There may have been any amount of drunken carry-on and shenanigans in the run-up. But no matter. I believe my poor boy took his own life.'

She nodded tragically, clutched her purse in both hands and walked out into the hall.

I followed her to the front door and tried to return the money she had given me.

'Barbara, I can't take this money,' I said. 'It's way too much. Besides, Linda has already paid me for the work I did.'

'It's only money,' she said, the beloved catchphrase of those who never have to worry about it. She looked around at the shabby, damp-stained walls, the grimy wallpaper, the chipped and rotting window jambs and the threadbare rugs, then turned her gaze on me, all of a sudden not bothering to disguise her contempt.

'Course, you were going to make a show of us all, weren't you?' Barbara said, a glint of malice in her smiling eyes. 'A doctor, wasn't it?'

I nodded.

'A doctor, indeed. And look at you now. The cut of you! You might have made Daphne proud, God rest her. And sent the few bob back to put manners on the house. Crumbling around her, it's a ruin so it is.'

Her teeth were bared, her smile a lurid mask, her trim, neat body shaking with passion.

'Gonna make a show of us all, weren't you? And now look at you! Well, I don't doubt you'll find some use for that money. I'm only sad I didn't give it to Daphne herself. 'Course, she wouldn't have accepted it. Too proud, you see. Pride, yes, pride.'

Her voice faltered. She brought the aubergine handkerchief to her bowed face and stood in the doorway, making sobbing sounds. I couldn't tell whether Barbara was on the level or faking, but her words had cut deep; the state of my mother's house had filled me with shame the moment I saw it; I should have helped her, and I hadn't.

Barbara dabbed her face. She was muttering something under her breath; it had the rhythm of prayer without the serenity; for all her willed composure, all her pantomimed gestures, grief was animating every breath she drew. How could it not?

'How is Linda?' I asked.

'In a terrible state, the poor child. She's going to stay with us for a while. She's been through so much, and of course, she's extremely vulnerable,' Barbara said. 'It's hard not to feel she's been taken advantage of. Especially recently.'

Barbara gave me a cold stare, then her face softened; she clasped my face with both hands and pulled it to hers, kissed me on the lips, hoped God would bless and save *and forgive* us all, then clipped out the door. As she walked down the drive and across the road to her car, she stumbled suddenly on the concrete, and was instantly transformed into an old lady, stooped and frail. She waited by the car for her chauffeur, in a black suit, to open the door for her; then, having regained a little poise, she sat in and vanished behind tinted glass. The car was a charcoal grey Lexus, and as it drove away, I came as far as the gate to check the licence plate. It was the same car I had seen parked outside Linda's house last night.

~

The perfume of night-scented stock hung thick in the garden air. I sat in the porch for a while, trying to sort through the details of the case, but they wouldn't arrange themselves in any order or pattern. A sheaf of junk mail in the letter box caught my eye, so I pulled it out and sorted through that instead: flyers for pizza delivery and garden maintenance, night classes, a local playschool and so on. I scrunched them up into a ball and went into the kitchen to trash it. The sight of the mackerel on the draining board reminded me I hadn't eaten all day. I put potatoes on to boil, gutted and cleaned the fish, coated them in oatmeal and fried them in butter. I shelled the peas and threw them in with the potatoes for the final few minutes, then drained the lot. I retrieved the ball of junk mail from the bin and read through it all again while I ate.

An ad for a new estate agent's announced: 'TO WHOM IT MAY CONCERN – and if you're a homeowner, it concerns YOU. Get the BEST PRICE on the market for your home. WE do all the work; YOU make all the MONEY.'

It went on in that delirious vein for a while, but I was stuck on that most conventional of openings: 'TO WHOM IT MAY CONCERN.' If you dropped it into lower case, you had 'to whom it may concern.' And if you were using that as the title for a document, you wouldn't want to go to the palaver of spelling it out each time, so you'd probably just use the initial letters of each word: 'twimc'.

That was what the document on Peter Dawson's computer was called, the one that had been wiped on Tuesday while Linda was at the funeral: twimc: to whom it may concern. The receipt from Ebrill's Stationery store in Seafield showed that Peter had bought envelopes, writing paper and address labels. Taken together, those two facts could mean a variety of things. But one of those things could certainly be that Peter intended to kill himself, and that he wrote a farewell note and posted it to somebody, or to several people.

And maybe that was it. Never mind about corrupt payments to councillors to influence planning decisions, never mind about Peter Dawson's links to Seosamh MacLiam's death, never mind about the part organized crime in the shape of the Halligan gang played, or why all Peter Dawson's and my family photographs had been stolen, or who moved Peter's body onto his boat; just mark it down to suicide, hush it up and move on. That was what Barbara Dawson wanted, that was seemingly what Superintendent Casey wanted too. Maybe it wasn't what Linda wanted. Maybe that's why she hired me: because she had an inkling of what was up, but wanted to get at the truth – wanted the truth, but was afraid of the truth. Well, too bad. Her husband was found, and there's an end to it. If you want the truth, maybe a private detective is the last person you should come to.

Night was falling fast. I dumped the dishes in the sink, locked the house, went to bed and slept for eight dreamless hours. When I woke up, rain was pouring from a slate-grey sky. That was more like it. That was the kind of Irish summer's morning I remembered. It made the previous few days seem like some kind of delirium, a post-funeral fever dream. As I drank a cup of tea, I knew exactly what I had to do. It was simple: I would have my father declared dead, then hand responsibility for the house over to Doyle & McCarthy. They could organize an executor's sale, subtract their no doubt exorbitant commission and send me the balance. In California. Because that was where I was going, as soon as I could get a flight. I'd had it with Dublin, where everyone was someone's brother or cousin or ex-girlfriend and no-one would give you a straight answer, where my da knew your da and yours knew mine, where the past was always waiting around the next corner to ambush you. 'It all goes back to Fagan's Villas.' Well, I wasn't going back there.

I was going to the place you went to when you'd had enough past, enough family, enough history, the place where they let you start again, make yourself up, be whoever you wanted to be. A happy orphan, in a land where no-one knew my name.

Blood.

You can't wash it away. Hot water only fixes the stain, and bleach turns it green. Cold water cleans the visible stain away, but it's still there, clinging to the floor, the walls, the curtains, the fireplace. And you can sand the boards and change the drapes, re-plaster and re-paint, you're still going to miss a drop, a splash, a smear. It's no longer even the same fireplace now, not the same as the one he was standing in front of when they shot him. And it's true to say they *shot him. He took the first shot, she did the rest. He was supposed to do it all. She was just there to watch. But you know how it is, when you're dealing with blood, things never work out quite the way you want them to.*

She said it would be cleaner if they used a gun. But that's only true if you know how *to use a gun, and he didn't. His hand was shaking, and the expression of shock, of disbelief, and then of fear, on his old friend's face made things worse. She was screaming at him to shoot, and for a moment, he felt like shooting her, but then he steeled himself, and closed his eyes, and pulled the trigger. The bullet hit her husband in the groin and punctured an artery. In an instant, there was so much blood it was like someone had stuck a pig. The gun fell out of her lover's hand and clattered on the floor. Her lover looked at his old friend, who was on his knees, screaming in pain, and threw up. The woman picked the gun up off the floor and pointed it at her husband. It was hard to make out what he was saying, or indeed if he was using words at all, but you could tell that he was pleading with her, begging for his life. Too late. Blood was spreading in a dark pool beneath him. She looked around her. Her lover had stopped puking; now he was weeping. She looked at him, not with contempt, but with resignation, the sense that she probably should have known she would bear the brunt of it.*

She was wearing open-toed sandals, and she could feel the blood between her toes. She thought momentarily of being a child, getting her feet wet walking home in the rain. Then she thought of the sea. Then she shot her husband twice in the back. He stopped screaming, but you could still hear his breath. Her upper arm and shoulder hurt from the pistol's recoil. The trigger was stiff, and she wondered whether she had the strength to squeeze it again. The sound of weeping told her she better had. She held the gun butt with both hands and shot her husband twice in the head.

She dropped the gun in the blood where the shell casings fell, and went to cradle her lover in her arms, wiping his tears away and kissing his cheeks. Now, she thought. Now, at last, her life could begin.

II

As a man gets older, if he knows what is good for him, the women he likes are getting older, too. The trouble is that most of them are married.

Ross *Macdonald,* The Zebra-Striped Hearse

11

I was on the point of ringing David McCarthy to set probate in motion when the telephone rang. Maybe it was McCarthy ringing me, I thought, somehow anticipating my plans. But of course, it wasn't.

'Is that Edward Loy?'

'Speaking.'

'Mr Loy, my name is Aileen Williamson. I understand you're a private detective.'

Here it was again, the old fever dream. You understand I'm a private detective, do you? Well, could you explain it to me?

'Mr Loy?'

'I'm here. What can I do for you, Mrs Williamson?'

'You know who I am, don't you?'

'Yes I do. I'm sorry about your husband's death.'

'My husband's murder.'

'Have the Guards declared it a murder investigation?'

'Do you think we could meet?'

'I'm not sure what good it would do, Mrs Williamson. You see, if it is a murder investigation, the Guards will be conducting it. And Seafield Garda warned me off, directly.'

'It's not a murder investigation. But it should be.'

'I still don't see . . .'

'I got an anonymous phone call. A woman. She told me you were searching for Peter Dawson, the builder's son. She said his death was connected to my husband's, but that the Garda investigations into Peter Dawson's case and my husband's were being undermined.'

'Undermined by who?'

'Senior officers, anxious not to offend powerful individuals.'

Superintendent Casey? Despite what Linda had said, did John Dawson still have the clout to influence a Garda investigation? And why were he and Barbara seemingly so keen to have Peter's death declared a suicide?

'And what has this to do with me?' I said.

'This woman said you didn't care about offending powerful individuals. In fact, she reckoned you'd relish it. If that's true, Mr Loy, I'd like to hire you to find out who murdered my husband, and why.'

Fever dream. Delirium.

'Who was this woman who called you?'

'As I said, it was an anonymous phone call.'

'No clue as to who she might have been? Her accent, her manner?'

'She knows you, not me. Sounded ordinary, soft Dublin accent. Friendly. A little nervous.'

'Anything else?'

'I have her phone number.'

'You do? How'd you manage that?'

'Joseph had caller ID phones installed.'

'Joseph or Seosamh?'

'No-one who knew him called him Seosamh. I think that was a sop to the Irish-language constituency. The Guards advised him to get caller ID to deal with crank calls, nuisance calls, menacing calls. Of which he received a number.'

This was my chance to escape, to get on a plane and never come back.

Apparently, I didn't want to take it.

'Mr Loy?'

'Give me your address, and I'll meet you in an hour.'

Aileen Williamson gave me her address. She also gave me the phone number the anonymous call came from. I dialled it, and a tired sounding woman said hello.

'Hello Carmel,' I said. 'It's Ed Loy.'

'Ed. Good to hear your voice.'

'Is it?'

'Very much so.'

'I assume your home number is unlisted.'

'Of course. All cops' phones are.'

'Aren't you curious how I got it?'

'Maybe Dave gave it to you.'

'You know he didn't.'

'Well. You're a detective, aren't you? I suppose you . . . detected it.'

'You know you can conceal your number from people with caller ID telephones.'

'You know you can turn that facility on and off.'

'So if you wanted someone to find out your number –'

'Yes, if you wanted that.'

There was a long silence. Carmel broke it.

'Dave is in a state over this, Ed. I'm not saying he told me to call Aileen Williamson . . . or that he'd be able to protect you in any way if you fuck up.'

'Don't you mean, when I fuck up?'

'I love men. They're always telling women what we mean.'

'Does Dave think there's a cover-up of some kind?'

'Dave would like the chance to find out. He's been pulled off the Dawson case.'

'Why?'

'Operational logistics, is what he was told. Because he believes in police work, is why. The whole thing stinks. But he's not giving up on this one. Will you help him?'

'I'll need stuff only the Guards have access to: forensic details, ballistics reports.'

'You'll get them.'

'You sure Dave will be up for this, Carmel?'

'I've already spoken to him. He'll be in touch. Mind yourself, Ed.'

Carmel hung up. I sat and listened for a while. The silence on the line sounded like the voices of the dead. If they knew anything, they weren't talking.

Aileen Williamson lived in Ballsbridge, on a broad tree-lined street of detached Victorian and Edwardian villas. There were half a dozen embassies and the occasional solicitor's office or dentist's surgery; the rest were private residences. Most showed the signs of recent building work: a tasteful extension, or a new perimeter wall, or freshly cleaned or painted stone and brick. The cars were expensive but discreet: Audis and Volvos, rather than Mercs and Jags: this was old money, Dublin 4 money, the kind of money that doesn't have to draw attention to itself. I couldn't imagine how much one of these houses cost; I guess it's like upscale shops that never display the prices of the goods: if you have to ask, you can't afford it.

The rain had been nothing more than a heat-weary cloud caught short; the air was so humid and the ground so warm that no trace of damp remained; blue and white rent the slate-grey sky asunder.

The Williamson house was a double-fronted three storey over basement red-brick villa. The drive crunched with those pale little stones that stain your shoes grey. Granite steps led up to the front door, which had stained-glass panes set around its elaborate architrave. A Filipina maid in a black and white uniform directed me around to the back of the house.

A gardener was training white jasmine up a trellis; another was weeding around a fine magnolia. They were talking to each other in a central European tongue, Romanian it sounded like. At the foot of the garden there was a raised wooden deck, on which sat a long maple table and chairs.

It sometimes seemed to me as if there was an entire generation of women who dressed almost entirely in black: Linda Dawson was one, and Aileen Williamson looked like another. She sat at the head of the table in a long black velvet skirt and a black silk blouse. A silver crucifix hung around her long neck. Her jet black hair hung straight to her waist; her oval face was pale and without make-up, her blue eyes gleamed. Her white hands rested on a stack of newspapers. With a small motion of her slender wrist, she bade me sit down; without a word she pushed the pile of newsprint towards me.

The top one – a tabloid – said DEEP POCKETS OF DROWNED POL. The story below it suggested, on the basis of 'Garda sources' that a substantial amount of cash had been found, wrapped in bin liners and taped to MacLiam's body, that this 'could well have been a corrupt payment' (no evidence was adduced for this), and that as a result the reputation of MacLiam as the incorruptible 'Councillor who Cares' lay in tatters. The next tabloid led with DEAD POL'S DRUG RIDDLE. It quoted sources 'close to senior Gardaí' and claimed MacLiam had enough heroin in his bloodstream to have caused an overdose. The remaining papers carried versions of one or other story. I looked at Aileen Williamson and waited for her to speak. She looked me in the eye, as if taking my measure, then spoke without waver.

'Joseph had an addictive personality, Mr Loy. Most people use the term as an excuse for weakness. But Joseph wasn't weak. When I met him, he was an alcoholic, and a compulsive gambler. But he conquered those addictions. We married, we had a family. With my encouragement, he went into politics. I was ashamed of what he had been, but so proud of what he became. And my pride outweighed my shame. I believed in him, you see. I still do.'

She smiled nervously at me, as if begging my indulgence for her sin of pride. I wondered if her husband's problems before he met her had been as serious as she claimed. Faced with such an intense and searching degree of regard from their wives, many men would take steps, secret or otherwise, to prove themselves unworthy of it.

The Filipina maid appeared with a tray of coffee and scones. She set it on the table and Aileen Williamson dismissed her with a quick smile and poured me a cup. I refused a scone; she poured half a cup of coffee for herself and continued talking.

'It's quite possible Joseph had relapsed. We're only human, after all,' she said, as if this was a regrettable but transitional state of affairs. 'The one thing I can't and won't bear is any suggestion that he might have taken a bribe. That for me is completely unacceptable.'

Ah yes, Jack Parland's daughter. The rectitude of rich men, the morality of money. All men are weak – Jack Parland was on his third wife twenty years ago, when his daughter was barely out of her teens – but money is strong, and demands strength in return.

'Do you think we can believe this overdose story, Mr Loy?'

'I can find out,' I said. 'Do you think it's believable? It's not unusual for a middle-aged family man to take drugs, but heroin is rarely his first choice.'

'Joseph – not long after the birth of our third child, Joseph was in a state of . . . well, I suppose you might say he had some kind of nervous collapse. I tried to snap him out of it, but he was extremely stubborn when he wanted to be. So I arranged for him to take a year out. I fundraise for a Catholic aid agency, and Joseph went on one of their missions to South-east Asia.'

'South-east Asia.'

'Cambodia, Laos, Vietnam. Thailand.'

'You think he developed a habit while he was out there?'

'I didn't want to think it. But something in him had . . . relaxed. At first, I thought it was just a new found calm. And he got caught up in the whole world of local politics – he said he wanted to make a difference – and everything seemed back to normal. Better than normal.'

'But?'

'But there was something about him – a look in his eyes, an attitude, as if nothing really mattered. As if, deep down, life were one big joke.'

'I'd have thought, if you were a local councillor with people pestering you about garbage disposal and broken street lights, you'd need a sense of humour.'

'It's serious work, Mr Loy. Local politicians are the people's direct connection to power – especially for those who have little else in the way of wealth or status. And Joseph took it seriously.'

'But nonetheless, you suspected him of being on heroin?'

'I knew he wasn't drinking. My mother was alcoholic, and you develop a radar for it in other people. But I worried that he was on *something*. And I know that, if one's life is not lived hand to mouth, a heroin habit can be tended for years.'

'What about gambling?'

'He didn't have the money. A councillor's salary is a pittance, six or seven thousand a year. I gave Joseph an allowance, of course, but it wasn't enough to gamble, at least, not on the scale he had been used to.'

'Maybe he got fed up having to make do with an *allowance* from his wife. Maybe he wanted some money of his own.

I have to tell you though that your husband was one of several councillors who were almost certainly being targeted by a land developer –'

'And I tell you, any hint of financial corruption on my husband's part is simply unthinkable!'

Her voice had risen to a shout. She clasped her hands together and bowed her head. I couldn't tell if she was praying or crying. When she looked up, her eyes were wet.

'My father built a business – an empire, some say – from nothing. But all along, there were the whispers, that he greased the right palms, took bribes here, gave them out there. That he dodged tax, and fiddled expenses. Even that he fleeced shareholders. None of it was ever proved – because it wasn't true – yet it stuck. People file him in their minds with the lads from the sixties and seventies, the smart boys in the mohair suits, the bunch of crooks who robbed us all blind with their secret land deals . . .'

I thought of the photograph of John Dawson with Jack Parland. There wasn't much money in Ireland back then, so anyone who had managed to acquire some was both revered and despised, often by the same people. I saw a guy on Venice boardwalk once selling T-shirts that read, 'The Rich are different from us – they get away with it.' No-one was buying any. What if they got rich one day themselves? Who knows what they might have to get away with then? Time enough to get all moral about money when they had some. And maybe not even then.

'I should tell you that any money I have is now invested in Church-approved ethical funds,' she said. 'And the greater part of the dividend – once the boys' education is paid for – a great deal of our income goes to charity.'

So despite maintaining that Jack Parland had come about his fortune honestly, his daughter still felt the need to give much of his money away – and to launder the rest, spiritually speaking. And to justify it all to me. And to clear her dead husband of the kind of allegations most people believed true of her father.

Aileen Williamson looked down at the table.

'I suppose you think it strange, that a wife would rather her husband was on heroin than that he had taken a bribe,' she said quietly.

'I think I understand,' I said.

'But you don't approve?'

'I'm not in the approval business, Mrs Williamson. Understanding is hard enough, don't you think?'

'It's important to be able to believe in people, Mr Loy.'

'Important not to believe in them too much though. They're only people, after all.'

She touched the crucifix that hung around her neck, rubbed it between fingers and thumb.

'You're not religious, Mr Loy,' she said.

'Not at the moment,' I said. 'But if I needed to believe in something, I'd believe in God.'

'Well, I suppose that's a start.'

'After all, He can't let you down if he doesn't exist.'

She shook her head and looked away, then looked back at me as if she had never seen me before. Suddenly she was all business.

'You'll need these,' she said, and pushed a set of keys across the table. 'The keys to Joseph's flat.'

'He didn't live here?'

'Of course he did. But he needed a residence within the Seafield council area. So I bought him a flat in one of the old houses on Victoria Terrace. The Guards have been through it, but I don't know if they found anything. Or if they even knew what to look for.'

'Did your husband ever mention Peter Dawson?'

'He spoke about Dawson Construction.'

'He didn't like them.'

'Joseph was anti-development. He didn't like builders in general.'

'Where are people supposed to live?'

'Everyone else thinks like that. Joseph was an idealist. He wanted everything that was built to be beautiful. He stuck to his principles. He was his own man.'

She was building him a mausoleum. I interrupted the eulogy to ask for a cheque. She baulked at the price, and tried to bring it down. I wouldn't haggle, and eventually she gave in. The rich aren't so different after all, at least, not from each other.

'One last thing,' I said. 'I understand your father is a newspaper proprietor.'

'He owns or controls just under half the press in the country,' she said, not without a flash of pride.

'I don't understand then – couldn't you get him to tell his editors to go easy, play the story down, cut you a break?'

'Jack Parland didn't get where he is by cutting people breaks.'

'Even for his own family?'

'Especially for his own family. I'm the only one of seven children living in this country, the rest couldn't stand being near him. Besides, he didn't like Joseph. He never really forgave me for marrying him. I was supposed to stay by his side. Daddy's best girl all my life.'

Her lips twisted in a thin smile that coloured her pale cheeks; her blue eyes flickered brightly with a fierce emotion I couldn't quite discern; somewhere between shame and pride, anger and grief; whatever it was, it had nothing to do with smiling.

Out on the street, I got a call on my mobile from Dave Donnelly.

'What do you need, Ed?'

'For now, Peter Dawson's bank details and phone records.'

'You've got them.'

'And anything you get on ballistics, forensic reports, so on.'

'I'll do my best. They won't come to me, but . . . I have my sources.'

'Is DI Reed –'

'DI Reed is playing politics with Superintendent Casey. DI Reed is not going out on a limb.'

'Explain something to me, Dave. Tommy Owens said Podge Halligan gave him the gun after the shots were fired. Surely that puts the Halligans in the frame?'

'Casey will do anything to avoid putting the Dawsons and the Halligans in the same frame. That's just not gonna happen. On top of which, the gun has conveniently disappeared.'

'The gun has what? The Glock 17?'

'Somewhere within the Technical Bureau in the Phoenix Park. Ballistics were done with it, and it was bagged and tagged. Then it just vanished into thin air.'

There was a long silence. Then Dave spoke, his voice a cracked, throaty rumble.

'I can't just keep looking the other way, Ed. If I do . . . I'm as bad as they are.'

12

'Move and you're dead.'

It had been years since someone had pulled a knife on me, but it hadn't gotten to be any more fun in the meantime. I had just let myself into Joseph Williamson's flat and closed the door behind me when I felt the point of a blade jab at the left side of my throat.

'The fuck are you?'

A reedy, nasal Dublin accent. I said nothing.

'Cat got your tongue? The fuck are you, bud?'

He was standing to my left, along the wall, his arm outstretched. The hand that held the knife was shaking. The serrated edge had already snagged my Adam's apple. It cut me again beneath my chin. I felt blood trickle into the fold above my collarbone. Coats hanging on the back of the door brushed against my ears and the back of my neck.

'Shaves you close, then closer still. Gonna answer me? Or'd you prefer to bleed all over your nice white shirt?'

His voice was strained, almost hysterical. He laughed, a high-pitched, grating sound, like a drill hitting metal. I feinted right and glanced quickly at him – a blur of navy sportswear, greasy cropped hair and grey skin. He jolted back as if in fear, then lunged forward with the blade again. His arm was at full extension from his shoulder. I braced myself back against the door, among the coats, and as the knife flashed past my face, I grabbed his forearm at wrist and elbow and jammed it up as hard as I could against the heavy brass coat hook. He screamed and tried to jab the knife back towards me, but I swung myself left into him, twisted his arm around and smashed it up into the hook again. There was a crack that sounded like wood smashing, then another, more prolonged scream, and the knife went skittering across the tiled floor. I followed the knife, pocketed it, then turned to see how its owner was faring. I thought the coat hook had come off its fitting, but it was still solid in the old door; the sound of smashing wood had been breaking bone; he crumpled to the floor, supporting his right arm with his left, whimpering in pain. I couldn't remember which bone was the radius and which the ulna, but the broken edges of one of them pressed red raw against the needle-pocked flesh of his forearm.

'You broke me fuckin' arm! You broke me fuckin' arm!'

A pool of urine seeped out beneath him and spread clear on the black and white tiled floor. Tears rolled down his heroin cheekbones, blood collected in his charcoal smear of moustache, drool glistened on his chin. Had I seen him before, or had I just marked his type, one among ten thousand Dublin smackheads and small-time hoods?

'There was no need to break me fuckin' arm. I wouldn've cut you.'

'You did cut me though.'

I ran the back of my hand across my throat. It came away smeared in blood.

'Just scratches man. You'd do worse to yourself shavin' sure.'

He was right. He hadn't planned to stab me. But if he had, well, junkie's defence, he didn't mean anything. As long as he was using, he never would.

'You gave me a fright, is all. I just wanted to know your name.'

'My name is Edward Loy,' I said.

Recognition drifted slowly across his streaming, bloodshot eyes.

'I know you. You're the smart cunt that had a go at Podge, aren't you? Ended on your knees, puking your ring up. Didn' look so fuckin' smart then, did you?'

I recognized him too; not from Hennessy's, although he must've been there, but with his family, weaving across the seafront plaza in Seafield, shouting obscenities into a mobile phone.

'About as smart as you look now. What are you doing here? You one of Podge Halligan's little friends?'

'I need to get to the hospital,' he said. Sweat was beading on his forehead, and he had started to shiver.

'Relax. It's just shock,' I said.

'It is in its hole just shock, you broke me fuckin' arm.'

'You're not losing any blood. You'll be grand.'

I crossed to the door and locked it from the inside, removing a scrap of blue and white police tape from the door jamb. I hunkered down beside him, took his keys and removed the set that were a match for the flat. In his wallet I found a driving licence and a social welfare card, both identifying him as Dessie Delaney, with an address in James Connolly Gardens. The wallet also contained about eighty euros in cash, a postcard from a Greek island I'd never heard of and a photograph of his children at a party in McDonald's.

The houses on Victoria Terrace were built in the 1830s in the spacious Georgian style. The grand hallway connected to a substantial galley kitchen; the doors to all the kitchen presses, the oven and even the fridge were open, and jars and cartons had been emptied onto the green marble work surfaces. A heavy door with stained-glass panels gave from the hall into a large, high-ceilinged living room. Cupboards and shelves had been ransacked, and cushions from chairs and couches disturbed. The bedroom/office was in a state of even greater disarray: the contents of two filing cabinets lay strewn about the floor, the bed linen had been tossed and the mattress upturned. The contents of the bathroom cabinet had been emptied into the bath. There was a half-full bottle of vodka in one of the filing cabinets. I got a glass from the kitchen, poured off a decent sized shot and brought it out to Dessie Delaney, who was still sitting in his own urine on the hall floor, moaning gently to himself.

'Here, drink this,' I said.

'I need to get to the hospital man. I'm in agony. Look at the fuckin' state of me.'

His right arm was swollen and inflamed around the break. He cradled it uneasily with his left, like a nervous father with a very small baby.

'You need to answer some questions first. Drink it down.'

I leant over the pool of piss and tipped the glass of vodka to his lips. He knocked it back in one and exhaled in quick bursts, as if his stalled heart had just been revived. Some degree of shame seemed to return to him also; he got slowly to his feet and moved off the ground he'd sprayed; his cheeks blotched crimson. His white Air Nikes squelched on the tiled floor.

'Ah fuck sake,' he moaned. 'Fuck this!'

'So what were you looking for, Dessie?' I said. 'And how did you come to have the keys?'

'I don't have to tell you shit! Now open the door, or I'll, I'll ring the cops and tell them I've been kidnapped.'

I looked at him for a few seconds to see if he'd laugh. He didn't.

'Off you go then,' I said. 'I'm sure they'd be very interested to have you explain what you were doing ransacking a dead man's flat.'

'And what are you doin' here?'

'I'm looking into Councillor MacLiam's murder, Dessie. And if I called Detective Sergeant Donnelly and got him over here now, what do you reckon he'd think? 'Cause what it looks like is, you loaded the councillor up on smack, took his keys, dumped him in the ocean and then, when the heat died down, you came round here to see what you could steal. Why's Dave Donnelly going to think any different?'

'I didn't kill him. I didn't . . . didn't *need* to take his keys, he, he gave me this set.'

'He gave you them? Why, because you were his best friend? His PA maybe, pop in three mornings a week for a little book-keeping and light burglary?'

'The fuck should I tell you anything? You're gonna call the cops one way or the other, call them and have done.'

'Depends what you tell me. I need information, Dessie. If I get it, and if you're not lying to me, then we'll see.'

'We'll see? That's what you tell your kids when you can't get them what they want for Christmas. We'll see means fuck you.'

Dessie Delaney, at maybe twenty-three, was little more than a kid himself. He grimaced and looked at me quickly, beseechingly, like maybe I could help him. Maybe I could, but I wasn't going to let him know that.

'Right now, we'll see means we'll see. If you fancy taking your chances with the Guards, be my guest.'

Delaney looked at the floor and muttered something about people thinking they were very fucking smart going around breaking other people's arms. Then he began to talk.

'I done a few jobs for Podge Halligan, right? I wasn't one of his boys, one of the lads that go round with him, not at first, I was just, I knew a couple of them and they were like, Dessie, you up for this man?'

'What kind of jobs?'

'Ah, drivin' mostly. They done a few ATM jobs, you know, raidin' the delivery truck. Couple of post offices down the country. I never had a gun or anything. Mad cunts, some of those cunts, shoot you for lookin' at them. You were lucky that day in Hennessy's, George Halligan came along, or you'd've been fuckin' done. Anyway, Podge comes over to me one night, has a job for me, this fuckin' politician cunt he knows has a little smack habit and he's finding it hard to get a regular supply without goin' places it's not a great idea for politician cunts to go. So I get the gig, bein' MacLiam's dealer, yeah?'

'On account of you having your own supply anyway?'

'I wasn't using then man. Swear. E and dope and whatever, but not smack. And the whole thing is, Podge doesn't deal in it either. So he knew to come to me.'

'Why?'

'The girlfriend's brother used to deal smack out in Charnwood, yeah? So Podge knew I had an in there.'

Delaney thrust his chin out and a glow of stupid pride lit up his dull eyes.

'Why doesn't your girlfriend's brother deal there any more?'

''Cause these cunts from Drimnagh threw him off a warehouse roof, broke his fuckin' back. Paralyzed from the neck down. Died soon after. Anyway, the Charnwood heads are sound if they know you, and they were happy to help me out on account of what happened, give me a decent rate an' all. Only thing was, they had me smokin' H too, each time I'd come to pick up the gear, just to seal the deal, yeah, and before I knew it I was shootin' up an' all.'

'How did you get in touch with the councillor?'

Delaney forced a grin.

'I went to one of his clinics, right? Don't know why they call them that, full of old dears moanin' about their neighbours' dogs shitein' on their lawns, anyway, came straight out and said I heard he'd had difficulties getting what he needed. He gave me this address there and then, and a couple of hours later, I dropped off the gear. Same story once a week, then a couple of times he couldn't be there, so he gave me a set of keys, said I could let meself in, have a drink, watch the telly, whatever, leave the gear behind.'

'And what, was Podge getting you to charge way over the odds?'

'No no, that was the whole thing, Podge was givin' me the cash to buy the H, but we were giving it to MacLiam for nothing, yeah?'

'No. Why were you doing that, Dessie?'

'George Halligan runs a book for all these lads who have cashflow problems, and can't get ordinary bookies to take them on. And the thing about MacLiam is, his wife's loaded but he's got fuck-all 'cept what she gives him, and she's some kind of Holy Mary who doesn't want him to be out drinkin' or gamblin' or whatever. Anyway, fuck her, soon the councillor's placin' bets with George bigtime, horses, dogs, football, all on tick. First he does well, up about twenty grand, but George wins all that back. Eventually he's down about a hundred and twenty, I'm worried for the cunt, you know? But nothin' happens, George is lettin' him go further and further down. I reckoned the smack was to get him gambling in the first place, like in a casino the high rollers get free drinks and rooms an' all.'

'And did George finally call in the debt? Is that what happened?'

'Not that I know of. But that's what I reckoned would happen eventually, he'd take it to the wife and say if she didn't pay, he'd let the press know about her husband's heroin habit an' all, yeah? And she'd probably be payin' off for years to come, first the debt and then for it all to be hushed up. That's forward thinkin', business thinkin'.'

Except George Halligan might want a little more for his time and money than a cash pay off every week.

'I mean, they owned him, yeah?' Delaney said. 'Eventually, that's what the Halligans like, to own people. Find a use for them sooner or later.'

'And if the people object, what do the Halligans do?'

Delaney looked at me with fear in his eyes.

'They do what they want man. They do what they want.'

'What did they do to the councillor then, Dessie? Try and get him to change his vote on the golf club rezoning?'

Delaney looked blankly at me, then shrugged.

'I don't know about any of that man.'

'Did you see Podge kill MacLiam?'

'What makes you think Podge done it? He put too much time and money into the cunt to go wastin' it like that.'

'Maybe the councillor wouldn't do what he wanted.'

'Sooner or later, he would've. Anyway, who said he was taken out? Could have been an accident, or suicide, or whatever.'

'Did he strike you as suicidal?'

'No, but . . . he was a junkie, yeah? You're never more than a step away from death, know what I mean?'

'Is that how you live, Dessie? One step away from death?'

'Ah, I'm all fucked up on it so I am. Sharon, the girlfriend, told me, don't go playin' the big man, stay away from Charnwood, they'll just fuck you up, and they have, them an' Podge Halligan together. I was just a driver, I was gonna get a taxi plate. 'Cause Sharon's brother had the virus an' all, if those cunts hadn've killed him, he'd've died anyway, I says no fuckin' way are we havin' the kids grow up round that, so moved out here, near the sea an' everything, rich cunts be needin' taxis all day. 'Course then, wasn't one of Podge Halligan's boys only in school with me, he's all Dessie the Driver like this, 'cause I used to boost cars with him years ago, and I needed the bread, that's why I agreed to do those jobs for Podge. Otherwise . . .'

'Otherwise you wouldn't be trashing a dead man's flat to see if there's anything worth stealing?'

'I was just lookin' for his stash, know what I mean? Just lookin' for . . . or if there was any dinars lyin' about . . . wasn't as if I was gonna rob the telly, yeah?'

He glanced at me quickly, a tight smile of shame on his face. The smile faded, and he flushed with the kind of harsh, merciless self-knowledge that only a bottle or a needle could dispel.

'I wouldn've cut you man, swear. Never use knives, I just reached for it. Just panicked, yeah?'

I looked at Dessie Delaney, sweating and shivering, and wondered whether he could change, whether he even wanted to. Then I thought of his kids at their party in McDonald's, smiling as if they didn't have a care in the world, as if the future looked bright, as if they'd have the same chances the other children whose parents lived by the sea would have.

I went in the bathroom and checked my throat in the mirror. Delaney had snagged me with the knife, no more; once I'd wiped the blood away, it didn't look like I'd done much more than cut myself shaving

I locked the flat up and put a bin liner on the passenger seat and drove Delaney to the Accident and Emergency Unit at St Anthony's on Seafield Avenue. I gave him my mobile number and asked him to ring me if he thought of anything else, or if he needed my help. He looked at his arm and then stared at me, as if to say I'd given him more than enough help for one day. His eyes receded into their sockets, beneath a brow corrugated with mistrust. He walked into the A&E without another word.

13

I parked on the coast road by Seafield Promenade. The midday sun was burning channels of blue through the slush-coloured haze that was the regular summer tenant of the Dublin sky; the yachts and the swimmers sported once more on the brimming sea; my shirt clung to my back in the heat. I took my jacket off and wandered across to the bandstand and down the central steps to the lower promenade walk. Where yesterday a dead man lay, now a gang of scrawny, sunburnt boys in green and white football strips stood with fishing rods, casting their lines into the sea.

I called Linda Dawson, but her mobile just rang off each time, and I couldn't leave a message. I rang directory inquiries and asked for John Dawson in Castlehill, but the number was unlisted. Peter's body was being brought to the church this evening, so I'd see Linda there. Strictly speaking, I was no longer working for her. But her husband's death and Seosamh MacLiam's death were all part of the same case.

I still had to speak to Brian Joyce and Mary Rafferty, and I needed numbers for Leo McSweeney and Angela Mackey, but the prospect of listening to more local politicians tell me less than I already knew wasn't tempting. I made a quick call to Rory Dagg and asked him a question or two about James Kearney; fortified by what he'd told me, I cut up by the Seafront Plaza and turned down the entrance to Seafield

County Hall and Civic Offices. In the foyer I headed for the desk and asked to see the chief planning officer.

'Do you have an appointment?' said the receptionist without looking up. She sounded like she was eating something.

'Special delivery,' I said, tapping my breast pocket.

She looked at me then, swallowing, her cloudy blue eyes sceptical. She was a bulky, shapeless woman in her mid-forties with chocolate stains around her mouth; her dyed-brown hair was cut in a bob that didn't suit her broad, pasty face; she looked like she was wearing a hat that was too small for her.

I tapped my breast pocket again. Her eyes seemed to deepen in colour.

'I can sign for that here,' she said uncertainly.

'Has to be the man himself,' I said. 'That's what we decided.'

'And "we" are ..?'

'It's a family matter,' I said. 'Mrs Joseph MacLiam. Aileen Parland.'

I watched her face quiver at the mention of the name. She looked nervously around her, picked up a phone and spoke quietly into it, said sorry a couple of times and replaced the receiver. Sighing extravagantly, she hauled herself out from behind her desk, crossed the foyer with a heavy tread and disappeared into an elevator. I leant over the counter to see what, apart from chocolate, had been absorbing so much of her attention. A puzzle book lay open by her keyboard, its chocolate-stained pages daubed with letters and numbers written in a broad, childlike hand. I felt sorry for her, and then ashamed of myself, an emotional sequence I recalled from all the divorce cases I had worked, where you always found out something about people you wish you hadn't, usually because you couldn't stop until you had.

By the time she got back, I had counted the money in the envelope. Barbara Dawson had been anxious to buy something from me: my silence, my assent to a verdict of suicide on her son, my agreeing to leave Linda alone, whatever; so anxious she'd been willing to pay me twenty grand. Even if you can afford it, that's still a lot of money.

The receptionist sat down hard behind her desk, her face flushed, her head down, her breath coming in steady gasps. There was a rustle of paper, and her hand went to her mouth.

'Top floor, through the glass doors, right down the corridor to the door at the end,' she said, her muffled words rising gradually from the oblivion of chocolate to which she had returned.

In the elevator, I could hear the rumble and clang from the builders below. I thought of the body that had been buried down there for twenty years, the concrete corpse: could it be my father? The timing fit, but the idea wouldn't take: he was in Australia, with a completely new family; he was living rough on the streets of London; he was fixing engines in a garage in Brazil. It was only because I was back in Dublin that I expected him to turn up; this was where I had left him, after all, not long after he left me. But he could be anywhere, and he probably was alive; it was morbid and sentimental to imagine otherwise.

At a desk outside James Kearney's office sat a slim sixty-something woman dressed in beige with a terracotta complexion and a blow-dried orb of pearl-tinted hair. As I approached she rose and said, 'Mr Parland?'

I didn't contradict her. She fixed me with a gleam of efficient charm, introduced herself as Mrs McEvoy and, ignoring the supplicants waiting on the two charcoal couches that flanked her desk, ushered me straight into Kearney's office, announced me as 'Mr Parland', and swished briskly out in a cloud of Issy Miyake.

If you couldn't be a millionaire, it seemed like the next best thing was to become the county planning officer, at least to judge by the view. From James Kearney's office you could see past Seafield harbour to the city, south along the coast all the way to Castlehill, and west across half the county to the mountains, and all over, as the sun burnt off the last of the grey, the great cranes stood black against the sky: one here, three there, half a dozen above the largest sites, as far as the eye could see and further, the cranes swooped and swung and loomed, hovered and turned and rose, until the ground beneath their feet seemed provisional, subject to their imperious whim. It was as if Dublin had become a city of cranes; like great steel titans of the property boom, they delved on the horizon, churning up the city's past and concreting it over, so some unknown but inevitable future could be built, some enticing, elusive dream of the new.

James Kearney was dressed like a national schoolteacher from the 1950s, in a tattersall shirt, herringbone jacket, cavalry twill trousers, polished brown brogues and bottle green knitted tie. His only concession to the weather was that shirt and jacket were of lighter material than the brushed cotton and tweed they impersonated; otherwise, he looked ready to thrust a shovelful of coal into a classroom stove. He was a tall man with a thin face stretched tight over high bones; his pale hair was side parted and fell lightly across his forehead, just as it must have done when he was eleven. He gave my hand a damp, loose grip, extended his sympathies on my sad loss and motioned for me to sit at a circular glass-topped table. He sat across from me and began unwrapping a package of sandwiches he had taken from a Tupperware box.

'Lunch-hour. I'd offer you one, but I've only sufficent for myself,' he said in a careful, peevish voice, biting into a thick wholemeal wedge filled with ham and egg mayonnaise. 'Prices have gone very dear these day. Better to make your own. Safer too.'

He unscrewed the top of a thermos flask and poured out a cup of steaming brown liquid.

'You might have a cup of tea – if we could find another cup.'

'I'm all right, thanks,' I said.

He looked relieved at this, and put the top back on the flask.

'Now, Mr Parland,' he said, 'just what is it I can do for you?'

That was the question I was still struggling to find an answer to. Never mind. When in doubt, barge straight in and give things a shake.

'We know that the late Peter Dawson was lobbying for a change in the zoning status of Castlehill Golf Club. We know he approached many councillors in the hope of securing their votes for the designation change. We know that he was not above offering donations to secure those votes to any councillor who showed willing. And we know that the last person on earth who would ordinarily have accepted such a bribe was Joseph Williamson. Yet the Guards claim to have found a substantial cash sum on his body. A sum the press are now describing as a bribe.'

James Kearney chewed his sandwich, washed it down with a mouthful of tea and, without lifting his gaze from the surface of the table, said, 'When you say "we", who else, exactly, do you mean?'

'The councillor's widow. Mrs Williamson.'

'Ah. Yes. Go on.'

I took the brown envelope of cash out of my breast pocket and set it on the table. Kearney's eyes locked on to it instantly.

'Now, I'm sure we're both realists. We know how wheels need to be greased in order to get things to happen. It's how the world works, everyone does it, and there's no need to get rigid about it. You might think the late councillor was something of a moral grandstander. But that was who he was, that was who Aileen married, that's how she wants him to be remembered. Now I want you to level with me – and I know you'll know, everyone has told me, there isn't much that gets past James Kearney – we know that Councillors O'Driscoll and Wall accepted so-called corrupt payments from Dawson – did Joe Williamson take one too? Because if he didn't, we'd be anxious to return the money to its rightful owner.'

I picked up the envelope, opened it so that the stack of notes were visible and tapped it against the palm of my hand.

'Obviously this isn't the identical money, the Guards are holding on to that as evidence. But it's the equivalent, twenty grand in cash. If the family could learn that there was a perfectly innocent explanation for how that money came to be on the body, it would be a great strain lifted.'

Kearney shifted in his chair. His remaining sandwiches lay forgotten, and a film of grease rippled across the surface of his cup of tea. His tongue slid between his parted lips as he gazed at the brown envelope, his eyes widening in a leer of avarice.

'Well,' he said, wresting his eyes away from the money, 'we all know Jack Parland of course, by reputation at any rate. Helped set this country on its feet. Cut through all the red tape that was holding us back. Man of vision. It's not going too far to describe him as a great man. Yes, a great man.'

'I'm sure he believes he still is,' I said.

'Oh, he is for sure and certain. But you won't find many to agree with me, I'm sorry to say, in these days where people expect business to be run like a, like a teddy-bear's picnic. Openness and transparency and codology! As if . . . you know the kind of men I'm talking about, of course you do, you're your father's son. If you bog these fellas down with rules and regulations and what have you, they'll just tell you to shag off. And right they are.'

Kearney jammed a hunk of sandwich into his mouth. Egg spilled on to his chin as his eyes locked on to the brown envelope once more, and sweat glistened on his brow.

'Right they are! Pygmies do not make the rules for giants! Am I right, Mr Parland?'

He was shouting now, frosting the glass table-top with crumbs of ham and egg. I assured him that he was absolutely right. I had a flash of Kearney and myself as the pygmies, high above the city, with the giant cranes advancing, angry and baying for blood. Kearney nodded in agreement with himself, drained his mug of tea, replaced the cap on top of his flask and cleared his throat.

'Now, about this money. I did, in fact, in . . . *point* of fact, have a number of financial dealings myself with Councillor MacLiam.'

'You did?'

'Indeed and I did. He recommended a, several times to me indeed, a, how do you put it, an ethical investment fund, something his wife dealt in, and I asked him if he was willing to invest a sum of money . . . on my behalf.'

'A sum of money?'

I wondered if he'd try for the whole twenty.

'Yes, fif, in fact, twenty thousand was the sum.'

A falter, but he made it. Rory Dagg had been right.

'It seems a very large amount to have given him in cash.'

Kearney's eyes flickered with suspicion, and he stared at me through a cloud of it. I'd shown an unhealthy sympathy with the pygmies' side of the argument.

The telephone rang. He crossed the room to his desk and took the call with his back to me. He listened for a while, then said, 'Thank you, as ever, Mrs McEvoy,' and hung up. When

160

he turned around, he looked more like a national school-teacher than ever, the kind who was looking for someone to make an example of.

'Well well well,' he said. 'All the things we know, what? About golf clubs and councillors and Jack Parland and so on. But what we don't know is, who the hell are you? Because Mrs McEvoy informs me Jack Parland may have been married four times, but his only son is fifty-eight.'

I furrowed my brow, as if that might add the necessary years to it.

'And completely bald,' Kearney said. 'And based in Hong Kong. So now. Maybe we'll see what the Guards have to say about all this.'

I smiled and nodded my head in agreement.

'Good idea,' I said. 'When in doubt, get the Guards in.'

I waved the envelope of cash in the air. Kearney held the telephone receiver for a moment longer, then replaced it.

'You misrepresented yourself.'

'I could be waiting out there yet, if I hadn't. Anyway, I never said I was Jack Parland's son.'

'You were announced as Mr Parland.'

'That was down to Mrs McEvoy. With some assistance from the receptionist downstairs. I said I was working for Aileen Williamson on a family matter. Between them, they made two and two equal seven. Of course, my suggestion that there might be a sweetener involved might have helped to force their hands.'

Kearney sucked in his lips and crinkled his eyes up, like an animal shrinking from a sudden blast of light.

'A journalist, is it?' he said, investing 'journalist' with an impressive degree of disdain.

I told him who I was, and that I was investigating Councillor MacLiam's death on behalf of his widow.

'And what were you hoping? That you'd catch me out taking the money?'

'How do you think we were getting on with that?' I said. 'You were in the process of remembering some kind of investment you asked the councillor to make for you.'

He took one last, lingering look at the cash, than shook his head.

'No,' he said.

'No?'

'Don't remember any such transaction. And I'm pretty certain I have no record of it anywhere.'

Kearney grinned at me suddenly. He was a piece of work, and easy with it.

'Don't follow much of the rest of your chat either,' he said. 'Corrupt payments to councillors, for example. And Peter Dawson being responsible for them. Far as the record goes, an outfit called Courtney Estates owns Castlehill Golf Club, and has applied for the rezoning. The named directors of Courtney Estates are Kenneth Courtney and Gemma Grand. So unless you can tell me how they might be connected to the Dawson family, I don't know how what you're saying even begins to add up.'

Kearney snapped the lid shut on his Tupperware sandwich box, picked up his flask and brought them both back to his desk.

'All we have here is a young man, a self-styled "private detective", attempting to bribe a council official,' he announced to the space above my head, as if a barrage of television cameras had suddenly arrived in his office for an impromptu press conference. 'Grief-stricken client, perhaps understandable they should stoop to desperate measures. In the circumstances, probably best to draw a veil over the whole shabby business.'

And James Kearney was seated behind his desk once more, uncapping a fountain pen, poring over planning applications, every inch the diligent public servant. Out past Seafield harbour, a crane turned suddenly, bisecting the sky with its dark steel limbs. A deafening barrage of drilling broke out in the basement, and the building seemed to shake to its foundations. James Kearney turned from his desk and examined a section of the map of the county that hung on the wall behind him, tapping at it with his pen, master of all he surveyed. Business as usual, at the County Hall.

14

To the rear of the Royal Seafield Yacht Club, the dock area is enclosed by high walls topped with four feet of spiked iron fencing. Access is through a heavy metal security gate, which has a smart-card and key pad code style lock system, the details of which Linda Dawson hadn't given me. I tried to get in when a couple of wet-haired yachtsmen came out, but they blocked my way and pushed the door closed. They were big wide-necked rugby-looking guys, so when one of them said, 'If you don't have your card' – he pronounced it *cord* – 'go in around the front, yeah?' I pretended to do as I was told. But I didn't want to go in around the front. I didn't want any more grief from Cyril Lampkin, entertaining though it would undeniably have been. Most of all, I didn't want Colm the Boatman to know I was coming: Colm who had let the Guards think I might have shot Peter Dawson on his boat while he waited a few feet away, Colm whom I'd seen greeting George Halligan in Hennessy's, Colm who, at very least, knew a hell of a lot more than he was telling.

A guy in blue and white checked chef's trousers and a white T-shirt was unloading kitchen supplies from the back of a navy Volkswagen Estate and lugging them through the entrance hall of the club: catering drums of ketchup and mayonnaise, giant slabs of cheese, jumbo cans of oil and tomatoes. Once he had vanished for a second time, I walked across and inspected the remaining contents of the boot. There were four crates of 'sports' drinks, so I hoisted one on my shoulder, cut briskly back around the side and banged on the security door. A tall old man in royal blue, naval-style trousers and matching shirt with a white beard that I guess you'd have to describe as nautical and a pair of field binoculars hanging around his neck opened the door. His face was pale and drawn, his eyes heavy-lidded and cloudy.

'Delivery for you,' I grunted, head down, leading with the crate. He turned his melancholy face away, stood to one side and let me through. To my left lay slipways and moorings, to my right a boathouse. I went straight on towards what looked like the changing rooms and showers, made a show of easing the crate down to the ground and turned around. The old man had vanished, and there was no-one else to be seen. Just inside the door of the changing rooms there was a soft-drinks vending machine. I slid the crate in against it and headed towards the slipways.

Seafield harbour looked like it had just run a very successful closing down sale: apart from a few bulky cabin cruisers and a couple of ramshackle old trawlers, there wasn't a boat within its walls. The sun was at its height now, all haze burnt away; the bay was a blue and white mosaic of sails and sea and spray; varnished by the sun, it glittered like crystal. The old man with the nautical beard patrolled the slipways and inspected the vacant moorings, his arms folded behind his back. He didn't have much in the way of company; on the terrace above us, a party of orange-faced blondes with skinny arms and false red nails sucked prawns and crayfish from their shells and swilled white wine; there was no-one else about. I went over to the old man and asked him if he'd seen Colm the Boatman that day. His thin face looked bewildered with grief, and I thought he was going to start crying. Instead, he peered through his binoculars and then pointed towards the pier, which was thronged with people. I followed the line of his arm, but couldn't make anything out much beyond an old Victorian shelter with a pale blue iron roof, so he passed me the binoculars. With them, I was able to discern Colm sitting on a pale blue bench in the shelter. He was smoking a cigarette and talking on a mobile phone. He looked at his watch like he was waiting for someone. I gave the old man back his binoculars. He nodded, and gave a slight bow, and resumed his patrolling, his lost eyes casting regular trawls across the lapping surface of the water.

I turned to go, and gave a start; Cyril Lampkin was standing behind me, an anxious smile on his plump pink face. He was wearing a fawn cotton drill safari suit and a mustard coloured ascot, and looked, as before, like he was costumed for the stage. But he was playing a different part from the first time I met him.

'Mr Loy. The Royal Seafield extends its regrets . . . deepest sympathy and support for the work you have done,' he said, or garbled, in an unctuous, priest-in-the-parlour kind of tone. 'If we had any inkling that day of what was to happen, or had just happened . . . that such a thing should occur at all . . . not in the collective memory of the Royal Seafield . . . any way I can now be of assistance to you or indeed, to the Dawson family . . . this very sad time . . .' he continued, punctuating his broken phrases with a great deal of plaintive simpering and batting of his carrot coloured eyelashes.

'Where's Peter's boat?' I said.

'In the boathouse. Once the Guards had finished their . . . technical inspection, we thought it best to . . . withdraw it from sight . . . always the danger of ghouls . . . prurient interest . . .'

'Who's that?' I said, pointing at the old man in the royal blue uniform, who had now come to rest at the waterline, hunkered down by the vacant moorings, staring out to sea.

Cyril Lampkin's face instantly retrieved the combination of superciliousness and martyrdom that was native to it; he sneered and rolled his eyes at the same time.

'He's known as the Ghost Captain. He's the longest serving member, can't get rid of him now. You'd have thought he'd get over it after all these years. But if anything, it seems to have become more real to him. Still, at least he only comes around once a year now, on the anniversary.'

'The anniversary of what?'

'His brother drowned. Fell overboard. Both drunk, I think, late at night, shouldn't have been out at all. Twins, it was their twenty-first birthday, they'd been given the boat as a gift. Just after the war, they'd both been Royal Navy. One was too drunk to swim, and drowned, the other was too drunk to save him, and survived. Mummy told me all about it. How he was jealous of his brother's fiancée, so he pushed him overboard, then impersonated his twin to marry the girl. And then she found out, and a year later, to the day, she took the boat out at high tide, to search for her lost love, Mummy said. Neither body was ever recovered. The boat vanished too. Not so much as driftwood.'

'So he comes here every year to . . . what?'

'He used to come here every *day*. But yes, to what? To search for them? Is it remorse, or jealousy that drives him? Because after all, he's alone, and they are reunited in death. And what about the binoculars? Does he really believe he'll spot them on the horizon, sailing home together, brother and wife come to forgive him?'

Lampkin's tone was hushed and tremulous, as if he were reciting the lyrics of his favourite aria.

'And if he did, what would he do? Welcome them, or murder them again?'

'Don't say murder, Mr Loy. There were never any prosecutions. And Mummy is such a gossip, she and her sewing circle may have made most of it up. But I suppose every great institution should have a dark secret, and the Ghost Captain is ours.'

'He certainly seems haunted by it,' I said.

'Yes. Well. It's all very sad, I suppose.'

Cyril Lampkin shook his head abruptly, as if sadness was a luxury busy people simply couldn't afford. The orange-faced blondes shrieked like a squall of gulls, their shrill laughter scrawling across the afternoon sky like nails against a blackboard. The Ghost Captain looked up at them in sudden fright, then turned back to his solitary vigil, his face staring down into the water now. I wondered whose face he saw reflected back at him, his brother's or his own. Maybe he couldn't remember which one he was any more.

~

Colm the Boatman's name was Colm Hyland, I learned from Cyril Lampkin. He was still in the pale blue shelter on Seafield Pier when I left the yacht club. By the time I reached the pier, he had gone, but he hadn't gone far. I climbed the wall that ran along the upper pier and spotted him walking towards the road. I followed, closing the distance between us to about fifteen yards. At first I thought he was going back to work, but he continued on past the Royal Seafield for maybe a quarter of a mile and turned right down towards the sea, crossing the railway bridge and descending to the entrance for the new ferry terminal, a sleek plate glass structure I had never seen before. Taking another right turn, he cut down a lane to a deserted road that had patches of grass and weeds growing in its cracks. A disused railway line lay to one side, behind a low granite wall; beyond the tracks stood a higher wall; beyond that, the harbour. Up ahead by the West Pier, I could see the flat-roofed semi-circular ferryhouse I remembered from years before, and the derelict terminal buildings stretching out on the dock behind it. A white van was parked outside, and as Hyland approached it, two men got out. One of them was carrying two full shopping bags and a two-litre plastic bottle of water. I vaulted the low wall and watched from the overgrown track as the three men knocked on the door of the ferryhouse. A security guard in a navy uniform opened the door and let the men in. I moved on down the warped and mangled track, working my way between bramble and nettle, through clumps of ferns and crackling gorse, until I was at the mouth to a blocked-up tunnel: the ferry-bound train used to run the passengers right down to the old terminal itself. I was about twenty yards from the ferryhouse door now. I hunkered down behind the wall, batted some wasps away and settled in to wait. It didn't take long; maybe fifteen minutes later, Hyland emerged with the two men. I thought I recognized one of the men by his blue baseball cap; then he turned around and I could see his face was bruised and his nose heavily bandaged. It was one of Podge Halligan's crew; the last time I'd seen him was in Hennessy's, when I broke his nose, and he suggested that they should do me in the car park.

Hyland got in the van with Blue Cap and the other man, who no longer had his bags, or the water. The white van pulled away. I waited a few minutes, then dropped to the ground and made my way to the ferryhouse door. When the security guard appeared, I asked him was this where I could get a boat to Holyhead. He directed me to the new ferry terminal. I thanked him, and walked back the way I came. The insignia on his uniform was the same as on the security gates that enclosed Linda Dawson's house: George Halligan's company, Immunicate.

~

If you know what you're doing, it's not too difficult to work your way through the pine forest on the coast side of Castlehill, climb the hill of scrub and gorse and scale the relatively brief stretch of quarry that leads up to Linda Dawson's house. It's not as if you have to climb the whole thing, after all, just the last fifty feet. You'd probably be better off with climbing boots, a hammer and some pegs for the quarry ascent itself, but if you find yourself halfway up without the gear, it may be easier to keep climbing than to come back down. And there are enough footholds and hand holds in the cliff face to do it too, although you might want to know where they are in advance, rather than casting around for them when you're two hundred feet off the ground. Still, once you make it up, there's a barbed-wire fence that isn't much of a trial, provided you haven't cut or callused your hands too badly on the climb. There's just another couple of hundred hardscrabble feet to go, and then if you can force your way through a hedge that's mostly hawthorn and holly, though there is a bit of laurel if you can find it, you're in Linda Dawson's back garden and you haven't breached the security system and Immunicate don't know you're there.

Of course, being in the back garden isn't much use when it's Peter Dawson's study you need, and even if you can pick a lock or smash a window to get in, chances are you'll set the house alarm off, so you won't have too much time. But maybe you won't need too much: your police source has confirmed that Peter Dawson's computer was left unexamined, so it's the work of minutes to gather up the G4's white globe-shaped CPU, find a spare set of car keys hanging on the hook in the kitchen and a security gate key pad in the hall cupboard and be out of sight by the time the Immunicate van arrives, even managing to avoid being spotted by Linda's pudgy, sunburnt neighbour as you go.

Then you just want to keep out of sight until the van leaves, open the gates and drive Linda's red Audi Convertible quickly up the hill. The van is out of sight by now, of course, but you play your hunch – you're always playing hunches, that's the business you're in, and you'll stay in business provided they pay off every now and then – and this time, it pays off, because you get to the top of Castlehill just in time to see the Immunicate van disappear behind the great black metal gates to John and Barbara Dawson's house.

15

The worst of a Catholic funeral isn't the day itself, it's the night before, the removal of the remains; grief that has been a private wound goes on display for the first time; the wound is still raw, and there's no telling what the air will do to it. When I stood by my mother's coffin in this church a few days ago, that line in the Nicene Creed about 'the living and the dead' kept repeating in my brain, like it was the only distinction that mattered any more, and the air and light rushed round my head like I was adrift on a storm-tossed sea.

Now Linda Dawson stood by her husband's coffin, adrift in her own storm; her colour was high and, when I filed past the front pew, she looked like she'd been sedated; when I mumbled my condolences, she stared at me without a flicker of recognition. Barbara Dawson thanked me for coming; her eyes seemed engorged, her teeth had aubergine lipstick stains on them; she looked more than half-mad. John Dawson, in navy suit and crisp white shirt, gripped my forearm with a liver-spotted hand; his rose-mottled cheeks were moist; his mouth fell open in apparent delight.

'Edward Loy,' he said, as if I were the very man he needed to see; 'Edward Loy,' he said again, and repeated my name until his wife took his hand back and gently nudged my elbow to move me on. I looked back to see Linda looking in my direction; the blankness in her eyes hadn't altered, but I felt at least she knew I was there.

The centre aisle was choked with people queuing to pay their respects: locals, many of whom had been at my mother's funeral, but also a bunch of very well-dressed, high-end types I assumed were the golden circle of developers and builders, and maybe more than a handful of rubberneckers come to catch a glimpse of the famously reclusive John Dawson. He had looked older than his years, I thought, old in a way that has little to do with years: his clothes hung from his bones, his brow was heavily ridged, his small eyes looked exhausted, their light nearly expired. Maybe he was ill, or maybe life hadn't delivered what it had promised; either way, no-one who knew John Dawson all those years ago would have expected him to end up looking like this.

I waited outside the church until the family appeared, but it was pointless; Barbara Dawson wasted no time in bundling Linda into the back of a black limousine. John Dawson, head now covered by a black fedora, looked around him blankly; before anyone thought to approach him, Barbara was by his side, guiding him into the safety of the car. She followed him, and the doors sealed them in; the tinted windows added to the appearance of perfect darkness. The car waited until the hearse moved off, then it followed silently, a black shadow in the glare.

~

I met Dave Donnelly in the churchyard and suggested a pint in Hennessy's.

'That'd look good, wouldn't it? And a joint round the back after,' he said, and made a noise that sounded like laughter, but not very much.

'We need to talk, Dave. Now.'

'I'll see you in the Gut in ten minutes, all right?' Dave said, and strode off.

The Gut had been our childhood secret place: three great oaks marked its corners, forming a great triangular riot of bramble and thistle, of hawthorn, fern and marauding fungus, bounded by the railway tracks on one side, and by the garden walls of newly built housing estates on the other two. You had to cram in through a hole in a hedge to get there, or brave the shards of glass embedded in the wall that ran by the railway, but once you were in, anything could happen. First cigarettes, first beers, first joints, first kisses, too many fights to count; Tommy Owens and I lost our virginity here when we were fourteen to two hard-faced Seafield girls who warned us afterwards that if we told anyone, their brothers'd come up and cut our balls off, which, combined with the joylessness of the event itself, made us feel like we'd lost our virginity but not really; I later found out that that's how it goes for pretty much everyone, even if you don't do it against the stump of a tree. Charlie Halpin's brother hanged himself from the oldest of the three oaks when he was seventeen, and Marko Henderson's brother Barreller did something involving masks and small children, the details of which I was never sure about, but which ended up with him doing five years in jail; when Tommy came to LA, he'd just been to Barreller's funeral; he'd soaked himself in petrol and lit a match. Where? In the Gut, of course. Tommy told me it was called the Gut because it was a perfect mid-point between Castlehill and the sea. And because all the poisons in the area ran through here, waiting to be converted or destroyed, although I think that was Tommy's own private interpretation.

I expected there to be nothing remaining of the Gut; maybe a bramble struggling for purchase in the flower bed of some semi-detached lawn, but there it was, in all its shabby, untrammelled glory. A wall of ash and elder had been planted around the perimeter, and had grown to hide most of the houses from view.

'Ah, you wouldn't be romantic about it if you lived here,' said Dave Donnelly, kicking the charred remains of a fire out of his way. Dave had never hung around the Gut back then. He was always captaining the hurling team, or training with the rowing club, or taking the scouts on hikes. He plucked a bramble off his trouser leg, and brushed poppy seeds from his sleeve.

'Every couple of weeks there's a cider party or a knife fight or a fire out of control or some fucking shenanigans up here,' he said.

'I can't believe they haven't built on it,' I said. 'I mean, it's hardly an area of outstanding natural beauty, is it?'

'There's a dispute between two old boys over who owns it. They've been locked in battle for twenty odd years. And as long as it goes on, neither will lift a finger to do anything about it, and no-one else can either.'

Dave stood in the shade of the younger oak, batting a caustic mist of pollen, hornets and midges away with a huge red hand.

I sat on a tree stump (maybe the same stump, I couldn't remember), leant the black watch tartan duffel bag I'd carried from the car on the ground beside it and lit a cigarette. I didn't always smoke, and some biological quirk meant I could go for long periods without, but I always seemed to need one after being in a church. Dave shook his head when I offered him one.

'Jaysus, state of your hands, Ed. That's not from the rose bush yesterday, is it?'

There were sores and lacerations on each finger to the knuckle, and abraded skin on the palms of my hands and on my wrists; I looked like I had eczema.

'Climbing up Castlehill Quarry. And a barbed-wire fence.'

'Right. Some kind of sponsored thing, was it?'

'That's right, in aid of the Garda Benevolent Fund.'

Dave grinned, but the grin faded like steam on a mirror. He made to speak, then stopped himself; he seemed to be having difficulties getting started. Plunge right in there, Loy.

'So any sign of the gun, Dave?'

'The story is, it must still be in there. There's no way anyone could have gotten it out of the Technical Bureau, security is too tight. No sign of a break in. So it's all some kind of administrative cock-up.'

'You don't think so.'

'I think it's very convenient. It suits people who want Peter Dawson's death to just go away.'

'Barbara Dawson told me she believes Peter killed himself. She claims Superintendent Casey agrees with her. What's all that about?'

Dave shook his head.

'Casey's doing what he's always done when he's got a case he wants to bury: he'll let it slide, until the trail's gone cold, then he'll dump it on the coroner and get an open verdict, death by misadventure, or somesuch.'

'But does he think Peter committed suicide? I mean, who moved the body onto the boat?'

'He has enough from the post-mortem to say it could be suicide. And now, no pesky gun to get in the way. But sure, even if Peter killed himself, where did he do it, and who cleaned up afterwards? That's what we should be asking. But Casey doesn't want to go there.'

'Why not?'

'Who do you think moved the body onto the boat?'

'Tommy Owens said the gun came from Podge Halligan. I'd say the Halligans have got to look favourite.'

'And that's just what Casey wants to avoid – making any link between John Dawson and the Halligans. There's to be no gangland connection in this case: that's official.'

'Despite the fact Immunicate runs security for Dawson Construction?'

'Immunicate runs security for lots of people, Ed.'

'So he's just going to block a potential murder investigation?'

'Oh, we're still to chase down Tommy Owens. But we'll end up ruling him out: no motive, no eyewitness, and the print on the weapon is a partial. If we had a weapon, that is.'

'So what, Dave, somebody's husband, somebody's son may have been murdered by gangsters. And the Garda Superintendent in charge of the investigation doesn't want an investigation. Talk to me here.'

'The important thing – the only thing that matters – is keeping the Dawsons happy.'

Dave rolled the great muscles in his neck and shoulders, then turned away and looked up towards Castlehill. The sun was setting now; flanked by two cranes, the wooden cross at the top of the hill seemed to glow. I'd forgotten the cross was there; it was the first time I'd seen it since I'd got back; it had been erected to celebrate some huge Catholic jamboree back in the fifties, when there wasn't much to do, and certainly little to celebrate. There was no chill in the shade now; the rain had made it more humid, not less. Dave mopped his brow with the back of his hand.

'And the Dawsons are happy with a suicide verdict. Can you imagine that? They're happier to think he killed himself than that someone murdered him. And we're happy to go along with it.'

'Is Casey connected to Dawson?'

'What, in some golden circle kind of way? I don't know. But John Dawson made a lot of friends over the years – not just the Jack Parlands who've been found out, but a lot more who haven't. And these fuckers like to please each other without having to be asked, you know what I mean? At the low end, it's a wad of cash. With the big boys, it's a lot more subtle. Being known as sound, as reliable. They never even have to meet, it's all understood – one good turn knocks on to another, the right words in the right ears, and suddenly there's an assistant Garda commissionership up for grabs.'

'You could leak it to the press.'

'What kind of a fuckin' thick do you take me for, Ed? There may be many things Casey is useless at: police work and man-management for a start. But getting good write-ups in the papers is his speciality, and he keeps enough journalists sweet to root out anyone who pulled a stunt like that. And there's me back directing traffic and signing dog licences.'

I waved my cigarette before my face to ward away the midges. Sweat was matting my hair and gathering at my throat, stinging the cuts Dessie Delaney had left there.

'Do you know a guy name of Colm Hyland, Dave? Boatman down the Royal Seafield? Because I think he's the link. I think he helped the Halligans get the body onto the boat.'

I told Dave about seeing Hyland in Hennessy's with George Halligan and about his rendezvous with Blue Cap down at the old ferryhouse.

'Who were the supplies for?'

'The Immunicate guy minding the place, I guess. What's he minding it for, is the question. Was Peter Dawson killed there? It's not far from where his boat was moored. And here's the other thing, I saw an Immunicate van running directly into John and Barbara Dawson's house.'

I filled Dave in on my trip to Linda's house, and gave him the duffel bag with Peter's computer hard drive in it.

'What did you do with Linda's car?' Dave said. For a moment I thought he was going to haul me in for stealing it.

'It's by the coast side of the pine forest, where I parked the Volvo. Can you have Peter Dawson's hard drive analyzed, Dave?'

'One of the computer lads will rush it through for me. I got him off a speeding thing there, he owes me a favour. Is there anything in particular you're looking for?'

'There's a document called "twimc" – to whom it may concern, I think it is. It was modified, but after Peter's death. Whoever did it didn't put the document in the trash. I'm no technohead, but if the content of it could be retrieved, it might be something.'

'I'll get Shane on to it tonight. Should have something on the bank and phone records in the morning. Would have had it today, there's just too many listening ears around the station, Casey's spies. What's the story on MacLiam?'

'He was in deep to Podge Halligan: gambling and drugs. The heroin wasn't coming directly from Podge though. The autopsy said what?'

'The heroin killed him, most likely.'

'And what, he was shooting up on the harbour wall, so when he OD'd, he just tumbled into the sea? That's convenient. What about the money?'

'Unmarked bills. No witnesses, no signs of struggle – certainly not after five days in the water. Toxicology reports can take months. Same story: they'll cruise it out to an inquest. Then death by misadventure. Or an open verdict.'

Dave took the duffel bag, looked me up and down and shook his head. He made to move off, then turned back, his broad face grim with unease.

'Thing I was going to tell you, remember the concrete corpse we found in the town hall? He was shot five times. So we've just got a report back from the lab. According to the ballistics report, they're Parabellum 9mm rounds from a Glock 17 – an identical match for the slugs they found in Peter

Dawson, and shot from the same gun – just twenty odd years in the difference.'

It all goes back to Fagan's Villas.

'I know . . . look, we didn't say anything the other day, but we both know there's a chance that it could be your oul' fella. And the fact that, well, he used to be in business with Dawson, and now the same slugs that kill Dawson's son are found in this corpse, well, I'm not saying it makes any sense yet, but – if it is your da – it's got to be more than a coincidence.'

Especially if you don't believe in coincidence.

'We got no match from dental records. Never had any for your da. The missing persons database from twenty years ago is in rag order anyway. We have a jacket though, with a label from a tailor in Capel Street. We may be able to trace who it was made for, get an ID that way. Ed? You don't remember if your da used a tailor, do you? Fitzhugh's, it was called.'

I seemed to have been robbed of the power of speech. The wooden cross above Castlehill looked starker now against the paling sky, suddenly flimsy next to the cranes that dwarfed it. The sweat had turned cold on my back, and I was close to shivering. I looked at Dave and shook my head. He brought one of his huge hands up and give my bicep a squeeze.

'Look after yourself, Ed,' he said. 'I'll pay Colm Hyland a visit, see what I can raise. I'll be in touch.'

Dave Donnelly strode off across the Gut and pushed out through a gap between two hawthorns, swearing. From my jacket pocket, I took the photograph of my father and John Dawson that I'd found on Peter's boat and looked at the two young men, their pints raised to the future.

~

I was eighteen, and had spent the summer working behind the bar in the golf club in Castlehill, listening to men lie about themselves and their lives and watching women pretend to believe them. Sometimes I'd try out my own lies on their daughters, and by the end of the summer, they were pretending to believe me too. I had money saved, and once I got my exam results, I was going to stay for a month with Kevin O'Rourke's brother, Brian, who had moved to California and was managing an Irish pub called Mother MacGillacuddy's on Main Street, Santa Monica. Then I'd come back and start at university.

The Leaving Cert. results came out on a Friday late in August, and we all went into school to get them. My physics teacher reckoned mine were good enough to secure me my first choice, which was a place studying medicine at Trinity College, Dublin. She was pleased for me, and she gave me a hug and kissed me on the mouth. Miss Stephens wore tight pencil skirts and heels and sheer blouses you could see her bra through, and everyone was scared of her, and I remember thinking that if Miss Stephens could kiss me, anything was possible.

We got to Hennessy's by about midday, and fed the jukebox and shouted and laughed and drank our way through the afternoon. At around five, a couple of the lads had been sick, and some of us went across to the chipper and sat eating our cod and chips in the church car park, watching girls from the local convent school playing tennis on the public courts and yelling half-witted remarks at them. Then it began to rain, and we went back to Hennessy's, but after a mouthful of my pint, I started to feel queasy. I told the lads I'd see them after, and walked home. In the house, I called out for my mother, but there was no sign, and I figured she hadn't made it home from work yet. I decided a shower would sober me up enough so I could go back to Hennessy's and drink some more. After all, you didn't get your Leaving results every day.

The immersion had been left on, unusually, but at least that meant there was hot water. We didn't actually have a shower, but you could attach a plastic shampoo spray to the bath taps and it did much the same job. I washed my hair and sprayed the grime of Hennessy's off my body and thought of how proud my mother would be when she heard my results. My father had walked out in April, and the house had been quiet without his drunken rages, his tantrums and sulks and peevish, embittered ranting. It wasn't the loss of his business that caused him to behave so obnoxiously. He had always been like that. 'Your father is a very disappointed man,' my mother used to say, as if that explained it. Neither my mother nor I had admitted yet that we were relieved that my father had left, that we didn't much care where he had gone, and that we hoped he would never come back, but I'm pretty sure that was what we both felt. My mother in particular seemed happier than she had ever been – younger and more alive.

I put clean clothes on in my room. My rucksack was packed, and my passport and plane ticket were in my desk drawer, along with dollars and some travellers' cheques. I was counting the twenty-dollar bills again, just to make sure a very selective thief hadn't broken in and stolen a couple of them, when I heard a noise from my parents' bedroom. I went out onto the landing and knocked on their door. There was no answer. I tried the handle, but the door was locked. I called my mother's name, and banged on the door, and shook the door handle. I heard urgent whispers, and movement inside, and then my mother came to the door. She wore a pale-pink satin robe I had never seen her in before. He hair fell in strands across her face, her lips were full and smeared with red and she had tears in her mascara-smudged eyes. She was frightened, and kept swallowing and trying to speak, but the only word she could get out was my name. I stepped into the room and saw a man on the other side of the bed. He had his back to me, and was pushing the tail of his white shirt into his navy suit trousers. He had a plume of grey-white hair, and smelt of musk and fresh-cut pine.

I looked at my mother. Her eyes were trying to explain, pleading with me to understand. But I didn't want to understand why

*John Dawson had been in her bed. I turned and went into my
room, got my rucksack, passport, money and ticket and hurled
myself downstairs.*

*That night I slept on a bench in the airport; the next morning I
flew to London, and then to LA. The night after I arrived in
California, I was serving beers and shots in Mother
MacGillacuddy's. I never went home.*

~

I was still in the Gut, smoking a cigarette, staring at the photograph of John Dawson and my father when my mobile rang.
It was Rory Dagg.

'I need to talk to you. I made a mistake earlier. Now I've
checked it out, I've realized that the new Seafield County Hall
was a Dawson job,' he said.

Of course it was. I nodded, and suddenly felt a little light
headed. My hands began to shake. I put the photograph back
in my pocket, threw my cigarette away and took a few deep
breaths.

'Hello? Mr Loy? Are you still there?'

'I'm still here. Where are you, Mr Dagg?'

He gave me his address. I said I'd be there in five minutes.

On my way back to the car, I let the thought I'd been sup-
pressing since I'd seen the concrete corpse take shape: did
John Dawson murder my father and hide the body so he could
be with my mother? Did my mother play her part in my
father's death? And if they had spilt blood to be together, why
did they remain apart?

183

16

Rory Dagg lived in the older of the two estates that surrounded the Gut. His road was built over a period of about
twenty years; detached villas and bungalows built in the late
thirties had segued into spacious semi-detached houses by the
1950s; mature horse chestnut and sycamore trees stood at
intervals along the street.

Dagg's house was a semi-detached about halfway along; the
attic had been converted, and there was an extension above
the garage. His black Volvo estate was hidden behind an enormous silver SUV. A pale, petite woman in her forties with
straw blonde hair swept back in an Alice band was in the front
garden, doing something tentative to some lavender plants.
She wore a black trouser suit and shoes with heels and looked
like she should be behind a desk or at a business meeting or
anywhere but out in a hot summer garden. She smiled at me,
a smile that did nothing to relieve the anxiety in her small blue
eyes.

'Gardener,' she said with a sigh, as if staff would one day be
the death of her.

'Edward Loy,' I said.

'Rory's in his office. The entrance is around the back.'

Her voice was high, nervy, schoolgirl-elocuted. She pointed
towards the garage. A black tongue-and-groove door opened
onto a narrow lane around the side of the house. The back
garden was scattered with tricycles, scooters and other toys; a

paddling pool in the shape of a big green car sat in the middle; a rusty old red swing took up the rear.

I knocked on the rear door of the garage, and Rory Dagg let me in, stumbling as he shut the door behind him. The front of the room had computers and year planners and box files and all the other components of a modern office. Step behind a green felt partition, however, and it was like stepping back in time. A pair of battered brown leather armchairs sat in one corner with a low oval coffee table between them; there were slatted blinds and angle-poise lamps and a wooden ceiling fan. There were two wooden drawing boards, with an inlaid covering of what looked like olive-green lino, several old filing cabinets and a worn oak desk and chair. Beneath the window at the far end there was a row of shelves; above that, a wire frame day bed. Everything in the room was weathered and seasoned and redolent of the past. Dagg bustled about, tidying up papers and files and straightening pieces of furniture. He rubbed his hands and exhaled loudly, as if we'd just come in after a long walk on a very cold day.

'Like a drink? I'm having a beer. But there's whiskey, gin, vodka. We have all the major booze groups covered.'

'No thanks.'

There was nothing I would have liked more then a good belt of whiskey, but I figured one of us might as well be sober. Dagg smiled blankly at me for a few seconds, as if I'd set him some moral conundrum by refusing a drink, then shrugged, went to a small fridge by the door and got himself a bottle of Warsteiner. While he was looking for the opener, which seemed to have gone missing, I turned my attention to the office walls, which were hung with draftsman's plans, all framed. Each was signed 'R. Dagg' in exquisite copper plate.

'These are very fine,' I said. 'Are they yours?'

'My dad's – I'm named after him.'

'I thought you said he was a foreman.'

'So he was. But a cat may look at a king. He had dreams, Mr Loy, dreams of rising in the world. Knew he couldn't make it himself. But here I am, the living embodiment of all those dreams.'

Dagg found the bottle opener and flipped the top off the beer. Foam spewed up over his hand and his tan chinos. He tipped the bottle to his mouth, drying the back of his hand on his green plaid shirt. Beer leaked onto his cheeks and trickled down his chin.

I looked around the room again. Almost everything in it looked like it had belonged to his father, or it could have, like his memory was being preserved. Dagg had sprawled in an armchair, legs and arms spilling out at angles, a half-drunk beer in his fist and a bored look on his face. He looked like he had regressed from capable family man to sullen adolescent.

'How'd you get on with Jim Kearney?' he asked, a satirical edge to his voice.

'He was very keen to claim some money that had nothing to do with him. But he lost his nerve at the last minute.'

'He doesn't usually. Mind you, the person doing the bribing should have something at stake too. Like adultery, isn't it, bribery: to keep it safe, both parties must have something to lose. You should ask Caroline about that sometime.'

'Caroline?' I said, stupidly, reflexively, already knowing who it would be.

'My wife, Mr Loy, my much better and for worse, 'til death do us mercifully part amen.'

I needed to press on, before Dagg vanished into the bottle for good.

'So you say Dawson's Construction built the town hall,' I said. 'How did you find out?'

Dagg reached for some of the papers he had tidied away earlier.

'Dad kept everything. And I haven't thrown any of it out yet. For reasons I don't like to dwell on.'

He riffled through a pile of papers and extracted a brown day book.

'It was my Dad's last job for Dawson's. This is the daily report book for the job. Who worked, what they did, what supplies they need, any expenditure, and his comments.'

A note of pride had entered Dagg's voice.

'Was that usual?' I said.

'It was for my father.'

'Is it conceivable that someone could have buried a body in the foundations of the building without your father's knowledge?'

'I wouldn't have thought so. I mean, he wasn't there twenty-four hours a day, but there would have been security. And in any case, if someone had stolen in at night and done it, he would have seen the work in the morning, there would have been an investigation, he wouldn't have let it slide.'

'Not even as a personal favour to John Dawson?'

'No. He was a meticulous man. He raised me on his own, after my mother left him. Because things were tough when they started out, and she didn't like having to scrape along. And he raised me, you know, as well as any mother could have. I never had the wrong clothes, I never went without, he'd check my homework, he knew in detail what I was doing in school. In detail. And the thing was, you couldn't . . . he wouldn't let something go. If I stayed out when I shouldn't have, or didn't try with an essay, he'd be after me, you know? Cross question me until he had the truth. And he was the same on the job. So . . . no, not even for John Dawson.'

'Why was it his last job?'

Dagg drained his beer and sighed.

'Because I failed, for the second time, to get enough points to do architecture. And I took a course in civil engineering instead. And I . . . well, it sounds ridiculous, but I broke his heart, Mr Loy. His dream for me was to be an architect. It didn't allow for any deviation . . . he gave up his job, and . . . gave up on life, basically. He drank, and sat around, and waited to die. He died . . . of a broken heart.'

Dagg shook his head. His eyes were damp. His reasons for building a museum in his father's honour were becoming clearer. He went to a filing cabinet, took out a bottle of Jameson, poured himself a slug and knocked it back. When he spoke again, it was in a drunk's voice: peevish, slurring, embittered.

'I mean, he was out of order, know what I mean? But we could have worked it out. But I just said, forget it, man; I was out of that house. We barely spoke for five years. And when we did . . . he was gone, know what I mean? Just . . . gone.'

Dagg rested his forearms on the filing cabinet and hung his head.

I looked through the day book; each day had been filled out in a neat printed hand, and signed 'R. Dagg'; I looked at the signatures and then compared them to those on the framed plans. They were identical. The shelves beneath the bed contained tens of identical brown-covered day books. I took one out: the same neat, printed hand, similar details, all signed by R. Dagg. But in this case, the signatures were freer and less meticulous.

'Where were these day books kept?' I asked Dagg.

'At home,' Dagg said.

'And these plans? Where did he keep those?'

'In his office at Dawson's. They used to have premises down on Victoria Terrace. Why?'

'I don't know why. Where was your father from?'

'Where was he from?' Dagg repeated.

'Yes. Don't you know?'

'From Clondalkin. Monastery Road.'

'You sure?'

'I'm sure.'

'Any family? Brothers or sisters?'

'No.'

'Anything else you want to tell me?'

There was plenty, but I wasn't going to hear it tonight. He wouldn't look me in the eye. I left him there, pouring more whiskey in his glass, lovingly tending his own pain.

The sun had dropped below Castlehill. The front garden was empty. I snipped a cone of lavender between finger- and thumbnails, rubbed it between my hands and inhaled; I needed to get the stench of self-pity out of my nostrils: Dagg's and mine. There was an entire history of feeling about my father that I had beaten down; I felt it welling up when Dagg was talking. I remembered his pride in my achievements at school, mingled with bewilderment that his son should shine where he never had. And I wondered whether he'd be prouder of me now – and I was astonished that I wondered.

There was a sheet of notepaper tucked beneath my windscreen wiper. It smelt of lavender too, or maybe my hands made everything smell that way. It had a mobile phone number and, at this stage it seemed, inevitably, the words FAGAN'S VILLAS written in capitals underneath. I walked back as far as the gate. The lights had gone off in the garage, and the blinds were shut; I guessed Dagg was settling in for the night. His wife stood at an upstairs window. I saluted her with the notepaper, and she turned away.

～

It all went back to Fagan's Villas, and finally, so did I. I walked around the horseshoe-shaped cul-de-sac with its ugly, boxlike semi-detached houses. When they were built, they were two-up, two-down affairs clad in dirty grey pebbledash with no bathroom and an outside toilet; now almost every house had an extension as big as itself slapped on the side, and a roof window for the attic room, and decking in the back garden, and an SUV or a brand-new hatchback on the kerb, or both.

I couldn't remember which house had been my mother's, which my father's, which John Dawson's or which his wife Barbara's. But they had all grown up here, tarred with the brush of hailing from 'the Villas', burning to move out and move up and leave it all behind. Now the houses sold to families who counted themselves fortunate to get them, and who saw Fagan's Villas as a destination, not a starting point. Home at last.

There were two houses that didn't have extensions, or new windows; the first was at the centre of the horseshoe, and its missing wing made its neighbour look lopsided. I walked up the path but before I reached the front door, I saw a 'Sale Agreed' sign lying on the ground by the side gate. The front door was opened by a blonde woman in her thirties with a baby in her arms and another on the way; the small hallway was piled high with brown cardboard boxes sealed with removals company tape. I couldn't remember if I had a cover story, or even if I needed one, so I told her the truth: that my late mother used to live around here, and I wondered whether there might be any of her old neighbours left. The woman said she had just moved in, that it was mostly young families, but that she thought she'd seen an old lady in the corner house on the left, the one with the absolutely gorgeous garden.

The corner house on the left had no extension either, but I suppose it did have an absolutely gorgeous garden, if you were an old lady or planned on being one eventually: there was a central circular bed of red and orange dahlias, yellow and pale-pink begonias and purple sweet pea, the lawn was well watered and thick with clover, and it was bordered on four sides by beds of pale blue delphiniums, white snapdragons and yellow-spotted orange lilies. I could hear the television from the road; by the time I got to the front door, I could practically follow the plot; it was one of those cop shows where male and female forensic pathologists trade flirty one-liners as they delve about in dead people's entrails. I rang the bell and thumped on the door for good measure, but the letter box snapped open immediately. I knelt down to see in. Amidst the yapping of a small dog, a pair of thick-rimmed spectacles peered out.

'I'm not deaf, you know,' an elderly woman's pert voice said.

'I'm sorry to disturb you at this late hour,' I said.

'What do you want, love? Only, me programme is on, I've been waiting all day for it.'

'My name is Edward Loy,' I said.

The letter box snapped shut, the door opened and a tiny old woman with a meringue of white hair stood there, her arms stretched open as if to enfold me in them.

'I saw you at the church. God love you, son,' she said, 'and poor Daphne not cold in the ground.'

The dog, a Jack Russell, nipped around my ankles. The television blared something about blood types and post-mortem putrefaction.

'Inside, Mr Burke!' snapped the woman, and the dog scuttled back into the house.

'Will you come in, son?' she said. 'I've nothing in the house, but you could have a cup of tea.'

'If it's not too much trouble. I thought . . . since you must have known my mother –'

'Didn't we all grow up together, me, your ma and your da, God help him. Come in out of that.'

Fluorescent strip lights made the house fantastically bright, and exposed the worn, frayed carpets and the torn, peeling wallpaper; there was a sharp smell of damp and dust and cleaning fluid and gravy. A gallery of photographs in cheap frames stood on a veneer sideboard in the living room.

'Eleven children we raised in this house, Mr Burke and me,' she said. 'Scattered all over now: Germany, Holland, the States, a couple in Cork. Grandchildren too, so many I lose track. There's a birthday present to send off every week, sometimes two.'

'Mr Burke?' I said, pointing at the Jack Russell, who had retreated beneath the sofa.

'Ah, bit of a laugh, you have to, don't you? And he reminds me of him, to be honest with you, sometimes, grumpy little shite that he is.'

The dog yapped. Mrs Burke went out to the kitchen. The television was still blaring, advertisements now: property investment opportunities in Budapest and Sofia. The English absentee landlord who exploited his tenants was a much-vilified figure in Irish history; little wonder, I suppose, that we had internalized out colonial master's methods and sought to emulate them, buying up cheap property in recovering countries so we could make a profit at the local population's expense. It was our turn now.

Mrs Burke reappeared with a gold metal tray laden with tea-things. She held the tray out to me; I reached to take it from her, but she shook her head.

'Underneath,' she snapped, 'the legs swing down.'

I reached underneath the tray and swung the legs down. She set it on a threadbare orange hearth rug and began pouring tea. The television began to shout about the urgent need to have a hot tub installed in your home today.

'Do you mind if I turn the TV off?' I said.

Mrs Burke looked as if I'd suggested tossing the set out the window.

'My programme is on,' she said in a quiet, hurt voice, and passed me a cup of tea. She sat on the sofa, which had a red throw on it, settled some patchwork cushions around herself and sighed. Her thin legs barely reached the ground; her eyes were improbably large behind her glasses; in her beige cords and fawn poloneck, she looked like a small child in a granny costume. Mr Burke scraped out from underneath and leapt up beside her. I sat on a stiff backed chair by the window. The television was showing the victim's coffin going into the ground.

'Poor Daphne,' she said. 'She was quite a beauty, you know. Broke a lot of hearts, so she did, but she was a good girl. Oh yes.'

'Whose heart did she break?'

'Johnny Dawson's, for one. He set his cap at her. But she only had eyes for your father. Still, no harm done. A gang of them there was, all friends really. Those lads were a holy terror, the three musketeers.'

'My father and John Dawson?'

'And the other lad, what's this his name was? Kenny? Kenny, that's it. But they were just lively young fellas, there was no harm to them, not like the other tramps, the Daggs.'

'Rory Dagg, was it?'

'Rory Dagg was all right. But his brother, Jack. Big Jack, they called him. That thrilled him, he'd strut about like a king to know someone was calling him Big Jack. Big eejit, more like.'

'I thought Rory Dagg was from Clondalkin.'

'He was originally, but he landed here when he was five. Some family trouble, brought up by the granny. Anyway, Rory done all right for himself, foreman for Dawson's, but the other blackguard? In and out of reformatory and jail and so on. And of course, some say Jack wasn't as bad as he was painted, that Rory did his fair share, at least when they were younger. There was no real way of knowing, I suppose.'

'Why is that?'

'Sure, even their granny couldn't tell them apart. None of the teachers could either.'

'Twins?'

'Peas in a pod. But what do you care about the Daggs, sure it's your mother you want to hear about. Very stylish young one now, 'course she had the job in Arnotts, all the girls on that counter had to look after themselves. But she was a dote. I used to mind her sure, and then she'd babysit the young ones for me.'

'And Barbara Dawson?'

'Barbara Dawson? Barbara Lamb as was?'

She gave a shrill, forced, anxious laugh, the kind of laugh women give when they're about to slight a rival, and know they risk making themselves look bad, but can't stop themselves.

'Barbara Lamb. The airs and graces of her. When you think of where she came from. She never had much time for baby-sitting, I can tell you. Not that a married woman'd want her in the house. Some cheek, that one had.'

Mrs Burke continued to speak, but silently, to herself, her head nodding vigorously, her eyes fixed on the TV screen. The forensic pathologists were pleading with the coroner to be allowed to exhume the recently interred body.

'Barbara was a fisherman's daughter, just like my mother, wasn't she?'

But Mrs Burke wasn't listening.

194

'In a red swimsuit in our back garden, because her da had theirs dug up for vegetables he couldn't make grow, the eejit. And Mr Burke home on his dinner hour, and me coming in from the shops with the three youngest dragging off me, and the pair of them flinging water at each other and laughing away, and she soaked through, *soaked* now, in a red swimsuit, with the big red lipstick lips and painted toenails on her and all. I sent her across the road fast enough, I can tell you. The nerve of her.'

She laughed again, and looked around as if for support from some invisible jury. Then she foostered around beneath the cushions until she surfaced with a naggin bottle of Smirnoff and, as if I wasn't there, poured a shot into her teacup and drank it down.

'Running round with Johnny Dawson one week and the Kenny fella the next. Never could tell that pair apart either. At least your da had the sense to steer clear. The airs and graces of her, that's what I could never get over. When everyone knew . . .'

Mrs Burke stopped herself. She looked across at me as if she had forgotten I was there.

'Another cup of tea, son?'

'No thank you. What were you about to say?'

'What's that?'

'About Barbara Dawson? That you couldn't get over the airs and graces of her, when everyone knew . . . ?'

'Everyone knew what, son?'

Mrs Burke's mouth had set in a slight smile; her eyes were sharper; her voice had a note of cunning about it once more. She had said enough, more than enough, when the national motto had always been, 'Whatever you say, say nothing.'

'And you're still in America, are you son? You're doing very well there, aren't you? What's this you are, a doctor? Everyone knew Daphne Loy's son got a very good Leaving and was going to be a doctor. Fair play to you now. Bless us and save us, they get up very early in the morning in America, don't they? Mine are out the door at six every morning.'

I asked a few more questions, but she answered blandly, in platitudes: my father was a decent man, and a hard-working man, and wherever he was, she prayed God he was happy; she thought Kenny had moved out of the area; any photos she had from that time were of her family only, and she wasn't sure where half of those had got to. I thanked her for the tea, and Mr Burke bounded from the sofa and nipped around my ankles when I rose from my chair. On the television, the grave had been dug up, and the lid of the coffin raised, only to find the corpse gone. In the hall, Mrs Burke dipped her finger in the small holy water font by the front door, and marked my forehead with a cross. As I left, she smiled and mouthed a silent prayer.

17

I lived in a city where the graves had all opened, and the dead arose and walked the streets and fields until they came to the houses in which they had once lived; their families opened the doors and the living and the dead looked at one another like strangers; then the dead moved off again, not permitted to find rest, while the living pursued them, trying to see in their faces some marks of familiar character, some bones of recognition. I thought I saw my mother and father, but when I caught up with them, neither had a face, or at least, a face I could discern; there were dead children too, but they were impossible to catch; I followed the legions of the dead as far as the coast, but when they reached the shore they changed course, in perpetual motion towards some unknown destination, and I was left alone, staring at the sea.

～

I awoke soaked in cold sweat, my hair matted to my head. Someone was hammering on the front door, and my heart pounded in sympathetic refrain. By the time I got down the stairs, the hammering had stopped; there was a brown jiffy bag on the doorstep and the sound of a car pulling away. The dawn air was almost cool; dew shone on the scorched grass; I shivered and went inside.

I had a hot shower, dressed and ate breakfast while I worked my way through the contents of the jiffy bag. Peter Dawson's bank statements made interesting reading. As far as I could make out, he seemed to be pulling down about eighteen thousand a month from Dawson's, plus another six or seven from assorted standing orders, presumably income from his rental properties, but his account was never less than forty grand overdrawn. There were continual cash transfers and withdrawals, along with many five-figure cheques. His outgoings otherwise were modest: the properties seemed to have been bought outright, without mortgages; there were no standing orders to building societies; he had utility bills to pay but little else. It looked not only as if Peter shared Councillor MacLiam's penchant for gambling and hard drugs, but that he spent the rest of his time tossing his money out the window. Or as if someone was bleeding him and good. In the last year, the situation had intensified; three properties had been sold, the proceeds – between three and four hundred thousand a time – lodged, and then within weeks, the money haemorrhaged from the account in tens, twenties and fifties. The sums were vast, way larger than what would be needed to bribe local councillors to vote in favour of rezoning a golf club.

I tried Linda's number, again with no success. I rang Rory Dagg's wife on her mobile.

'Caroline Dagg?'

Her voice sounded strained and wary. I pressed ahead.

'Hello, this is Edward Loy here, I was wondering if I could talk to you about your uncle by marriage, Jack Dagg? Rory's father's twin brother?'

'Mr Loy. I . . . hold the line a moment, would you?'

After a muffled exchange, Rory Dagg came on the line.

'He's dead,' he said.

'Your uncle, Jack Dagg, is dead?'

'Yes.'

'You see, I was talking to someone who remembers your family from Fagan's Villas –'

'It's not a good time to talk, Mr Loy,' Rory Dagg said, and hung up.

I rang a body called the Private Security Authority, and asked them a few questions which they were happy to answer. I rang the airline to ask about my luggage, and was told by someone who made it clear she felt I was being an unreasonable pest by expecting them to find it in the first place that there'd been 'no sign of it' for days; finally she hung up on me. I slammed down the receiver and the phone rang immediately, as if on contact. It was Aileen Williamson, and she wasn't happy.

'Mr Loy, as far as I'm concerned, you have breached the terms of our contract; I want you to cease all further investigations on my behalf.'

'Why the sudden change of heart?'

'The office of Seafield County Manager contacted me yesterday, claiming that you presented yourself as my brother –'

'They chose to believe I was your brother.'

'With no assistance from you?'

'I didn't contradict them until they found out otherwise.'

'They said you were rude and abusive to the point of slander. That it could be highly compromising for me and for my father if it emerged that I had hired you –'

'Sounds like a threat. Was Kearney looking for a bribe, do you think?'

'Mr Loy, I can't afford any more negative comment to surround the name of Parland!'

'I thought it was the MacLiam name you were anxious to clear.'

'Don't be insolent. Did you assault a person called Desmond Delaney?'

'I broke a person called Desmond Delaney's arm. But there was a knife on the end of it at the time, pressed up against my throat. What, is Dessie Delaney putting the bite on you too?'

'He said he felt I should know what was being done in my name. He said my husband had been a good friend to him.'

'Dessie Delaney kept your husband supplied with heroin. How much money did he squeeze out of you?'

'He said the only course open to him was to go to the press. I can't –'

'I know, you can't have the good name of MacLiam Parland Williamson dragged through the mud –'

'How dare you speak to me like that? Do you know who I am?'

'I know who you are all right, and how many names you have too, although I don't know yet if you have a different personality for each of them. The problem is, you don't know who I am. Because you hired a private detective, and no-one wants to know who a private detective is. He's too shabby and disreputable and hustle-a-buck ordinary to make the grade at your charity balls and grand-a-plate dinners and that suits him fine, because that way, he can get on with what he's been hired to do. That's the only point of him really, like a dog that's been bred to work, he can't relax by sitting around. He's got to be prying and poking and stirring things up until somehow, out falls the truth, or enough of it to make a difference. Now, so far, I've found out that a criminal gang was supplying your husband with heroin via Dessie Delaney, that he'd run up huge gambling debts to the same gang; what they hoped to get for their time and money I can't say yet; possibly they wanted to bribe him, or blackmail you. I know it was the heroin overdose that killed him, but not what he was doing in the water. But I'm going to find out; his death is connected to at least two other deaths, and one of them is my father's. And if you're so upset about the bad press your late husband's getting, why don't you take it up with *your* father: if he can't mount a little press campaign on behalf of his widowed daughter, either he's not much of a father or he's no kind of newspaper baron – or Superintendent Casey's decision not to dig too deep on this and the Dawson case suits a lot of those powerful people you claimed you didn't mind me upsetting. And by the way, you can't fire me. I work until your cheque runs dry, and it's got plenty of juice in it yet.'

I stopped for breath, ready to hang up. Aileen Williamson was too quick for me.

'You haven't lodged the cheque yet,' she said.

'Not yet, no.'

'I've cancelled it. Goodbye, Mr Loy.'

And she hung up on me too. It was the latest craze, people hanging up on me. Three of them this morning, and it wasn't ten o'clock yet. Dead bodies piling high, but God forbid anyone should help me find out why. Well, it didn't matter any more if I didn't have a client. I had a stake in this that went beyond the job. It was time to stop waiting for this case to solve itself. It was time to stir things up.

I dialled another number.

'Who are you and what do you want?'

George Halligan had a crisp Dublin voice with a dangerous edge, matured in whiskey and smoke and casual brutality.

'It's Ed Loy,' I said. 'Isn't it time you bought me that lunch?'

~

Strictly speaking, it was accurate to say Podge and George Halligan were neighbours, but the six properties that went to make up the exclusive development called 'Redlands' where the brothers lived had gardens the size of football fields, with mature broadleaf trees dotted throughout, so not only were the chances slim of hearing the couple next door have a row; the chances of seeing them at all were pretty remote. The land was a chunk the golf club had sold off ten years earlier, when the commercial rates they had been avoiding finally caught up with them. Building starts had been at a low ebb back then, so there wasn't much fuss about the development.

We were seated at a black glass table on a black marble deck shaded by lime trees. A South-American girl, dressed in pretty much the same servant's livery as the Filipina in Aileen Williamson's house, served champagne and orange juice. An Eastern-European blonde who looked like Grace Kelly's hard-faced sister and whom George introduced as one of his 'wives' appeared briefly, and giggled dutifully at the assorted lewd propositions George made to her. George counted off fifteen hundred euro from a platinum bill-fold and she clipped off on steel-heeled stilettos, trailing all manner of intoxicating odours in her wake. A couple more women in bikinis, who looked like models and might well have been 'wives' also, were sunbathing by a marine blue swimming pool. There would be scallop and clam salad for lunch, followed by lobster. I could see an enclosure with a couple of horses down the way, and a tennis court over by the pool. It looked like it might be fun to live in, George's world. The major drawback was, George'd be living right there alongside you.

'Orange juice with it? Do you know what you call that Ed? Mimosa. Sounds better than Bucks Fizz, doesn't it, Mimosa? Bit of class. Cristal this is, none of your sparkling rubbish. No juice for me. Wine we're having with lunch now is French, from the Loire Valley, a Château . . . Château . . . ah, Château whatever-the-fuck. I like wine and all, spend a lot of dinars on it these days, but, in my not very humble opinion, it's impossible to talk about wine without sounding like a cunt.'

George Halligan was wearing a cream single-breasted suit, pale blue shirt with a white collar, red silk tie with a diamond tie pin and gold cufflinks. His one concession to the heat was to drape the jacket over the back of his chair; his red braces had a pale blue trim. He looked at my black suit and white shirt and shook his head.

'You look like some drunk cunt on his way home after a dress dance. Have you no other clothes?'

'The airline lost my luggage.'

'We'll have to see about a new wardrobe for you. Dress sense. Lacking in this town. Fucking lamentable. Changing, yes, but too fuckin' slowly, still look like a shower of culchies up for the day. Anyway, down to business: Ed, I hope you're serious about this, because I need a serious man here; I'm surrounded by yes-men, gobshites and savages.'

'What exactly would you want me to do for you, George?' I said.

'I'd want you to be the public face, the legitimate face, of the Dawson – excuse me, the Halligan, eh, empire. Because things are evolving. Maybe in the past, I acquired a pub or a bookies as a way of giving certain monies a bit of a rinse. But now, pretty much everything is profitable in its own right. I'm pulling in more above board than otherwise. So it's time to phase otherwise out.'

'And how does Podge feel about that? I mean, he is Mr Otherwise, isn't he?'

'Ah, Podge is a bit of a nostalgist all right. He likes the old ways. But change is ruthless, know what I mean, Ed? It doesn't take account of individual preference: it runs roughshod over us all. Podge will have to, eh, make an accommodation with it.'

'I don't know that I'd be keen on making an accommodation with Podge.'

'Leave Podge to me, Ed. Leave Podge to me. Now, drinks. Where's the girl from Ipanema? Jaysus, you've hardly touched yours, what's the story, are you playing games here, Ed, letting me get langers while you sit there beady-eyed, takin' notes? I don't like that.'

George's tiny eyes narrowed, and the expansive fug of boozy bonhomie vanished in an instant. Veins stood out on his temples; the sinews in his neck corded and pulsed with sudden tension.

'Bit early in the day, George. Anyway, I've already been picked up once for drink-driving,' I said.

'Fuck *that*,' George said, wielding his rasp of a voice like a scythe. 'Sure we can always have you driven home. You're well in with the Seafield Guards there anyway.'

The Brazilian servant arrived and refilled George's glass with champagne. George stared at me until I emptied mine, then he nodded for it to be refilled.

'Letting a man drink alone, your *host*, no less, the height of bad manners,' George said in a tone of mock-outrage.

'Leave the bottle, and the juice,' he said to the Brazilian girl, touching her lightly on the forearm, his eyes fixed on mine. The girl flinched, and pulled her arm away as if it had been scalded.

'My apologies,' I said.

'Accepted,' he said solemnly, then cracked a grin that dispelled little of the menace he had suddenly invoked. It was an impressive reminder that the difference between him and his brothers was merely one of style. George Halligan snipped the end off a large Cohiba, ran it under his nose and sniffed. It made a scrabbling sound as it chafed against his moustache, like a small animal trapped behind drywall. I thought of ramming the cigar up his nose. It would pass the time, but it wouldn't help to crack the case.

'So would I be involved with your burgeoning property empire, George?'

'That's exactly what I had in mind for you, Ed. Right now we've apartments, a few pubs, some commercial units, a small office block – but what we're getting into now is development land: parcel it up, hold on to it for long enough, get it zoned the right way and then release it back on to the market at the right time. That's easy money – the legal way.'

'And my role would be . . . ?'

'I'd want you to piece together consortiums – *consortia* – of investors. All those nice lads you were at school with, the dentists and the barristers. Respectable citizens with plenty of money who want to make more. Not that I haven't done well without those cunts in the past. But the only way I'm going to do well in the future is with them on board.'

George lit his cigar, exhaled a large gust of smoke and winked at me. I was suddenly sick and tired of George Halligan, of his delusions of business respectability, his air of casual menace, his fantasy lifestyle copied from a Robert Palmer video.

'Is the golf club development first on the list then?' I said. 'The one you and Peter Dawson were trying to get rezoned? What's the status of that, now that Peter Dawson's dead?'

The beam froze on George Halligan's face; his coal-black eyes bored into mine.

'Down to business straight away. Good sign, Ed, shows willing. Predicament attached to this kind of conversation however; can't go disclosing highly sensitive business details to non-employees.'

'Can't really think about accepting a job unless I know some of the details, George. Maybe you should have your solicitor present. Set your mind at rest.'

George considered this.

'Maybe. Nah. Trust the important thing. And you'd be well aware, the consequences of a breach of trust. Wouldn't you?'

'Absolutely,' I said.

'Good man,' George said. 'Trust we must.'

George stirred the orange juice with a long silver bar spoon, and held up his glass. I drained mine, and he took it and filled it with champagne and juice.

'A toast to the future, Ed,' he said.

'The future,' I agreed.

We both drank. George was drinking champagne without the juice. His head was stronger than mine, or maybe it was the heat: already I was feeling a little hazy.

'So there must be a council meeting coming up soon?' I said.

'Friday.'

'And you're confident it's going to go your way?'

'How's that?'

'You're confident you'll get the golf club rezoned for high-density development?'

'Business is all about confidence, Ed. You know that.'

'And were you Peter Dawson's business partner in Courtney Estates? I mean, you weren't giving him money to bribe councillors just for the crack, were you?'

'Why would I give money to Peter Dawson? Don't you think he could have afforded to bribe his own councillors? They're not short of money, the Dawsons, case you hadn't noticed.'

'Someone was into Peter Dawson for a lot of money, bleeding him dry. If he was going to put this deal together, he needed cash to persuade the necessary councillors to come on board. Cash he didn't have access to day-to-day.'

George looked at me, his eyebrows raised. I felt hot, and my throat was dry. I drank some more of the Mimosa. I was thirsty, but I needed to stop drinking. What did that mean? I couldn't think straight.

'I mean, this is the kind of stuff I'm going to have to know, George, if I'm going to run things for you. Need to know stuff. On a need-to-know basis.'

There was fur in my mouth, and panic-sweat on my brow and in my hair, and a catch in my throat like I had swallowed sand. I drained my glass. The bubbles felt like sulphur in my chest. George leapt up, bottle of Cristal in his hand. I shook my head.

'No thanks.'

'Are you all right there, Ed? You look a little flushed.'

'I'm fine. Maybe just some orange juice. I feel a bit weird.'

'No bother. I'm beginning to think you just don't have the head for booze. Sure the last time I saw you on it you were scuttering your guts up, weren't you?'

George Halligan stirred the jug of orange juice again and poured me a glass.

'Now, knock that back, do you the world of good. Vitamin C, the business.'

Something was happening to my eyes; it felt like cold cream had been daubed on them. I reached for the glass, but couldn't quite seem to connect with it; George guided it into my hand. I brought it to my mouth and bent my head down to meet it. I tried to lift glass and mouth together, but my co-ordination was shot; the juice spilt down my cheek and on to my jacket. I was moving in slow motion; the air boiled in my ears like a river in full spate. George tipped the rest of the juice into my mouth and then tossed the glass away; it detonated on the marble tiles like a small explosion.

My head felt like it was made of lead; I lifted it slowly, in case it tore itself from my neck. Engulfed in cigar smoke and sunlight, George Halligan's face had contracted into a series of furrows and clefts; with no lips or eyes, it looked like a grinning fist. He leant into me. I could smell cigar smoke sour on his breath, and I felt the pit of my stomach churn. George Halligan laughed, then slapped me once, very hard, across the face, knocking me from the chair.

He said something, but all I caught were the words 'orange juice'; I could sense the rhythm though, vindictive but exuberant, like a boxer in triumph. I could hear him laughing, a grinding sound, like a small engine that wouldn't catch. I thought I could see people approaching; they looked too burly to be George's wives. The marble deck was cool on my cheek, the other cheek from the one George Halligan slapped. 'Turn the other cheek,' I thought. I would have said it if I could have spoken. I think I laughed, though. The last laugh. Not the last thought, though. There was a taste of cheap perfume in my mouth. The last thought was, 'Whatever he slipped me, they must have cut it with talc.'

~

I woke to the sound of male voices raised in laughter. The laughter broke apart in a flurry of obscenities, and subsided to a low rumble. I could smell creosote, and paraffin, and the stale musk of tobacco smoke laced with the sweet tang of burning hashish. I was lying on some kind of sofa or day bed, and my hands and feet weren't tied. I opened my eyes, or at least, my right eye; there was something wrong with my left. Above me there was a vaulted wooden roof. Weathered garden implements hung from hooks on the raw timber walls: rakes, scythes, shears. The voices were coming from the other end of the room. I looked to my right: there was a workbench with toolboxes and cartons of nails and screws and drill bits and so on stacked above and beneath it. A long-handled sledge-hammer and a disused green motor mower leant against a door by the bench; the door bolts had been painted shut with several coats of creosote and resin. I hoped there was another door, then cursed the stupidity of the thought, then welcomed it: at least it meant whatever I'd been drugged with had worn off. I lifted my head off the sofa to see further into the room and a searing pain shot through my sinuses. My nose was running, and when I wiped it, a smear of fresh blood came away on the back of my hand; crusts of dried blood clung to my nose and chin. I was having trouble opening my left eye, and a soft opening from my temple to below my ear smarted on contact. My tongue traced torn flesh and shattered root remnants still embedded in the gum on the lower left side of my mouth: the gap felt like at least two teeth were gone. My hair had felt dry when I came to; now it was soaked; I ran my fingers through it, but it was sweat, not blood. The rest of me felt bruised but not broken; I figured I could move when I needed to.

I attempted to move my head again, but this time keeping it on the sofa; twisting it to my right and bringing it around in a slow arc, I got a fisheye view of the room: long and narrow, an old garden shed, with machinery, paints and brushes. The floor was stone; there were what looked like cupboards or cubicles on the right-hand wall. At the other end, swathed in a fug of smoke, three men were playing cards around a white garden table. I watched them for a while, training my right eye to focus, trying to ignore the throb of pain in my head, until I was satisfied I recognized them: Blue Cap, Nose Ring and Dessie Delaney. At least my head was still attached to my neck. I lay back and looked at the rafters. The light was soft through long, narrow windows above head height: early evening, maybe, of the same day, I hoped.

Someone got up from the table. I heard a door opening, then the sound of a man pissing.

'Ah, that's it.'

'Check on your man, will you?'

'He's goin' nowhere.'

'Check on him anyway. Podge wants to know as soon as he comes round.'

'Podge wants, Podge wants.'

'And don't forget to wash your hands.'

'Fuck off.'

The sound of laughter again, then steps coming towards me. No sense in delaying the inevitable. I looked up at a tall, skinny man with a shaved head, a ring in his nose and green and yellow bruising around his throat.

'Cunt's awake,' said Nose Ring, grinning down at me. 'Maybe we should get a mirror, let him see his new face.'

Blue Cap appeared. He had lost his bandages, but his nose was a blue and purple mess. He grinned too. My face was first-rate entertainment today.

'This looks like a job for Podge Halligan,' he said, in a bad American accent. 'Give him a shout there Dessie.'

Nose Ring and Blue Cap both laughed again. Their laughter was getting on my nerves. I sat up and swung my legs to the ground, gripping my knees for balance. Nose Ring and Blue Cap both stepped back when I moved; Blue Cap fell on top of the disused motor mower. I nearly blacked out as the blood left my head; I nearly threw up as my stomach lurched with the unaccustomed motion. My head felt like someone was hitting it at regular, metronomic intervals with a rock. Nose Ring had gone to help Blue Cap up; Blue Cap was pushing him away. I sat where I was and worked on lifting my head up. Blood was flowing freely from my nose now; I pinched it hard below the bridge.

'Lucky he didn't break it so you are,' said Blue Cap peevishly.

'Maybe we should finish the job,' said Nose Ring. He looked towards Blue Cap, who shrugged, picked up a heavy wooden-handled spade and tossed it to Nose Ring. Nose Ring fumbled the catch, and it clattered to the ground.

'On you go,' said Blue Cap.

Dessie Delaney appeared behind Blue Cap. His right arm was in plaster.

'Podge said nothing happens until he gets here,' he said.

Dessie looked authoritative, presidential, almost, when contrasted with Blue Cap and Nose Ring.

'I owe this fucker,' said Nose Ring, leaning down to get the spade.

'You think I don't?' said Dessie Delaney. 'Let's wait for Podge. I'm pretty sure Podge has a plan.'

'He's lucky Podge didn't break his nose, so he is,' said Blue Cap.

'He's lucky Podge didn't do a lot of things,' said Dessie Delaney, grinning.

Blue Cap and Nose Ring laughed.

'Yeah, must be the first fucker Podge slipped Roofies to didn't wake up with an ache in his hole,' said Blue Cap.

'Don't speak too soon, lads. The night is young. Anything can happen,' said a reedy whine of a voice.

Podge Halligan had arrived.

Podge dressed like a loyalist paramilitary: muscle shirts, low-slung jeans, a white baseball cap. He greeted each of his men with a backslapping embrace, kissed Nose Ring on the mouth, then twirled around and smashed me in the face with his left fist, getting his shoulder behind the blow. I was flung back on the couch and my head thumped off the wall behind me. My nose spurted a jet of blood over Podge's white top. He immediately whipped it off and used it to wipe my blood from his tattoo-laced, steroid-swollen torso.

'Little bit more work on that nose and I'll be able to fuck the hole!' Podge Halligan shouted. He laughed, but it took a while for the others to join in; Dessie Delaney pursed his lips, Blue Cap looked uneasy, Nose Ring simply looked scared.

Podge wasn't bothered; he twisted himself around and strode off down towards the other end of the room, head bobbing and fingers snapping to a tune only he could hear.

I felt my nose: miraculously, although it was a mess of cartilage and bloody flesh it wasn't broken. I pinched below the bridge again to stanch the flow of blood. I clocked the spade on the ground where Blue Cap had thrown it; I checked the positions of the implements hanging from the walls; I looked at the anxious faces of Podge's gang. If I was going down here, I was going to take Podge with me, at the very least.

He returned with a can of lager and a cigarette; he drank half the can of lager, belched at Blue Cap, then came towards me and waved the lit cigarette in front of my face.

'Not finished with this fucker yet. Not by a long shot,' he said, his bloated face contorting itself into a succession of leering fright masks. He took a long drag on the cigarette, then brought the red tip close to my closed left eye, then to my open right one. The heat and smoke made it water and smart; I tried not to flinch, got ready to dive for the spade.

'Podge. Podge, George said . . .'

Podge Halligan flashed the cigarette away and turned on Dessie Delaney, who had spoken.

'George said *what*?'

Delaney tried to draw Podge close to him, so he could talk in his ear. Podge shook Delaney's hand off like he was a bothersome fly.

'Fuck away off out of that, telling me secrets, whisperin' like a girl. What did my brother say?'

'That we shouldn't take things too much further. Find out what he knows, then . . . just a scare thrown into him, that's all he wanted,' said Dessie Delaney.

Podge moved close to Delaney then, forehead to forehead.

'I think he's scared, Dessie. Are you scared? Are you?'

Dessie Delaney shook his head.

'No, Podge,' he said.

Podge took a step back.

'Good man,' Podge said, and headbutted Dessie Delaney. Delaney shouted out in pain and dropped to his knees, blood dripping out between the fingers he held to his face.

'You should be. My brother. *My* brother,' Podge said, nodding violently to the beats inside his head. 'The fuck does it matter what this little prick knows? Comin' back here from the States, thinks he's fuckin' *it*, pokin' around like a fuckin' . . . I mean, if he knew anything – if he knew where Tommy Owens was, or what happened that night with MacLiam and Peter Dawson, if he knew anything – and even if he did – and even if he *does* – he can disappear, can't he? Not too fuckin' difficult. People vanish all the time, don't they? No-one misses them. 'Cept the cunts that do, and they don't matter. Strictly day-to-day. No big deal.'

Podge seemed to deflate all of a sudden. His head drooped, his chin rested on his chest. He kept talking, mumbling to himself. Then, just as abruptly, he perked up again.

'Just 'cause George wants to carry on like some kind of business cunt, doesn't mean I do. Me own plans. Not some fuckin' . . . like I'm his fuckin' waiter. "George said . . . George wants" . . . what about *me*, eh? What about *my* plans?'

Podge Halligan's upper body was shaking, rippling with tension. He pivoted and made a surging run up to the far end of the shed, like a fireman plunging into a burning building. I braced my left leg on the floor, ready once more to make a dive for the spade. Podge returned with four cans of lager and passed them around. Nose Ring and Blue Cap cheered and high-fived each other and opened their cans and drank. Dessie Delaney sat on the stone floor hunched up in a ball, leaning against one of the broad wooden legs of the work bench, dabbing at his nose; he pushed the can he was given to one side.

'Waiting for something to drink too, Dessimond? Proper order. Let's do this fucker once and for all, eh?'

Podge Halligan was too quick for me. He flung his beer can at my head; by the time I had slapped it out of the way and wiped the beer from my face, he had scooped up the spade and pressed it into Blue Cap's hands. Then he stepped onto the back of the sofa and unhooked the scythe from the wall. I sprang up and looked around for a weapon, but Blue Cap blocked my path with the spade; now Podge began to close me into the corner, slicing the air with the scythe. His eyes were clear and wide and full of light; his grinning lips were swollen with the prospect of blood.

'Harvest time. Don't fear the reaper, isn't that right, Dessie? Never used a scythe before. Still. Think it might be one of those things you pick up along the way.'

There was a sound from further down the shed.

'Podge,' said Dessie Delaney.

'Fuck away off now or you're next, Dessie,' Podge said. Drool ran down his chin. He swung the blade of the scythe again; it sounded like death in my ears.

'Podge, it's your one,' said Delaney. 'It's the Dawson girl.'

I saw the flash of Linda's golden hair between Podge's head and Blue Cap's baseball hat. What was she doing here? Where were we, anyway? This shed was fifty years old, at least; the Halligans' houses had been built ten years ago.

'Ed, is that you?' she said.

Linda's voice sounded sluggish, affectless: sedated.

Podge slipped the scythe beneath his left arm and turned back towards Linda.

'Have you made a wrong turn, love?' he said. 'Lads, see that Mrs Dawson here gets back up the house.'

Nose Ring made a move towards Linda; Dessie Delaney stood up but didn't budge; he stared from Podge to me and back.

It was all the time I needed. I gripped the workbench with my right hand for ballast, braced back and hit Podge right-side on, mid-chest, with both feet. He tumbled onto the sofa, the scythe still tucked beneath his left armpit, and screamed. Blue Cap stared at Podge open-mouthed; the blade had cut into his chest, and the point into his shoulder. There was a lot of blood. Podge got onto his knees and tried to work the scythe loose; each way he moved it was worse than the last; he was screaming in pain. Blue Cap was still absorbed by Podge's agony; I kicked him in the balls and took the spade off him, then kicked him twice in the head when he was down. Linda was standing in the middle of the room, her eyes cloudy with medication; it was hard to tell how much she was taking in. Nose Ring made a move towards Linda, then a move towards me, then he grabbed the sledgehammer that lay beside the motor mower. He didn't have the upper-body strength to wield it properly, so he came at me holding it high on the shaft. He would need to get in close to use it; with the spade handle at full extension, I jabbed him in the face until he fell, then hit him on the head with the flat of the blade. Podge was still screaming; in between screams, he swore he'd have me executed, but the scythe had him hooked; he wasn't going anywhere without medical help.

With his mobile in his hand, Dessie Delaney nodded at me and looked towards the door.

'Go on,' he mouthed silently.

'All right, Podge, we'll get someone for you now,' he said out loud.

I threatened Delaney with the spade, to make it look right, crooked an arm around Linda's waist and backed us both towards the door.

'I want that fucker's head,' Podge screamed.

I grabbed Linda's hand and we plunged through the door towards the fading light.

18

We came skidding out onto fine, coral-coloured gravel, and I ran the outside bolt on the shed door. A dense copse of beech trees faced us, and beyond, a baize green lawn sloped out of view.

Linda reached a hand up and gently stroked my left cheek, then drew the knuckle of her forefinger across my mouth.

'You OK to run?' she said, and smiled.

I nodded, and tried to ask her something, anything, but she stopped my lips with her fingers, and shook her head.

'Talk later. Follow me, Edward Loy,' she said.

There was a wild glow in her eyes, as if this was all a great game. She set off at a run across the lawn, and I tried to keep up with her. We were in the grounds of a very large house, high above the sea. The lawn was set in tiers, leading down to a great granite wall encrusted with ivy and topped with jagged shards of glass. Linda leapt the tiers without breaking stride, reached the wall and hooked right along a gravel path; she was wearing a white summer dress with red roses and black leaves printed on it and flat black shoes; her lean brown legs moved with an athlete's efficient grace. Each time my left leg hit the ground a jarring pain shot through my side and exploded behind my left eye. I halted by the wall to stanch a fresh jet of blood from my nose. From behind, I could hear commotion from the house; lights were flashing, and I could see men running down towards the shed and fanning out across the lawn. Linda reached a hedge of tightly-packed red and green laurel and hawthorn trees that must have been twelve feet high; she turned, beckoned to me and then disappeared into it. I made it to the trees, but the gap Linda had passed through seemed too narrow; I pressed sideways between the tangled branches of two laurel trees that were close enough to be one. Halfway in I got stuck, but Linda urged me on; by lowering my head, sucking in my gut and pushing hard with my hip, I managed to force my way through with just an average set of scrapes and tears; getting out, a hawthorn branch snapped back and smacked me in the eye, but it was the left eye, so no fresh harm done.

We found ourselves in an unkempt wilderness of thistle and bramble, with dark pools of stagnant water bordered by dock leaves and clumps of nettles. Voices and shouts came from behind us; they sounded as if they were on the other side of the trees. The granite wall still ran to our left, and, having checked that I was in one piece, Linda took off at speed once more; she ran bare-legged through thistles and nettles, taking care to avoid the marshy ground, until she reached a point where the wall had collapsed and formed a rudimentary stile. We climbed over the shattered granite and broken glass and sank down onto a soft incline of dead ferns and pine needles. A few feet further down and it was dark under cover of a pine forest; further down again and I could see fluttering ribbons of greyish blue in the distance, and I knew where I was and where we had been: this was Castlehill, and the pine forest that led down to the sea at Bayview, and the house in whose grounds I had been imprisoned belonged to John Dawson.

We worked our way down the forest for about a hundred feet or so, then clambered onto a steeper ridge of gorse and scrub and dropped the last few feet to a cliffside path. Another ridge of gorse and ferns led down to the road, then another to the railway, and below that a sheer drop to the water. Night had fallen, and the moon loomed above the glistening slate-grey sea. Linda turned around and looked at me for the first time since we'd gotten away.

'Oh Ed,' she said. 'You came for me.'

She pulled me close, and pressed her face to mine; I could feel her tears damp on my neck. When she looked up at me, her face was smeared red; I made to rub it off, but she shook her head, and kissed me; her tongue darted into my mouth and caressed my broken teeth, my torn gums; it hurt, but it was worth it. She looked up at me again and smiled; her lips were black with blood, like the rose leaves on her dress.

'Where can we go?' she said.

'I don't know. I'm not even sure what's happened yet.'

There was a sound above us, a crackle of gorse, a rustle in the ferns. A rat or a rabbit, maybe. Maybe not. Linda's eyes flickered with excitement and fear.

'Ed, we have to keep moving. Where can we go?'

'We're not far from your house.'

'Are you crazy?'

'No. Come on,' I said.

We ran along the cliff path about a quarter of a mile, until it turned inland and we reached the base of the quarry. Linda blocked my path.

'What do we do now, scale the quarry face with our bare hands?'

'It can be done,' I said.

'Don't you think they'll be watching my house?' Linda said.

'We're not going to your house. Come on.'

And I tramped down the mud path that led to the road, hoping Linda's red Audi would still be there. It was. I started to explain how it got there, but she interrupted me.

'Have you got the keys?' said Linda.

I checked my pockets: phone, keys, wallet, change, even the twenty grand in its brown envelope, all there. Maybe Podge preferred to rob people after he had murdered them.

I gave Linda the keys. She unlocked the car, turned to me and burst into tears.

'It's all right,' I said. 'It's all right.'

'Oh Ed, it's not all right,' Linda said. 'It's never going to be all right again.'

She looked up towards the quarry.

'We've got to get out of here. They're probably searching for us now.'

'What's Podge Halligan doing in John Dawson's house, Linda?'

'I'll tell you everything once we're on our way. Can you drive? I'm still whacked out on whatever shit they were feeding me,' she said. 'And I've been drinking the whole time. Can you see properly?'

'One eye's fine,' I said. 'But I've got to get home, get cleaned up.'

'We can't. They'll be watching your place too.'

'I can't go anywhere else. Look at the state of me.'

'I'll get you fixed up. Come on.'

We got into the car and I drove down to Bayview and pulled over behind the trees at the back of the public sports field.

Linda had an assortment of make-up bags scattered around the car. She found some cotton wool in one, took a half-full bottle of Stoli Limon from the glove compartment and cleaned me up. The vodka stung like hell, but it felt good: like every trace of the Halligans was being wiped from my face. Linda laughed each time I winced.

'You're fine,' she said. 'The eye will be grand, and I don't think this gash needs stitching, it'll knit together itself. Don't think you'll need a doctor. A dentist, maybe.'

She passed me the bottle, and I rinsed my mouth and spat blood and crumbs of teeth into the street. The pain was suddenly excruciating, and I knocked back a hefty slug of vodka to chase it away.

'A dentist, definitely,' she said. 'In the meantime . . .'

She found a pack of Nurofen Plus in a silver sequinned bag and handed me four. I washed them down with another slug and passed her the bottle. She took a long drink, and wet her glistening lips with her tongue. I could smell her again, deep inside, that tang of grapefruit and summer sweat and smoke. She took my hand and placed it on her breast; I could feel the rise and fall of her breath, the rustle of her dress as she shifted in her seat and moved her legs apart, her tongue hot as she whispered in my ear.

We drove south and west, past lead mines and through dense pine forests until we were in the mountains. We climbed as high as we could, on roads where gorse and ferns gave way to marsh and shallow bog, and parked in the shadow of the communication masts that dotted the summit of the highest peak. We started kissing in the car, tearing at each other's clothes, hoarse with silent lust, but it was too hot and too cramped, so we got out and I sat on the car hood and Linda sat above me. I could see the lights of the city beneath us, see them over Linda's shoulder as she moved with me in the night, sense them pulsing in the haze as I came inside her and she cried out and I held her bright head close to mine. We stayed like that for a while, for as long as we could, until a white van blazed past, with the horn honking and its loutish occupants yelling cheerful obscenities out the windows. We dressed and lit cigarettes and smoked them in the precarious still of the night. Linda didn't want to talk at first, and I didn't want to force her, didn't want to dispel whatever it was we had summoned up, so we sat on the hood and looked out at the city below, at the glowing channels of heat and light that coursed through its arteries like blood.

When Linda began to speak, it was in a low, steady voice.

'It didn't feel like I'd been kidnapped,' she said. 'I mean, it was right that I should be with the Dawsons, after Peter's body was found. And I needed the downers, God knows. Barbara has a pet doctor who gives her anything she wants, he was feeding me them with a spoon. But it went from Valium to something stronger, I don't know what. And I ended up in a total fog. So it wasn't as if they had to lock me up or anything. Though there always seemed to be someone around, someone watching. And then that evening, there wasn't. I walked out of the house, and I got some air, and I heard sounds from the outbuildings, and I pushed open the shed door, and there you were.'

We drove to a hotel Linda knew, where sympathetic staff seemed used to her arriving at unusual hours with unfamiliar men; a dapper manager with a camp Dublin manner called Val took her aside and they embraced and commiserated; soon they were laughing, and Val was casting appraising looks at me. I pulled the lapels of my coat over my bloodied shirt as we rode the elevator. Linda said Val would see to it that a clean one was sent up. Food was sent up too: steak sandwiches and tiger prawn salads with Thai dressing and bottles of ice-cold Staropramen. It was a nice set-up, so I felt an overpowering need to fuck it up.

'Come here often?' I said, almost wincing at how pinched and unpleasant my voice suddenly sounded.

'I come here when I want to,' Linda said. 'Or at least, I did, when my husband was alive.'

'But you didn't bring him here, did you?'

'No, I brought other men here, Ed. That was then. Now could be something else. That depends on you, as much as me.'

She looked at me straight, unashamed of who she'd been, ready for who she might become. At forty-three, I'd be lucky to find anyone else with half what she had. I couldn't hold her gaze, and turned away, and muttered something about a shower.

I stood under the hottest water I could bear for as long as I could stand, until my body had begun to forget what had been done to it. Then I ran it cold until my head felt numb, and the throbbing in my temple had almost abated.

Linda was on the phone when I came out of the bathroom.

'Could we have some vodka? Stoli, or Absolut, and a jug of freshly squeezed grapefruit juice? And some ice and lemons, room 146. Dawson, thanks.'

I took a long hit on what remained of my beer, and Linda began to talk.

'They don't let Podge in the house. But they let George in the house. George Halligan, chatting to Barbara Dawson, helping himself to John's scotch, walking around as if he owns the place. For all I know, he does. And Podge and his pack of savages lurking around the grounds, sitting in their vans smoking and barking at each other.'

'What are they doing up there, Linda?' I said. 'What are the Dawsons doing with the Halligans?'

'It started with Peter, I think. Because Peter needed help. And instead of asking his father, he asked George Halligan. John Dawson owns the golf club lands. And he presented it to Peter as a gift. Well, he meant it as a gift, but it ended up being a test.'

'What do you mean?'

'I think John felt sorry for Peter: the way he tried so hard to impress him. John tried to let him know he didn't have to, but of course, Barbara made it very clear she thought he was a failure, not a patch on his father. That's why John wanted

Peter to have the golf club lands. So he could make his mark. Barbara wasn't supposed to know about it, but she found out. And she said that this was his last chance, that if Peter didn't come good this time, she was finished with him.'

'Meaning what? That he'd have no job? Or that she wouldn't see him again?'

'Maybe both. Maybe neither. Barbara always argued like it was the last throw of the dice. She'd cry, or rage, slam doors, the whole Joan Crawford routine. Sometimes she'd turn the tables and apologize to Peter, beg his forgiveness. That was even scarier. But soon enough she'd be sniping at him again. So it could have meant anything. But Peter took it seriously: he was going to do it this time.'

'He told you that?'

'Yes. It was his last chance. And I think . . . I know . . . that he hoped it would give us one last chance too.'

'Would it have? Or were you too close to his father for that ever to have worked?'

Linda's lip quivered in hurt surprise, and I thought she was going to cry. She looked at me as if I had betrayed her. I had, but that had started when I took her money, and then fell in love with her, and then made myself believe I could do both.

'I saw his car on its way to meet you the night they found Peter's body. You were dressed for . . .'

'Yes, Ed? Dressed for action, is that what you thought? Not so evolved after all, are you, you can form the thought but you don't have the spine to say the words.'

'This is not about you and me, this is about the case: if you were having an affair with your father-in-law –'

'Is that what you think of me?'

'I don't think. I ask questions.'

'Ask your question then.'

Linda's face was flushed but defiant, so beautiful it made

my pounding heart sore. Maybe if I'd stopped there, and taken her in my arms, and let the case fade away, maybe she'd still be alive. But how could I have done that?

The vodka arrived. Linda drank a shot straight off, then made herself a screwdriver. She gestured to the bottle, as if to say, 'If you want one, make it yourself,' walked to the window and looked out at the night.

'All right Ed. Shoot.'

'Were you having an affair with John Dawson?'

Her voice, when she spoke, was low and melancholy.

'John Dawson is a lost and lonely man. His marriage has been dead for years. In a way, it's like *he's* been dead for years, he seems to take no pleasure in the present, in living, in his achievements. He and Barbara exist in a kind of total war. But it's a cold war. He . . . I could never work it out, him and Peter: John seemed to like him so much, you know? He'd sympathize with him that Peter hadn't made the big impact he thought he should. It wasn't like . . . well, you hear about successful men giving their sons a really hard time if they don't live up to their expectations. John wasn't like that. Barbara was. Actually, it was like John wanted Peter to do well so they could get Barbara off both their backs. But beyond all that, there's something . . . detached about him. As if John was dealing with Peter, with Barbara, with the day-to-day of his life, but that it was all faintly unreal. I don't know, I guess a lot of people get like that when they're older, like the people they knew in the past are their true reality. But with John, maybe there was something more. One night a few months back . . . they were just starting the work on Seafield Town Hall, and Peter was working late all the time, and John arrived. Just, out of the blue . . . and asked me to sit with him, and . . . make him tea, or a drink, and sit and listen to him, you know? Like I was his daughter.'

'His daughter?'

'That's what it felt like. And then it became a regular thing, he'd come over when Peter was out. He'd want me to dress up, and then he'd sit and talk. It was . . . it was really weird, I suppose. An affair, you could call it. A family affair. I liked it. I liked being a daughter. Never got the chance – my dad walked out when I was five. And he spoke as if he had a daughter, or that one day he hoped to have one. About the funny little games and songs they'd sing, and how she liked her hair in plaits, not pigtails.'

'You said he talked about people from the past. What people? Did he talk about my mother?'

'Not your mother, no. He talked about your dad. And a guy called Courtney. Kenny, I think it was. How they were the wild boys, the three musketeers, all this stuff. That was actually pretty boring, how they robbed this orchard, or bunked into this cinema, or how they set a goat free once.'

The three musketeers. My father, John Dawson and Kenneth Courtney. And Courtney estates, directors Kenneth Courtney and Gemma Grand.

'Did he say what happened to Courtney?'

'He died. Wouldn't tell me how. As if it upset him too much. Your Dad disappeared, and Courtney died, and that was the end of that. End of everything.'

'Is that all?'

'Well, apart from the fact that he asked me to hire you.'

'He what?'

'Peter disappeared around the same time your mum died. By the time you got home, and the funeral was set and everything, there was still no sign of him. We knew about you in LA, that you were a private detective and everything. John said I should hire you, that you'd find Peter. And more besides.'

'And more besides. Did he say that?'

'Yeah. That you were your father's son, and you'd know what to do.'

Linda stepped away from the window and stumbled as she crossed the room. She made another screwdriver, lit a cigarette and sat on the bed, looked up at me beneath long lashes.

'Do you, Ed? Do you know what to do?'

'What about the Halligans? You said Peter turned to them for help.'

Linda shook her head and sighed.

'The sins of the fathers. You know all the talk about John Dawson with those houses on Rathdown Road, how Jack Parland helped get him the votes on the council to get the land rezoned? And how that help was doled out of John's back pocket? Well, that was Peter's first idea: bribe everyone. Only trouble was, he didn't want to use the money he earned from Dawson's.'

'He didn't have the money. I've been through his bank accounts, money was going through them like rain through a sieve. The Halligans must've had him laundering cash for them or something.'

'That's why Tommy Owens was bringing him money the night he disappeared.'

'Money to bribe Joseph Williamson.'

Linda looked away at the mention of his name.

'Do you know what happened to him, Linda?'

'He wouldn't budge. He was the vote Peter needed. And of course, the vote the Halligans needed. Because now they were in on the deal. They soon got a couple of councillors to accept "donations". Then George went to John and Barbara, told them what was going on, and made it clear he'd let the press know the attempt to rezone the golf club lands was dodgy. The Dawsons realized they were trapped: they couldn't go to the police, they just had to just suck it up and hope for the best.'

'I thought they had Superintendent Casey looking out for them.'

'Barbara said with the Halligans involved, there was no way you could control the information.'

'And how did the councillor die? Do you know?'

'Peter met Williamson somewhere, then he contacted the Halligans, I guess to tell them Williamson wouldn't play. After that, well, whether the heroin was a deliberate overdose, or just that they were trying to get him to change his mind and gave him too much by mistake, I don't know.'

'And Peter?'

'Barbara said Peter came back that night in a state. He was upset by what had happened, and personally ashamed – after all, he had involved the Halligans in the first place. She said she tried to calm him down, told him it wasn't his fault.'

'Why? I thought she despised him. And it was his fault.'

'Yeah, but she said she didn't want him doing anything stupid.'

'Like ringing the cops.'

'Exactly. I mean, it's a total cover-up, the whole thing. She said she gave him some Valium, he went into the garden to get some air. Next thing, they hear shots. It's so fucked-up the way she talks about it, like she's proud of him now, like it was some kind of noble act. But she didn't seem to think it was a good idea to have his body found in the house, so I assume the Halligans had to come to the rescue. And now the Dawsons can't get rid of them.'

'Do you think Barbara encouraged Peter to kill himself?'

Linda drained her glass, and quickly shook her head.

'No. No. I mean, she's a monumental bitch, but she wouldn't have done that.'

'And what about John Dawson? He must have known all about this the night he came to visit you. What did he say? Did he show any sign of upset that his son had just killed himself?'

'No, not at all. He seemed . . . serene. Almost euphoric.'

'Euphoric?'

'Yeah. Kept telling me not to worry, everything would work out for the best. That, somehow, you would sort it out.'

'And what about you? The night this happened, you narrowly missed meeting Peter in the High Tide. You did meet Tommy Owens. What did you do then?'

'I went home. And drank until I fell asleep.'

'What did you and Tommy Owens talk about? Did Tommy tell you anything about what was going on?'

'Am I a suspect too, Ed?'

'I'm just trying to work out what you knew and when. I had the impression when we spoke earlier, before Peter's body had been discovered, that you knew a lot more about what had happened than you were saying.'

'It wasn't that, it was . . . there was something Peter used to say about you.'

'About me? I never met the fellow.'

'I know, but he knew all about you. He . . . the whole family thing became something of an obsession with him, especially after we discovered we couldn't have kids. He kept going through old photographs, and visiting Fagan's Villas and so on. And he said he thought you and he were related. That . . . well, John Dawson was your father too. And that he killed Eamonn Loy so he could be with your mother. That's what I didn't want to tell you, Ed.'

I went to the window and filled my lungs with air; I felt like I was going to suffocate. I'd become more and more convinced that my father had been killed, and that his killer was John Dawson; could it be that that was true, but that Eamonn Loy's killer had been my real father? I poured myself a shot of vodka and knocked it back. It tasted like water, and had the same effect. I did it again.

'Who did Peter visit in Fagan's Villas?'

'I don't know. I don't know that he visited anyone. I think he just went there to soak up the vibes. The past.'

'A Mrs Burke?'

'Doesn't ring any bells.'

'All that stuff was in his files, Linda, remember? The boxes Family 1 and Family 2? And this is something else that was there. I found it on Peter's boat.'

I showed her the photograph of Eamonn Loy and John Dawson, a photograph I didn't seem able to hold without my hand shaking.

'My God, look at John, he's so young. Is that your father with him?' she said.

'It is.'

'This photograph has been cut, hasn't it? Look, the edge here is frayed and torn, but not all the way around. And it's been cut on a curve. It looks like there was a third person there, the curve is cut in the shape of a head. As if whoever it was had been deliberately removed from the picture. Or someone wanted a picture of just the other person.'

'Kenneth Courtney. The third musketeer. The other dead man.'

Linda turned it over and noted what was written on the reverse of the torn fragment:

ma Courtney

3459.

'The directors of Courtney Estates: Kenneth Courtney and Gemma Grand,' I said. ' "ma Grand." Maybe Gemma Grand was Kenneth Courtney's wife. Or Ma Grand was his mother, her maiden name.'

Linda looked at me as if I was going to explain. But I didn't have anything more to say.

19

I woke in the grey pre-dawn. Linda was kissing my eyes; her tears were wet on my forehead. She moved down my body and got me hard with her mouth, then she rolled beneath me and guided me inside her, and all the time we looked each other in the eye as if to break gaze would be the worst thing, and we moved long and slow, and both came hard, and cried out together, and fell back asleep almost at once.

When I woke again, it was half five, and the sun was hoisting itself above a pale red horizon. I felt like I'd slept twelve hours through, though it had been barely half that. I washed my damaged face and peered at it; yesterday you'd have thought I'd walked into a glass door; now, you'd just reckon it was just a door. My clothes had been left in the corridor: my suit sponged and pressed, my white shirt bloodless and starched, my shoes polished. I thought about how frequent a customer Linda must've been to get service like that. Those thoughts weren't very pleasant, so I put them out of my mind. It was easy to do, looking at her. She lay deep asleep, her mouth in a slight pout, her honey-blonde curls framing her pale-brown face. I could still smell her on my body; I needed a shower, but I didn't want to be without her scent. I thought about leaving a note, but I'd be back before she woke up.

The sunrise was an orange blaze now, above a band of deepening red; it looked volatile, incendiary, like it was ready to engulf itself; I thought of the death-soaked canvas Linda had hung in her bedroom. It was time to go.

Last night, Podge Halligan had assumed I didn't know where Tommy Owens was. He was wrong. I took a taxi down to Seafield. I asked the driver to go past my house. Last time we'd clashed, the Halligans had trashed the place; the only thing left for them to do was burn it down. Instead, they'd returned my car. I paid the taxi-driver off and inspected it. There was a tube of cream for securing false teeth and a packet of plasters under the windscreen wipers: George Halligan's way of saying sorry. He was going to have to say it again, and mean it.

I drove through Seafield and left the car parked across from the new ferry terminal. I headed for the west pier, walking along the old road by the disused railway track until I reached the abandoned ferryhouse. I knocked on the door repeatedly, until I heard someone stirring. A voice came from behind the door.

'Who is it?'

I didn't think I could get my voice high-pitched enough for Podge, so I tried George.

'The Count of Monte Cristo, the fuck d'you think it is? Open the fuckin' door.'

I heard the sound of a bolt being drawn, and as the door opened, I heard a voice say,

'Colm's down there, he's —'

The security guard had a navy uniform and a shaved head, and a black baton in one hand. When he saw I wasn't George Halligan, he lifted the baton and came at me fast. I stepped in so close to him that he had no room to swing it and headbutted him in the face as hard as I could. His nose gave way and he screamed in pain and I pushed him back inside and closed the door behind me and steadied myself against it. My head was reeling, and the wound on my left temple had opened up, and blood was coming out of *my* nose; I hadn't wanted to nut him but it was the only thing I had room to do, and now I wasn't sure if I had the strength to do anything else. The security guard was on his knees, holding his face in his hands; I took a step towards him and he retreated behind an oval brass counter that had formed part of a ticket kiosk; there was bedding and a radio and assorted beer cans and pizza boxes scattered; he huddled in a corner and held his baton in front of him.

The entrance hall had a crumbling marble floor of brass-flecked coral, with a small waiting room to the left of the door; past where the kiosk would have been, a brass rail bisected a semi-circular set of steps that led to two swing doors with porthole-style window frames without glass. I went through one of the doors and found myself in the old double-aisled departure hall with windows on the left looking out at the West Pier. There were old chairs and tables piled about at random, and a dilapidated wooden corral halfway along on the right that might have been a customs post. Matching swing doors at the bottom of the hall led to a stairwell that smelt of smoke and diesel and brine; I clattered down the steps to the disused railway station. The grey-and-blue-tiled platform was still intact; old railway sleepers and fragments of sleepers were piled onto the mangled tracks; a rusting buffer lay twisted beneath them. I got an intense flash of travelling with my father on the ferry, a daytrip to Holyhead to get I don't know what, duty-free booze most likely; I remember I got precious sweets you couldn't get in Ireland. The force and vividness of the memory took me aback, and I sank to my hunkers to bear it: my hand in his, the flat green and white package of Major cigarettes that he'd take from a pocket of his khaki-brown corduroy jacket, his smell of Brylcreem and Old Spice and alcohol and motor oil and smoke, the dark look in his eyes that, even as a child, I recognized was defeat, self-hatred, surrender. Maybe we didn't get along so well. Maybe he was not a nice man, or a good one. Maybe he wasn't even my father in blood. But he was a man, and John Dawson was going to pay for his death. If the cops wouldn't make him, then I would have to.

Colm Hyland must have moved with the silence and grace of a cat, or maybe I was momentarily deafened by the swirl of blood that memory had sent to engulf my brain, but I only saw his shadow, only felt the rush of air above me, only moved in a quick forward roll an instant before he brought a short length of railway sleeper down where my head had just been. He was left off-balance, and the heavy wood slipped from his hands; he stretched his long torso to reach for it, and I stood and kicked him hard in the stomach. He grabbed my foot by reflex, but couldn't hold it, and dropped to his hands and knees, wheezing and gurgling, desperate for breath.

'Colm's down there,' the security man had said. 'He's –'

He's what? But I knew. I knew since the Halligans had trashed my place and Tommy had vanished that they were holding him somewhere; I knew since I had seen Colm and Blue Cap bringing supplies in here that there was a good chance that somewhere was here; I knew after my encounter with the Halligans last night that they would probably try and move him. Colm's down there. He's on the job.

'Get up,' I said. 'Show me where you're hiding Tommy Owens.'

Hyland said nothing, just did some more wheezing.

'Get up, Colm.'

'Go fuck yourself,' he spat.

I kicked him in the face, and in the side, in the ribs, and in the balls, and I had to stop before I went further, stop before

I took it all out on Hyland, every humiliation I'd suffered at the hands of the Halligans, who at least had some genetic rationale for their behaviour, unlike this bastard of a boatman who must've had a choice and chose badly, stop before I literally kicked his fucking head in.

'Show me where he is,' I said, looking away quickly towards the down stairway, blocked up with old baggage trolleys, and the derelict escalators, and turning back to see the knife flashing as Hyland lunged forward and cut into my trouser leg, aiming up but lacking the strength to lift his arm; I felt a flash of pain along my calf, and stamped on his arm with my other foot until he dropped the knife, and slapped his head hard against the tiled floor until he was out. I sat beside him and inspected the damage he'd done: a clean slash along the muscle, a lot of blood, surprisingly little pain, a trouser leg that did not look to me like it could be mended. Hyland was unconscious; I rolled him on his side and took his knife with me.

The escalators were coated with rust and sand and what could have been mud, or shit, or blood, maybe all three. They led to the passenger boarding deck, with access doors that opened onto thin air, thirty feet above the water; a second set of escalators, even filthier than the first and stencilled with wet footprints, led down to a partly covered L-shaped dock recessed at the rear of the harbour. The open side looked out at the West Pier curving into the bay; the other side, dark and dank beneath a corrugated iron roof, was where repairs had presumably been carried out, or where a second ferry might have docked. A line of buoys blocked access to any craft that might wish to explore it. I shouted out Tommy's name, and heard nothing but my own voice back, hard and metallic. There was a rusting ladder attached to the wall at the corner of the L shape, and I climbed down as far as the waterline. The dock was supported by steel girders encased in concrete;

235

beneath it, Colm Hyland's wine-coloured motor launch was tied to a ladder rung; further in, three weathered rowing boats were tethered together and moored to steel rings fixed to the girders; they rose and fell in the swell of the tide. The contents of the three boats were concealed beneath tarpaulins.

'Tommy? Tommy, it's Ed.'

There was no reply. I thought I heard a thumping or a kicking, but that could have been the slap of the water against the boat hulls.

'Tommy?'

This time the sound was unmistakable, five steady knocks on wood, accompanied by a low moaning. I tugged on Hyland's boat and sat into it and untied the rope that secured it and angled myself towards the rowing boats and pushed off beneath the dock. It was only a few yards, using my hands to pass between girders and keeping my head low, and I floated alongside the first boat and grabbed hold of the side and lifted the tarpaulin. There were oars in it, and white plastic containers of what could have been oil or water. I tied Hyland's boat to it and climbed aboard and leant across and hauled the other tarpaulins away: in a second boat there were life belts and fishing kit; in the third, Tommy Owens lay, his trousers round his knees, gagged and bound at wrist and ankle with ropes that were tied to the oarlocks of the boat. I took the gag off and used Colm Hyland's knife to cut the ropes. There were knife cuts around his bruised thighs and buttocks and blood around his genitals; he had soiled himself, and reeked of urine and faeces; the gag was stained with blood and semen. Once I'd freed him, he sat up, flexed his wrists, grabbed the side of the boat and vomited into the sea. He dropped over the side and submerged himself completely, then surfaced and clung there, moving his legs in the water. He didn't speak, and I didn't know what to say to him, so I looked out towards the bay, where the

Holyhead ferry was approaching. When I looked back at Tommy, he had tears streaming down his face. There was a bottle of water in Hyland's boat. I passed it to Tommy and he drank as much as he could, and poured the rest over his head. He began to cry harder, shock working through his body in great heaving sobs.

We stayed like that a long while, and would have stayed longer if Colm Hyland hadn't had such a hard head, because here he was now, hanging off the ladder to see where his boat was. I didn't use the outboard motor before because I didn't know how; now there wasn't much of a choice. I was looking for a switch to flick, or a cord to pull, and Hyland was in the water, swimming the few yards towards us, and I figured the engine must need a key, but suddenly it didn't matter what it needed because Tommy Owens was standing up in the rowing boat with an oar in his hands, Tommy Owens back from the dead, his eyes all fire and blood, and he swung the paddle hard against Colm Hyland's forehead, and I had to grab the oar to stop him doing it again, because the first blow had sent Hyland under. When he surfaced, he was out cold, and I had to grab him quickly by the collar before he went down for a second time. Tommy didn't want to help me but I didn't want another dead man on my conscience, no matter what he'd done; I wouldn't let Hyland go, and eventually Tommy pitched in, and we got Hyland onto his boat and tied it up. He was breathing, and I put him in the recovery position, and Tommy tied his legs and hands and tossed the outboard engine over the side. We left him there by the old ferry dock, the Halligans' deadly boatman, sleeping in the dark.

20

I untied one of the rowing boats and channelled it out from beneath the dock and rowed towards the mouth of the harbour. Tommy sat astern of me and trailed a hand in the water, his sodden clothes dripping, his wet hair blowing back in the first breeze there had been for days.

'It was grand up until last night,' he said, suddenly, astonishingly, capable as ever of saying the thing you least expected. He said nothing more for a while. We came out of the harbour in our rowing boat, and were immediately rocked by the wash from the incoming ferry. Children up on deck waved to us. The first yachts of the morning were appearing in the bay. I felt like the last survivor of some savage tribe, escaped at last from his cave, dazzled and bewildered by the cold glare of civilization.

I narrowed my focus, concentrated on getting as far away from the old ferryhouse as we could. When I next checked our position, we were drawing level with the Royal Seafield, and Tommy had begun to talk.

'It was the night they trashed your house. I was in the garage, giving your oul' fella's tools a once over. Good equipment, but in a shockin' state. They came and got me. I told them where I thought the Glock was, but you'd moved it. They found it in the hire car though. Anyway, they took me and brought me down to the old ferryhouse, and it was grand, you know? Said they had to keep me out of the way. Podge was all smiles about the Glock, which I didn't trust, but still, he didn't come near me, not then. And it was grand, really, I mean, not great since I was bein' kept against my will, but they kept bringin' pizza and beer and all, and initially, I was up in the ferryhouse, wasn't chained up or anything, just locked in. Big Hyland was looking after me. Decent enough bloke, I thought.'

'Which is why you tried to kill him,' I said.

'Hyland could have stopped it. He just let it happen.'

'Podge Halligan? Was it Podge, Tommy?'

Tommy flushed, and instantly there were tears in his eyes again; he twisted his face into a fierce smile to hold them back, and nodded.

'How could Hyland have stopped Podge? The guy's out of control, a fucking savage.'

Tommy looked at my face as if he hadn't noticed before.

'You have a run-in with him too?'

I nodded.

'I thought I'd cut him up pretty badly,' I said.

'He had bandages around his chest and his shoulder all right. But that explains . . . he kept saying, "I won't let your little friend off this easy."' Tommy shook his head. 'Fuck's sake! They're just supposed to be dealers and blaggers, not the, not the fucking SS,' he said.

He looked out to sea, his lips trembling, his gaunt features creasing in tight folds as his jaw worked to master his emotions. The ferry had manoeuvred its stately progress past the mouth of the harbour, and we churned about in its wake, heading south.

'Tell me about Peter Dawson the night you met him in the High Tide, Tommy.'

'I told you. I gave him some money from George Halligan. Had a drink. His mobile rang, he said he had to go, asked me to wait and tell Linda he'd been called away. So I did, end of story.'

'This thing of George Halligan giving Peter the money. I mean, I know Peter was in a bad way financially, I've seen his bank records, but how? What was he spending it all on?'

'Horses. He was gambling with George Halligan. Ran up huge debts, kept trying to pay them off, couldn't, so he let George in on the whole golf club development thing instead. It started off as Peter trying to impress the old fella, 'cause John Dawson was a great man for the ponies. Ended as another rich kid's mess.'

'All right, back to the High Tide: anything about Peter you can remember that night, anything strange or unusual, or just a detail that sticks in your mind?'

'He had a blue plastic bag with him. You know, the kind they have in small newsagents and sweet shops. I remember thinking it looked weird, 'cause he was all collar and tie, Mr Business, should have had a briefcase or something, but no, this plastic bag full of . . .'

'Full of what?'

'I thought at first newspapers, like that madman who's always riding the DART with, you know, two plastic bags full of all the papers, but it looked like photographs, and old envelopes, the big ones, and cardboard folders, the kind they used to put photographs in.'

'Very good. Anything else?'

'He was nervous. Excited nervous, acting the gobshite. I remember the last thing he said, he said, "Make sure and tell Linda I've business with Lady Linda." I was like, yeah, sure I'm gonna tell her that.'

'"Business *with* Lady Linda?" Are you sure that's what he said?'

'Yeah. No, you're right, actually, it was business *on* Lady Linda.'

'And did you tell her?'

'I did in me shite. What am I gonna say, oh, your husband says he can't see you now, but don't worry, he'll give you the ride later?'

Tommy pursed his lips, and I remembered, despite the seeming chaos and abandon that surrounded him, what a puritan, what a hippie roundhead he had always been.

'The *Lady Linda* is the name of his boat.'

Tommy's bloodshot eyes widened.

'Fuck,' he said. 'That means he must've gone out there.'

'He met MacLiam, brought him on board. Maybe our friend Hyland helped him. Sail about with the good councillor, get him all relaxed, hopefully he'll prove amenable. And then who was waiting there? Podge and friends?'

'And they killed him there?'

'They fed him enough smack to kill him, or he OD'd by accident and they did nothing to help. Then tossed the body over the side. But that's all just what we think. We'd need a witness to know for sure.'

We let the likelihood of finding a witness willing to testify to a murder Podge Halligan had a hand in mock us in silence for a while. We were level with the Royal Seafield, and I wondered briefly whether Colm Hyland could be forced to testify, then, remembering how hard his head was, dismissed it out of hand.

'Podge never offered me the gun, you know?' Tommy said, his hair falling in his eyes, his expression as close to sheepish as it ever got.

'Say again,' I said.

'The Glock. He never offered it to me. I just took it out of Podge's gaff. And the clip. I knew there was something goin' on. I was at the party, you know? They were all still up to ninety about it, so they were? Sayin' things and then shushing each other, whispering, giggling, all this; they were like a pack of girls talking about young fellas. Anyway, I was pissed off being their fucking errand boy, oh very good Tommy keep the change you crippledy prick you. Hopalong, some of them called me. All very smart. And I knew you were back, with your ma an' all. And Podge told me, just leave the gear upstairs in his bedroom. And I needed a piss, Podge's ensuite bathroom, a fucking black bath an' all, black toilet, black sink, gold taps, fuck sake, the bad cunt. Anyway, there's the gun lyin' on top of the cistern. Checked the clip, two shots missing. So I thought, I'll take it and give it to you and see what you can come up with, see who's fucking smart then.'

'Just because they called you names?'

Tommy's eyes flashed with anger.

'If I'd known what Podge was gonna do, I'd have piled downstairs and emptied it up his fat hole,' he said.

He was breathing heavily, and his body went into something like a spasm.

'But you didn't know that then, did you?'

Tommy waited until he stopped shaking. It took a while.

'Podge and George were having a lot of rows, on account of George wanting to go legit, pay Podge off. They'd've been having even more if George knew what Podge was planning.'

'And what was that?'

'To team up with Larry Knight out in Charnwood and start dealin' H all round the Southside, down the coast as far as Wicklow, Wexford even. That's his plan now, anyway. What he originally wanted was to have me picking up the smack for him in Birmingham. Build up a connection, a regular route. Only I said no. He was furious, started makin' all these threats, my daughter's safety, all this. I told him I'd tell George what he was up to if he didn't back off. He said he didn't care what

George thought, but he did. Still, you never know what Podge is gonna fuckin' do. So I took the gun, so I'd have something on him.'

'Why didn't you tell me that in the first place, Tommy?'

'Ah, I didn't wanna make it too easy for you man, you know?'

And Tommy grinned. A little sheepishly, but it was a recognizable grin.

'And maybe I didn't want to tell you any more about how in I was with the Halligans.'

It wasn't quite an apology, but it would have to do.

'Anyway, something got Podge riled up last night, he came storming in and, and . . . well, you saw what he did to me. I thought he was gonna kill me when he was finished. Most of me wanted him to. But he said he'd keep me around. In case you kept sticking your nose in, he said.'

'What, that he'd use the threat of killing you as a way of warning me off?'

'Yeah. And he said he'd keep me around also because – said this as he was zipping himself up – because he didn't realize before how much he liked me,' Tommy said, his voice breaking. He began to shiver now, and a rattling sound came from his chest.

We had gone the length of the Seafront Plaza, and I turned the boat towards the shore. There was an old beach-house a canoeing club used to own with a patch of stony strand in front of it. I ran the boat up as far as I could, and we both stepped out in the shallows.

Tommy sat on the beach and tossed pebbles into the sea, and I went up on to Seafield Road. I passed three women's clothes shops, a fancy deli, two restaurants and an art gallery before I located a man's shop around the corner from a Mercedes dealership. It sold preppy-looking stuff at preppy-looking prices, no item of which Tommy Owens would normally have worn in a million years. I picked out a pair of beige chinos, a pale blue button-down shirt, a blue blazer and a pair of brown deck shoes. When I caught sight of myself in the mirror – my trouser leg ripped, my suit spattered with brine and blood and sand, my shoes soaked – I figured the assistant would think I was buying clothes for myself; the assistant, meanwhile, seemed untroubled by thought of any kind; beneath an electric shock of highlighted hair, his eyes never budged from his mobile phone, which was fielding text messages at a frantic rate; the only thing he looked at was my money.

'I'm not wearing those fucking things. I'll look like an accountant on his yacht,' Tommy said when I handed the bags to him.

'Clothes, Tommy. They're the latest craze. They won't let you on the ferry without them,' I said.

Because, once we had established that, while there were many things Tommy wanted to do to Podge Halligan, pressing rape charges was not among them, the plan we agreed was that Tommy should jump the Holyhead ferry and keep out of sight for a few days. So, with a full body shudder, as if he was being made to wear his soiled clothes again, Tommy put on the preppy outfit. He looked like several things when he was dressed; an accountant on his yacht was not one of them. We walked along the coast road to the new ferry terminal. Cloud was seeping across the sky like foam. The breeze was building, and there was a lick of cold in it, the first hint that summer wouldn't last for ever. I bought Tommy a return ticket and gave him a wedge of cash from Barbara Dawson's brown envelope, then I watched as he limped through to the departures lounge. It came to me then what he looked like: a boy who'd been bought his first grown-up clothes. They didn't suit him, didn't really fit him, usually made him look as lost and confused as Tommy looked, but what they said, emphatically, was: the old life is on its way out, to be replaced by the new. It may not be as much fun, or even fun at all, but it's inevitable; it doesn't fit yet, but it will. I thought that, and then Tommy turned and threw a few hard man shapes in my direction, and grinned like he had just gotten away with something, and all he looked like was the latest version of the old joke: what do you call Tommy Owens in a blazer? The defendant. And when it came to Tommy, it wasn't much of a joke. Still, he'd be safe from the reach of Podge Halligan, and out of my way for a while.

I sat into the Volvo and thought of Linda. It was still only eight fifteen, and the roads were busy now with the morning rush. I figured she'd sleep until ten at least, and I had one last stop to make. I knew Peter Dawson had visited Fagan's Villas; I wanted to see if he'd ever spoken to Mrs Burke, and if so, what she might have told him about the old days.

But if he'd been there, what they'd said had gone to the grave with the pair of them. A hearse was outside the corner house, and as I got out of the car, two burly grey-suited men carried a stretcher with a black body bag on it. They opened a trunk that lay beneath the main body of the hearse, pulled a rail out, positioned the stretcher upon it, slid the rail back in and shut the door. A woman of about thirty-five stood crying in Mrs Burke's lovingly tended garden. She watched as the hearse pulled away. No-one was standing at their gates, or on the pavement, the way they would have been in the old days. The few who passed on their way to catch the DART, or to the shops, turned their faces away, as if it would have been in bad taste to notice, or to reach out a hand in comfort. But the bereaved need all the help they can get, and, smiling as if that was my only intention, I walked up to the gate.

'Miss Burke? I'm sorry for your loss.'

The woman looked at me in surprise, then smiled and nodded. Her thick dyed-auburn hair looked the way hair looks when it's been up all night: like an exotic plant, or a modern sculpture. She came down to the gate, her broad, open face stricken with shock, her round hazel eyes kind and warm.

'Kay Preston, but yes, I'm the youngest Burke. Thank you, eh . . .'

'My name is Loy. My parents grew up here.'

'Of course,' she said. 'Quarry Fields, you lived in. And then your da . . .'

She left it unfinished.

'That's right. I'm not long home. My own mother died a few days ago,' I said.

Kay insisted I come in for a cup of tea. If she noticed my dishevelled appearance, she didn't mention it. We sat in the dusty, fuggy living room, and I told her I had visited her mother, and she started to cry: she hadn't seen her since last Christmas, although they spoke regularly on the phone; she drove up from Cork yesterday. Meals On Wheels had found her; she'd died in her sleep. The dog was up in the room, wouldn't leave it, not a bark out of him. I talked a bit about my mother, and we drank the tea, and she said a couple more of the family would make it over for the funeral, but not all of them: it was too far, and even if you could get time off work (and not all of them had the kind of jobs that allowed that) you couldn't always afford the fare. That was when my mobile made the double bleeping sound it makes when you receive a text message. I didn't look at it, didn't think it could be urgent, not urgent the way a call is. Kay raised her eyebrows as if to say it was all right by her if I checked it; I shook my head and asked her about Peter Dawson, whether her mother had mentioned him visiting. She said she had, she was quite excited, one of the Dawsons, although of course she knew his da when he was nothing.

'Did she say why he had visited her? Was there something in particular about the past he wanted to know?'

My question had been a little direct, and for a moment I thought she was angry with me, but she was too caught up in her own grief to be suspicious. I was just someone from the old neighbourhood, another local, and I knew from my mother's funeral what a comfort their mere presence could be.

'She said he wanted her to look at a load of old photographs. His da, and yours, probably, and a load of others. Ma said she got a bit bored, other people's photographs and all that, even if they had all grown up together, so she got out hers, but he was thrilled, started to ask loads of questions about everyone, even the Daggs she said.'

'Even the Daggs? Are you sure she said that?'

'Absolutely. Because when we were growing up, she'd always say, oh if you don't eat this or wear that, you'll end up walking the roads, a tramp like one of the Daggs. Which I always thought was unfair, because Rory Dagg, the son, was a fine thing, always was, you wouldn't have minded, put it that way. Anyway, Ma said she had to practically throw him out, you'd swear he was writin' a book he asked so many questions.'

I finished my tea, and declined a second cup, said I would have to go. Kay clearly wanted company, but just as clearly realized that she couldn't expect me to stay. She bustled about for a bit opening windows, then said in an improbably bright tone that she had to go to the funeral home shortly to pick out a coffin. Then she sat down hard on the old sofa with the red throw and the patchwork cushions and began to cry like a child that needs her mother, a convulsive, inconsolable sound. I tried to say something, but she waved me away; I wanted to tell her where the vodka was hidden, but I'm sure she found it; as I left, the dog – Mr Burke – scuttled downstairs and across the living-room floor, only to stop, screeching, when he saw it wasn't his mistress; he slid beneath the sofa and began to whimper.

I sat outside in my car and rested my forehead on the steering wheel. I felt exhausted, and like nothing I had done since I had got back had made a difference, like all I was doing was wandering among the dead, like Dublin was a city of the dead, a vast necropolis, and if I couldn't shake them off my trail, I'd be next. And then I looked at my text message. It read:

'Gone to house, meet me there NOW! Love LXxx.'

I was there in four minutes. I rang her number on the way, but it went straight to voicemail. I still had the key pad to open the security gates, the key to her house; I got sixty-six out of the old Volvo on the way *up* Castlehill. Four minutes.

I was too late. When I got to Linda's house, her beautiful corpse was still warm, but as dead as if it had lain in the cold earth for a thousand years. Outside, the police car sirens howled a *Dies Irae* that blew about the hills like dust on the wind.

Blood.

Sometimes it's all down to blood.

Blood can be wrong in itself.

The presence or absence of A and B antigens (molecules found on the surface of your red-blood cells) helps to determine whether your blood is Type A, Type B, Type AB or Type O. The Rh (Rhesus) factor is another antigen present in 85 per cent of the population, meaning they are Rh+; the remaining 15 per cent are Rh-. Rare blood types are defined by the presence of uncommon antigens, or more usually, the absence of minor antigens commonly found in most people's blood. About one tenth of 1 per cent of the population have a rare blood type; about one hundredth of 1 per cent of the population have a very rare blood type. And of course, there's nothing wrong with that – unless you are seriously injured and need a blood transfusion. If two incompatible blood types are mixed, the results can be deadly. In general, everyone can receive Type O blood. But the other antigens you possess or lack go to determine how rare your blood is, and the rarer your blood, the more likely it is that you'll need a transfusion of blood of that precise type. And if you don't get the right blood, you'll die.

Blood can go wrong so easily.

These are the diseases of the blood: anaemia, which is low red-blood cell count; leukaemia, which is cancer of the white-blood cells; haemophilia, where your blood won't clot properly; and hepatitis, a viral disease of the liver. Some forms of them are treatable, even curable. Some forms are simply death, pulsing in your veins.

Blood can be wrong from the very beginning.

Your blood type is your genetic inheritance. You have two genes, one of which you inherit from your biological mother and one from your father. A and B genes dominate, while O is recessive. That means that if you have Type O blood, your parents must each have possessed at least one O gene, and that must have been the gene that you inherited from each of them. If you inherit an A and an O, the A dominates; similarly with B. So for example, if you have Type O blood, and you discover the man you thought was your father has Type AB blood, or if you have Type AB blood, and your child has Type O blood, then the man cannot be your father, the child cannot be your child. The blood was never right in the first place.

III

Lost but not forgotten, from the dark heart of a dream.
    Bruce Springsteen, 'Adam Raised A Cain'

21

DI Reed was the first officer on the scene. I thought she was going to arrest me – the Guards at the scene certainly seemed to feel that someone should be arrested, and that I was the most likely candidate, and I agreed with them – but they don't make you a detective inspector for nothing. Fiona Reed was cool and careful, and she wasn't going to waste an arrest if she didn't have enough evidence to bring charges. She listened to a brief, highly edited account of how I'd spent the night with Linda in a hotel, how I'd had to go to my house for clean clothes, how I'd met Kay Preston née Burke and commiserated with her on the death of her mother, how I'd responded to Linda's text by driving here to meet her, only to find her dead body. I showed her the text on my mobile, and she noted the time of the call. Then she asked if I would accompany one of the Guards to Seafield Garda Station to make a voluntary statement.

Maybe neighbours didn't turn out for a hearse any more, but you can depend on a crowd if the cops show up. As I walked down Linda's drive alongside a uniformed Guard, and got into a blue, white and yellow-marked squad car, it must have looked like I was being arrested anyway: the sporty blonde stood by her black Mercedes convertible in a pink jogging suit, a manicured hand to her open mouth; the bloated tanned man in the white towelling robe had come right down to the pavement and stood with his arms folded on top of his protruding belly, his lips compressed in a righteous smirk; two men in business suits were frozen on their lawns as the car swept around the development and drove up the walled slip road. The sky was low with cloud and darkening; I could feel the damp air cold in my bones.

The Guard took my statement from me, and then I spent the rest of the morning in an empty interview room at Seafield Garda Station. Dave Donnelly came in early on and asked for my mobile, which I gave him. For a while I was moved to a cell, but they kept the door open, to make it clear I wasn't under arrest. I didn't care. I didn't care about anything except the fact that Linda was dead. I sat and stared at the dirty ochre walls, numb to everything except the sense of outrage I felt. I could still smell her on my fingers, on my arms; her scent clung to me like grief. My face was in my hands when Dave Donnelly stuck his head around the cell door. He came in and stood by me and gave my shoulder a brisk rub with his knuckles.

'That's another fine mess you've gotten yourself into,' he said, his tone as dry as an undertaker's. I shook my head. I didn't want to talk to him, or anyone else. But it wasn't really up to me. When I looked up, his face was blank.

'The NBCI are here, and they'd like to ask you a few questions,' he said.

'The NBCI?' I said.

'The National Bureau of Criminal Investigation,' he said. 'They're coming in to, uh, lend us their assistance. With the Linda Dawson murder. And with cases associated with it.'

I couldn't tell whether Dave was annoyed or relieved, or whether he had given up altogether. And then he winked at me, and I had a pretty good idea.

I was led to the interview room I had been in when I was told that Peter Dawson's body had been discovered. Two plain clothes detectives were waiting for me. DS Myles Geraghty was about medium height, heavy build, maybe three stone overweight; he had salt and pepper hair the consistency of wire wool and a shiny tan suit that looked like he had slept in it. DI John O'Sullivan was lean and tall with close cropped brown hair; he wore cream chinos, an olive-green linen shirt and a bottle-green cord jacket; his shoulders and arms were powerfully built. O'Sullivan nodded and Dave left the room.

They had a routine: Geraghty played the clown, while O'Sullivan was strict but fair. I had already decided I wasn't going to tell anyone about how Halligans were all over John Dawson's house, maybe not even Dave: I wanted to take this case down alone. Dave could take any credit he wanted afterwards, especially if it helped his career, but this case was about my dead now, and I needed to put them to rest myself. Geraghty had already started his schtick; when I tuned in, he was on his feet, riffing on the subject of private detectives.

'A private dick, is it? Fast cars and bourbon chasers and a forty-five, what? Is that the way it is, Ed, shoot-outs and double-crosses and dames?'

He turned up the collar on his tweed jacket, narrowed his eyes and bared his teeth. He looked like something carved out of stone on the roof of a medieval church.

'No,' I said, 'that's not the way it is.'

'Ah go on out of that,' he said, 'there must be some crack to be had. Did you ever say, "I'm taking this all the way to City Hall"?'

'No, I didn't.'

'Did you ever crack and take the bribe and say to hell with the job, or is it mostly a case of settling in for the long lonely nights alone, just you and your integrity?'

'Mostly it's a case of sitting in a car all night drinking stale coffee and eating damp sandwiches and pissing in a bottle so you can photograph a husband leaving his girlfriend's apartment and give his wife the shots in the knowledge that the only ones with a happy ending coming are the lawyers,' I said.

I raised my eyebrows in O'Sullivan's direction. I'd had as much of Geraghty as I could take. Maybe O'Sullivan felt the same.

'I take it you were licensed to work as a private investigator in Los Angeles,' he said.

'In California, yes.'

'Is that licence valid for the whole state?'

'It is.'

'And who's in charge of that?'

'The Bureau of Security and Investigative Services. It's in Sacramento.'

'And do you have to be a US citizen?'

'A green card will do.'

'Are you going back? We understand you came home to bury your mother.'

'Yes. I don't know. I . . . a lot has happened since I got here.'

'You might say trouble follows you.'

You might say that all right. How could I disagree?

'That licence doesn't entitle you to work here. As a private investigator. Not in this *jurisdiction.*'

Geraghty, bullying now, the brow furrowed, the clown after-hours.

'No, I don't suppose it does,' I said.

'So you admit, you've been working in this jurisdiction, accepting money as a private investigator, when you've no legal entitlement to do so,' Geraghty said.

'I admit it, yes.'

'So what are you going to do about it?'

'Well – you tell me where I can get a licence, and I'll apply for one.'

'You should have thought of that before you started sticking your nose in, shouldn't you?'

'I did.'

'What?'

'I did. I rang the Private Security Authority. They're in charge of regulating the industry. Or at least, they will be, once they've reported back from all their committees and worked out how they want to go about it. For now, there's no such thing as a licence for a private investigator in this "jurisdiction". But sure, you knew that already, didn't you?'

Geraghty stared at me a moment, the eyes all fire and menace, then he threw his head back and snorted like a bull, whether in laughter or rage it was impossible to say.

'What happened to your face?' said O'Sullivan.

'I tripped,' I said.

'You tripped?' said Geraghty, getting his leering face close into mine.

'That's right. What happened to yours?' I said.

'Did you kill Linda Dawson?' he yelled.

'You know I didn't.'

'You're the great man for what I know and don't know, aren't you now?'

'How do we know you didn't?' said O'Sullivan.

I looked at them across from me: Geraghty's bloodshot grey eyes bulging, O'Sullivan's tired blue eyes watching me with interest and full attention. I couldn't tell whether I was a suspect or not.

'I had no motive, for a start. I had no way of getting away with it, number two. And number three . . .'

My voice faltered, maybe from emotion. Or maybe because I couldn't believe what I'd actually been about to say. Was I really about to tell these cops that the reason I couldn't have murdered Linda was because I loved her? How they'd laugh about that down at the CopBar. They'd include it for light relief in CopSchool. Because the prime suspect is always the husband, always the lover. And he always says, but I loved her. Geraghty was grinning. He wanted me to say it.

'And number three?' he leered.

'You were in a relationship with Linda Dawson?' said O'Sullivan.

'Yes, I . . . we were only at the beginning, really.'

Get out of there, Loy, there'd be time to mourn what might have been. Plenty of time.

'Did Linda drive herself or take a taxi?' I said. 'From the hotel.'

Neither of them said anything.

'Because if she drove herself, then that's your line of inquiry: find her car. It's a red Audi convertible, and it wasn't there when I got to her house, and it wasn't in the carport when I was leaving, so the chances are the killer drove away in it.'

'And how did the killer arrive, on foot?'

I shrugged.

'Hey, I don't even have a licence. You're the guys in charge around here. In this "jurisdiction".'

Geraghty's eyes flared; O'Sullivan gave me a thin smile. He picked up my statement and tapped it on the table between us.

'We spoke to the night manager at the hotel, and to Mrs Preston in Fagan's Villas. They bear out your story. And of course, there's the text message Linda sent you.'

'He still could have done it,' Geraghty said.

I looked from one to the other.

'You're right,' I said to Geraghty. 'I made it from the Burke house to Linda's in four minutes. When I got there, she was dead. But she could still have been alive. And I could have strangled her as the police sirens were approaching. Technically, I'm a suspect. But it doesn't look likely, does it?'

'What can you tell us about Peter Dawson's death?' said O'Sullivan.

'Anything I find out, I tell Detective Sergeant Donnelly,' I said.

'Like shite you do,' Geraghty snapped.

We sat in silence for while. I didn't know whether Geraghty had taken against me, or whether it was an act, whether O'Sullivan's pained expression was embarrassment at Geraghty's carry-on or simply concentration on the job in hand. Then something occurred to me.

'Who phoned it in?' I said. 'Do you know?'

'It was an anonymous call. No caller ID.'

'What time did the call come through? Was it before the text message was sent to me?'

Geraghty and O'Sullivan looked at each other.

'It was, wasn't it? And if it was, that text wasn't written by Linda at all. It was written by the killer. Because who could have known about the killing? There was no-one else in the house. A neighbour might have complained about a car being driven too fast. But that's not going to bring squad cars with their sirens wailing, is it? And she was strangled, so no gunshots or screams.'

Geraghty didn't want to give up.

'That means you could have sent the text from Linda Dawson's mobile to yours. Still puts you in the frame.'

'And then I rang the police anonymously, but waited around so they'd catch me? Whoever texted me was trying to set me up for the murder.'

'Or maybe you took a gamble,' Geraghty said. 'Maybe you banked on getting away with it because it looked so like a frame. Maybe you were too fucking smart for your own good, Mr Bigshot Private Dick from Los Angeles.'

I looked at him. He held my gaze and flung it right back at

me, his face glowing with a grin in which derision and devilment mingled. He was good at this.

'I'm going to ask you to surrender your passport while our investigation is underway,' DI O'Sullivan said.

'Indefinitely?'

'I don't mean the investigation to last indefinitely. We can review it when we've made some progress.'

'Sure, why not?' I said.

DS Geraghty stood, smiling and stretching his arms, as if we'd just played a hard-fought game of squash and now it was done with and we were all friends again. Then he made a gun of his fist, index finger extended, and pointed it at me.

'Don't forget, you'll have to apply for a licence to the Private Security Authority soon enough,' he said. 'I'd say they'll be very particular about who they'll want in the private detective business. Very particular indeed.'

And using his middle finger to pull the trigger, he shot me in the face.

∼

The Custody Officer gave me back my mobile. A uniformed Guard had driven the 122S from Linda's house; now he was going to follow me home to collect my passport. We went out together to the car park. It was raining, and we ran to our cars. Dave Donnelly was sitting in the passenger seat of the Volvo. He handed me a brown A4 envelope.

'Phone records. All right Ed?'

'I think so. Thanks. You? You don't resent the outsiders barging all over your patch?'

'At least we'll see some action now,' he said. 'And Casey's going to end up in the shite when it comes out he was trying to block any murder inquiry into the deaths of Peter Dawson and Seosamh MacLiam.'

'I suppose it's beyond even him to make out Linda Dawson strangled herself.'

Dave looked at me.

'You spent the night with her. Something there, was there?'

'Don't want to talk about it,' I grunted, and shook my head.

'Sorry all the same,' Dave said, relieved we didn't have to do any more of that.

'If Casey does end up going, it could work out well for me: Reed could step up, and I could take her job. DI at last, not before fucking time, but I won't resent it 'cause I should've had it five years ago.'

The rain was coming down in sheets. I wondered about the windscreen wipers: the kind of feature that mightn't work so well on an old car, the kind of detail Tommy might easily have neglected. I switched them on, and realized I had been unfair to the car and to Tommy: they clacked like knitting needles but they did the job. I filled Dave in on the interview with O'Sullivan and Geraghty, and told him they knew I was dealing directly with him. But I didn't tell him about the Halligans' hold over the Dawsons, or about finding Tommy and getting him out of the country; I suggested he have a look around the old ferryhouse and left it at that.

The Guard who was to follow me flashed his headlights from across the car park. I told Dave I'd better be off, and he nodded, but didn't move.

'Ed, I don't know if this is good news or bad – because I can imagine you'd like to get the whole thing wrapped up one way or another, but – anyway, we got an ID on our concrete corpse, Fitzhugh's tailor in Capel Street has records that go back thirty years. It wasn't your da, our party had an address off the South Circular. His name was Kenneth Courtney.'

22

I gave the Guard my passport and watched him drive away, then I stood in the kitchen, looking out at the rain. It spumed on the rotting sills, it flashed in sparkles off the flagstone path and drenched the parched grass; it washed the hard green fruit on the apple trees clean of a long dry season's dust. As a child, I always believed that the male and female trees would grow together, that their branches would touch one day. It didn't seem likely any more. Linda's scent felt stronger on me now: the grapefruit tang, the damp musk, the intoxicating sweet salt reek of her. I kept turning to greet her; the idea that she would not come again wouldn't lodge in my blood. Finally I went out in the rain and stood between the apple trees until I could smell nothing but the softening earth and the drenched stone. It took a long time.

I went back inside the house. I had a hot shower and dressed. The sky was darkening; even though it was only four o'clock, it felt like a November afternoon. There was nowhere to sit but the stairs, so I sat there and worked my way through Peter Dawson's telephone records. Two things caught my eye: one was a mobile call to George Halligan's number at 21.57 on Thursday night, the night Peter was last seen alive. It was the last call Peter Dawson made. The second thing was a number sequence: 3459 showed up as the last four digits of an 086 mobile number Peter called several times over the last couple of months, the last time two nights before he died. I checked it against the numbers I had collected on my mobile, but it didn't match them. Then I looked at the legend scrawled on the back of the torn photograph of my father and John Dawson:

ma Courtney

3459.

I called the number and went straight through to voicemail: a youngish sounding woman with a broad Dublin accent identified herself as Gemma and asked me to leave my name and number, which I did. As I hung up, I could hear my heart beat. If this wasn't a break, it was close to it. But this case wouldn't break by itself. I couldn't afford to make any mistakes now, which above all meant keeping out of the Halligans' way. Twice I had handed them the advantage; twice they had punished me for it. Third time would be for keeps.

I checked my mobile to see if I had missed any calls, and found I had inadvertently turned it off. I switched it on and locked it. I was waiting for Gemma Courtney's call, but sitting by the phone isn't good for the soul. Using the landline, I got a number for a waste disposal firm from directory inquiries and ordered a skip to dispose of all the trashed furniture that was piled in the garage; rain like this wasn't going to do a car manufactured in 1965 much good. I was assembling a bag of clothes that needed washing when my mobile rang. It was a woman, just not the woman I hoped it would be.

'Ed Loy? It's Caroline Dagg here, you remember, Rory Dagg's wife?'

I did remember, but she sounded like a different woman: chipper, brisk, resolute.

'Mr Loy?'

'Yes, I'm here.'

'Rory wants to talk to you, Mr Loy. He's remembered something he thinks could be helpful.'

263

'About his dead uncle, is it?' I said.

'It is about his uncle, yes, and the sooner you know about it the better.'

I said I was free now, and told her where I lived; she said they'd come straight over. I drove to the cleaners on Seafield Road and left in a bag of laundry. I picked up some whiskey and beer in the off-licence, and some cold food in the fancy delicatessen. On the way back, my mobile rang again, this time to tell me I had two messages in my mailbox.

Message Number One: 'Ed Loy, this is Gemma Courtney, I'm free tonight nine until midnight, love to see you then, ring me back to arrange a time.'

Message Number Two: 'Ed, what can I say about Podge, something must be done, no hard feelings, wanted to invite you to a breakfast at the Royal Seafield in the morning – I have a feeling the council will make the right decision tonight, and we'll be celebrating in style tomorrow – and don't worry, Podge won't be there. Come along and I'll make it up to you, big time.'

When I pulled into the drive, I saw Caroline Dagg's silver SUV parked on the kerb. Dagg held a golf umbrella over his wife for the short walk into the house. We crowded into the living room and stood around in an awkward triangle while I explained about the furniture. Rory Dagg pitched his look somewhere between sheepish and shifty; he hung his head and let his wife do the talking. Caroline Dagg, in a navy suit and candy pink lip gloss and eye shadow, spoke her over-enunci- ated words through a fixed smile that made me feel like she was telling me off.

'Rory is – well, I'm not going to speak for my husband, Mr Loy, except to say, I think Rory wants to tell you – there I go again!'

She laughed a tinkling, mirthless little laugh. Rory Dagg stared at the threadbare carpet.

'Except to say, Rory was mistaken about his uncle being dead, he is in fact alive, and Rory . . . actually, Rory knows where he is, in a nursing home, isn't that right, Rory?'

Dagg grunted.

'The poor man. And I think what Rory wants to say most especially, because the whole point is that you make a clean breast of it, it's a public programme after all, a declaration of intent to the world – and this is why he probably had some trouble coming clean about his uncle, about his *background,* because – Rory?'

She looked towards him, smiling and nodding and gesturing with her hands, like a teacher coaxing a recalcitrant child to apologize. Dagg's gaze remained fixed on the floor, but his shaking hands balled themselves into fists.

'I'll let him tell you himself. Nothing to be ashamed of, perfectly treatable. So! There you have it! Now, I have children to collect from a girlfriend who won't be a girlfriend for much longer if she has to put up with my three on top of her two, so I'll just leave you boys alone to talk things through, shall I?'

Rory Dagg would not meet his wife's worried eyes. Her forced brightness hung in the air between them like smoke. She flashed her eyes at me, eyebrows raised, as if her husband had joined the gardener in the ranks of those sent to try her inexhaustible patience, then gave me a very brave smile and left.

Dagg didn't move until he heard the SUV kick into life. He turned to the window and watched his wife sail off in the rain, high above the ground in her silver chariot. Then he looked up at me, his face a mixture of anger and embarrassment.

'We've decided I'm an alcoholic,' he said. 'Apparently that's easier than deciding we just don't like each other any more.'

'Would you like a drink then?' I said.

'Fucking sure I would,' he said.

We had glasses of Jameson and chased them with bottles of Guinness. I realized I hadn't eaten anything that day – they'd given me some kind of rubber chicken and mushy chips combination in Seafield Garda Station, but I didn't have the stomach for it. I ate a sundried tomato, fresh basil and parmesan pizza, some chicken wings in black bean sauce and a tub of avocado, tomato and red onion salad. It tasted good, which was just as well, as it had cost more than the booze. Rory Dagg didn't want any food; he poured another whiskey and had to stop himself knocking it back in one. Maybe he *was* an alcoholic; I didn't care: I wasn't his social worker, or his shrink. Maybe I'd be an alcoholic if I were married to Caroline Dagg. Maybe I was one anyway. Who gave a fuck? Things could be worse; we could be dead; we would be soon. I joined Dagg in a second whiskey, and began to feel calmer and clearer about everything. Dagg started to say something about how his wife had changed since she gave up her job to look after the kids full time, how her horizons had narrowed, how she needed something or other to stimulate her, but I wasn't listening; I was enjoying the bursting illusion of insight that the whiskey gave me. It wouldn't last, but while it did, it gave the world a pattern and a coherence, an order that made me feel my task was simple, and its accomplishment inevitable. I tuned in when Dagg began to talk about his uncle.

'I wrote down the address of the nursing home,' Dagg said, handing me a sheet of lined paper.

'You'd better come with me,' I said. 'They may not let me see him otherwise.'

'I've never been to visit him,' Dagg said. He flushed, and reached for the whiskey bottle with a shaking hand. My hand got there first. An alcoholic was one thing, but a sloppy drunk was no use to me. I handed him another Guinness instead.

'I've paid his nursing home bills. But I don't have to see him.

266

That's above and beyond. After what he put my father through.'

'What was that? Forging his signature on your father's day books for the town hall construction job?'

Dagg looked at me as if he was still weighing whether he'd talk. I wondered whether I should have made his wife stay. Then he turned his head away and nodded briefly.

'How did you know?' he said.

'The signatures in the general day books vary a good deal within a certain pattern – that chimes with the way most people sign their names. But the signatures on the town hall day book are all identical, and they're identical to the signatures on your father's framed plans. It makes sense that he'd be more careful over those, since they were going on display. But why should one day book diverge so substantially from all the others? Because the signatures in it were forged – careful copies, deliberately done. Maybe if it had been just one or two, it would have been a brilliant forgery.'

Rory Dagg gave a quick, sour smile.

'A brilliant forger is not one of the things Jack Dagg was. A brilliant house-breaker, a brilliant extortionist, a brilliant pick-pocket – none of those either. He was good at lying though. And he had a real talent for taking advantage of my father's generosity.'

'By impersonating him, was it?'

'Jack had money troubles all the time, spent it like water, gambled or drank it away. In the early days, when my Dad was a general labourer, he'd let Jack stand in for him the odd day, if he was desperate for cash. Then as Dad moved up the scale, got his skills, did his exams, he'd still have to find Jack work. Jack didn't have the qualifications or the abilities, but when it came to bossing people around, he could always get away with it – he had a lot of swagger, a lot of front – more than the old man, actually – not to mention the common touch, so when Dad was foreman, Jack could slip in and earn a few days' drinking money. But the town hall job was different.'

'Why? Because he let his brother do it all?'

'For one. And he wasn't happy about it. I told you before, he went into a depression because I failed my exams and gave up on his big plans for me to be an architect. Well, that was just part of it. The rest was fallout from the town hall. He never spoke to Jack again, wouldn't acknowledge him in the street.'

'What happened? Could your uncle have blackmailed him in some way?'

'I don't know. It could have been as much John Dawson's fault. I mean, he left Dawson's there and then, having worked with them for years. He wouldn't tell me. And to be honest, part of me wanted to put it behind me, you know, all this brothers falling out and not speaking to one another for years is from the ark, isn't it, it's real old Irish tribal bullshit. At least, that's how I saw it. Then I got a call about a year ago. Jack Dagg, destitute, no health insurance, no other family – he had a wife and kids in England at one stage, but he left them long ago, and I've no idea where they are – anyway, "Big" Jack Dagg has leukaemia, he's asking me to help him. He needs palliative care, a nursing home, whatever. My first instinct was, not my problem. But . . . well, it's blood, isn't it? I mean, he has nobody else. He's my father's brother. You can't just walk away.'

'Did you ask him about the town hall, what happened there?'

'I tried. He said no-one who'd grown up in Fagan's Villas expected life to be easy. He said he did what he had to do and no more. He said he'd never been a fucking tout and wasn't going to start now. And if I didn't like that, I could fuck off.'

'And you still helped him?'

Dagg shrugged, as if he was embarrassed.

'Like I said, he'd no-one else. And I suppose a part of me thought, maybe he'd tell me eventually.'

'Why did your wife have to force you to come here then?'

'Because a bigger part of me thought, I don't want to know, just let the old fucker die and that's the past done and good riddance.'

I nodded. I could understand that at least.

'But then the nursing home rang last night. Sister Ursula. Uncle Jack'll be dead in a matter of days. Hasn't asked for me, but she thought I'd like to see him. And Caroline starts in, of course you must, it'll bring you "closure", all this. And I started to drink. And she won't shut up, about talking to you again, about my drinking, so on. And there's some shouting. The kids are there, getting upset. I go out, drink some more, come back, wake everyone up, do some more shouting, break some stuff, pass out on the living-room floor, everyone's crying. And now I'm an alcoholic and I'm joining a twelve-step programme, or I can get out of the house.'

I looked at him now, drink-sweat beading on his brow, eyes boiling red, hands still shaking. I'd been hasty in dismissing Caroline Dagg's opinions, just because her manner got on my nerves, or because the last thing I wanted to hear was the notion that simply because a great deal of your life would be impossible without booze, it meant you were an alcoholic. But I didn't have time to think about that now.

'Let's go and see your uncle,' I said.

23

St Bonaventure's Nursing Home was a large Victorian red-brick villa set in a quiet square on the west side of Seafield. Neo-Gothic in style, with its turrets and stained-glass windows, its conical towers and spires, it looked in the rain like a haunted house from a child's story book. A stone carving above the front door showed angels guiding a three-masted ship through stormy seas. Sister Ursula was an angular, brisk, gleaming woman in her sixties in a blue-grey uniform that looked like a nurse's; her grey and white headdress and the silver crucifix around her neck displayed her other allegiance. She led us up a great staircase to the first floor, and along a wood-panelled corridor to Jack Dagg's room, and brought a still-reluctant Dagg in to see his uncle. I walked back to the stairwell and waited. The stained-glass window that lit the stairs on this floor depicted the ninth station of the cross, the third fall; the window at the turn of the stairs had shown the fourth station, the meeting with the Virgin; I wondered if there was a logic to their placement, or if they were scattered about this house of the dying at random. I heard a woman crying, and the sound of a television commentating on a horse race, and the sibilant colloquy of two elderly women hissing about oncologists and tests and a blessed release.

Rory Dagg was out in minutes. As he passed me, he waved an arm back in the direction of his uncle's room. He didn't say a word. Sister Ursula joined me on the landing and we both watched as he clattered down the stairs and flung himself across the entrance hall and out the door. When I looked up, Sister Ursula was shaking her head.

'What do you think he's afraid of, Mr Loy? His uncle? Or himself?'

'The past,' I said.

Sister Ursula walked me to Jack Dagg's door.

'That's where Jack Dagg lives, Mr Loy, for his sins. The past.'

Her eyes twinkled fiercely. I liked her vigour, her gaiety of spirit; I wanted to breathe it in, to absorb it; I wondered if the dying found it an inspiration or an agony, to be confronted by such forceful life as theirs ran out.

Jack Dagg's life was running out, and it showed in his sunken cheeks, the waxy pallor of his complexion, the dimming light in his dark eyes. Red blotches marked the glands in his neck; his hair had the dull glow of wet cement; his bony hands sat splayed on the bedspread like two antique fans. His eyes closed and his head lolled. I sat on the chair by his bed, took a naggin of Jameson from my jacket, poured some of it into a glass tumbler on his bedside table and passed it beneath his nose. His eyes flickered open and turned in the direction of the whiskey. I brought it to his mouth and tipped it in. He drank it all down and sighed.

'God bless you son,' he said, and closed his eyes again.

'Rory told me. Is it the garage?' he said after a while, his voice a thin reed in his throat.

'No,' I said, 'it's the town hall. They found a body.'

He nodded.

'The town hall, yes. Excuse me if I ramble. Blood's all wrong, you see. They have to give me someone else's. Right down to the marrow. But they can't do that now. Too late for that now.'

'Kenneth Courtney,' I said. 'Did you know him?'

'I knew them all, son. Knew them all, back in the day.'

'John Dawson?'

'Me and Mr Dawson. I did a job or two for him.'

'What sort of job?'

'All sorts. Chaps who'd got a tender we wanted. I'd disappear their trucks and mixers, their tools and all. Sometimes, the brickies'd have their arms broken, labourers get warned off. I took care of all that for him.'

'Did you bury Kenneth Courtney in the basement of the town hall?'

'I buried a body all right, but I didn't know who it was. Ask no questions, isn't that right?'

'The corpse wasn't hooded. If you buried him yourself, you'd've recognized him. From Fagan's Villas.'

'He was on his face when I saw him. I just lobbed the concrete in over him.'

'And was that another job for John Dawson?'

'Mr Dawson rang me up, yeah.'

'What, he rang you up and told you there was a corpse at the site, go down and bury it?'

'Take care of it, yeah. Wasn't the first time. None of my business who it was.'

'You buried someone else?'

'Beneath the garage, yeah.'

The garage. John Dawson and Eamonn Loy's garage.

'Do you know who that one was?'

'Didn't want to know, son. Bad for the health. In a green tarp. Quicklime an' all.'

'Would you be prepared to swear out a statement about all of this? For the Guards?'

'Would you have any more of that whiskey on you?'

I helped him drink another glass. His eyes were closing as he got to the end of it, but when I asked him a second time if he'd make a statement, his hand gripped my forearm with surprising force.

'If I'm still alive, son, I'll even tell a copper. Blood down to the marrow's what I need. But it's too late to do any good.'

His eyes flared briefly with an afterglow of menace, then sputtered out. He was asleep before I left the room.

I rang Dave Donnelly from St Bonaventure's and gave him the details, then I found Sister Ursula and told her to expect a Garda detective. She muttered a quick prayer, touching her crucifix.

'Would he make a confession now, do you think?' she said.

I knew there was only one kind of confession she cared about.

'If he'll talk to me, and to the police, I don't see why he shouldn't talk to a priest,' I said.

Sister Ursula affected to find this shocking and scandalous, and shooed me out the door with one hand over her open mouth, and all the while her eyes twinkled like flint. She told me she'd pray for me, and I thanked her, and felt like I meant it.

~

The garage my father used to run stood across from a roundabout amongst the maze of sixties and seventies housing estates between Castlehill and Seafield, about a mile up from the sea. The roundabout was still there, but the garage had been replaced by something called the 'House Beautiful Retail Park', according to a little brass plaque on a granite block by the entrance: there was a DIY superstore, a carpet showroom, a garden centre, a bathroom and tiling store, an electrical goods warehouse and outlets that sold furniture and lighting. The forecourt was thronged with determined shoppers loading their cars with crates and cartons. Rapt faces huddled in the stores, studying carpets and gazing at tiles and worshipping fridges and washing machines. The atmosphere was hushed, reverent, devotional. The kingdom of the house beautiful was at hand. I stood there and tried to feel something. I knew my father's body lay buried beneath all this strip-lit splendour. For years I had dreamt of finding him, alive or dead, imagined the moment I'd uncover the truth. Now it was here, and I felt nothing; worse, I felt what the bustling congregation around me felt: an overwhelming desire to buy something.

I bought a box of white candles. I took one and set it on the granite block by the gates, and lit it. By the time I reached my car, it had blown out in the wind.

24

Kenneth Courtney's daughter Gemma lived in Charnwood, just off the Grand Canal, a couple of miles south-west of the city centre. I took the N11 north towards the city. My jaw ached where my teeth had been kicked out, my left ear throbbed, and my left eye had a twitch I couldn't seem to shift. I tried to focus on the pain; it felt better than thinking about Linda. I drove through Donnybrook, turned onto Grand Parade at Leeson Street bridge and followed the slow evening traffic along the canal until I came to Fogarty's pub. I found a parking spot and fed the meter. Past Fogarty's there was a chipper, a bookie's, a 2 Euro shop, a newsagent's, an off-licence and another pub, the Michael Davitt. Breaking the terrace between the newsagent's and the euro shop, a pedestrian lane ran down to a gate that led into a small park. The rain had eased off, was little more than a thick mist now; the sky was a dirty white, like coal-dust in milk; there was a burr of cold in the air, the first evening chill I'd felt since I'd come back. The park was a desultory affair that looked like it had been put together late on a Friday afternoon: laid mostly with broken flagstones and surrounded by high mesh wire fencing, it had a small children's playground with swings, slides and climbing frames, a couple of vandalized wooden benches, some parched green lawn and a few clumps of hardy shrubs, Hebe and St John's Wort. Most of the space was clogged with garbage: crisp and cigarette packets and sweet wrappers, discarded condoms, cigarette butts, dog shit, beer cans, broken bottles, plastic bottles, plastic bags full of bottles. Through a second gate at the other end of the park, I crossed a narrow lane to the wide pedestrian entrance to the Charnwood Estate. Footpaths at either side led down to a square of small terraced houses built in sandstone with shabby off-white cladding on their upper storeys. Eight red-brick pillars were positioned at three feet intervals between the two footpaths, and a badly kept oval patch of grass and mud lay beyond them, running a third of the way down the square. The pillars were about three feet high, and a bunch of teenage kids in navy and white sportswear were hanging around smoking and drinking Rolling Rock long necks and tossing the bottles in the mud. They muttered something about me as I passed and cracked up laughing.

I was in Charnwood Square; a lane at the bottom left-hand corner led me down onto Charnwood Drive. The breeze-block walls of the lane were daubed with slogans: IRA, and DRUG SCUM OUT, and NIGGERS GO HOME. Charnwood Drive was a bigger square with a larger patch of sun-blasted grass and mud in its centre. Some of the houses I passed were clean and well-cared for, with flower gardens and new cars out front; others were dilapidated, crumbling and oozing neglect; others still had front gardens full of garbage. The garbage was everywhere: along with the paper and plastic and glass, there were discarded buggies and children's bicycles, bedsteads and electrical equipment, a coiled-up rug and a wooden tea tray, all just tossed in the street. Small kids were running about kicking water out of puddles at each other and screaming. A very fat woman in a burgundy robe and blossoms to match on her greasy face stood in her front doorway smoking and drinking cider from a can; behind her, a stereo played 'A Nation Once Again'.

There was another lane at the end of Charnwood Drive; I thought I saw Dessie Delaney standing in it, but it was just someone who looked a bit like him, dressed in the inevitable navy and white tracksuit. Two men stood with him: one, in black leather jacket and jeans and thick soled boots with a boxer dog on a lead, looked like an off-duty bouncer. The other was about fifty, with silver hair swept back, black track pants and a snow-white hooded top; he had gold on his fingers and around his neck, and looked like the Boss.

'All right brother? Looking for something are you?' said the Tracksuit.

'Charnwood Avenue,' I said.

'Right at the bottom of the lane, hook back around and you're onto it. Bit of a maze round here, isn't it?'

'Thank you,' I said, and made to move on.

The Bouncer crowded me as the Tracksuit barred my way. I looked at the Boss, who shrugged. Tracksuit quickly frisked me, up and down, and I stood and took it; I had no choice. He leant into me.

'You're not a copper anyway. Know how I know?'

'How?'

He held my jacket between finger and thumb.

'They wouldn't spend the steam off their piss on a decent swatch of cloth man.'

He looked at the Boss, who nodded, then looked back at me and grinned.

'Numbers 52 and 53. Brown on the left, white on the right. You look like a white man yourself, but Liberty Hall, whatever. All right bud?'

'All right,' I said.

Tracksuit stepped aside, and I walked on down the lane. On a sodden patch of green to my left, amidst the dog shit, someone had dumped a beige-and-brown-and-yellow-striped three-piece suite. It looked like an outdoor room, and I found myself wondering what had happened to the family who'd lived there.

At the end of the lane, a final terrace of a dozen houses sat opposite a bus shelter; the road curved up to a roundabout; overhead, great trucks and container vehicles thundered along an old main road of industrial estates and service stations. I wheeled around to the right and doubled back into the estate, this time along Charnwood Avenue. Gemma Courtney lived in number 36: she didn't have garbage all over her front lawn, but she didn't have a flower garden either. A weak stream of yellow light trickled down onto her door from a lamppost that had bent from upright like a young tree in the wind.

Gemma Courtney was twenty-four, or forty-nine, or eleven; it was hard to tell. She had huge, Bambi eyes, full, prominent lips and short snow-blonde hair; she was skinny and tall with heroin cheekbones. She was wearing a black leather miniskirt and what I thought at first was a red bra-top, but which turned out on closer acquaintance simply to be a red bra; it took a while for my eyes to adjust, because there were only two lamps in the tiny living room, and both were swathed in red silk scarves; there was incense burning also, and smoke from her cigarette, so it was only when Gemma Courtney sat back on the sofa and spread her legs to reveal lace stocking tops and red pants that matched her bra that I worked out what was going on. She parted red lips to smile, and patted the seat beside her.

'I'm not a client, I'm sorry,' I said. 'I'm a private detective.'

Gemma Courtney's smile disappeared. She looked at her watch.

'You're what? I could be earning, this hour. You said an hour.'

She didn't sound angry; if anything, she seemed relieved.

'I'll pay you for your time. What do you normally charge?'

'A hundred,' she said.

I doubted whether Gemma Courtney normally charged a hundred an hour, but I didn't think bargaining with her would get me anywhere, so I gave her the money and asked her to turn the lights on. She put the kettle on too, then she went upstairs – the stairs were in the middle of the living room – and came down in a tight pink velour tracksuit and pink sandals to match. With her face wiped clean of make-up, and her rail thin body without buttocks, hips or breasts, she definitely looked eleven; in the harsh light, the lines on her face told an older story. While she was in the kitchen making tea, I looked around the small living room: magnolia stipple ceiling and walls cobwebbed with damp at the corners, cheap veneer floor split and buckling, flame-effect electric fire, TV and VCR, furniture shabby but clean. The only individual touch was a set of framed photographs lying face down on the mantelpiece; I sat them up and saw they were of a child at different stages: as a baby, a toddler, a smiling three-year-old boy. When Gemma Courtney saw me looking at them, she came across the room so fast I thought she was going to hit me. She scooped the photographs up and laid them face down on the sofa, then sat beside them, lit a cigarette and blew the smoke out quickly, as if it was some kind of physical exercise.

'So what do you want then, Mr Detective?' she said. Her legs were crossed at the ankles; her feet tapped against each other.

'There's no easy way to say this: your father, Kenneth Courtney, is dead. His body was found a week ago.'

I explained the circumstances in which the corpse was discovered, and how long that meant he must have been dead. All the while, she stared at me, her head nodding, her huge eyes expressionless. When I had finished speaking, she set her lips and shook her head.

'And what do you think this has to do with me?' she said, her voice like a whip.

'He was your father, wasn't he?'

'What if he was?'

Her eyes narrowed. A mantilla of smoke veiled her face. She was closing down on me. I needed to reach her, fast.

'I . . . my father vanished around the same time as yours did. His body hasn't been found yet, but I believe he's dead, that he was killed by the same man who murdered Kenneth Courtney. They were all great friends once upon a time. But something happened, and I still don't know what. I'm trying to find out. You could help me. I need you to help me.'

Something that looked like human feeling rippled across Gemma Courtney's wide mouth and flickered in her eyes. She breathed deeply for a while, as if she was working up to a decision. She rubbed her wrists together suddenly, ferociously, as if she hoped to break the skin. And then, with her head nodding and her feet tapping and her eyes blazing through the smoke that wreathed her pale head, it all came tumbling out, words that sounded like they'd been waiting years to be spoken.

'Kenneth Courtney was not my father in any way that counts. I never knew him. He left when I was a baby. Left my ma to cope. And she couldn't, could she? She fell apart. We had a house back then – I don't remember it, but Ma always did – a proper house, up off the South Circular. 'Course, Ma had a nervous breakdown when Courtney took off, couldn't pay the mortgage. She lost the house, and we ended up having to be "housed". That's what they call it, not having a house, being "housed". Abandoned mother with a baby, top of the list. And this place had just been built, lovely new houses, green spaces, all this, so they lobbed a load of people on the priority housing list in here together. Trouble was, number one, too many families that had been evicted from other estates for anti-social, they thought, stick them in here when it's new and there's no-one to object, the place was like a fucking zoo; trouble was, number two, cheap heroin then and now, went through the place like a scythe through corn; trouble was, number three, even if there hadn't've been troubles one and two, my ma wasn't able for a place like this, where you can hear your neighbours whispering through the walls, if anyone round here ever whispered, she was raised to better so she was, and she couldn't cope with the shame of it. Not that she was the only one on pills round here, sure there still does be women in their bathrobes at lunchtime, even in the midst of our great economic boom, but Ma made it clear she thought she was a cut above, so they started calling her Lady Muck, and Queenie, and all this, only slagging, they'd say, when what they were doing was twisting the knife, if you're so great, why are you down here with the rest of us? And I grew up with all that, the girl with the mad ma, the girl who thinks she's it, little princess posh pants, only slagging, only slagging. Grew up to be ashamed of her, to see her illness as weakness and hate it, wishing my da had never left but understanding why he had. But that's the wrong way around. And now you say he was murdered, what am I supposed to be, sorry? Because he left Ma before that, he was gone a while before anything happened to him.'

'How do you know that?' I said.

'He wrote her a letter. Said he was sorry, but he had to go away. Said some day, he'd try and make it right.'

'Do you still have the letter?'

She stared hard at me, as if double-checking I was on the level, then she clopped up the stairs for a second time.

Outside I heard shouts and commotion and the screeching of brakes. I went to the front window and pulled the curtain to one side. Further up the way, the Avenue swung left into a another square, and that seemed to be the source of the rumpus. Gemma Courtney joined me at the window and replaced the curtain.

'Rule one, don't twitch the curtains round here. What you don't see can't hurt you,' she said. 'Specially if it involves Larry Knight.'

'Is that Larry Knight's set-up in 52 and 53?' I said. 'Smack on the left, coke on the right?'

'Pass a checkpoint in the lane, did you?' she said.

'Chap with grey hair and a white hoodie looked to be in charge.'

'That's Larry himself,' Gemma said. 'Must be something big on tonight if he's gracing us with his presence.'

'Why? Does he not live in Charnwood?'

'He does like fuck, he's a big house in Ranelagh and kids in fucking boarding school. He used to, he started off in 52, but Larry's moved up. He's got some cousins in there now, running the day-to-day, while he plays golf and goes racing and whatever. That's what a lifetime in the smack trade gets you. But no-one'll say a word against him here. We're all bought and paid for. Or scared to fuck, what's the difference? Now come here and have a look at this.'

I followed her back to the sofa, where she showed me a large brown-paper carrier bag with cloth handles full of photographs.

'The letter's in there somewhere.'

She thrust the bag at me. Her hands were shaking. I took the bag, and held on to one of her hands, gently, but firmly. She didn't try to pull it away. Her wrist was red raw. I pushed up the sleeve of her pink top. Her forearm was a mass of scabs and sores, some open and bleeding.

'Are you still using?' I said.

'No,' she said.

'No difference to me one way or the other,' I said, trying to sound like I meant it.

'I open them myself. To feel something. Anything. I won't let them heal.'

She sat down hard on the couch and pulled the photographs of the little boy into her lap.

'Is he dead?' I said.

She shook her head.

'I sometimes wish he was,' she said. 'But that's not right. All that is, so I could get over him. But he's alive, and out there, and better off without me.'

'Do you think so?'

She lit a cigarette, forced out the smoke as if she'd run a fast mile.

'I was incapable. Out of it all the time. I let him run into the traffic. He was found, and they took him into care. If I'd come off it in time, I could have had him back. But I didn't want to kick. You know what the worst thing is? I didn't want him back. I was so strung out, my first reaction was, good, at least the little bollix won't be under my feet any more. And by the time I realized what I'd done, it was too late. So yes, I think he's better off without me. I think to have felt like that rules me out of the mother club, don't you?'

'I'd say it was the heroin doing the feeling for you.'

'How do you know? Maybe I'd've felt like that anyway. You can't keep blaming it all on smack.'

'Did it come from Larry Knight?'

She shrugged.

'If it wasn't him, it would've been someone else.'

'That's not a law. If you can't get hold of heroin, you don't go around seeking it out. Everyone knows how evil it is – especially the fuckers who deal it. That's why you get it free at first. Smoke a little, work up to your first shot, 'cause that's gonna feel so much better. And then everything else except another shot feels so much worse. And *then* they make you pay.'

She nodded at me, and looked at the photograph of her little boy as a three-year-old, and began to cry. I didn't blame her. She had a lot to cry about. I felt like joining in. She was close to me, Gemma Courtney, even though we'd only just met; history had made cousins of us. I looked through the bag of photographs, searching first for the letter. When I found it, it was scrawled on the lined pages of a child's exercise book:

> *Darling,*
> *I'm sorry for the hurt I've caused you. But I had to leave. Think if you got a chance to go back to a time when you were at a crossroads. You had a choice and you took the wrong path. Well that is what happened to me. It was before I met you, but it meant everything was wrong after.*
> *Well I got handed a second chance and I said, I cant mess it up again. I know its hard, but your better off without me, and little Gemma is too. Look after her for me. You were not happy without your job, well you can go back to the service and get your Ma to look after the baba. One day we will look back and wonder what the fuss was.*
> *God bless,*
> *Kenny*

'Your mother was in the Civil Service?'
Gemma nodded.
'Department of Education. But she couldn't get her job back. They'd filled it and there was nothing else around. And anyway, her mother reacted to Da taking off as if Ma was some kind of loose woman – you know, why else would a husband

walk out on his wife, it must've been her fault. She didn't want to help. I suppose she would have come round eventually, but Ma cut her off. So she had no-one to mind me, no support system, no job, nothing. And down we went, the pair of us.'

'What happened?'

'Booze, pills, not a good mixture. A few hospitalizations. Then she worked out how many pills she needed to do it right. Saved them up and took them all. She was younger than Da, she was only in her forties. Didn't look it.'

Gemma got up and went into the kitchen, and I heard the metallic roar of the kettle. Suddenly there was a blast of noise, music and a voice announcing 'News Headlines on Sky'. It was as loud as if it had been on in the room. Gemma stuck her head around the door.

'That's just the oul' one in 37, she's half deaf. Better than the crowd on the other side, the young fella wants to be a DJ. But they're on holidays at the moment.'

The news blared on. I thought of Mrs Burke, the last of the old Fagan's Villas, and *her* TV, yelling out its tale of exhumed corpses, of revelations beyond the grave. She had called my father and his friends the three musketeers, and here I was, looking at a photograph of them. It was a complete version of the fragment I had been carrying around in my pocket. The missing man had been Kenneth Courtney. And John Dawson was to blame. It was strange looking at the two men together, the murderer and both his victims: Dawson had a slightly stronger jaw, a fleshier face, a colder eye, a more pronounced sense of physical power; Courtney had deeper set eyes, and a fuller mouth; but the resemblance between them was what you first saw: if not like twins, they certainly put you in mind of brothers. And there was my father, glass aloft, dark eyes glittering. The four beaming girls gathered behind looked out of place, like a chorus line at a funeral.

Gemma came back in with more tea, and looked at her watch.

'I've someone coming at ten, you better shift soon,' she said.

'This is my father, Eamonn Loy, and a man named John Dawson,' I said.

She looked at John Dawson.

'God, he was the spit of Da, wasn't he? And you think he killed both of them?'

'I think so. Gemma, did your mother ever speak of my father, or John Dawson?'

'Ma didn't know any of Da's old friends. He'd been in England, he was working on the buildings there, saved his money. He came back here, they met at some dance, I don't know, and got married soon after.'

'Who was at the wedding?'

'People from Ma's work. No-one on his side, I don't think.'

'And these photographs –'

'I didn't even know we had them, until your man rang up, Peter Dawson – is that whatdoyoucallhim, John Dawson's son?'

'Yes. What did he say?'

'Pretty much like you. Our fathers were friends, did I have any photographs from that time, all this? I said I didn't think so, but he left his number. I hunted around, found this under the mattress. It's all stuff of Da's. I guess Ma didn't want to see it around, but didn't want to get rid of it either.'

'What else did he say?'

'He said he'd pay me for them, if I didn't want them.'

She tried that on for a moment, then shook her head.

'Take them if you want. But you'd better go. I don't like men crossing over at the door, it doesn't look well.'

She smiled then, a crooked, crinkle-eyed smile that seemed to fill her great eyes.

'You don't need to do this. I can give you money,' I said, thinking of Barbara Dawson's bribe. What better recipient of her conscience money could there be?

'I do all right,' Gemma Courtney said. 'I do it on my own. I don't need anyone's help.'

At the front door, she touched my arm.

'Let me know what happens,' she said.

I told her I would, made to leave, then thought of something.

'Gemma, were you ever called "grand"?'

She smiled that crooked smile again.

'Grand not too bad or grand la-di-da?'

'No, your name: "Gemma Grand".'

'No. No, the only thing that's grand around here is the canal, and even that's seen better days.'

25

It was dark when I came out of the house; the mist had billowed up to choke the light, and overcast had segued into night. I walked up to the point where the Avenue opened left into a square. Larry Knight's operation looked liked it was centred in two houses on the opposite corner. The garden walls of the houses had been augmented by ornate metal railings, and spotlights positioned on the roofs made the high black- and gold-spiked gates blaze and shimmer like a drug dealer's ensign. Lord of the Manor, tribal chieftain: Larry Knight.

A thin trickle of bodies was leaking in from the lane at the far end of the Avenue and making their way to 52 and 53; I guessed there was another 'checkpoint' up there. I began to pick my way across the obligatory patch of mud and moss and weeds that passed for green space in Charnwood. Halfway across, I saw Tracksuit in position by the gates, checking out the customers. At least, I thought it was Tracksuit, who had reminded me of Dessie Delaney; when I got closer, I noticed he had his arm in plaster: it *was* Dessie Delaney. I cut back towards the lane at the far end. Halfway there, I ducked into a house that had boarded up windows and doors and a skipful of household debris in its front yard. I settled down behind the skip, set my mobile phone to mute and waited. It was damp and cold, and smelt of plaster dust and mildew and dog shit. Much of the square was shrouded in mist, but the roof spots lit 52 and 53 like a stage set.

Delaney's mobile rang; he took the call, then went inside.

When he came out again, it was with his tracksuit-wearing look-alike and the leather jacketed bouncer with the boxer dog. Tracksuit went to the lane at the far end of the Avenue, while the Bouncer headed up past Gemma Courtney's house. After that, the flow of customers heading for 52 and 53 abated, and then stopped altogether. About twenty minutes passed, during which no-one entered the Avenue from either end. Tracksuit and the Bouncer returned, conferred with Dessie Delaney, and then all three went inside. A few minutes later, the spotlights went off. Nothing happened for a while, except a) it began to rain again, and b) a rat ran over my feet and I had to bite my lip to stop myself shouting out. Rain ran down my face and down my back, and I began to doubt whether anything worth seeing was going to happen. But waiting around until nothing happened is part of the job; sometimes it feels like it's what the job's all about.

The first car was a BMW, navy, or black; it set the roof spots off as it pulled up outside the big gates. The second car was one of the new Jags with the fuller hood and the chunkier, curvier styling; it was silver, and it slid into place nose to nose with the BMW.

Larry Knight got out of the Jag, his grey hair plumed back, his white hooded top fluorescent in the sparkling rain. Podge Halligan, in baseball cap and sleeveless biker leather over denim jacket, got out of the BMW and shook Larry Knight's hand. Each man carried a sports holdall. The gates swung open, and as the men went inside, Dessie Delaney stepped out and took a look around the square, then closed the gates again. After a few minutes, the lights went off and it was back to waiting. Dogs barked, and in the distance, a couple were having the kind of wheedling drunken argument that seems like the weather, it lasts so long. The thunder of heavy vehicles along the main road was constant; I tuned in and out of its rattle and boom.

At midnight, a flow of people appeared from both directions of the Avenue and scuttled quietly into their houses; the 'check-point' must have been suspended, although only temporarily, because there was no more movement for another hour; at one, the same thing happened. At twenty past one, the lights came on as Dessie Delaney opened the spiked gates; Podge Halligan and Larry Knight emerged from the house and went through a reprise of their dumbshow, shaking hands and swinging holdalls in cars. Larry Knight pulled away first and Podge Halligan fol-lowed him. Dessie Delaney didn't join Podge in the BMW; he went back inside the gates. Then, a spill of people appeared in the Avenue, including a handful of baseball-capped youths who were admitted to 52 and 53. These must have been the lads who had manned the checkpoints, as there was a now steady, random footfall along the street.

I needed to talk to Dave Donnelly, but I didn't want to let Dessie Delaney go. But maybe he wasn't going anywhere. He had told me how his girlfriend's brother used to deal in Charnwood, how Delaney was connected there; maybe he hadn't gone back in Podge's car because he was acting for Larry Knight on this deal. The level of noise on the Avenue had returned to normal, now that business had been concluded; hip hop boomed bass heavy from one open window; The Wolfe Tones droned monotonously from another. I figured that gave me enough sonic cover to make a call. Dave's mobile was off, so I rang his home. Dave answered.

'Dave, Podge Halligan is coming from Charnwood with what I'd lay odds is a bag of smack in the car.'

'Charnwood? Larry Knight? What the fuck?'

'Podge has been planning this for a while. Flood the area, under his control. Tommy Owens told me.'

'Have you seen Tommy Owens? Where is he? Ed –'

'He's safe.'

'You're fucking me around, Ed –'

'You'll get everything I have, I swear –'

'Because if those NBCI fuckers think I'm protecting you –'

'Wait until you serve them up Podge Halligan on a plate. You're gonna need three interception points, and fast.'

'Three? I don't know if I –'

'Get Geraghty and O'Sullivan involved, why not? Anonymous tip-off, your own private intelligence gathering. Podge's house, the old ferry terminal in Seafield.'

'And what's the third?'

'John Dawson's house.'

'Ed, are you serious? Even Geraghty and O'Sullivan don't want to question John Dawson unless they're certain they've a case.'

'You don't have to question anyone, just wait outside.'

I gave Dave the BMW's description and plate number. Before I hung up, he told me Seafield Council had voted by a majority of three to rezone the Castlehill Golf Club lands for high-density development. The Halligan brothers were all business tonight.

It began to look like Dessie was settling in for the night. When another rat began to check me out, I dislodged myself from my place behind the skip. I stretched and stamped my feet, then walked as far as the lane and had a piss. Then I walked towards Gemma Courtney's house. When I was at the corner of the square, the roof spots flashed on, and I heard the gate slam. I doubled back along the mud patch, covered by the mist, and spotted a figure in navy and white sportswear turning into the lane. I followed, hoping it was Delaney. The other end of the lane gave onto a short terrace which swung right into Charnwood Square. The mist let me stay close. We left the estate, cut right by the park and left down a cross street. I could see a sign for Fogarty's up ahead. I broke into a run, and as I closed in, spotted the plaster on my quarry's right arm. He turned as I was on him, a few yards from the pub; I put him against the wall with my left forearm across his windpipe; my right arm held his left at the wrist.

'Hello Dessie,' I said.

'No way,' he said, shaking his head.

'Way,' I said. 'Podge is finished. The cops are waiting for him. Podge is going down for a long time. And I could help put you there with him, unless you'd like to help.'

'Yeah yeah yeah, talk to the hand,' Delaney said.

'Give me enough, you could walk. For starters, where's Podge bringing the heroin tonight: John Dawson's or the old ferry-house?'

Dessie Delaney shook his head.

'Forget about it. If it's not Podge, it's Larry Knight: either way, I know nothin'.'

'They'll only have Podge's say-so on Larry Knight. It'll be inadmissible. Anyway, I don't even have to hand you over if I don't want to.'

'And Podge won't know it was me who talked? Yeah, right.'

'It won't be you, it'll be me. You're just narrowing it down.'

'You've got nothin', just a big fuckin' mouth, that's all.'

Dessie Delaney's pupils were distended and his teeth were grinding; he was cresting on some kind of uppers and feeling no pain. I needed to reacquaint him with his fear. I pressed hard against his Adam's apple, then released him and held my hands up. He bent over, holding his throat and retching. I waited until the pain had subsided.

'Of course, the other side is, Podge finds out you're talking,' I said.

'How's he gonna find out if I'm not?' Delaney shouted. His voice was shrill, and fresh blood streaked his eyes.

'We tell him you are. About Podge's new best friend Larry

Knight – everyone knows you and Larry go back. And each time one of Podge's dealers is picked up in Seafield, or in Wicklow, or Wexford even, the cops give you the credit, Dessie. Drip drip drip into Podge's ear. And what are the odds one morning – maybe you've just dropped your kids to school – you take a bullet behind the ear? Or you open the front door, a balaclava and a sawn-off are the last things you see on this earth? What are the odds? Too short for a punt, Dessie, too short for a punt.'

Delaney's brow was soaked in sweat; his nose was running; drool leaked from his shaking lip. He looked at the ground, and in a strained, remote voice that sounded as if it had been beamed in by satellite, said, 'He's dropping the smack off at Seafield ferry terminal, the old one.'

'You gonna tell me the rest, Dessie?'

His head still bowed, he nodded.

I rang Dave Donnelly and told him. Then I walked Dessie Delaney to my car. Childlike excitement rippled across his face at the sight of the old Volvo.

'A 122S,' he said in wonder. 'She's in great shape man. Where'd you get it?'

I told him about my father and Tommy Owens.

'Say what you like about Tommy Owens, he knows his way around a fuckin' motor,' Delaney said, an unconscious echo of what Tommy had said about my father. The freemasonry of petrolheads.

'Dessie the Driver,' I said. 'You want to take the wheel?'

'Serious?'

'You up to it, with that arm?'

Delaney bent the arm at the elbow, flexed his hand at the wrist.

'No bother man.'

I sat in the passenger seat. Delaney couldn't shut up, he was so excited.

'An Amazon, they call it. Nice handling. And easy stick action, they're built to last. People say they're boring now, but back then, they were a class act man. Nineteen-sixties, '64, '65? Swingin' sixties. Very Swedish, very gnick. Your man, Simon Templar. The Saint, he had one. In white it was. No, it wasn't an Amazon, it was a P1800, an earlier model. Sportier and all. But this is the business, this is the fucking *business*!'

'What are you on, Dessie?'

'Coke. Lotta coke, waiting for all that to go down. I had to be the linkman, 'cause Larry knew me. In case Podge wasn't on the level. And Larry wanted it all to be in Charnwood, 'cause that's where he feels safe, no-one'd say boo to the cunt there. But don't worry, I've some H to bring me down later.'

'Up at the shed in the Dawson house –'

'I'm sorry about that, I did my best for you man, but Podge was out of control –'

'No, and thank you, but there was nothing you could do. You know Podge raped Tommy Owens later on that night?'

Delaney turned and looked at me, eyes wide.

'The road, Dessie, the road!'

But he had it covered. He *was* a driver.

'Ah, that is fucked up man. I heard things, you know, about Podge. Young fellas, all this. Never tried it on me. I knew he was a mental bastard, but . . . ah, that's fucked up man.'

'That's why we've got to put him away for a long time, Dessie.'

'I thought you said he is going away for a long time.'

'Not as long as he'd do for the murder of Councillor MacLiam. You were there that night, weren't you? Out on Peter Dawson's boat?'

Delaney twisted his head around again, mouth open.

'How'd you . . .'

'I wasn't sure – until now. But it doesn't make any sense for you to be missing, does it? You're MacLiam's supplier, you're the one he trusts. He's into Podge for all sorts, sure. But you're the one who can coax him. You're the one who can help him change his mind.'

'I told Podge the dose was for both of us, I fuckin' *told* him.'

We drove in silence for a while. I imagine Dessie was thinking pretty much what I was thinking: that given his position as the councillor's connection, given that he was on the boat that night, there was no way he was going to walk away from this. Maybe there was no way he deserved to either.

There was a service station coming up, and I told Dessie to pull in. I got coffee and chicken and bacon sandwiches, and we stopped by park railings in a leafy red-brick square somewhere between Rathmines and Ranelagh, and as we ate and drank, Dessie told me how Joseph Williamson died.

'The set-up was, Peter Dawson would take your man out on the boat, offer him the money, explain what it was for – his vote in the rezoning of the golf club lands – and also, tell him George'd be willing to have MacLiam's gambling debts written off in return for that, and for the guarantee of his vote in favour of any future Dawson developments. And your man says no way. I knew he would, he was like . . . he was a real smackhead, he had a totally unreal sense of who he was. I mean, he was shooting up this free heroin he was getting from people he knew were criminals, you know, 'cause who the fuck else is going to get you it, and he's running up these debts gambling like some fucking madman who must think he's going to be dead a week on Thursday the way he's layin' it out, and then in the middle of all this, he thinks he's got his integrity: I am the man who says no to developments, I am the man who doesn't take bribes, I am the man you can trust. I mean, it's fucking whatyoucallit, self-delusion, know what I mean? I liked the guy, I'd sit up with him . . . he had a lot to fucking say for himself, about liberation theology and the Irish language and Fianna Fáil and all this, but in the end, it was all just talk, you know? His wife was like his ma, and he was like a really smart kid, but one of those . . . you know, they're smackheads waiting to happen, they're already hiding from things, from people, the truth, the world, everything except ego, and heroin is the worst drug they can take, it just pulls the covers right over their head.

'Anyway, we're waitin' around, we're the persuasion squad, 'cause if Peter Dawson can't get MacLiam onside, we're to go in.'

'Who's we?'

'Me and Podge.'

'Just the two of you?'

Delaney nodded.

'So Peter calls Podge, and Podge calls big Colm Hyland, and Colm takes us out to Peter's yacht, out in the bay, and we go aboard. And MacLiam doesn't have a clue, you know, he's delighted with himself, he's out on a yacht on a summer's night, with all his new friends who let him do what he likes.'

'Where's Hyland?'

'Hyland doesn't get onto the yacht, but he must be still there, 'cause he comes into it later. But I don't know where he is. Now I'm brickin' it man, 'cause I can see Podge thinks MacLiam is a fuckin' flake, so I'm talkin' all about councillor this and councillor that, and George's business plans and all this shite, talkin' like a cunt, know what I mean, just so Podge remembers he can't simply shank this fucker and get away with it. And we're drinkin' whatever it is, this fuckin' . . . *wine* Peter has on the boat. And it's a bit of crack for a while, 'cause Peter's sailin' the fuckin' yacht, and we're gettin' speed up and it's a beautiful night an' all. I'm thinkin', this is gonna be grand, you know? No worries. Then we can see the baths, you know, the old outdoor swimming pools there between Seafield and Bayview, and MacLiam starts into it, how they're not going to bow the knee to the developers, how

296

they'll restore the baths as a public amenity, how kids – we were all up on deck, it was like he was making a speech to the world, fair play to him, it was very good – how kids will one day swim again in the Seafield Baths, 'cause the sea belongs to us all, not just those who can afford to pay for it. Anyway, he's delighted with himself, shouting into the air, but I could see Podge turning, you know, the head's nodding, the feet are tapping, the eyes are buggin' out, all the danger signs, so before he can do anything, I move into MacLiam, how about a little hit, and he's yeah great, you know. So we go downstairs, or below deck or whatever the fuck you call it, just the two of us, and I light the little gas ring he has down there and start to cook up the stuff, we're both gonna do it together. And I remember, MacLiam has found this blue plastic bag, and he's looking through it at a load of old photographs, I don't know what they were, but he was mouthin' on about them anyway. And then Podge comes down, bouncin' and clickin' and all, up to here on speed and coke and whatever, you saw him like that, and of course, MacLiam, instead of being fucking terrified like a normal person, he's all Podge this and Podge that, excited 'cause he's gonna score, oh Podge maybe *you'd* like to try some of this, oh Podge can you lay some bets for me at Leopardstown tomorrow, Podge Podge Podge, almost takin' the piss he's so friendly, and Podge looks at me – upstairs. The eyes are gone. Nothing I can say. And who knows, maybe he's just gonna rattle the fucker's cage, slap him around a bit till he sees sense. Wouldn've done him any harm.'

'So you prepared two shots, one for MacLiam and one for yourself.'

'That's right. And I'm up on deck with Peter, and he's asking me what Podge's gonna do, and I'm saying he's just gonna try and get MacLiam to change his mind about the vote. And Peter says, maybe we should ring George, I don't trust Podge, let's ring George. And then Podge comes up on deck and says, ring

George about what? And Peter says, where's MacLiam? And Podge says, he's down below, sleeping it off. And there's something about Podge's voice – he's fucking thrilled with himself is what it is, he loves the moment after there's been any kind of action – and Peter hands over to me and makes to go below. Podge is blocking him, you know, you're the only sailor here, we don't want to be left in the hands of Delaney, we'll be in Holyhead before we know it, making a joke of it, and Peter loses the head, he's screaming about his boat and his plan and how he wasn't going to be bossed around by some Neanderthal, and I thought Podge'd do him then and there, but no, he steps aside, and Peter goes below.'

A group of drunken kids came lurching along the street. One of them fell against the car, then clawed himself up by my window. When he saw me he got a momentary fright, then recovered and made a gurning face through the window at me. I nodded at him, and he pulled back, made a loud shrieking sound, flapped his hands beneath his arms like a monkey and sprang off after his friends.

Dessie Delaney was starting to look rough. The coke was wearing off, and he didn't have any more. If he wasn't going to get somewhere he could shoot up, he wanted to snort some of the heroin he had with him. But I wouldn't let him, at least not until he had finished his story. I lit two cigarettes and gave him one, and pushed him to keep going.

'We were out past Bayview by now, and it's dark, and you could see all the big houses lit up around Castlehill. I remember thinking, that'd be nice. Up there, looking out at all this. Having a drink, and some, some ice cream, wearin' one of those, you know, those white towelling robes like you get in a hotel. Looking down on it all. Very nice. I can remember thinkin' that. And then I heard Peter cry out, "Oh my God", or "Jesus Christ", or something. Then he comes up, and he's crying.

Actual tears. He's dead, he's dead, he says. He can't be, says Podge. He's no pulse, he's not breathing, says Peter.

'And Peter gets his mobile out, right, and Podge says, who are you ringing, and Peter says, 999. Smack! One to the head and Peter is out. Podge calls George on Peter's mobile, then thinks better of using it; he tosses it in the sea and calls Colm Hyland on his own. When Colm appears, they talk for a few minutes. Then Podge is on his mobile again. And it's decided, myself and Podge will get in Colm's boat and take Peter in and George will have us met at the old ferryhouse. And this is because Hyland is the only one who can take Peter's boat into the Royal Seafield and not arouse suspicion, and also the only one capable of taking it in at all, of sailing the fuckin' thing.

'So we get Peter into Hyland's boat, and Podge and me sit in, and we start the outboard and off we go.'

'Didn't you say anything?'

'To who? To Podge? What would I've said? Because the first rule is, when something goes off, don't say a fuckin' word. 'Cause what are you gonna say? What did you do that for? I don't like you now? Let's call the cops? Give me a fuckin' break man, I said yes Podge no Podge three bags full Podge otherwise I would've joined the cunt and still could, the stories about that fuckin' ferryhouse I'm not coddin' you man.'

'And Hyland was left on Peter's boat.'

'And he dumped MacLiam overboard. I mean, I assume he did, I didn't *see* it.'

'And you get to the ferryhouse.'

'Yeah, and George is there himself, and a few of the lads, and George is like a fuckin' madman, he takes Podge into a corner, and it's not that he's shoutin' at him, you can't hear anything, just the hand going, the finger in Podge's face, you know?'

'Does Podge care what George says?'

'What do you think? I mean, he would've done you that night

up in the shed. And now, settin' up his own heroin route all over the south east – that's gonna look good to all George's new business friends, isn't it?'

'So what is Podge up to?'

'He's just doin' what he wants. He doesn't give a fuck. He doesn't want to be a businessman, he wants to be a criminal. He likes it, end of story. And of course, he likes hurtin' cunts too, because he's a fuckin' mental bastard.'

I lit two more cigarettes. The smoke sluiced out into the mist and the slow dawn light; silver wisps curled around horse-chestnut leaves heavy with moisture.

'All right, so George is giving Podge a bollocking, what then?'

'George has the lads put Peter Dawson in a white Immunicate van, so he can bring him up to his folks' house.'

'Why his folks' house? Why not his own house?'

'Don't know.'

'And was that it?'

'No, Hyland came in then. He brought Peter's yacht to the ferryhouse. And MacLiam is gone. And he has a chat with George, how he'll see it's all cleaned up, and that's it.'

'Anything else you can remember, Dessie?'

Dessie sucked smoke into his lungs as if it could satisfy his craving.

'The blue plastic bag full of photos I saw below deck, Hyland had them now, gave them to George Halligan. George took off with Peter Dawson. That's it. And then Hyland and me spent the night cleaning off Peter's boat with cleaning fluid and bleach an' all. Perfect end to a perfect day.'

'So Podge murdered MacLiam.'

'He killed him anyway.'

'He knew it was a double dose of heroin, he sent you out and he made sure MacLiam took it. That's intention. And you say you could see in his eyes he was going to do it.'

'So why didn't I stop it?'

'How could you, without losing your own life? If you give evidence, Podge could do life.'

'I thought you said your mates in the Guards were gonna pick him up tonight. I'm not saying I will or I won't, but there's no way I'm saying a word if he's on the streets.'

I realized there'd been no word from Dave Donnelly. I checked my mobile. I had set it to mute in Charnwood and had missed four calls, all from Dave. They had picked Podge up in possession of twenty kilos of heroin, with a street value of 2.2 million euros.

I told Dessie Delaney what had happened. I also told him that, if he didn't tell Seafield Guards everything he had just told me, I was going to make it clear to Podge that Delaney had been the one to betray him. Just because Podge was in jail didn't mean he couldn't order a hit. On the other hand, if the Guards were looking after him, a bit of witness protection for the key witness in a high-profile murder would be in order. And for his family too.

Delaney was anxious, and scared, and upset. But that wasn't my problem. I'd wanted to help him. I felt bad for his kids, I felt sentimental about them. But there was nothing I could do. He had got himself into this fix, and there was only one way out. I didn't know if he was going to serve jail time. I thought he deserved to, if not for MacLiam's death, for the fact that he assisted Podge in buying a stash of heroin that, if it had gone onto the streets, would have caused a lot more deaths, left a lot of kids without their parents. Maybe he'd get out of it, and clean up, and get a taxi plate, and bring up his kids right, and they'd all go on holidays one day to that Greek island he had the postcard of in his wallet. Maybe in all of this, someone should have a happy ending, even if no-one deserved it.

26

'Who are you and what do you want?'

'You been listening to the radio, George?'

'Edward Loy, glad to know there's no hard feelings. I had a sense you wouldn't bear a grudge when it comes to business. Well, my offer still stands.'

'Have you been listening to the radio?'

'Yes I've been listening to the radio. House prices rise again, Exchequer receives tax take boost, banks announce record profits. Nothing about Seafield Council's timely decision to rezone the Castlehill Golf Club for high-density development yet. First report will probably come when the usual shower of socialist layabouts and university muppets mount a picket –'

'Item one on the 7 a.m. bulletin. Over two million euro worth of heroin picked up in Seafield. Man held. They didn't say who it was, or where exactly he was picked up.'

I could hear George's fibrous, tar-rich breath crackling down the line.

'Go on,' he croaked.

'He was arrested outside the disused ferry terminal. On his way in. He was driving a blue BMW.'

'I'll kill the cunt!'

'You might have to. Because the cops have a witness to Councillor Seosamh MacLiam's murder. He's going to give evidence against Podge, and in the course of things, your name will inevitably come up in relation to what they were trying to persuade the councillor to do out there.'

'Who is it? Not Hyland. Fuckin' *Delaney* –'

'They have Podge cold on the smack, George. And they're going to offer Delaney a deal that keeps his family safe. So if I were you, I'd be thinking limitation, not elimination.'

'You're very smart all of a sudden, aren't you son?'

George Halligan, a year younger than me, short of breath, sounded suddenly like an old man.

'What the fuck did he want with all that heroin?'

'Meet me on the beach across from the Bayview Hotel and I'll tell you.'

'I'm meeting an investor for breakfast at the Royal Seafield,' George rasped.

'All right, I'll meet you there. Is he up on the narcotics trade, this "investor" of yours?'

George called me a variety of names, then said he'd see me on the beach.

'And come alone, George,' I said.

～

I had handed Delaney over to Dave Donnelly earlier that morning. Dave wanted me to bring him into the station, but I wasn't convinced if I came in, I'd succeed in getting out, so we set the meeting for six thirty in the pine forest car park in Castlehill. Before I took Dessie there, I let him talk to his girl-friend. I was in two minds about this, as I wasn't sure he could be trusted, but I was in two minds anyway about why I liked Delaney when there was so much to dislike. Maybe it's just that the good in him seemed to outweigh the bad. I always thought that was worth taking a chance on. I was often wrong.

I stood in the tiny hall of the house in James Connolly Gardens while he went upstairs and spoke to his girlfriend.

After a few minutes she came downstairs and went into the kitchen. Delaney came down and nodded at me to follow her.

Delaney introduced her as Sharon. She had a hard thin face and cold green eyes and dyed-copper hair and her cigarette looked like a part of her hand. I had seen her before, with Dessie on the seafront plaza. I wondered if she was using too.

'What about us?' she said. 'Where are we going to go? We can't stay here.'

I said it wasn't up to me, it was up to the Guards to work out whether they'd be offered witness protection.

'Yeah, but now, where do we go now? Word gets out, Podge could have someone down here in five minutes, even from jail. The kids, anything.'

She wasn't panicking, she was just looking for the right word. She wasn't using, not smack at any rate. Those hard eyes were clear and smart. Delaney was lucky to have her.

'What about Collette?' he said.

'In Galway? How do we get there?'

Delaney looked at me. I nodded to whatever it was. He took a brick of money from his pocket and offered it to her. She looked at it like it was dirt, then she looked at him the same way. Delaney was coming apart as it was from the lack of heroin; I thought her gaze might send him under.

'Is that drug money?'

She spat the words out.

'It's money I gave him,' I lied. 'Use it. Get a taxi to Heuston, take a train to Galway. I'll see what the Guards offer, and then I'll get in touch.'

She turned the gaze on me. It was strong stuff to take, particularly when you'd been up all night. I liked her. If Delaney wasn't strong enough to make it, she certainly was.

'If rehab for him isn't included, forget it,' she said.

I nodded.

The fridge had a freezer section on top, with three drawers. She pulled open the third drawer, took out packs of fish fingers and peas and potato waffles, then produced a plastic sandwich box, which she handed to me. I opened it. Inside, in a sealed sandwich bag, was a blood filled syringe.

'The murder weapon, isn't that what they call it?'

I looked at her in astonishment, and she almost smiled.

'When I was cleanin' up Peter Dawson's boat with Colm Hyland, I slipped it in me jacket,' Delaney said.

'Go on, wait in the hall a minute till I say goodbye to this bollocks,' she said.

From the hall, it sounded more like a mother with her son than a woman and a man.

When we left the house, Delaney was crying. It seemed like the right thing to do.

I took the wheel. On the way to the pine forest, Delaney took a wrap of heroin from his pocket. He was sweating and fidgeting; I could see he needed it badly. Then he wound down the window and tossed it out of the car.

'Why'd you do that?' I said.

'Cops hate junkies bad enough as it is. If I'm out of it, it's only gonna make it worse.'

It was a grey morning, and the mist was cold and damp enough to make you shiver.

'Dessie, do you still have the postcard of that Greek island in your wallet?'

Delaney nodded.

'What's the story with that?'

'My brother part-owns a restaurant and bar there. Fifty grand and I could buy into it. Dream on, yeah?'

Dream on.

Dave Donnelly was standing by his car among the pines. I pulled in beside him and turned to Delaney.

'Do me a favour. Leave George Halligan's name out of it.'

'He's hardly in it.'

'At the ferryhouse. Just leave him out.'

'Why? You're not workin' for him, are you?'

'No. But I need a favour from him. OK?'

'OK.'

I got out and greeted Dave.

'You're looking pleased with yourself,' I said.

'Things turn around,' Dave said.

He told me that the National Drug Unit boys had shown up trying to take the case over, but that he'd brought O'Sullivan and Geraghty in, and they were making sure Dave got the credit.

I gave him the syringe and told him what it was.

Dave punched me in the arm, he was so happy.

I asked Dave about rehab and witness protection and he said he'd have to work it out with DI Reed, and maybe O'Sullivan and Geraghty too.

'What about Superintendent Casey?' I said.

'If Casey spends the rest of his days playing golf, he'll be a lucky man,' Dave said. 'Casey's finished, he'll do well to stay out of jail. The NBCI boys couldn't believe the decisions he made on the Dawson and MacLiam cases.'

'He will stay out of jail though,' I said.

'Of course he will,' Dave said. 'I was just imagining we lived in a different country there for a minute, where bad cops get what they deserve.'

I got Delaney out of my car, and Dave put him in his. Then he leant in at the driver's seat window.

'Ed, there's something Jack Dagg said –'

'Ah listen, away with Jack Dagg, Dave; I don't have the time for it now.'

I started my engine.

'Go easy on Delaney,' I said. 'He's not all bad.'

Dave's face was expressionless.

'If he helps send Podge Halligan down for murder, I'll buy him a teddy bear,' he said.

~

The strand at Bayview was broad and stony and sloped down to a foaming grey sea. I stood on the shoreline and looked towards the land. The lights of a train flashed out through the mist as it snaked around the edge of the cliff. Its sound seemed muffled by the roar of the surf as it vanished silently into a granite tunnel on the northbound line.

George Halligan crunched his way through the pebbles in a navy suit and matching raincoat. He took a handkerchief from his top pocket and wiped the pebble dust off his black penny loafers.

'Fucking beaches. This is what people build swimming pools for,' he said, and coughed. The coughing went on for a while. I waited until he was finished, and then I waited some more. He took a Cohiba from its thick foil tube and bit the end off and lit it and threw the foil tube away.

'Pick it up,' I said.

'What?' he said.

'Pick it up.'

He looked at me warily for a second, then he picked it up and put it in his coat pocket.

'About that business up in the house,' he said. 'I didn't mean it to go that far. Truth be told, I was called away, and word got out you were there, and Podge got hold of you and . . . well, it shouldn't've happened.'

'What should've happened? You slipped me the knockout juice yourself. What was it? Rohypnol?'

'Roofies and GHB cut together. Podge uses it.'

307

'Not any more. What was the idea?'

'Just to scare you off. Stop you poking around. You'd've ended up in your car down here or somewhere, with a big headache, and a message: watch your step.' George shook his head, like it was nothing to do with him. 'Podge got carried away. It was wrong.'

'You could've killed me. Rohypnol and GHB mixed, you could have fucking killed me.'

'Send me the bills. Dentist's or whatever.'

George's black eyes looked like shiny little bugs. He spat bits of tobacco over one shoulder, then turned away from me, as if the matter had been dealt with. I looked at his Italian shoes, his silk tie, his perfectly pressed suit, his pale blue shirt with the white collar. He was the boss who never gets fired, the killer who never gets caught, the general who never gets shot.

'Now, tell me about Podge,' he said. 'I can't hang around here all day.'

That seemed to make up my mind, or what was left of it. George was about six inches shorter than me, and maybe fifty pounds lighter. I picked him up by his coat lapels and flung him backwards into the sea. The slope on the shore was very steep. He stumbled trying to keep upright, but I followed through and knocked him down, and then I was on him. We were in about a foot of water, and I held him under for a while, then let him up. I had a rock in my hand, and I was going to use it. I could see the fear in his eyes, and the shock that anyone would dream of laying a finger on him, then I felt the barrel of a semi-automatic hard under my chin. I don't know whether I was too quick to react or too slow, or whether my synapses were simply refusing to pass vital information on, but instead of backing off, I just rammed George down again while whipping my head to the side of the gun. He got one shot off into the air, and I smashed the rock against his hand, and the gun dropped in the water. His legs started to kick frantically now, and his arms clawed at mine. Time seemed to slow down, and I tasted salt water cold on my lips and I wondered whether it wouldn't be simpler just to drown him and have done. Then that wondering passed, and I let him up and dragged him ashore. He sat on the stones, coughing and wheezing and spitting, getting his breath back so that he could curse and threaten me. I went back in the water and found his gun. It was a SIG Sauer Compact, with seven shots remaining from an eight shot magazine. I showed it to him, put it in my pocket, lit a cigarette and watched him. After a while, he reached out a hand. I lit another cigarette and passed it over. He looked at me for a few seconds, his eyes cold and tight, then took the cigarette.

'Dessie Delaney was getting the heroin they were feeding Councillor MacLiam from Larry Knight across in Charnwood,' I said. 'And last night, Podge bought a big supply from the same Larry. Story goes he was ready to start dealing all around the south east. That's not going to help the blind eye the Guards were turning on the Halligans, is it? And it's not going to help your business schemes either.'

'How much is Delaney going to say?'

'Everything. How they hooked the councillor, the gambling, the heroin, the potential for blackmail, the need for him to change his vote, the night on the boat, Podge administering the double dose, you supervising the clean-up.'

'That's the only place I'm connected to it, in the ferryhouse. Everything else is Podge, or deniable. And I'm at the ferryhouse to collect Peter Dawson and bring him up to his parents' house. If I'm drawn into it, the Dawsons are as well. And that's not gonna happen.'

'The NBCI are running the case now. And Superintendent

Casey is going to be promoted out. That means the Dawsons are no longer off limits.'

'What do you want? I don't even know what I'm doing here, I should be briefing Podge's solicitor –'

'You're here because I know more about what happened than anyone else. Because I'm one step ahead of the cops on this one, and if we share information, you'll be one step ahead too.'

'What information? What do you know?'

'I know that after you brought Peter Dawson up to his parents' house that night, you hung around. I know that when he killed himself, or when he was murdered, you took the body, or you directed Podge to take the body, and stashed it somewhere and then stowed it on his boat a week later. I know the murder weapon was lying around Podge Halligan's house, that Tommy Owens stole it, that it was in my hire car, that you got it back when you trashed my house, that you planted it with Peter's body on the boat. I know that you're up to your neck in the cover-up of Peter Dawson's death.'

George Halligan shook his head.

'There's nothing there. A lot of words, but no case.'

'It's not about a case against you, George. It's about finishing you as even a semi-legitimate businessman. Do you think all those nice lads from the good schools with the few bob to invest are going to consider you for a second? Bad enough you've got a psycho for a brother, but to know the full extent of your connections to how many murders? Three? More?'

'I didn't kill Peter Dawson. Podge didn't either.'

'And Linda?'

'Why would we? What'd be the point?'

'She knew too much.'

'About what? I don't get it. Listen, tell me what you want.'

'I want you to pull the Immunicate boys out of the Dawson house. It's in your interest too, the cops will be all over there soon enough, and if the place is overrun with Halligan gang members masquerading as security guards, well, that's another link in the chain that binds you to all this. But whatever about you, I want to go in there alone, before the cops get there. I want an hour with John Dawson, alone.'

'Why?'

Why? Because he started all this when he had an affair with my mother. Because he cheated and bribed his way to a fortune he doesn't deserve. Because he killed Kenneth Courtney. Because he killed my father. Because he's sitting there at the top of the hill, waiting for me to come and tell him it's over at last. 'Because I need to know the truth.'

'And you think you'll get it from him? Good luck.'

George stood up and shook himself like a dog. He took off his coat and wrung it out.

'You know how much these clothes cost? I should have you killed,' he said.

I took the gun out of my pocket and held it out to him. He looked at me uncertainly, then took the gun and pointed it at me.

'Remind me again why I shouldn't have you killed,' he said.

'Because you'd be caught,' I said. 'Anyway, look at all I've done for you.'

'What's that again?' George said.

'I've been doing it. I've told you about Podge, about Delaney. No-one else did. None of Podge's boys picked up the phone. Neither did Podge. They were all preparing to become smack dealers. That wouldn't have been good for business at all, George. Now you're equipped to brief your own solicitor. And you're advised to go into quarantine, and not be making a show of yourself with the kind of people who won't want to know you. And then in a few months, you can quietly sell the land on again. Now it's rezoned, it's not going to drop in value.'

George slipped the gun into his pocket. He ran a hand over his face and through his hair, leaving a grin on his creased features.

'I'd do well with you on my side,' he said. 'Situation's still vacant, I'm not coddin' you. But I don't know that there's enough there for a deal.'

'Delaney's not going to mention you.'

'In the ferryhouse?'

'In any of it.'

'Why not?'

'Because I asked him not to. Of course, I could change my mind.'

'Don't change your mind.'

George Halligan picked up his mobile and spoke first to his solicitor, and then to someone who took orders without asking any questions. And then he told me what he knew. 'It all goes back to Fagan's Villas,' he began.

By now, the words sounded like the tolling of a bell.

27

The black iron gates to John Dawson's house were open. I parked on the road outside, and walked passed the granite gate-lodge and down the long tree-lined gravel drive. The house was an enormous red-brick mansion in the Victorian Gothic style; it reminded me of St Bonaventure's, but it was larger and more forbidding than the nursing home; the towers and turrets were higher and more numerous; the stained-glass windows were grander; as I approached it through the mist, the yellow-and-slate-coloured brickwork seemed to glow, making it look like some unreal castle in the clouds.

The charcoal Lexus was parked in front of the house; there were no other cars visible, nor were there any Immunicate vehicles. I went to the side of the house where the sheds and outbuildings were. An old-style garage with wooden doors for about six vehicles looked like it had been recently abandoned. Other garages were closed; some with locks on the doors. I spotted three cars: a black Volkswagen Polo, a racing-green Jaguar XJ6 and Linda's red Audi convertible.

The heavy front door was ajar, and I pushed it open and walked into the marble-floored hall, which was of double height; a mahogany stairway rose and turned at the far end, while a crystal chandelier hung from the landing above. The walls of the hall were covered in portraits of dour-looking individuals from the nineteenth and early twentieth centuries: merchants and professionals, rather than royalty; they wore dark clothes and sported complacent expressions of well-to-do respectability on their well-fed faces. I wondered who they were, and who they were intended to be, and what on earth connection they had to the people who lived in the house.

One of those people stood by the mantelpiece in a living room that was about half the size of a football field. The room was a riot of styles: every twelve feet you moved from regency stripes to paisley swirls to Chinese patterns; there was leather and silk and wool, ruched curtains and slatted blinds, carpet and rugs and polished boards, sofas and chaise longues and armchairs and, behind a white upright piano, a pink corduroy bean bag. It was as if whoever lived here refused, or had been afraid, to make a decision about what kind of room it was, what kind of house it was. It was a study in visual uncertainty, in social insecurity. It was a mess.

The fire was lit; pine logs crackled and hissed in the grate. The mantelpiece above it was a large, carved wooden affair. The man who was leaning on it wore a hound's-tooth check jacket, beige cavalry twill trousers and brown suede shoes. I could see his gaunt, mottled face reflected in a gilt-frame mirror, and he could see mine.

'Eamonn Loy,' he said.

'Edward,' I said.

'My apologies,' he said. 'Your father was Eamonn. Now why do you think he called you that? Edward being the English for Eamonn. Was he trying to be modern?'

'My mother told me it was because *his* mother had wanted him to be christened Edward. But the priest was a De Valera man and wouldn't name a child after an English king. So Eamonn it was.'

'And he made it right with you, son. That's how it should work, the present washing away the sins of the past.'

A smile spread across his worn face, a smile that made his small, watery eyes look even more desolate.

'You don't look surprised to see me,' I said.

'I've been waiting for you. Longer than I realized.'

He made a gesture towards a white sofa that sat before the fireplace. I shook my head, took the photograph Gemma Courtney had given me and showed it to him. He sat down in the white armchair to the side of the fire and studied it.

'The three musketeers,' he said, fondly. 'I don't remember who the women were.'

'That's 'cause you only had eyes for me, John,' said a woman's tart, sarcastic voice. The accent was broader than I'd heard Barbara Dawson use before; maybe she didn't feel the need to disguise it when she was carrying a gun.

'There's no need for that, love,' the man said. 'Nothing to be gained at this late stage.'

'I like the feel of it in my hand,' she said.

Barbara Dawson, in a black trouser suit with an aubergine scarf around her neck, sat in a white armchair at the other end of the fireplace, a dull blue-black SIG Sauer Compact in her hand.

'George Halligan has one of those too,' I said to Barbara. 'He's been good about keeping you supplied with firearms, down the years. First the Glock 17, now that.'

She weighed the pistol in her hand, her face giving nothing away.

'Do you remember a Mrs Burke, from Fagan's Villas?' I said to Barbara.

Barbara shook her head.

'Well, she remembered you. Remembered you running around with two men. John Dawson, and Kenny Courtney. Couldn't tell them apart, she said. I'm not sure if I knew then, or when I realized someone didn't want me to see a photo of Dawson and Courtney together, or when I found out that Courtney had abandoned his wife and daughter not long after my father disappeared. He had a second chance with the love of his life, he said. To be honest, I don't think I knew for certain until I saw his face in the mirror a minute ago.'

'Knew what?' Barbara said.

'That John Dawson is dead, his body buried under concrete in the town hall. That the man who's been impersonating him all these years is Kenneth Courtney.'

The room was still after I had spoken those words, the silence roaring in my ears like wind through a tunnel. The first sound I heard was the spitting of the fire; then the click of the safety being removed from a gun; then outside, a sudden squall of gulls, keening in the distance.

'Good,' said Kenneth Courtney quietly. There were tears in his eyes. 'Good man. At last.'

'The Guards have identified the body found in Seafield Town Hall as Kenneth Courtney,' Barbara said.

'Courtney was identified by the clothes he was wearing. They're running a check on John Dawson's dental records now. I think they'll match.'

Kenneth Courtney smiled.

'I know they will,' he said.

The mist swirled against the great sash windows, and I had a flash of the Ghost Captain, waiting on the shore for his twin brother and his lost love to return.

'Shut up,' Barbara hissed at him. 'Not another word.'

'What's the point? It's all coming out now. Least we could do is tell the poor lad where his father is buried.'

'I don't know where he's buried.'

'We should have found out, before we –'

'Shut up, I'm warning you.'

316

'Or you'll what, shoot me? I'm happy to go at any time, you know that.'

'And leave me here alone, in a house full of ghosts?'

'So then. No threats, if you don't mind. And put the safety back on that gun, please.'

Kenneth Courtney got up, went to an ornate table beneath a great sash window, and collected a black- and white-labelled bottle of whisky, a bottle of water and three crystal tumblers. He poured whisky into each glass and handed them around.

'Laphroaig,' he said. 'Like drinking burning turf.'

He drank his off in one. Tears appeared in his eyes again. He couldn't seem to stop smiling, but the smiles had nothing to do with happiness, or pleasure. He looked confused, like an actor without a script, an impostor in a life that was no longer his. He poured himself a second drink. Barbara ignored hers, but she did put the safety back on the gun. I didn't feel I should drink, but I couldn't resist. The taste brought me back to the night I drank with Tommy Owens, the night of my mother's funeral. It seemed like a very long time ago.

'John Dawson did kill my father, didn't he?' My voice nearly cracked.

Barbara looked into her drink and nodded. I knew it, had known it for some time, but to have it confirmed made me realize I had still been holding out some kind of hope. I took a belt of whisky and kept talking.

'You see, that's what I couldn't figure. If John Dawson was prepared to kill my father to be with my mother, how could he spend the rest of his days with the wife he had abandoned, had spilled blood to leave? It wouldn't add up.'

'That's what he thought he could do,' Barbara said. She had begun to drink, and it had moved her to speech. 'He thought he could come crawling back here because his precious Daphne had rejected him. And me with a nine-month-old

317

baby in my arms. Thought he could take whatever advantage he liked. Found out he couldn't.'

Courtney stared at her in surprise.

'Is this your "not another word"?' he said.

'I'm tired keeping it in,' she said. 'It's been hard for me too, all these years.'

'Harder than for me, perhaps,' he said sadly. 'Harder than for me.'

They looked at each other and smiled. There was still a strong charge between them, whether of love or hate or simply shared guilt I couldn't divine; as they reached back in time, I began to feel they were doing it for each other as much as for me: the past was food and drink and sex, was life itself to them now.

'We'd moved up here, and we'd had the baby – Peter – and suddenly John wasn't around. Well, he was working, and when a baby comes, there's often little room for a man, at least that's how it was back then. I didn't suspect a thing to be honest with you until it was over, the affair. He burst out crying one night right over there by the window, told me how he'd been seeing your mother. I was so stupid, I kept asking why, what did he mean seeing, had he been going into Arnotts? He had to spell it out to me. And then he blurted out how he had a fight with your da, and it escalated, and he ended up killing him.'

'Like it was an accident?' I said.

'That's what he tried to make out. But sure that's what they all say, isn't it? He knew what he was doing. And then your ma gave him the heave-ho.'

'Did he tell her he killed my father? Do you think she knew?'

'Oh no. Don't get me wrong, even though she's in her grave, I could never forgive your mother for taking my man from me. But she had a lot to put up with in your da, and anyway, she would never have . . . she wasn't –'

'Daphne Loy was a real lady,' said Courtney. 'Always was.'

Barbara stared at him, her lips set, her eyes blazing with sudden rage.

'And so Dawson came back to you,' I prompted.

'Came crying back to me,' she said. 'And my first instinct was, put it from you. Sleepless nights, crying baby, your man took a little walk and now he's back. But I couldn't let it go. He killed a man for love. And not for love of me, for love of another woman. I couldn't let him near me after that. I wasn't born to be second best. And how could I know it was over? I began to hate the baby he gave me. And it was one night, looking at that photograph – we had a print of it too – it was then I had the idea.'

'She waited outside my house,' said Courtney. 'I'd forgotten she knew where I lived.'

'You put it on a Christmas card, when you moved back from England.'

'She had me under her spell.'

'I knew I'd made a mistake, that Kenny was always the one.'

'It was wrong to leave herself and the little one, but I didn't care. I didn't care.'

'We killed Dawson here, against that fireplace.'

'Not that exact fireplace, we had to get a new one built.'

'And the plastering redone, and the carpets thrown out, and the floorboards sanded. There was so much blood, you see.'

Their faces glowed with passion as they brought it back to life, the crazed music of their shared blood-crime sounding like a lovers' duet.

'You threw up,' Barbara Dawson said, not unaffectionately, to Kenneth Courtney.

'I didn't expect there to be so much blood. I thought I'd have the guts. Especially since I knew he had killed Eamonn, your da. Killed my friend. I thought I'd be up to it – but you never know whether you'll have the stomach until you're in the thick of it. I fired the first shot.'

'I had to finish him off.'

'And then we cleaned it all up.'

'Dawson told me Jack Dagg took care of your da's body, so we got him to do the same thing. Kenny called Rory Dagg to tell him he wanted his brother on board.'

'I was nervous on the phone,' Courtney said. 'But why would they have suspected anything? They were used to doing what they were told.'

'Where was the baby that night?' I said. 'Where was Peter?'

Barbara looked irritated at my question.

'Here, I suppose.'

'Did he not cry? On account of the gunshots?'

'That child was always crying on account of something or other, he didn't need gunfire as an excuse. I'd just leave him, he'd always drop off again. If you pick them up when they cry, it becomes a habit with them.'

Barbara shook her head, as if to dispel the inconvenience of having to think of her son, and looked towards Courtney again.

'So we took a long holiday in America. And while we were there, Kenny gained the bit of weight – he's lost it again – and he had some plastic surgery.'

Courtney pointed to the photograph.

'They thinned out the lips a little, took some furrows around the eyes away. Minor stuff. But combined with the weight gained, I was a ringer. I was John Dawson.'

'You *are* John Dawson,' Barbara said.

Courtney shook his head.

'It's all over, Barbara. Too many dead.'

'You didn't have the guts back then, you don't now,' she spat.

'You heard the lad here, the Guards know.'

'We can deal with the Guards. We always have. There's plenty more like Casey. Sure who'd believe a story like the one we've just told in anyway? They'd never take it to a jury, it'd be laughed right out of court.'

The whisky had given Barbara renewed confidence. Courtney seemed relieved to be escaping the prison of their shared past. But Barbara still thought they were free. I needed to make her see clearly the bars of the cell she had made for herself.

'Let's talk about the night Peter came up here – the night Podge Halligan murdered Councillor MacLiam,' I said. 'He wanted to call the Guards. He was in a panic about MacLiam, about the Halligans, about all the mistakes he had made on the Castlehill rezoning project.'

'He went off half-cocked,' Barbara snapped. 'Offering bribes before he knew what time it was.'

'He was just following his father's example in that,' Courtney said. 'John Dawson never made a penny without making sure the right palm was greased first. Council officials, building inspectors, local and national politicians. Jack Parland wrote the rule book back in the sixties, and Dawson copied it all the way. Just, he didn't use the Halligan family for anything other than the occasional hired muscle.'

'Peter had run up massive gambling debts as well,' I said. 'He probably felt he had no option but to give George Halligan a piece of the company. He was getting drawn in deeper and deeper. And then that night, after MacLiam's death, he wanted to confess it all. You couldn't let him do that, could you?'

'He could have been persuaded out of it,' Barbara shrugged. 'That wasn't the problem.'

'The problem that night was, on top of everything else, Peter was on to us,' Courtney said. 'George Halligan brought

321

a blue plastic bag full of photographs up to the house that night. Photographs Peter had with him on board the *Lady Linda*.'

'Photographs he had stolen out of this house,' Barbara said. 'Photographs I had kept hidden in case he'd find them. Not that they were hard evidence. But I was afraid, when he was older, and maybe he began to have doubts about his Da – I mean, these days kids wonder about their parents even when there's nothing up – so I never let him see those snaps.'

'So needless to say, he was a bit interested in his past,' Courtney said. 'The only thing was, he had it all wrong.'

'He thought John Dawson was my father,' I said.

'That's what he said that night,' Courtney started. Barbara interrupted him.

'You don't know what he said. You went to bed with a pill. You don't know what happened that night. No-one does – except me,' said Barbara.

There was a gleam in her eyes that scared me. She was teasing us with the riddle of how her son died. She clicked the safety on and off the handgun like it was a cigarette lighter. It was time to bring this to an end.

'I know what happened, Barbara. George Halligan was supposed to leave the house that night. But he didn't, he hung around the grounds. It was a hot night, the windows were open. Easy to hear a scene played out between mother and son. Especially when both parties are screaming their heads off.'

Barbara was shaking her head, Courtney was nodding his.

'Peter'd had enough, hadn't he? He was fed up being told what to do. He knew how his father played the game: crooked. He didn't mind that. But he baulked at murder. Maybe he could be persuaded not to go to the police. Maybe he could be persuaded MacLiam's death was an accident. But he knew

322

the Halligans were scum. And who had suggested he use them? His mother. Barbara Dawson said the Halligans were useful men to have around when the going got tough. Well, he told you you were wrong, didn't he? And he told you why. "It's no surprise you should think that way," he said. "You're a Halligan yourself. Everyone knows. It all goes back to Fagan's Villas," he said.'

'No,' Barbara cried out. 'No, no, no, no, no!'

'"God only knows what's kept my father with you all these years. You've poisoned his life, just like your filthy Halligan blood has poisoned mine," your son said, and then there were two loud shots.'

Barbara was sobbing now, repeating the word 'no' softly through her tears.

'I couldn't be sure until now,' I said. 'The Glock 17 that killed the body in the town hall also killed Peter. If that was my father, if that was Kenneth Courtney, there was no connection. But if it was John Dawson who was dead, then the same gun killed father and son, and chances are the same person pulled the trigger. Chances are it was you, Barbara.'

Barbara Dawson's eyes burned defiance; her face was grey.

Courtney poured another whisky, drank most of it down and stood, swaying but possessed, accusatory finger pointing at Barbara Dawson's shaking frame.

'Your own son,' he said, his voice shaking. 'Your own flesh and blood.'

Barbara wouldn't look at him, wouldn't give him the satisfaction of acknowledging his sudden bid for the high ground.

'I thought it *was* suicide,' he said, turning to me. His weak eyes pleaded for understanding, for forgiveness, for an absolution nobody could give him. He drained his glass and refilled it and sank back into his chair. I turned to Barbara.

'Why Linda?' I said. 'Why did you have to kill her?'

'She knew. Or she was close to knowing. Or she would have led to you knowing,' Barbara said.

'I know, Barbara,' I said. 'And the Guards know. They know about the faked text message, so it would look like I did it. What they've been looking for is Linda's car. And now I've told them where that is, they're ready to bring you in.'

'I didn't intend to . . .' Barbara said, and faltered.

'To what? To strangle her?'

'I just wanted to talk to her. To try and explain. She screamed at me to leave. She turned her back on me, began to call the Guards on her mobile. I didn't know what else to do.'

'You didn't know what else to do but murder her. That was a cold place to find yourself, wasn't it? Or did you notice? Let me guess how you did it. Easy, really. You always wear a scarf around your throat, don't you? Plastic surgery can't fix that. You took it off and strangled her with it,' I said.

Barbara's lips quivered, and tears glistened in her huge eyes.

'Poor Linda,' Courtney announced loudly, as if he had just woken up. 'I loved her very much. She was like a daughter to me.'

His voice was hollow, hoarse with booze; the words sounded like a prepared statement. Whisky tears slipped down his blotchy face.

'You should cry for Gemma, the real daughter you left behind,' I said.

'Don't you think I do? Don't you think I regret the choice I made every single day?'

'She needs your help,' I said. 'Gemma Grand. Does that mean you knew where she lived, in that hellhole down by the canal, and still you did nothing?'

'I've taken steps to look after her, once I'm dead,' Courtney said. 'I would have made it up to her long ago, but I was prevented by this woman, this Barbara Dawson, Barbara Lamb – or should I say, because Peter spoke nothing but the truth, Barbara Halligan.'

Barbara lifted her head and looked at Courtney, her tear-stained face riven with hurt. Courtney crossed the room and bore down on her now, his words jabbing hard, wanting to finish her off.

'We *all knew*. Barbara Lamb, that's Old George Halligan's little bastard. That's why she was so wild, that's why she had so much go. That's why you'd get more off her than you'd ever get from the rest of the Holy Marys around the Villas. Let you ride her, she would, when none of the others'd give you a decent kiss. But deep down, beneath the looks, she was rotten. And she's rotten still. When it's deep in the blood, you never escape it.'

There was a moment when I saw what was going to happen but before it happened; a moment where Barbara Dawson's face seemed to collapse back through time until it was the tear-stained face of a child again, hurt and smarting from yet another humiliation; a moment when Barbara's journey from Fagan's Villas to the top of Castlehill finally ended, right back where it began.

Barbara Dawson shot Kenneth Courtney three times. Her first two slugs hit him in the chest, the third cut his throat, and drove a sluice of blood out the back of his neck. He was dead seconds after he hit the floor.

She stood up and turned to me, her eyes ablaze, her lips engorged.

'I'm not,' she said, shaking her beautiful head. 'I'm not. I'm not. I'm not.'

She kept repeating it, a threnody of denial and shame, a negation of – what? her birth? her life? Still it kept up: *I'm not, I'm not, I'm not.*

Outside, for the second morning in a row, police sirens echoed around the slopes of Castlehill. I got up and headed for the door.

'Where are you going?' she said.

'I'm going home,' I said.

I was at the door to the hall.

'I am Barbara Dawson. I am at home,' Barbara Dawson announced to no-one. 'I am Barbara Dawson. This is my home.'

I heard the shot, but I kept on walking. There was a muffled sound, like a coat falling to the floor. I walked through the hall hung with Barbara's imaginary ancestors and pushed past the front door into the mist and light of day.

28

Everyone was there: DI Reed and DS Donnelly of Seafield Garda, DI O'Sullivan and DS Geraghty of the NBCI, any number of uniforms. Once they'd taken a quick look in the house, the tape came out and the scene was secured. While they were waiting for the Garda Technical Bureau and the State pathologist to arrive, we stood in the front garden and I gave an account of what had happened. I left out my meeting with George Halligan. Geraghty kept interrupting me, trying to get me to implicate myself, until O'Sullivan told him to shut up. It was either that or Dave Donnelly would have hit him. After that, Geraghty contented himself with scowling and throwing shapes at me, trying to psyche me out. Given what I'd just been through, Myles Geraghty was kid's stuff. When I was done, two uniforms were summoned to take me to Seafield Garda Station, where I could make a formal state-ment. DI O'Sullivan, who had senior management stamped all over him, assured me that I would be advised about a range of counselling options. This was too much for Myles Geraghty, who snorted, wheeled away and stalked off down the drive in disgust, but not before he had said, 'Counselling? A good boot in the arse'd be more like it.'

For some reason, this cheered me up enormously, rooted as it was in a world where all problems had simple solutions; as I waited in the great tree-lined garden for the uniforms to collect me, I found myself pining wistfully for it, that place and time where nothing was so grave that it couldn't be sorted out by a good boot in the arse. A couple of times Dave Donnelly said he needed to speak to me but I told him he could get me later. I was losing my sense of urgency. There was no-one left to die, was there?

In Seafield Garda Station, I was dealt with swiftly: they taped my statement, I waited until it had been typed up and then I signed it. Then they gave me a lift home.

~

There was a yellow skip in the drive; I had signed for it that morning between handing Dessie Delaney over to Dave and meeting George Halligan. I had thought I should try and get some rest, but there was nowhere in my house to sit down, and I knew I wouldn't be able to sleep, so I rolled up my sleeves and opened the garage doors and began to load all the broken furniture and upholstery and other debris from the house into the skip. It took me a couple of hours. There was plenty of room left in the skip, so I went upstairs and threw all the beds out too; the Halligans hadn't really set on these with such determination, but they were in a bad way as it was: ripped and sagging with protruding springs and mould stains. Out they went, and the homemade plywood and chipboard bedroom furniture with them. There were hordes of old toys and children's books my mother had never thrown out: I stashed them in boxes to take to a charity shop, along with the paperbacks and magazines my mother had accumulated.

It felt good to do this, to strip the house down; or if not good, it felt fit, like the only possible course I could take. I got some tools from the garage and set to taking the carpets off. This wasn't as easy as it seemed; the carpet tacks were rusted and bent, and the batons that held them down splintered or stuck, and the carpets and underlay were filthy; my fingers were soon cut to ribbons and my nose and chest were clogged with dust. But I got them out, and rolled them up in the front garden and tossed them in on top of the rest. Mrs Fallon, the lady who had found my mother on the doorstep, went past with a Pekinese; she nodded and smiled at me, and I waved and smiled back. The mist had lifted, and while it was still overcast, the day didn't feel quite as notional, quite as fragile as it had.

There was nothing left in the house to throw out, unless I made a start on the kitchen and the bathroom; I figured it was a bit too early to start thinking about that level of refurbishment. I went upstairs and collected the tools – hammer, chisel and a crowbar – and brought them out to the garage. I closed the garage doors at the front. There were tools hanging on the walls, and a few metal toolboxes piled by the back door. I wanted to check what was there, but I couldn't see properly; there was a bulb in the light fitting, but it didn't work. I went inside and took a bulb from the back room downstairs. I went back into the garage, piled the toolboxes beneath the fitting, balanced on top of them and fit the new bulb in. I switched on the light and laid the toolboxes out on the floor. The third one was heavier than I remembered, and I was at an odd angle, and it came down with a great crash. Only for that, it might have been years until I'd noticed – and by then, maybe I wouldn't have made the connection. The floor beneath the toolbox that fell had cracked, and some of it came off in a cement sheet, about a centimetre thick. Beneath it lay another floor. I prised some more of the cement away: it lifted in shards. The floor it revealed was made of concrete. I chipped away some more, then looked around and saw a sledgehammer hanging on the wall.

I went into the house and telephoned St Bonaventure's and asked to speak to Jack Dagg. I waited for a while, and then Sister Ursula came to the phone.

'Mr Loy, it's so kind of you to call, but you're a few hours too late. Poor Jack died in the night, no trouble at all, just drifted away. And do you know, I think your visit made a big difference – and I'm not just talking about smuggling in the whiskey, for which you should be ashamed – after you'd gone, and that nice Garda Detective had come and gone, he asked for a priest. Made a full confession, took the Blessed Sacrament, dropped off to sleep like a happy infant. So you may have played a part in helping to send a soul to his saviour Mr Loy – there's some credit in the ledger for you!'

'When you say a full confession –'

'To the priest of course, to Father Ivory.'

'Sister Ursula, I'm afraid as a Catholic, I've been stalled for years now at a station somewhere between lapsed and out of practice, but I don't suppose the Church has relaxed its strictures any on the sanctity of the confessional?'

'Ah go on out of that Mr Loy, you're a terrible chancer so you are, almost as bad as poor Jack; I see I'm going to have to pray a lot harder for you than I thought. God bless now.'

I wasn't going to find out from Jack Dagg, alive or dead. I went back down to the garage. Using the sledgehammer, I loosened up the remainder of the cement floor, and then cleared it into a corner with a shovel. With a yard brush, I swept the dust into the corner too. I still couldn't see what I was looking for, so I went out into the back garden. An old garden hose lay coiled up against the back wall of the house. I attached it to the kitchen cold tap, turned it on, ran it around the passageway and sluiced it over the concrete floor. And there it was, in the midst of the concrete, a stretch of cement about eight-feet long and about three-feet wide. The shape of a grave. The shape of a man.

I turned off the hose and went back inside and started in with the sledgehammer. I worked around the concrete at the edges. I didn't know how deep the cement was laid, and I didn't want to puncture it. I cracked the concrete around the perimeter, then worked it loose with a garden fork, picking out chunks and tossing them in the corner with the cement, until I saw a flash of green. I started to prise up cement with a clawhammer and chisel now, chipping and cracking until it lifted, and I saw the green tarpaulin in the shape of a shroud.

Dagg *had* told me. In a green tarp, he said, in the garage. Not Eamonn Loy's motor garage, his garage in Quarry Fields. Dave Donnelly had tried to tell me too; Dagg must have included it in his statement.

I knew I should call the Guards in. But the Technical Bureau would be busy up in Castlehill for hours. And anyway, I wasn't going to stop now.

Jack Dagg probably thought quicklime destroyed corpses. In most cases, it has the reverse effect: there's some superficial scorching, but then the intense heat dries out the body and preserves it in a mummified state. It doesn't smell great, but it doesn't smell like a putrefying corpse. It doesn't look perfect, but it can still look like the person.

There were stab wounds all over the body, which was weathered and browned; the face was slashed and twisted in pain; the eyes were gone. There was a gold wedding ring on his shrivelled left hand. It came off easily; inside the ring was engraved the name Daphne. My mother's name. I put the ring back on the man's finger.

It was my father.

29

The Garda Technical Bureau lived in my garage for about a week. They prepared diagrams and graphs that charted the patterns of the various bloodstains. Comparing these with the angle and depth of the various wounds as described by the forensic pathologist's team, they were able to figure out pretty much how John Dawson's attack on my father proceeded: the variety and sequence of the wounds, the duration, and so on. One forensic chap who had seen me so often in Seafield Garda Station and hanging around crime scenes that he must have confused me with someone who didn't give a fuck, told me excitedly that there were six kinds of bloodstains, and that Green Tarp's crime scene (that's what they called my father, Green Tarp) exhibited all six, and did I know how rare that was. I said I didn't, and he told me that it was very rare.

It's all on file, should I ever want to reconstruct my father's murder, blow by blow.

~

I spent a lot of my time talking to the Guards, and a lot of the rest of my time at funerals. One of these was Jack Dagg's. I went back to the house afterwards. Caroline Dagg smiled glassily at me as if I was there to steal the silver. Rory Dagg was drinking sparkling water. He told me senior management at Dawson's were organizing some kind of takeover, and that he would do very well out of the shake up. He said he regretted not telling me all he knew earlier. I said it wouldn't have made any difference. He said anytime he could do me a favour, he'd be happy to. I said how did right now sound.

We drove to Quarry Fields. The Technical Bureau had pulled out. The only trouble was, they'd had to leave the garage behind. We stood in the drive, and I pointed to the garage.

'I want to get rid of it,' I said.

He looked at the garage – flat concrete roof, attached to the side wall of the house on one side, a side lane on the other – turned to me and nodded.

'Not a problem. What about the floor?'

'Especially the floor,' I said, and he flushed. 'I want earth there.'

'Once we pull out the concrete – and there's probably some hardcore down there, whatever – we'll turn whatever's left. It'll probably be very sandy though, so we'll throw in some topsoil for you. That'll work well if you want grass, or plants, whatever you want to grow.'

'What's it likely to cost me?' I said.

'You're not paying for it,' he said. 'I should have told you what I knew first thing. This is my way of not feeling guilty.'

'Not feeling guilty,' I said. 'Sounds good to me. How do you think that's going to go for you?'

'You've got to start somewhere,' he said, got into his battered black Volvo estate and drove away.

I looked at the garage, and tried to imagine what it would look like, just a patch of earth, and what I would grow there. Whatever I wanted. I didn't know how to grow anything. I was going to have to learn.

~

On Bayview Strand, George Halligan had almost been embarrassed talking about his putative blood tie with Barbara

Dawson. He told me that when his father was dying, he summoned George to his hospital bed in private and made him swear that, if ever Barbara Dawson needed anything, George was to supply it, no questions asked. Hence the Glock 17, years ago. He'd never tried to exploit the relationship until Peter came to him with the golf club deal. He didn't know whether she was his father's half-sister. He didn't have an opinion one way or the other. Family was a pain in the bollocks.

Barbara had asked him to take half a dozen files out of Peter's office, and to wipe anything recent off his computer. There was a cold room in one of the outbuildings on the Dawson property in Castlehill. That's where they'd kept Peter's body. It was Podge's idea to move it back on board the boat. George had simply asked him to retrieve the gun, and, again at Barbara's request, take any photographs he could find in Loy's house. Podge took it upon himself to make a clumsy attempt to set me up. They'd've been better off dumping the body in the woods. Trouble always started whenever Podge started to think he had brains.

George had told Colm Hyland to tape the bribe money on Councillor MacLiam's body. Deflect attention away from the councillors who actually had taken backhanders. Spread the blame around a little: if everyone was on the take, it cancelled itself out; as good as if no-one was. According to George.

$\sim$

The Guards found Barbara Dawson's prints all over Linda's Audi. Linda's mobile phone, the one Barbara sent the text from, was in a drawer in her bedroom. The mobile also registered the call Barbara made to Seafield Garda Station reporting a murder that morning. And the tape of that call was Barbara Dawson with her grawndest accent on. In another of the Dawsons' myriad sheds and outbuildings they found the contents of the box files that had gone missing from Peter Dawson's home office: the photographs from Family 1 and 2, the golf club papers, and all his bank statements, itemized telephone bills, share certificates and mortgage statements. They found all my family photographs too. They also found, printed out on white A4 and put in envelopes with labels addressed to the editors of newspapers, prominent politicians, every detective in Seafield Garda Station and assorted other community leaders and public figures, the following letter:

To Whom It May Concern

I, Peter Dawson, only son of John Dawson, builder, have been following a family tradition in recent weeks. I have been attempting to secure the rezoning of the Castlehill Golf Club lands, which my family owns, by means of bribery and corruption. This is how my father built up the business all those years ago, himself following the illustrious example set by Jack Parland and his merry men back in the sixties. I have succeeded in bribing Seafield County Councillors Eithne Wall and John O'Driscoll so far. Each cost thirty thousand euro; for this, it is understood that they will support, or if you're reading this after the vote has taken place, have supported the application to have the land rezoned from agricultural to high-density residential. I have hopes for other councillors, especially Councillor Seosamh MacLiam, Jack Parland's son-in-law, as at the time of writing the vote is still in doubt. I have not neglected my mother in all of this. In attempting to further my business ambitions, she advised me to involve George Halligan, best known as the head of the Halligan crime family. My mother places no trust in what she calls such scurrilous rumours. This is probably because she is the illegitimate daughter of

George Halligan's grandfather. Therefore she is a criminal by
blood, as opposed to my father, who became one by
inclination and greed. There isn't a great deal of difference
between the two; you might say they are just around the
corner from each other. Of course, the Halligans are very
dangerous, and do as they please, and George's brother is a
disturbed and volatile individual who should be in some kind
of institution. But I wouldn't make any great claims for the
degree of sanity in my own family either. In any case, if
anything happens to me, or to my family, then it may well be
the fault of the Halligans. But equally, it may be that we
Dawsons have brought it on ourselves.

I remembered the receipt from Ebrill's Stationers I found in
the trash at Linda's house. Dave Donnelly told me the friend
in the Garda IT division who was going to scour Peter's hard
disk had gone on sick leave; the virtual version of the above
letter, under the file name 'twimc', was eventually located and
printed and sent to Dave three months to the day after Peter's
body was found.

There was a reference in Peter's letter that only a few of us
would have got: when he says that criminality by blood is 'just
around the corner' from criminality by greed. He was thinking of John Dawson in Fagan's Villas, just around the corner
from the Halligans in the notorious Somerton flats. And
Barbara somewhere between the two, or rather, with the worst
of both. Peter's letter was never made public. There was something glorious about its recklessness and its honesty, something terrifying about its nihilism. I think he wanted to die, but
only if his family was publicly shamed in the process. But it's
sometimes hard to imagine what would be deemed shame in
Ireland: financial crimes don't seem to figure. Murdering your
son and daughter-in-law would certainly qualify. But at the

inquests into each death, despite the best efforts of Seafield Garda, the National Bureau of Criminal Investigation and Edward Loy, private detective, juries returned open verdicts. Nobody wanted to believe a mother would do such a thing, so nobody did. All the papers Jack Parland controlled wanted to steer clear of any Halligan–Dawson connection for fear that the papers he didn't control would revive the charge sheet against Jack Parland's adventures in the property world. So nobody reported it. It was as if it had never happened. Whatever you say, say nothing.

The documents and computers were taken for examination by the Garda Fraud Bureau and the IT Division, and the Criminal Assets Bureau prepared to launch another investigation into George Halligan's wealth. Dave told me if CAB believe you are living off the proceeds of crime, and you can't prove you're not, they can confiscate your assets.

Before that happened, George's solicitor released a statement saying George wanted to cooperate fully with any Garda investigation, that he regretted any stain of impropriety surrounding his legitimate business dealings with the Dawson group, and that his holdings in the Castlehill golf club lands and other properties were all legitimate and above board. What came next was inevitable: Podge's solicitor, who happened to be George's solicitor's partner, in life and in practice, announced that her client would be pleading guilty to the manslaughter of Seosamh MacLiam. The Director of Public Prosecutions hadn't felt confident in Dessie Delaney as a witness to pursue a murder charge; the murder weapon had Delaney's prints all over it; now Delaney was surplus to requirements. There would be no trial, no public account of any of the details of the case, or any of the embarrassing connections with George Halligan. Just a drunken party on a yacht, with tragic consequences. George Halligan's black sheep brother. No story here. Dave said Leo Halligan, who makes Podge look stable, had sent word down; otherwise Podge wouldn't have gone for it. Leo is due out next year.

~

Colm Hyland wouldn't say a word, he just stared at the wall. He got five years for conspiracy to pervert the course of justice. His solicitor has lodged an appeal.

~

Councillor Seosamh MacLiam, or Joseph Williamson, as the priest referred to him, was buried after a funeral service in the ProCathedral in Marlborough Street in the centre of Dublin. The Palestrina Boys Choir sang Duruflé's *Requiem*, and everyone was there. At least, I assumed everyone was there; I hadn't been home long to know who everyone was, but to go by the coats and the suits and the cars, they looked as rich and powerful and quietly pleased about it as that type of everyone everywhere else. And if I hadn't recognized the type, I would have suspected some high profile folk were abroad when I got out onto the street to find it barred to traffic. The ProCathedral has no churchyard, so there's usually no place to hang around after a funeral to commiserate if you're just an acquaintance who's not going to the grave afterwards. Aileen Parland's family got the street sealed off so people could do just that. I waited while she was surrounded by mourners paying their respects. She noticed me, and made a gesture with her hand, beckoning me to her. She didn't look any different from when we had first met: all in black, no make-up (or no-make-up make-up), the silver crucifix in place.

'I owe you an apology, Mr Loy,' she said.

'Accepted,' I said.

'But you don't know what it's for,' she said.

'Doesn't matter,' I said. 'I'll save it up, and next time I need one, I'll cash it in.'

'I shouldn't have fired you. I should have trusted your methods, however . . . unorthodox. I was wrong. Detective O' Sullivan of the National Bureau told me it was your work that led to the arrest of my husband's killer.'

'I'm only sorry we couldn't get a murder charge.'

'If there's ever anything I can do to help, I'd be glad to.'

There was, and I told her what. I thought she would baulk at the price, but the deal must have attracted her do-gooder instincts.

'Isn't that the person whose arm you broke?' she said. 'I'd have to meet the family first, to see if they're . . . and if they are, I'll do it.'

Seventy-five grand, just like that.

Nice to be rich.

See if they're what?

～

Dave Donnelly had a party to celebrate being promoted to Detective Inspector. Fiona Reed had a party the night before to celebrate being promoted to Superintendent. I wasn't at that one, and I wasn't at the one the whole Seafield station held to celebrate Superintendent Casey being moved to some made-up job in Garda Headquarters while he sat out the eighteen months to his pension. But I was at Dave's party. There was a wind in off the sea that made it too cold to be out in the garden, and the barbecue wouldn't start and then flamed too much, and most of the cops there were too partied out to handle another big night and left early, until eventually all that was left was a hardcore of three: Dave and Carmel and me. We sat by the big outdoor heater and ate underdone meat and drank too much beer. In no particular order, we had a laugh, a cry and a fight. The laugh I can't remember. The cry came when I broke under questioning about my romantic history in LA. I heard myself telling them that I had been married, that there had been a daughter, and that she had died. Carmel burst straight into tears. Dave set off and started laying into one of the giant rose bushes that stood at the bottom of the garden. He was shouting and kicking at it. The neighbours looked out their bedroom window, and Carmel had to go quiet him down.

The fight came because we began to drink whiskey to cheer ourselves up. It was between Dave and me, after Carmel had fallen asleep. I can't remember exactly what it was about, but I think it went something like:

How much of a bottle of whiskey can two Irishmen drink before they have a fight?

This much, you fucker.

No, this much, you cunt.

I woke up in the garden. All Dave's kids ran away when I sat up and opened my eyes.

～

I had a DNA test. I am Eamonn Loy's son. Better to know.

～

I wondered a lot about how much quicker I might have gotten to the truth. Courtney had left clues: calling the property company that bought the golf club lands Courtney Estates. Making the directors Kenneth Courtney and Gemma Grand. And Barbara had denied knowing anyone named Courtney when she visited me at home.

But I couldn't have made the connection with Gemma Courtney until I had Peter's mobile records, and matched her

340

number with the digits scrawled on the back of the fragment of photograph I had found on the boat.

And then a finger-sized scrap of the photograph, just large enough to show Kenneth Courtney's face, showed up when the Guards went back to take one last look at Peter Dawson's boat to see if they could find any fingerprint or DNA connections to Colm Hyland. It had been wedged tight between two seat cushions, and had evaded the first forensic trawl and my examination. It had been there all along: the third musketeer. If I had found it first off, Linda might still be alive.

There was no sense in thinking that way. If Linda had told me everything she knew straight off, she might still be alive too. If the Seafield cops hadn't been corrupt, if Peter hadn't joined forces with the Halligans, if my mother and John Dawson hadn't been lovers, if it hadn't all gone back to Fagan's Villas.

No sense in thinking that way. But in the long nights that followed, that's the way I thought.

~

My father's funeral was the last. Linda's funeral was the worst. I was living among the dead, in the church, at the gravesides. The scent of incense in your nose, like gorse.

Heaven's morning breaks, and earth's vain shadows flee;
In life, in death, O Lord, abide with me.

30

My mother had left enough money for her grave. How she did this was, she part-re-mortgaged the house. She must have had money problems. She never told me. Or it's possible she did tell me, and I was too drunk to take it in. She hadn't spent all of the money she'd borrowed, so once I'd paid for the grave and a headstone, I paid the rest of the money to the bank and took the mortgage on myself. David McCarthy ushered me gingerly through the process like I was some kind of chemical experiment that might erupt at any moment. It worked out that I owed the bank six hundred a month for the next twenty years, so I'd need a job soon. I asked Aileen Parland to recommend me to all her wealthy friends. She thought I was teasing her. I wasn't; who else could afford me? She said she thought I'd have too much integrity to make a habit of taking money from the rich. I said I preferred my integrity with a roof over its head, and anyway, who better to take money from than people who had too much of it?

~

The Dawson/Courtney estate was a shambles, with hordes of lawyers setting siege to it all; David McCarthy told me with barely suppressed glee that it would be twenty years before anyone sees a penny, and by that time, the lawyers will have it all anyway. I still had eighteen grand of the twenty Barbara Dawson had given me. I subtracted the remainder of what I was owed for finding Peter's body, and then his murderer, and sent the rest by courier to Gemma Courtney on the Charnwood Estate, with a note giving her a broad outline of what happened. She rang me and we agreed we should stay in touch. That's what cousins always say.

∿

Tommy rang me one night from Wales, cartoonishly drunk, to tell me that he'd remembered where my hire car had been dumped, only that was earlier in the evening, and by the time he got around to phoning me, he'd forgotten again. I hung up, and he rang back and repeated what he had said before, word for word, as if the first call hadn't taken place, so I hung up again, and left the phone off the hook. The next day, I reported the car stolen from outside my house. The truth, if not the whole truth.

∿

Aileen Parland flew to Galway where Sharon Delaney was staying with her sister Collette. It turned out that, in a brief flirtation with egalitarianism during Aileen's childhood, or as a reaction to Jack Parland leaving her, her mother had sent her for two years to a non-fee-paying convent school – the same school Sharon had attended fifteen years later. So they had nuns in common. And a certain lack of sentimentality. And so Dessie Delaney got his rehab, and his family got their fifty grand stake in his brother's restaurant, and I got a postcard from a Greek island I've still never heard of, and someone got a happy ending out of all this.

∿

The cemetery lies between the sea and the Wicklow hills, a couple of miles south of Bayview along the coast. My father's coffin had gone into the same grave as my mother's, and the earth was packed in a fresh mound above them both, with a wooden cross as a marker. I had ordered a roughcast oval granite headstone, and when it was ready, they would take the cross up and put the stone in.

It was one of those bright, cold nights that tell you summer's turning. I threw my cigarette away and left my parents' grave and cut across to the path that leads from the cemetery down to the sea. A fresh breeze was churning surf up in the dark blue water, and gulls raised a clamour that sounded like keening.

I walked along the pebbled shore towards Bayview and thought of all the dead: of Barbara Dawson and Kenneth Courtney, of Linda and Peter Dawson, of Seosamh MacLiam, John Dawson and Jack Dagg. And my mother and father, Daphne and Eamonn Loy. It was like the weekly litany read off the altar at mass, the priest urging prayers for the repose of each soul, and then 'for all the dead'.

For all the dead.

Dagg had died of leukaemia. His blood was all wrong, he said. Maybe that's how they all died. Maybe everyone connected to Fagan's Villas had the wrong kind of blood, right back to Old George Halligan's little bastard daughter Barbara. Either their blood was corrupt, or they weren't the person they claimed to be, or thought they were.

But that wasn't all the dead.

I thought of how we had been in the mountains on vacation, my wife and daughter and me, and my baby girl, Lily, her name was, had put her hand through a pane of glass and opened an artery, how I tied her arm above the wound with strips of my shirt as we drove to the hospital, how they told us in intensive care how rare her blood was, how they didn't have any blood of her precise type for a transfusion, how I said they should check to see if mine would match, and my wife imme-

344

diately said no, it wouldn't, not to waste time, and I tried to argue her down, both of us shouting now, scared ourselves, scaring everyone around us.

'Test my blood,' I said, 'it's worth a try.'

'It can't be a match,' she said.

'Why not?' I said.

'Because she has O type blood, and you have type AB.'

The nurse looked quickly at my wife, then she left the room.

'I don't understand what that means. What does that mean?' I said.

'It means you're not her father,' my wife said. 'You're not . . . her blood father, Ed.'

It didn't matter, not just then, there were so many other factors complicating my girl's blood that I could have been her father and it still mightn't have matched. But they couldn't find her blood father, and they couldn't find any blood that matched either. They tried a transfusion with the closest O blood they could get, but it was the wrong kind. She had already lost so much, and her little heart couldn't take the strain of it all. She died before we had fully taken in what was happening. I remembered how my wife and I scattered her ashes in the ocean at Santa Monica, how, in our helpless, hopeless grief, we couldn't hold each other, couldn't even look each other in the eye, and how nothing I had done since had mattered a damn to me, and still didn't until now.

∽

I *was* her father. Blood can't tell the whole story.

∽

You can't outrun your past. I spent twenty years hiding in a country dedicated to that very idea. But it doesn't work. Your blood might be wrong, but it's your own. Your past is always waiting for you, and the longer you leave it, the less prepared you are. I had left it long enough.

I climbed up the cliffside through the gorse and scrub as far as the edge of the old pine forest. Dublin lay before me, waiting. I could see the city lights up ahead, connecting with each other in the dark, like the quick breath of the living amidst the souls of all the dead.

Closer, I could see the great harbour of refuge at Seafield, built with granite hewn from the old quarry on Castlehill. In between lay Quarry Fields.

I turned into the wind and walked down the hill towards home.